Cape Light

The Cape Light Titles

CAPE LIGHT
HOME SONG
A GATHERING PLACE
A NEW LEAF

Cape Light

THOMAS KINKADE
& KATHERINE SPENCER

JOVE BOOKS, NEW YORK

A Parachute Press Book

CAPE LIGHT

A Jove Book / published by arrangement with the authors

PRINTING HISTORY
Berkley hardcover edition / March 2002
Berkley trade paperback edition / March 2003
Jove edition / May 2004

ISBN: 0-515-13732-4

A JOVE BOOK®
Jove Books are published by The Berkley Publishing Group,
a division of Penguin Group (USA) Inc.,
375 Hudson Street, New York, New York 10014.
JOVE and the "J" design
are trademarks belonging to Penguin Group (USA) Inc.

PRINTED IN THE UNITED STATES OF AMERICA

10 9 8 7 6 5 4 3 2

WELCOME TO CAPE LIGHT

~

I AM OFTEN ASKED WHY THERE ARE NO PEOPLE IN my paintings. And some "experts" have even come up with weighty answers to that question. But the truth is, my paintings are full of people. They are there. I see them when I paint. They sit in the windows reading a bedtime story to their children. They tend the flowers that line the paths to their warm and inviting homes. They work in the shops. They play in the parks. They pray in the churches. They struggle. They rejoice.

They live.

They love.

They can't stop their lives to pose for a picture. But if you come with me now, you can meet some of them. Come with me to Cape Light.

Located just an hour's drive north of Boston, some call it the town that time forgot. But Cape Light's slow-paced, old-fashioned atmosphere is valued and protected by its residents. In this close-knit community, neighbors help neighbors, and storekeepers greet their customers by name.

Up on Main Street, the storefronts and restaurants look much the same as they always have. First stop at the Clam Box where Lucy Bates and her husband still make the best clam chowder and the strongest coffee in New England. Then, you'll be ready to wander down through to the Village Green where Cape Light residents, led by Mayor Emily Warwick, gather to celebrate each season. A Christmas tree is lit for the winter holidays. There are band concerts on soft spring nights, fireworks on the Fourth of July, and the Harvest Festival in the Fall.

Walk down to the harbor and you'll probably see Digger Hegman. The old fisherman is never too far from the water. Let your gaze follow the coastline and you'll see Durham Point Lighthouse whose beacon has guided ships for more than a century.

Cape Light is a place where people have the time to savor life's simple pleasures. Where they have learned to find joy in the simple—but extraordinary—blessings of everyday life. Their lives are not without challenges, fears, even sadness. Light cannot exist without shadow, and neither joy nor love can be experienced without dark times as well. But day by day, the people of Cape Light struggle to make the right choices—choices that will lead them toward the paths of deep, satisfying lives. They learn how the power of faith and hope can work to change them for the better. And in the course of their journyes, they also experience the unexpected miracles that bring events full circle—and feel like a gentle, guiding push from some unseen hand.

I know you will enjoy meeting the people of Cape Light. Their stories remind us that it is possible to overcome challenges and learn to live again in the light of love and faith.

Welcome to Cape Light, a little town you've never been to, but you know it by heart.

Welcome home.

—Thomas Kinkade

CHAPTER ONE

✦

*I*T WAS HARD TO COME BACK AGAIN.

This time, for some reason, it was harder than usual. As Jessica Warwick headed north on the thruway, she could almost feel the pull of Boston behind her. She was already missing the city—her friends there, the stores, the restaurants and galleries. She loved the city's excitement and sophistication. She couldn't quite believe that she was once again leaving it for Cape Light.

Jessica fought back a surge of frustration. The thruway was thick with traffic, and the air conditioner in her aging hatchback was no match for the late-afternoon heat.

What were all these people doing, driving around on Memorial Day, anyway? They should be at barbecues or at the beach. Or even in shopping malls.

I never should have promised Mother I'd visit her tonight, she told herself as the traffic inched forward. *I could have gone to Rita's party and breezed up here later. When the roads were clearer and I was in a much better mood.*

When was the last time she'd been to a party? Jessica honestly couldn't remember. But it had to be when she was living and working in Boston. Before she moved back to Cape Light. She'd returned to her hometown nearly six months ago to help care for her mother, Lillian, who'd had a stroke. Except for working at the bank every day and helping her mother, Jessica found very little in Cape Light that interested her. All her old friends had either moved away or were married with children and living very different lives. Or they had changed so much they didn't have a lot to say to each other anymore.

Maybe the problem is that I've changed, Jessica thought. She didn't have much in common with the people in the small village. Maybe she never did. It was difficult to make new friends, even among her co-workers at the bank. Although she had lived in Cape Light most of her life, Jessica now felt very much the outsider.

Finally the exit for Cape Light came into view, and Jessica turned off the highway. At the last minute she decided to take the back road to her mother's house instead of driving through the village. It would take a little longer, she knew, but there would be a big crowd at the harbor and village green by now, everyone waiting for the fireworks display due to start at sundown.

Of course, there had been a parade down Main Street that morning, and Jessica's older sister, Emily, had made an appropriate speech as the town's mayor. Jessica could already imagine the full report she'd receive from their mother, praising Emily's many accomplishments.

Well, that wasn't Emily's fault, Jessica told herself. Her older sister was, in fact, quite modest. Emily also seemed to have endless patience with their elderly mother, which was no small feat. Emily was a genuinely caring person, Jessica thought, though Emily had no one close to look out for, except for their mother. And her, Jessica. The two of them were nine years apart, and Jessica figured

Emily's protectiveness toward her was only natural. Sometimes it irked her, though, as if Emily didn't quite realize her little sister was not a child anymore but a thirty-two-year-old woman.

Jessica had expected that she and her sister would become closer once she returned home. She wasn't sure why, but so far that hadn't quite happened. They were both busy with their jobs. Still, there was something more to it—some wall of reserve they could never quite break through. Their mother didn't help, either, with her sly way of pitting her daughters against each other. Jessica was aware of it now, as an adult, and Emily was, too. Sometimes they even joked about it. Though Jessica wondered if the damage done over so many years could ever quite be undone.

Driving along the Beach Road, lush and overgrown already in late May, Jessica slowed as she came to a long line of cars parked along the shoulder, just before the Potters' orchard. Sophie and Gus's annual barbecue, she realized. There was quite a crowd there. Jessica had gone to a few of their parties when she'd been very young. While the Potters were never close friends of her family, they'd always been kind to the Warwicks, even when it felt as if the whole town had turned against them. Jessica had been invited to the barbecue this year, as well, and as she approached the orchard, she was tempted to park and stop in for a minute, just to say hello.

But she decided against it and continued to drive by. The Potters' grand old Queen Anne–style house caught her eye as she passed, only partly visible through the trees. She spotted children running around beneath the apple trees and caught just a hint of the smoky scent of grilling food carried on the breeze.

Jessica sighed. Well, there was another party she'd missed today. Now it was on to her mother's house, where she was sure to be greeted with a litany of complaints and demands.

THE PARTY HAD BEGUN IN THE EARLY AFTERNOON. By dusk it seemed at least half the population of Cape Light had gathered in the field behind the Potters' orchard. Family, friends, and neighbors of Gus and Sophie Potter had arrived from near and far, as they did every year on Memorial Day weekend, for as long as anyone could remember. They came for the company, the music, and even some dancing. And, of course, for Sophie's renowned cooking.

When darkness finally dropped over the harbor like a heavy curtain, a hush would fall over the crowd as well. Everyone would find a comfortable spot, then settle back to watch fireworks explode in the night sky. Set high on the bluffs north of town, the orchard was an ideal viewing point for the show. An unofficial but indispensable village tradition that marked the start of summer.

This year the evening was unseasonably warm for late May, the air heavy with the scent of barbecue. There was also a drift of fragrance from the flowering shrubs, honeysuckle and early roses, mixed with the faint, intrinsic scent of the sea.

Beneath a star-filled sky and a full moon, the open field looked luminous. Magical. Paper lanterns had been strung in the trees, and small candles glowed on tabletops. Long tables stood under a makeshift canopy, covered with an array of homemade dishes. No one had come empty-handed, and the guests could be heard exchanging compliments and recipes.

Sophie had prepared several of her specialties, including poppy-seed coleslaw, red potato salad, johnnycake, and twice-baked beans with seven secret spices, which no one had ever quite figured out. Notoriously secretive about her recipes, Sophie would only confirm five.

Real-estate maven Betty Bowman, who was quite well traveled, suspected the missing ingredients were ground cloves and a dash of paprika. Charlie Bates, who owned the Clam Box Diner, insisted it was chili powder and Seaman's Boiling Spice. But then again, it was common knowledge that Charlie put chili powder and boiling spice into nearly every dish he served, so few took that guess too seriously.

It didn't help to ask Sophie. She claimed she was writing a cookbook and wasn't about to give away her secrets for free when she and Gus could be living off her royalties in their old age. Sophie had reportedly been working on this manuscript for years, though no one had yet seen a page of it.

At the dessert table there was another bountiful spread of confections. A huge strawberry shortcake held center stage, the berries fresh from the Potters' pick-your-own patch. The chorus line included lemon-meringue and strawberry-rhubarb pies, chocolate layer cake, and carrot cake with cream-cheese frosting, all baked by Molly Willoughby. Chocolate chip cookies, gelatin molds, and watermelon slices rounded out the offerings.

Some time after dinner, instrument cases appeared—a guitar, a fiddle, and even a banjo this year. A space was cleared for dancing, and the music began, floating out over the field and vine-covered trees to the shadowy spaces beyond, where children chased each other through the dark orchard, miraculously tireless.

Sophie moved among her guests with a regal air, dressed in a long summer gown. The beads and bangles around her neck swayed and glittered with every step. Her hair, a faded strawberry blond mixed with silver gray, was arranged in a braided coil and studded with fresh flowers. She paused to chat with each group, making sure everyone was having a good time.

Gus watched his wife from a distance, his large chest puffed with pride as he stood beside the reverend Ben Lewis.

"She's the queen bee tonight, all right," Gus noted with an admiring shake of his head. "Sometimes I think we'd be better off running a banquet hall instead of keeping the orchard all these years. Sophie sure loves throwing a party."

"It's a good one, Gus," Ben said. "The best ever, I think."

"Thanks, Reverend. That's kind of you to say." Gus hooked a thumb in his suspenders, a patriotic red, white, and blue pattern he'd received as a Christmas gift from one of his grown children. "Sophie and I were just saying last night, we'll keep doing this as long as we're able and the Lord is willing."

"And we'll all keep coming as long as you keep inviting us," Reverend Ben replied with a smile.

Gus laughed. "Well, it wouldn't feel like summer's really started around here without it, I guess."

"No, not at all," the reverend agreed.

When Gus drifted off to visit with other guests, the reverend joined his wife, Carolyn, seated at a nearby table with their friend, Harry Reilly. Harry, who was busily eating, answered the reverend's greeting with a nod.

"Enjoying yourself?" Ben asked Carolyn as he sat down.

"Yes, very much," Carolyn assured him. She was already on her dessert and about to take another bite of strawberry shortcake. "The shortcake's perfect."

Harry looked up. "Try the rhubarb pie," he managed around a mouthful of pie. "You'd better get up there," he advised the reverend. "It's going fast."

Carolyn laughed and turned back to her husband. "Wait, dear, don't go yet. Harry has some news. . . ." She turned to Harry with a prompting smile.

"You tell him." Harry shrugged and speared a large strawberry with his plastic fork. "It's no big deal."

"All right, then, if you don't want to, I will." Carolyn's blue eyes sparkled. "Harry's giving Digger a job at the boatyard," she announced.

"Really? That is news," Ben replied. Removing his round wire-rimmed glasses, he wiped them on a paper napkin and glanced at his friend. Harry met his gaze for a moment, then looked away, clearly reluctant to offer any explanations.

Harry had never been an easygoing man, Ben knew, nor the most accepting. Grief over the loss of his wife, Nora, ten years ago, had caused those traits to harden. Maybe this news about Digger was a good sign, Ben mused. Maybe Harry was turning a corner.

"And how did that come about?" the reverend finally asked. "From what I hear, Digger's the last person you want around the yard."

Harry shrugged one large shoulder. "He's always hanging around. I thought I'd put him to work, is all. He'll be scraping hulls mostly. Painting, patching. That sort of thing. I need a hand. Temporary, I mean. He was more than willing."

Yes, Digger Hegman probably was eager to work, Ben thought. The old fisherman had been the best clammer on the Cape in his day, hauling up shellfish faster than any man on the water. Nearly eighty and still strong in body and spirit, Digger tended to be a bit absentminded these days. Often wandering the village as early as dawn, he'd watch the fishing boats leave the harbor, then turn up at Reilly's Boatyard.

"Does Grace know?" Carolyn asked Harry.

"I think Digger is old enough to do as he likes without his daughter's permission." Harry sat back and rubbed his hand through his bristly gray crew cut.

Carolyn glanced at Ben. His look told her to let the subject drop.

"Looks like Digger is showing the children his tricks," Ben said.

Harry turned to see his new employee a short distance away, entertaining a group of kids with a handkerchief and a coin.

"And that's another thing," Harry added. "He showed me some knot tricks the other day. He's entertaining when things get slow."

"Digger is full of surprises," Ben agreed.

Harry dabbed his mouth with a paper napkin. "Well, he starts at the yard tomorrow. We'll see how it works out."

"Yes, you'll just have to see," Ben agreed. He turned to watch Digger again. Grace was approaching her father, her slim body seeming lost in her long, loose blouse and patterned skirt.

She said something to Digger, interrupting one of his magic tricks. Digger nodded at her. Then he smoothed down his long beard and took a small bow for his audience. As the children applauded, he left them to follow his daughter.

Digger, a widower, lived with Grace, who owned the Bramble, an antique shop in town. The old man had a long-standing heart problem, and lately he tended to get confused and forgetful. Grace kept a close watch over him. Sometimes perhaps too close, Ben thought.

Work might be good for him, Ben told himself. If his daughter lets him take the job, this idea of Harry's might be good for all three of them.

After Harry picked up his ever-present Red Sox cap and left to get coffee, Carolyn moved her chair closer to her husband.

She had more news for Ben—news she was bursting to share. But she'd been waiting until Harry left. Now she wondered if she should wait until they got home.

"Look, Rachel and Jack," Ben said, pointing out their daughter and her husband dancing together to a slow ballad. He was quiet for a moment, then added, "They look happy, don't you think?"

Carolyn nodded. "Yes. They seem very happy together. That's a blessing."

"For all of us," Ben agreed. "And we're lucky that the two of them decided to stay here in Cape Light. Some parents aren't so fortunate." He thought of the Potters and other couples they knew who had to be content with visits from their children two or three times a year.

Carolyn's smile slowly grew wider. "And it's going to get even nicer."

Ben turned to his wife with a questioning look.

"In about seven months, to be exact," she said. "Another blessing for us all should be arriving."

Ben's mouth hung open in shock. "Rachel's expecting?"

Carolyn nodded happily. "You're going to be a grandfather, Reverend Lewis. What do you think of that?"

Ben sat up straight in his chair. He took his wife's hand. "When did you hear?"

Carolyn put her finger to her lips. "Just tonight. I wasn't supposed to tell you yet, so act surprised. Rachel took one of those home tests. She's seeing a doctor next week to make it official."

"What wonderful news." Ben's face glowed with happiness, and Carolyn resisted the urge to give her husband a hug. Instead she squeezed his hand even tighter.

Ben was happy that his wife and daughter shared such a close relationship. It might not have worked out that way. But Rachel had matured into a very special woman. And in his eyes Carolyn had always been special.

"The baby is due at the end of December, just in time

for Christmas," Carolyn went on. "Maybe Mark will come home for a visit."

"Yes, maybe he'll come to see Rachel's baby," Ben said, nodding. "He's always been close to his sister. He might come for her."

"Yes, he might," Carolyn agreed quietly.

Ben reached over and took her hand again. They glanced at each other but, by unspoken understanding, agreed not to discuss the matter further. At least, not now.

They had not seen their son in several years, ever since he'd dropped out of Brown University in his junior year. For the past four years Mark had been wandering from town to town in the Southwest, working odd jobs. A period of finding himself, some might call it. Ben and Carolyn had both tried to be patient with him. To understand that he needed his own space to work things out. But over time their patience had slowly worn down to frustration. They simply yearned to see him, to talk things out. To understand what he was going through. But how could they help him if he only pushed them away? Mark even went so far as to deny that there was a problem, any rift at all.

Maybe with the arrival of Rachel's baby, this precious new link, the Lord will mend the broken places in our family circle, Ben thought hopefully. A scrap of a quote came to mind that lifted his spirits, though he couldn't recall the author.

" 'A baby is a messenger of peace and love, a link between angels and men,' " he said quietly to his wife. "I can't remember where I heard that. I think it might be part of a poem."

Carolyn smiled, taking in the words. "I don't recall that one. But I've often felt that way myself."

The couple sat quietly, holding hands as they listened to the music and watched the dancers. Although their conversation about Mark had touched on a sensitive nerve,

Carolyn felt a comforting silence draw them together.

She stole a sideways glance at Ben. Her husband didn't look like a grandfather. Somehow, he still looked the same as the day they'd met—especially his bright gaze and easy, warm smile. His medium height and hardy wrestler's build suited her, and she loved his thick, reddish brown hair, now threaded with gray. He'd always worn glasses, she recalled, but he didn't have the beard back then, which was now neatly trimmed, close to his cheeks and jaw. It was mostly gray now, as well. She could hardly remember what Ben looked like without it.

When the slow ballad ended, Joe Morgan took over the banjo. Carolyn saw Joe's son Sam leading his thirteen-year-old niece, Lauren, out to dance. Sam's dark good looks and muscular build were typical of the Morgan men, as was his wide, warm smile. With her big brown eyes and curly dark hair, Lauren resembled her uncle so much that they might have been mistaken for father and daughter. Sam was certainly a father figure to his nieces, Carolyn knew, ever since his sister Molly had gotten divorced. Sam helped a good deal with Molly's two kids. And Molly needed the help. The girls' father wasn't giving either financial or emotional support.

Lauren had started piano lessons with Carolyn a few months ago and was making great progress. Sam often brought her or picked her up from the house. Carolyn suspected that he also footed the cost of the lessons and other "extras" for the girls. Carolyn wouldn't have charged at all, under the circumstances, but Molly had insisted.

Carolyn wondered why Sam didn't have a family of his own by now. He seemed to love children. Tonight he'd come without a date, she'd noticed. But his entire family was here at the Potters'—six sisters and brothers altogether—most of them married. The Morgans were a wonderful clan, from hardworking Yankee stock. Their ancestors had been among the town founders, and many of the current generation had remained on Cape Light, living in the village or nearby. Carolyn knew Joe and Marie well from church. And Sam, who attended Sunday service regularly, was always quick to lend a hand when the church required carpentry or other repairs.

"I like the sound of a banjo," Carolyn remarked to her husband. "It's perfect for a summer night."

"Yes, it is," Ben agreed, enjoying the lilting music. "I didn't realize Joe was so good."

"Mmm . . ." Carolyn was looking at Sam Morgan dancing with his niece. "I wonder why Sam is still single," she said.

Ben laughed. "Now there's a non sequitur if I ever heard one," he teased. "How did you jump from the banjo to Sam getting married?"

Carolyn gazed at him and smiled. "It would make perfect sense if you were a woman," she told him. Ben heard a trace of her southern accent in her words, a trait that still made his heartbeat quicken.

"Many things would make more sense, I have no doubt." He squinted as he tried to remember what he knew about Sam. "I think Sam had a girl a few years back. I believe they were even engaged. But it didn't work out."

"Yes, I remember," Carolyn said, still watching the dance. "But that was several years ago. Long enough to try again, don't you think?"

"Well, I think it depends on the person," Ben replied. "Are you plotting some matchmaking, Carolyn?"

"Who, me? Not at all," his wife said innocently. "I'm not the type, you know that by now. Besides, I'm sure Sam has no trouble finding his own dates. He's certainly handsome enough." Then she glanced at Ben and added, "Not as handsome as you, dear. Of course."

"Of course," the reverend agreed.

"I just wondered, is all. Sam is such a nice young man. The settling down type, I mean. I would think he'd have found someone by now."

Ben hadn't really thought about it before, but he had to agree. Sam was a good man, mature and responsible. Generous with his time and friendship, giving in a true Christian spirit. He was a fine-looking man, too. No doubt about that. It did seem curious that he wasn't married, or at least attached.

The reverend's conversations with the younger man had never touched upon matters of the heart. Perhaps Sam's failed romance had hit him harder than he'd ever revealed. Maybe he was afraid to try again.

"To everything there is a season," Ben reminded his wife.

"Yes, of course. That part goes without saying." She glanced at him briefly and squeezed his hand.

Now she and Ben were about to enter a new season in their lives together—as grandparents. Though she'd long looked forward to it, she found that notion remarkable. How had the years passed so quickly? She'd turned around and her children were grown. Rachel, married now, having her own baby. Carolyn felt a bit older, it was true . . . but not that much. Not deep down inside, in some immutable part of the self untouched by time. Some days it felt as if she and Ben had just arrived here in town, when in fact, it had been nearly twenty years now.

But to the good people of Cape Light, even two decades of residence still made one a newcomer, without generations of ancestors buried in the cemetery outside of town. Carolyn sometimes still felt like an outsider. They were fleeting moments, to be sure, but vivid ones. Especially at a gathering like this one. She'd been raised in the South and knew she was different from many of her neighbors. They were superficial differences, for she truly believed that inside, everyone shared the same spirit. Still, those small differences sometimes set her apart, set her at a distance from others. She'd tried to reach across that breach her whole life.

But tonight Carolyn was truly enjoying herself, part of the flow of life around her. Sitting beside her husband, she focused on the moment: the music, the company, the night sky above, and the reassuring touch of Ben's hand in her own. She pushed aside unhappy memories of the past and fears about the future. She was here now, happy and at peace, with plenty of faith and love to sustain her.

EMILY WARWICK WAS THE LAST TO ARRIVE AT THE Potters'. She parked her blue Jeep at the bottom of the hill, then started up the long gravel-covered drive, her gaze fixed on the old house that sat atop the hill. Each passing year seemed to bring the place some new indignity, Emily thought, noticing the crooked shutters, the peeling paint, and the sagging front porch. But in the darkness, with every window glowing with a warm golden light, the pale yellow Queen Anne–style home was a remarkable-looking piece of architecture.

A few families with small children were already on their way home and greeted Emily as they passed by. A few languid party guests, seeking a break from the music and revelry on the wide porch, also waved to her. Emily waved back, but she didn't stop to chat.

She had been mayor of Cape Light for the last two years, but most of the citizens addressed her by her first name. That was the way she preferred it. Emily had lived here nearly her entire life and knew that her familiarity was a large part of the reason she'd been elected. Unmarried and without children, her job was her life, a twenty-four-hour-a-day commitment. Or obsession, depending on how you looked at it, she reflected wryly.

While Emily hated to think of herself as a politician in

the worst sense of the word, it was hard sometimes to separate her public persona from her authentic inner self. But tonight she'd come to the gathering as a longtime friend of the Potters—and just another fan of Sophie's famous shortcake.

She moved past the house and followed the path through the cutting garden. It was filled with waves of pink stasis and daisies, blue and purple bearded iris, and the bold-faced lilies. Tufts of greenery promised plenty more to come: black-eyed Susans and pink coneflowers, Sophie's glamour-girl dahlias, and for the summer's grand finale, rows and rows of sunflowers.

Sophie always cut her bouquets early in the morning. Then she set them out at a roadside stand, along with pies, jars of honey from her bees, and baskets of fruit. There was a shoe box, too, for the money. It was the honor system all the way, but it worked around here, Emily knew. That was one reason she'd stayed in Cape Light all these years.

Emily reached the end of the garden and gazed ahead. The field, with its glowing lights and happy crowd, was just a short distance away. She hardly noticed the man in the shadows nearby.

"You're late, Mayor."

Emily turned to see Dan Forbes standing behind her on the path.

"Was it a full roster of appearances today? I didn't think the campaign kicked off until August."

Emily greeted him with an easy smile. "Who said I was even running again? I don't believe I ever did."

"Sorry, I stand corrected, then." Dan's tone was serious, but he gave her a knowing grin.

Emily had known Dan for years yet couldn't really say she knew him well. He owned and ran the local newspaper, *The Cape Light Messenger*, first published by his great-grandfather. Now that she was mayor and he was

"The Press," Emily was Dan's official moving target. They got along relatively well, despite some conflicting opinions on town issues. Still, Dan kept her on her toes, from an unbiased distance. Sometimes Emily wondered if that was due to his professional training or simply his personality.

"On your way out?" she asked.

"Just taking a break before the fireworks. Being my typical unsociable self," he admitted.

Dan fell into step beside her, and they continued walking toward the gathering. "I hope you find something left to eat. It was a pretty good spread."

"I've already eaten. At my mother's," Emily told him.

Dan felt a guilty twinge for needling her. Of course, she'd been keeping her bitter pill of a mother company tonight—just about the only person in town who would. Emily was a good daughter. Too good, Dan thought, for Lillian Warwick, who was now—and always had been—an emotional tyrant. The old woman's recent health problems had only made a bad situation worse. Emily had born the brunt of it, Dan suspected.

Her younger sister, Jessica, had returned to town a few months ago to help out. He was sure that the Potters had invited Jessica tonight, as well, but the younger sister was more like her mother. Probably thought she was above the company.

Emily wasn't that way. Dan had to hand her that. She was easygoing and unpretentious. Straightforward, too. He liked that about her. She seemed to have real concern for the town and genuine connections to its residents. Considering her upbringing, he sometimes wondered how she had escaped the Warwicks' exalted mind-set.

Sophie came up to them and enveloped Emily in a huge hug, her beads and bracelets jangling. "Emily, dear. I've had my eye out for you."

"Hello, Sophie. Better late than never, I hope," Emily apologized.

Dan politely stepped aside, preparing to slip away, when he noticed a group of children racing from the orchard.

He could tell immediately that they weren't playing a game. Something had happened. Something bad.

The kids' high-pitched shouts and desperate faces quickly drew everyone's attention. The dance music abruptly stopped, and everyone ran to see what was wrong. One of the Bates boys, Charlie Junior, commonly known as C.J., was leading the pack of children. He ran straight to his father.

Charlie Senior bent low and took firm hold of his son's shoulders. "What is it? What's the matter? Are you hurt?"

The boy was breathing so hard he could barely speak. "Bees got loose," he managed. "Some kid knocked into the bee house and it tipped over."

Charlie stood up and frowned. "What do you mean, some kid? Did you do it?" he demanded.

"No, it wasn't me, Dad. Honest," his son promised, sounding on the edge of tears. "They're flying around the orchard, Dad. Maybe they won't come this way," he added lamely.

C.J. glanced from his father to his mother, Lucy, who had quickly stepped over. The boy looked up at her hopefully. Her pretty face took on a tight look, and she slipped an arm around her son's shoulders.

By now Gus and Sophie had heard the alarm. "Everybody into the house!" Gus shouted. "Head for cover!"

But the guests milled around, confused and unwilling, or simply not understanding why they had to disperse.

"The bees are loose!" Gus called. "Get to the house. Or into your cars. Please."

Sophie was the first to spot a few of the vanguard bees. They were headed straight for the dessert table.

"Heaven help us, here they come," Gus said in a strained tone.

"Just keep everyone back," his wife instructed. "I can take care of it."

She moved forward and he grabbed at her arm. "Are you crazy? You'll get yourself stung to death."

"Calm down. I know what I'm doing," Sophie insisted, brushing him off.

She then took the gauzy overslip layer of her dress and tossed it up overhead from the back to the front, so that it covered her face and hung down to her chest, like a Spanish mantilla. By now, all of the guests who had not run for safety stood in a tight knot at the far end of the field.

As Sophie walked with slow, deliberate steps in the opposite direction, some of her guests cheered on her on. "Go get 'em, Sophie! That's the way!"

But others soon hushed the cheerleaders, and even Gus stopped urging people to seek cover. Everyone stood perfectly still and silent, mesmerized by the sight of Sophie in her long gown and makeshift veil, bathed in moonlight, striding across the field as purposefully as a bride.

Finally the swarm approached, wafting out from the orchard like a humming black plume of smoke. Sophie stood still, waiting, her arms stretched up to the sky.

Later some would say they'd heard Sophie Potter call the bees to her with a special song. Some would even argue that she did a special dance. But they would all agree that she slowly turned, her arms stretched out to either side. The swarm of bees settled over her body, twisting around like a small black tornado. And when Sophie stopped turning, she stood covered with a teeming, buzzing black mantle, which coated her arms and chest, back and shoulders, even her head.

In awe, Dan Forbes watched silently. But he still managed the presence of mind to grab a camera from a nearby table and snap a photograph.

Then Sophie started walking into the orchard, her steps painstakingly slow, as if she balanced a stack of crystal goblets on her head.

Some couldn't watch and covered their eyes. Sophie's oldest daughter, Evelyn, watched but bit down on a finger until she tasted blood. Fearing that the bees would be disturbed and start to sting, no one dared to utter a word while Sophie stood in sight. Gus kicked at the dirt and berated himself silently for permitting his thick-headed wife to attempt such a thing. And the Reverend Ben, staring at Sophie wide-eyed, whispered a prayer.

When Sophie finally disappeared into the shadows—headed for the bee house, no doubt—Gus and Evelyn dashed across the field to follow her. Dr. Ezra Elliot ran after them, too, with the black satchel he'd quickly retrieved from his car.

The crowd murmured with astonishment. All agreed they had heard about folk who had the ability to charm bees, but no one had ever actually witnessed such a feat.

Nobody seemed to know what to do. The guests milled around, talking about Sophie. The young culprits who had started the trouble were pulled aside by parents, questioned, and scolded. But no one could really determine who had turned over the hive. It didn't seem that important now.

"Here she comes!" Harry Reilly shouted suddenly, the first to spot Sophie returning.

The over-slip of her gown was back in place, but Sophie's hairdo had shifted to one side. Gus held her arm protectively, watching her every step. She looked flushed and breathless but otherwise unharmed. Dr. Elliot and Evelyn followed close behind.

"It's all right, everybody. I got them back in, safe and sound," Sophie reported. "Everything is fine."

Her guests started clapping: Sophie shook her head. "Go on, stop that," she said, waving them away.

But the clapping and the cheers didn't stop. Blushing, Sophie tried to right her lopsided hairdo. Then she smiled, squared her shoulders, and took a deep, graceful curtsy, holding out the corners of her gown as she'd been taught at Miss Dinah's School of Dance, so many years ago.

Her guests applauded even harder as Sophie stood up once more. Then, as if it had been carefully planned, the first of the night's fireworks streaked across the sky and burst into a sparkling shower of light above Sophie's head.

Everyone looked to the sky, their attention drawn by the noise and light. They gasped in delight and felt the deafening boom of the explosions down to their bones.

But, for many, the light show seemed rather anticlimactic this year after Sophie's remarkable performance.

JESSICA WAS IN HER BEDROOM, UNPACKING HER BAG from the weekend, when the fireworks began. She left her task and went outside to watch. Her apartment was on the first floor of an old house in the village, and she had the use of the small backyard.

She sat on the steps leading down from a narrow back porch and looked up at the sky, grateful for the diversion. She lived only a few blocks from the harbor, and the fireworks seemed to be exploding right overhead.

The visit to her mother had been draining, as usual. Emily had been there earlier and had even left a light supper that Jessica served to Lillian out on the patio. Still, the back-to-back visits from her daughters were apparently not satisfactory to Lillian. Her mother remained touchy and querulous, finding fault with everything from the bread Emily had bought, which she claimed tasted stale, to the purple spiderwort in her back garden.

"What's wrong with the spiderwort?" Jessica had ventured to ask. The flowers looked fine to Jessica, just coming into bloom.

"What's wrong?" Lillian echoed. "I thought you knew something about gardening. Obviously not. It shouldn't be drooping that way," she added, poking a few floppy stems with her cane. "It needs to be thinned or it will choke out everything."

"Don't worry, Mother. I'll take care of it for you."

Her mother cast her a dark look. "You said you'd work in the garden last week, but you never came."

"I was busy at work. But I promise I'll come this week," Jessica had assured her.

She would try, she thought. Maybe one night after work. She didn't have much to do in the evenings around here anyway. Now that it stayed light so much longer, Cape Light's lack of entertainment had become more obvious.

Besides, Jessica felt obliged to do what she could. She wouldn't be living here too much longer. Her mother had nearly recovered from her stroke. Most likely, by the end of the summer, Jessica would be free to return to her real life again.

It wasn't so bad to be stuck here for the summer, Jessica told herself. The beaches were beautiful and rarely crowded. Maybe she could persuade some of her friends from Boston to visit. She hoped they would. Sometimes the weekends seemed very long. She never had a date. So far she hadn't met one single guy in Cape Light . . . at least, no one who met her standards.

Then there was Paul Copperfield, the man she was seeing occasionally . . . too occasionally for Jessica.

They had met a few months ago while she was in Boston on business. He'd come out to Cape Light to see her once or twice, and they went out when she visited the city. So far it was still a casual thing. Nothing steady or serious. They were still getting to know each other.

Paul was different from most of the men she'd dated lately. He was older, more mature. And quite sophisticated. He'd recently started up his own firm, doing corporate systems analysis. He was ambitious, successful, and interesting. Jessica liked Paul a lot and was fairly certain he liked her. If only they didn't live so far apart, Jessica was sure the relationship would have progressed further by now.

She hadn't been able to see Paul this weekend, but he would be driving through town tomorrow, on his way back to Boston from Vermont. They had a date for lunch, and Jessica was looking forward to it.

The fireworks ended in a resounding burst of light and color. Jessica heard a few lingering *pops*, and then abruptly it was over. The stars were visible again, and the soft warm night closed in around her.

Time to go inside, Jessica decided. It was getting late. Then she heard a sound from under the stairs, like a baby crying.

She leaned over to take a look. It was hard to see in the dark, but after a moment or two on her knees she could distinguish a soft feline shape, wedged in a frightened ball under the bottom step.

"Hello, cat," Jessica murmured. "What are you doing down there? Did the noise scare you?"

The cat didn't make a sound. Yellow eyes glowed at her in the darkness. Then the cat squirmed, fitting itself even more compactly under the step. Jessica knew instinctively that if she reached out to it, she'd end up scratched.

Still, she felt sorry for the cat and stayed hunched over, kneeling in the dirt, watching it for a while. She couldn't see a collar and she guessed it was wild. There were a lot of feral cats in the woods outside of town. She couldn't tell the animal's coloring in the dark. Maybe orange and white. Or a calico. The creature had a long bushy tail and one ear looked crumpled, probably chewed in a fight.

She'd found a cat this way once, when her family had moved in to the new house in the village. She'd slowly won it over and cared for it in secret. With few friends at school, she'd had a lot of time in the afternoons for taking care of the stray.

"Okay, pal. Stay put. I'll be right back with some food for you," Jessica told her timid visitor.

She didn't need a pet right now. And certainly not a dirty wild cat. But she would leave it a little food. The poor thing was probably hungry.

CHAPTER TWO

❧

*I*T WAS BUSINESS AS USUAL THE NEXT MORNING AT the Clam Box, with plates clattering and batter sizzling on the grill. The rich smells of coffee, bacon, and home fries were so thick in the air, hungry customers were tempted to take an invisible bite.

Charlie Bates manned the grill, stepping up to the counter to exchange a few words with the regulars or shout an order at his wife.

Lucy ran around with the coffeepot, jotting down orders, bringing the food to the tables, and cleaning up in between. The other waitress had walked out in a huff two weeks ago—she couldn't put up with Charlie's temper—and they still hadn't found a replacement. A Help Wanted sign hung in the window, alongside the sun-faded poster that read, "Try Our Famous Clam Rolls and Blueberry Pancakes—Box Lunches To Go."

A number of customers had been at the Potters' party, and that morning Sophie's bee charming was being widely discussed. Especially since a photo of Sophie in all her insect-covered glory had made the front page of the *Messenger*. "Cape Light's most charming hostess entertains some uninvited guests," the caption read.

Tucker Tulley, senior officer in the town's police force, who'd been on duty during the party, seemed disappointed that he'd missed the action.

"I bet Gus was nearly having a heart attack," he said to Lucy. "I'm surprised no one called for EMS."

"Dr. Elliot ran right into the orchard after Sophie," Lucy explained. "But Sophie came out just fine. Said she didn't get one sting. It was amazing."

Charlie came up to the counter and served Tucker a side of bacon. "Never mind Sophie Potter. What about this . . ." He quickly turned the page to an advertisement that announced the Grand Opening of the Beanery, complete with a clip-out coupon.

"I saw them out in the street, giving out free samples," he told Tucker. "Blocking the sidewalk, serving food outside the premises—isn't there some law or ordinance prohibiting that?"

His mouth full of doughnut, Tucker chewed slowly before replying. "Nope . . . I don't think so. As long as they clean up the litter. I wasn't going to tell you, Charlie," he added, "but I tried one of those gourmet coffee drinks on my way over. What do they call it? A Lottie? A loddy?"

"A latte," Lucy cut in. "It's coffee with steamed milk."

"Whatever." Tucker shook his head. "I don't get it. That coffee's all foam, like drinking a cup of shaving cream. People around here won't pay two dollars for a cup of foam."

"Let's hope so." Charlie wiped down the counter and straightened the napkin holder. "Or I'm out of business."

"Oh, Charlie, stop exaggerating. They're not serving real food. It's just coffee," Lucy said.

"And cakes and funny little sandwiches. And this and

that," Charlie argued. "I heard Molly Willoughby was baking for them. That's the last time we buy from her," he told Lucy.

"Charlie, she's a single mother, for goodness' sake. The woman has to earn a living. Why shouldn't she sell to them, too, if she can?"

Charlie scowled at his wife as she left to take an order. *"The Beanery."* He drew out the name. "Felicity and Jonathan Bean and their gourmet coffee beans. Cute, right? What are they doing up here anyway? Where did they even come from?"

"College professors from Cambridge, I heard. They're retired," Tucker said.

"So? Why don't they just buy a boat or something, like everybody else who retires up here? Who says they have to go and open a coffee shop two feet from my place? They look like two burned-out old hippies, if you ask me."

"Gee, Charlie, that's real open-minded and friendly of you," Tucker chided him.

Lucy returned with two orders. She clipped them to the pass-through near the grill, then struck the bell a few times. "Cheese omelet, rye toast. Fried egg sandwich to go."

"Yeah, all right. I heard you." Charlie scratched the back of his neck, then glanced at Tucker, who was quietly laughing. "Stop laughing at me, Tucker. This could be serious."

Tucker chewed a bite of bacon. "Don't get yourself worked up over nothing. It's just coffee, for Pete's sake."

Lucy exchanged a glance with Tucker as she filled his mug again, but left him to read his newspaper. She moved down to a customer who had just entered, a young woman sitting where the counter curved.

"Care for some coffee?" she asked.

"Yes, please." The young woman put aside her book

and pushed her mug toward Lucy. She'd been reading a tourist guide to the area, Lucy noticed, and also had a map out.

You could tell a lot about people by watching them, Lucy thought. She liked to study the customers and try to guess about their lives. Lucy could tell the young woman wasn't from New England just from the way she answered about the coffee. She looked about college age, with long dark hair pulled back in a ponytail and bright blue eyes. Her T-shirt read University of Maryland, and Lucy guessed she was a student there.

"Ready to order?" Lucy asked.

The girl looked at the menu, then back at Lucy. "How about the famous blueberry pancakes?"

Lucy glanced over her shoulder, then turned back to the girl. "It's not really blueberry season around here for another month or so. I think he's using frozen ones now," she confided. "The French toast is very good, though."

"I'll have the French toast, then, please." The girl handed the menu to Lucy and smiled. "Thanks."

"No problem." Lucy jotted down the order. She reached under the counter and brought out silverware and a napkin. "Are you here on vacation?"

"Oh . . . uh, sort of." The girl seemed shy. She tucked a strand of hair behind her ear. "I always wanted to see New England, and I thought I'd just come up here and drive around."

"Well, there's plenty to see," Lucy told her. "We have a nice historical center across from the town hall, just down the street. Then there's the Warwick Estate on the Beach Road and the Durham Lighthouse out on the point. It's nice there around sunset," she added.

"Thanks. I'll check it out."

The girl smiled again and looked back down at her guidebook. Lucy suddenly saw a flash of something familiar in her face, though she was sure they'd never met before. She couldn't quite place it.

Then the door opened and Emily Warwick came in, distracting Lucy from the question.

"You're running a little late today, Mayor," Lucy noticed.

"Just plain running as usual," Emily replied with a smile. She put down her briefcase and sat on a stool next to the young woman. "I'll have an order to go, I guess. Large coffee, small orange juice, and a cranberry muffin, please."

"You got it." Lucy poured Emily a mug of coffee to drink while she waited and then left to fill the order.

Seated a few stools away, Tucker turned to Emily. "Morning, Mayor," he said respectfully. "Did you see this yet?"

He pushed his copy of the *Messenger* across the counter. Emily picked it up and looked at the photo of Sophie.

"Maybe we ought to put that picture in the town archives or something," Tucker suggested.

"Good idea." Emily looked up at him. "It happened so fast, I almost thought I imagined it."

"Yup, I heard. Too bad I missed it," Tucker said.

Emily sipped her coffee and glanced at the paper's headlines. Aside from Sophie, it was a slow news day in Cape Light. A good sign for the start of her week.

She looked up to see Charlie coming toward her with a plate of French toast in one hand, her take-out order in the other, and that telltale cantankerous gleam in his eye. A bad sign, Emily thought as she braced herself for their usual morning debate.

Charlie planned to run against her in the next election, and for months now he'd been using the diner as a soapbox. People had come to expect it, free entertainment along with their breakfast. Emily could have easily avoided him by picking up her breakfast elsewhere, but she didn't want anyone to think she was afraid of Charlie Bates. She absolutely was not.

She would bet dollars to doughnuts that this morning's diatribe would involve the question of parking meters on Main Street. She took a long sip of her coffee and met his eyes.

"Mayor Warwick," he greeted her. As he set the French toast down in front of the young woman seated beside her, Emily noticed the girl's wide-eyed stare. Emily briefly met her glance, then turned back to Charlie.

"A large coffee, a small juice, and a muffin," he said, peering into the bag. "Is that it?"

"That's it." She watched as he slipped some napkins into the brown paper bag but didn't hand it to her.

"I heard some news this morning you ought to know about," he said with authority. "Dr. Elliot is selling that property he owns outside of town, where he rents those cottages. Betty Bowman is already lining up buyers for him." Betty was the town's leading real-estate broker.

"Actually, I do know that." Dr. Elliot had told her about his plans to retire a few nights ago, when he stopped in to visit her mother. He'd mentioned that he had started referring his patients to other doctors in the area and planned on selling his property on the Beach Road. Emily had been sorry to hear he was giving up his practice. He'd been their family doctor for so very long, and a great help to her mother.

"Okay. So you know." Charlie sounded irritated. "What do you plan to do about it?"

"Give Dr. Elliot a retirement party?" she asked innocently.

"Cute," he said. "You know what I mean."

Emily took another sip of coffee. "A private citizen puts property up for sale. What would I have to do with that?"

Of course she knew what Charlie was driving at. She knew the way his mind worked by now. He could make an issue out of repainting the yellow line down Main Street. But she wasn't about to jump at his bait.

"Elliot could sell that land to anyone. Some builder could come along, knock down the cottages, and put up some ugly eyesore that would ruin the whole town. You're the mayor. You got to talk to him. Make sure he's selling to the right kind of people."

Emily raised one eyebrow. "The right kind of people?"

"The land borders right on the Warwick Estate. I'd think you'd be concerned about that, at least."

The last jab had been targeted to strike a nerve, Emily noticed. And it had, although she was adept at hiding her feelings. The Warwick Estate had been in her father's family for generations, until necessity had demanded that her parents give it up. Her mother had worked out a deal, selling the mansion and the property with its beautiful gardens to the town to be preserved as a historic site.

Emily didn't need Charlie to tell her that the estate was important to the village. She squelched the urge to stuff his mouth with one of his famous clam rolls.

"Charlie, you're way off base on this one. For one thing, I wasn't elected to regulate real estate transactions. And for another, I think you're panicking. You don't know who's going to buy that land. Betty might find someone who wants to make a bird sanctuary out of it."

Emily heard some muffled snickers behind her and realized that people in the diner had been eavesdropping on the debate. Sounded like she'd scored a point. Though getting laughed at had only made Charlie madder.

"Betty Bowman doesn't deal much with bird lovers, from what I can see," Charlie argued. "She deals with money lovers. Big, greedy contractors who'll put up anything to turn over a dollar, then take off." He leaned toward her, his face red. "It's not just me. People aren't going to like this once it gets around, I guarantee you."

"I disagree. But we'll have to wait and see, won't we?" Emily stood up and held out some bills. "Is that my coffee?" she asked pointedly, looking down at the paper bag he'd been so reluctant to hand over.

He handed the bag across the counter and took her money.

"Thanks. Have a good day," she said evenly as she left.

"Yeah, you too, Mayor," Charlie grumbled at her back. After she'd left, he looked over at Tucker. "You believe her? Some kind of mayor, that's all I have to say."

Tucker stood up and brushed some crumbs off his uniform.

"I think she does a decent job. You're hard on her, because you keep thinking what you'd do in her shoes. But you're not in her shoes yet, pal," Tucker reminded him.

"I will be if people in this town have any common sense." Charlie crossed his arms over his chest. His scowl suddenly turned to a wide smile. "You'd better be nice to me, Officer Tulley. I might be your new boss soon."

"Yeah, you might. I'd better start looking into early retirement," the police officer replied as he carefully placed his hat on his head.

Charlie went back to the grill, and Lucy walked around with a pot of coffee, giving refills. She reached the girl with the tour book last. Lucy noticed she'd finished her French toast and was now writing in a notebook. "More coffee?"

The girl looked up, appearing distracted or rattled about something, Lucy thought.

"Um . . . no, thanks. Just the check, please."

"Sure, hon." Lucy pulled the girl's check from a pad in her pocket, tallied it up, and placed it on the counter next to the girl's plate. "Here you go. How was your breakfast?"

"Very good, thanks." The girl closed the notebook and slipped it in her backpack along with the guidebook. She drew out a wallet and pulled out some bills. "That woman who was in here a few minutes ago talking to the cook. That was the mayor?"

"That was our mayor, Emily Warwick," Lucy confirmed. "And the guy giving her grief was my husband," she added with a laugh. "I think she's doing a good job. Though obviously, Charlie does not agree."

"I noticed. He seemed pretty upset with her."

"That's just his way." Lucy glanced over her shoulder again, checking to see if Charlie was out of earshot. "If it's not one thing, it's another."

The young girl didn't reply. Her thoughts were whirling. She'd come all this way looking for Emily Warwick, thinking she might have to stay in town for days to track her down. Then she'd practically sat right in her lap. And she turned out to be the mayor here. It . . . wasn't what she had expected.

She glanced up as she realized Lucy was staring at her. "Oh, sorry. Here you are." She handed over the bills. "My name is Sara, by the way."

"My name is Lucy. Lucy Bates." She looked down at her hand, wiped it on her apron, and extended it to the girl. "Nice to meet you. Maybe I'll see you again before you leave town."

"Maybe you will. It's very pretty here. I might stay a few days. I'm not sure."

"Got the summer off?"

"Sort of. I graduated a few weeks ago and I don't have a job yet."

"Don't worry. You'll find something," Lucy assured her.

"Yeah, well, first I have to look, I guess," Sara replied with a grin.

Lucy laughed. "That might help. What did you study?"

"I was an English major. Not a big career track," Sara added.

"Oh, but that's interesting. Do you want to be an English teacher, like in a high school or something?"

"I'm not sure. I like to write."

"Well, maybe you'll be a writer, then." Lucy rang up the check and handed Sara the change. "Hang around here awhile. You'll find plenty to write about."

Sara laughed. "Maybe I will." She tucked a tip under the edge of her plate and picked up her knapsack again. "Bye, Lucy," she said as she headed for the door.

"See you," Lucy replied, smiling.

LUCY WAS TAKING AN ORDER AT A LARGE TABLE WHEN Grace Hegman walked in, her yellow Labrador retriever, Daisy, following close at her heels. Dogs were not allowed in the diner, but Grace and Daisy were an exception to the rule. Besides, Grace rarely ate at the Clam Box, though her father Digger often did. Lucy had a feeling she was looking for him.

Grace stood at the door and looked around. Then, as Lucy had predicted, she asked very loudly, "Anyone see my father?"

"Try Reilly's Boatyard," Warren Oakes, an attorney in town, suggested.

Grace looked skeptical. "Reilly's? I doubt it."

"I saw Digger headed that way myself," another voice agreed.

"But he knows he's not supposed to go wandering around Reilly's anymore," Grace said to no one in particular. Looking worried and confused, Grace met Lucy's gaze. "Harry Reilly said he was going to get the police involved next time he caught my father trespassing."

Lucy picked up a glass and wiped it with a towel. "Maybe you ought to just go take a look," she said gently.

Lucy had heard that Harry had hired Digger to work in the yard. Digger had been in earlier, when the diner opened at half past six, looking proud to be on his way to his new job.

Grace wouldn't like it when she heard, Lucy was sure. And Lucy wasn't going to be the one to break the news to her, either.

A customer at a back booth waved for service, and Lucy went to check on his table. Grace remained in front of the door, standing perfectly still, her lips pursed in a thoughtful expression. Warren Oakes smiled at Daisy and held out a tidbit of bacon. "Here, doggie," he coaxed gently.

Daisy licked her chops and replied with a canine smile, but remained solidly seated at Grace's feet.

Warren met Grace's stare. "Can your dog have a little bacon?"

"No, she cannot," Grace replied firmly. She turned on her heel and opened the door. "Come, Daisy," she said. The dog rose instantly and followed her.

Lucy watched Grace go. She'd like to be a fly on the wall when Grace caught up with Harry Reilly and Digger. There would be more fireworks at the harbor this morning, for sure.

Charlie met her as she turned back to the counter. "Just saw another one of our regulars pass with one of those Bean drinks. You've got to get out there, Lucy, see what's what."

"Me?" Lucy stared at him. "Why me? I don't want to go spy on those people."

"Of course you have to go. I can't leave right in the middle of breakfast," Charlie insisted. "Here, take this thing off. You have to look like a normal person." He

reached out and untied her apron strings. "Just run down
the street and see what they're doing. Take a look inside
and see if any of our regulars are there."

"But I can't just—"

"This is an emergency. They could put us out of business. How would you like that?"

Lucy glared at him and snatched her apron back. She
pulled a tube of lipstick out of the front pocket. Checking
her reflection in the mirrored wall behind the cereal boxes,
she added a little lipstick and poked her fingers in her
curly blond hair.

"Go on," Charlie said. "You don't need to primp, for
goodness' sake."

"I'm going, Charlie. Just calm down." Lucy shook her
head at him and hooked her purse over her shoulder, then
left the diner in a huff.

JESSICA WARWICK WALKED QUICKLY DOWN MAIN
Street in her best black heels, headed for the bank. The
fancy shoes were already starting to pinch a bit, but she
willed herself to put up with them, at least until after her
lunch date with Paul.

She noticed Lucy Bates rushing out of the diner, root-
ing through her purse as she walked, but didn't really pay
attention until the other woman nearly walked right into
her.

"Jessica . . . oh, I'm sorry." Lucy grabbed Jessica's arm
to steady herself.

"That's okay." Lucy had dropped a pair of sunglasses,
and Jessica bent to retrieve them. Lucy looked even more
harried than usual, she noticed. "Are you okay?"

"Me? I'm fine. Just got to check on something for
Charlie. You have a good day now," she added. She
slipped on the dark glasses and rushed off in the opposite
direction.

Jessica often stopped at the Clam Box for coffee in the morning, but she had no time today. She'd hit the snooze button on her alarm one too many times and then had dressed in a rush. She hoped she looked right for her date. The gray-blue suit—a sheath with a matching long jacket—was simple but elegant. She'd added gold earrings and a bracelet. But maybe the earrings were too much? Too big? She'd ask her friend Suzanne Foster at work.

Why did some people think dating was so much fun? Jessica wondered as she entered the bank's cool interior. Dating was definitely high stress. Sometimes her job seemed a lot easier than trying to have a social life.

Jessica hadn't expected it, but there had been distinct advantages in her transfer from Boston to this backwater branch. Her career had actually advanced here. She wasn't lost in a large staff; her experience and hard work were noticed. She'd even gotten a raise and a promotion last month, along with a new, larger office space that included a window.

Or rather, she *would* have a window once the renovations were done, converting a space on the second floor that had previously been used for storage. As she walked down the corridor toward her office, she heard a loud, ominous noise coming from inside. She pulled open the door and gasped. Her office was a complete wreck.

A workman stood in the middle of the mess. His broad back turned to her, he was attacking the far wall with a loud, serious-looking piece of machinery, the battle giving off swirling clouds of white dust.

Jessica remembered then that the office manager had told her a carpenter was scheduled for Wednesday morning.

But today was Tuesday.

And there he was.

And she was already behind, due to present a report

that she hadn't completed at a staff meeting this afternoon. The last thing she needed was to be surrounded by a dust tornado and an irritating racket.

"Excuse me . . ." Jessica called out. "Uh . . . sir? Could you please stop that a minute? . . . Please?"

If he'd heard her at all, he gave no sign. He didn't turn or shift a bulky muscle. He was concentrating intently on slicing a hole in her wall with his machine, which looked fairly heavy and even dangerous. He wore protective goggles and a mask over his mouth.

"Hey . . . could you shut that off a minute?" Jessica called out more loudly.

Still no response. Jessica stepped out from behind her desk and approached him. Puffs of white powder filled the air as the tool cut into the plasterboard wall. His dark curly hair was coated with it, she noticed. *She'd* be coated with it in a minute if she didn't watch out. Just what she needed to complete her high-style look—a coating of plaster dust.

She reached out and tapped one broad shoulder.

Suddenly the buzzing noise stopped. The workman pulled the machine away from the wall, and looked down at her. He was just slightly taller than she was in her heels. They stood practically nose to nose. Still, his broad shoulders and powerful build gave a solid, almost intimidating impression. He quickly pushed down the mask to talk.

"Yes?" he asked politely.

"You're not supposed to be working in here today," she stated flatly. "I was told you would be here on Wednesday. As in tomorrow."

He pushed the eye gear up on his head and took a long look at her. His tanned skin was covered with a fine layer of dust. Still, she couldn't help but be struck by his strong, ruggedly attractive features—lean cheeks, square jaw, and blunt chin.

"Sorry, that's not what I was told." His expression was

perfectly polite, yet something in his dark eyes hinted at amusement.

He pulled a slip of paper out his back pocket and read from it, "Room thirty-five, double window in the southwest wall, Thermopane glass, exterior crown molding, white polyvinyl framing . . . so on and so forth. . . ." He handed her the work order, which was signed by the office manager and showed Tuesday's date. "Official enough for you?"

Terrific. She had to get a wise guy besides.

"I was told you wouldn't be in here until tomorrow," she began reasonably enough. "I would have prepared for this—taken work home or something. What am I supposed to do now?" Jessica heard her voice rising, but she couldn't help herself. "Look at this place. It's a total mess!"

"Absolutely," he agreed. "Unfortunately . . . it's going to get worse before it gets better."

"Great . . . that's just great." Not only a wise guy, but a wise guy with a philosophical streak. Jessica turned in a half circle, taking it all in. "I need to get at files and things. I need to use my computer. . . . Where *is* my computer?" she asked suddenly.

"Hmmm, let's see. It's around here somewhere." His face took on a thoughtful expression as he nimbly stepped over tools and equipment. Surprisingly agile in his large boots, she thought vaguely. Then he smiled again. "Okay, I remember now, I rolled the whole cart into the office next door. Even with a cover on top, I thought it might get too dusty."

Well, that had been considerate of him. "Thanks, that was a good idea."

She felt a bit calmer and, as she surveyed the mess, somewhat resigned to having her day turned upside down.

"This big gray lump over here is your desk," he went on, "and I pushed the file cabinets back against this wall.

I just covered the bookcase," he added, pointing to more drop cloth–covered shapes.

Jessica nodded.

"I'd rather not stop right in the middle," he admitted, glancing at the partial hole in the wall. "But, of course, I can if I have to."

She glanced at him and then away. She felt an urge to be imperious and demanding. She didn't like having her well-ordered office, her personal territory, turned inside out without any warning at all.

Then she squelched the reaction. She didn't want to act like a Warwick. It was bad enough that some people in town expected her to.

Besides, she realized, there was no sense tossing him out now. It would only make the mess last longer.

"The place is already a disaster. You may as well stay and try to finish," she said as graciously as she could.

"I should be done by the end of the day. Except for the finish work. Might have to come back for that. But I'll have everything back the way I found it by five o'clock tonight. Don't worry."

Jessica met his dark-eyed gaze. Despite the plaster dust and the goggles on his head, she couldn't help noticing again that he was handsome. Incredibly handsome. He wasn't her type, of course. Still, if she looked at him long enough, he sort of took her breath away.

Suddenly feeling self-conscious, Jessica turned to her desk and started to raise the drop cloth so she could open the drawers.

"Let me do that for you," he offered. "You'll get all dusty."

She stepped back and watched as he carefully rolled back the cloth.

"Thanks." She pulled open a side drawer and tried to ignore him. But she was keenly aware of the fact that he was standing less than a foot away, watching her. She grabbed some files that she needed for the day and stacked them on her desk. Somehow her nameplate slipped off the desktop and dropped to the floor.

He quickly picked it up. "Jessica Warwick, Assistant Manager," he read her name and title aloud as he handed it back to her. "Jessica Warwick. Of course. I thought I recognized you. But I wasn't sure."

Jessica stared at him, puzzled. Did they know each other? She was sure she wouldn't have forgotten a man with his looks. Unless early senility was setting in. Still, she couldn't place him and felt embarrassed. He clearly seemed to remember her.

"You don't remember me, I guess," he said. "Sam Morgan. I was a few years ahead of you at school."

"Oh, sure. I'm sorry," Jessica apologized.

It had been at least ten years since she'd last seen Sam Morgan, and they'd moved in different social circles back then.

"That's all right." He didn't seem offended. "It's been a long time. I didn't recognize you at first, either," he admitted. "When did you come back to town?"

"A few months ago. Around Christmastime."

"Really? I had no idea you'd moved back."

Jessica glanced down at her files again. That wasn't surprising. They probably still moved in different social circles.

"Where were you living?" he asked.

"In Boston. But my mother had a stroke last fall, and I decided to come back to help take care of her."

"That was good of you."

"My sister needed some help. But my mother has improved a lot. I may be able to move back to the city soon."

Sam looked surprised. "Oh, so it's only short-term?"

"That's right. Just temporary."

If he had any interest in her at all, she had just sent him a message, loud and clear. He was attractive enough, that was for sure. But he was definitely and absolutely not her type. She turned her back to him and lifted up the heavy pile of file folders, her calculator balanced on top.

"Here, I can carry those," Sam offered.

"That's okay. I can handle it."

Jessica knew he was just trying to be polite, but she didn't want any more of his help. She swept past him and out the door, carrying her load to the coffee room at the end of the hall. She'd work there today. That was all there was to it. She could borrow a laptop if she needed a computer. She'd check her e-mail somewhere, too. She'd just have to get by.

She settled down to work, but her thoughts wandered back to Sam Morgan. They'd never been friendly in school. But, of course, she'd had a certain notoriety back then. The poor little rich girl who wasn't so rich anymore. She'd been a real honor-roll grind then, partly because Lillian would accept no less, but also because keeping her head stuck in a book had been the perfect way to hide out.

Jessica didn't like being recognized by people she grew up with. She was sure that once they remembered her, they remembered the scandal that had toppled her family from their social perch. Even now, with Emily being an extremely respectable mayor, memories of the way people had talked about their family still made Jessica uncomfortable. That was one of the reasons she'd moved to the city.

Sam had to be about three or four years older than she was, Jessica remembered. The Morgans were a big family with maybe five or six kids. He had a sister her own age, she now recalled. Margie? No, it was Molly. Molly had been sort of a wild type.

Molly still lived in town, too, Jessica was sure of that. Her last name was Willoughby now. She was a single mother, divorced, who took a lot of odd jobs to make ends meet. Emily had mentioned something just last week about hiring Molly to do some cooking and cleaning for their mother, the latest entry in a long parade of household help that had come and gone. Well, Molly had always been pretty tough. Maybe she was even tough enough to put up with Lillian.

"Hi, Jessica. What are you doing working in here?"

Jessica looked up to see her friend Suzanne pouring herself a cup of coffee. "My office has turned into a construction site. In case you didn't notice."

"Believe me, I noticed. Who's the masked man? He looks like a superhero with power tools."

Jessica laughed despite herself. Suzanne was a great friend but had a completely different perspective when it came to men.

"His name is Sam Morgan. And the faster he disappears, the happier I'll be. Though so far, he seems like a nice guy." Jessica didn't know why she felt obliged to add that last part. It had just popped out.

"I'd put up with a little sawdust to hang out with him," Suzanne said as she stirred her coffee. "Maybe he'll have lunch with us."

The idea surprised Jessica. Suzanne was a lot bolder than she could ever be. She'd never think of inviting a guy like Sam to lunch, though there was really nothing wrong with it.

"Sorry," Jessica said. "I already have a lunch date."

"I thought something was going on with you." Suzanne sounded intrigued. "Either a date or a job interview. By the way, your hair looks really nice like that."

"Thanks. It wasn't easy," Jessica admitted. Her long, reddish brown hair had a strong, natural curl; it was always a challenge to get it looking neat and "professional." She'd worked hard this morning to pin it up in a sleek French twist.

"Of course I expect a full report," Suzanne added in an official tone.

Jessica laughed. "I'll come straight to see you when I get back. Promise."

"Meanwhile, maybe I can talk somebody around here into sending Sam Morgan to work in my office tomorrow. I could really use some bookshelves," Suzanne mused. "If you don't mind, of course."

"Mind? Why should I mind?"

"Well, he was in your office first," Suzanne teased her.

"Don't be silly. I don't have any feelings about it, one way or the other." Jessica shook her head and turned her attention back to work.

But try as she might, she had trouble concentrating on her spreadsheets. For some unfathomable, irritating reason, Sam Morgan kept drifting into her mind.

Okay, Jessica told herself. So he was extremely attractive. In that muscle-bound workman sort of way. And yes, he was even pleasant to talk with. But he absolutely didn't qualify as a romantic possibility for her. How could she even consider such a thing, especially when Paul was on his way to take her out to lunch.

No question. Suzanne could have Sam Morgan.

For some reason this final conclusion irked her. She didn't know why . . . but it definitely did.

Five minutes before Paul was due to arrive, Jessica brought her file folders back to her office. Sam was still working, measuring something that looked like it would be part of the window frame. "How's it going?" she asked.

He looked up. "Fine. How's it going with you? Did you find someplace to work?"

"Yes, I did. Out in the coffee room," she explained as she placed the folders back in the desk drawer.

"Wise move," he said, glancing at the huge hole in her wall. "It got a little drafty in here."

"Well, it is going to get worse before it gets better, right?"

He met her gaze. "Very good. I can see why you rate a window, Jessica Warwick, Assistant Manager."

It might have been a flash in his eyes, or the way he'd said her name, or even his slow, warm smile. Jessica felt it in the pit of her stomach, like an elevator dropping a floor. Or two. His dark gaze locked with hers, and she couldn't look away.

She noticed that he was no longer wearing the eye gear and mask. And the dust was gone from his face and hair. And the way he smiled at her made her smile, too.

"Jessica, someone's here to see you." She heard Suzanne in the doorway, and she turned to see her friend standing there with Paul.

"Paul . . . oh, I'm sorry. Have you been waiting long?" Jessica felt taken by surprise, as if Suzanne and Paul had interrupted something private.

"The receptionist told me to come back. But I couldn't find your office," Paul explained. "Your friend was kind enough to help me out," he added, glancing at Suzanne.

"You guys have a good time," Suzanne said as she strolled away—but not before casting an interested glance at Sam, Jessica noticed.

Sam had been standing in a relaxed pose, surveying the scene, his arms crossed loosely over his chest. But he now crouched down to sort through some tools, the heavy muscles in his back and shoulders straining against his white T-shirt.

"Is this your new office?" Paul peered inside, careful to stay away from the dust. "Very nice."

"Well, it looks like a demolition site today. But I'll have it in order soon."

"Congratulations again on your promotion." Paul smiled at her approvingly. "I brought you some flowers. They're out in the reception area."

"Thank you. That was sweet of you, Paul."

"It was nothing, really," he replied. "It's good to see you again, Jessica. You look great. I think Cape Light agrees with you."

"Thanks . . . but I spent the weekend in the city."

Paul laughed. "Well, you look wonderful either way." He leaned over and gave her a friendly kiss on the cheek. She was glad for some reason that Sam's broad back was still turned.

"I made a reservation for twelve-thirty," Paul said, glancing at his watch. "We'd better get going."

"Yes, of course." Jessica picked up her purse. As she turned to go, Sam caught her eye. Something in his bland expression made her feel he was smirking at her. She felt her cheeks redden and quickly looked away.

That's it, she decided as she and Paul walked out together. *I'm going to put Sam Morgan totally out of my mind.*

"SO WHERE ARE WE GOING?" JESSICA ASKED, intrigued.

"A little waterfront restaurant in the next town," Paul answered. "They got a good write-up in the *Globe*. They're supposed to have outstanding crab cakes, and I know you've got a weakness for crab cakes, so I thought you might like to try it."

"That sounds lovely," Jessica said, pleased that he was so thoughtful.

Paul's silver Mercedes coupe was the kind of car people noticed, especially around Cape Light, where most people drove pickup trucks. Jessica felt a little conspicuous, but she also couldn't help enjoying the ride. The Mercedes was so much smoother, so much more luxurious than her hatchback; it almost felt like another form of transportation.

"The last time you came down here, you were driving a Saab," she said. "So this one is new?"

"Yes, very. As you can see, I went for the works," he said with a resigned but happy sigh. "I don't know, I guess it was a bit self-indulgent," he added, sounding almost apologetic, "but I do work very hard. And you know what they say, 'Life is short . . . let's have dessert first.' "

Jessica laughed. "Not a bad philosophy, though my mother always warned me about spoiling my appetite."

"But you can do as you please now," he reminded her.

"Very true." She smiled and tucked a loose strand of hair behind her ear. "Let's skip the crab cakes and go straight to the crème brûlée."

"Maybe we will," Paul said with a laugh. After a moment he added, "By the way, you look very good in this car. It really suits you," he noted with another admiring smile.

"Umm—thanks."

What did he mean by that? Jessica wondered. Did that mean she fit into his future? Or did he just have strong feelings about his car? Paul was charming and sometimes very flirtatious, she reminded herself. She shouldn't read too much into these offhand remarks.

They were soon seated at a table on an airy, awning-covered deck. "We'll need to order and get our food fairly quickly," Paul said to the waiter who brought them menus.

"Sorry," he said to Jessica. "I've got to get back to Boston for a late-afternoon meeting. It can't be helped."

"That's okay." Jessica was a bit disappointed but tried not to show it.

They ordered crab cakes to start, which they would share, and two salads with ginger-soy dressing and grilled mahi-mahi.

"So what have you been up to?" Jessica asked.

"Downsizing one company, finding funding for another," Paul reported. "Actually, I'm really excited about a little start-up I took on six months ago. It's a woman who developed a new super-comfortable seat for power-boats. We put together a group of investors for her and drew up a five-year business plan. She's already exceeding her second-quarter goals. When I see someone take off that way . . . it's my favorite part of the job."

Jessica smiled as the waitress brought their crab cakes. "Sounds like the way I feel when I'm able to give a loan to someone buying their first house."

We really do have a lot in common, she thought as Paul told her about a few of the other projects he was working on. *We have a similar work ethic and a similar excitement about our careers. And,* she thought, biting into the crab cake, *we both enjoy excellent food.*

Still, for some inexplicable reason, Jessica found her thoughts wandering back to Sam. Staring at Paul across the table, she couldn't help but compare the two men. Paul's sandy hair, blue eyes, and tall, lanky build were almost the physical opposite of Sam's dark coloring and broad shoulders. She tried to picture Paul wielding the machine Sam had used to slice through the wall this morning, and couldn't imagine it.

But Paul was in very good shape, she reminded herself, for his age, which she guessed to be about forty. He was athletic and liked to play golf and sail, an interest they had in common, though so far, they hadn't gone sailing together.

"So what's up with you?" he asked.

She told him about work and her weekend in Boston. What she didn't tell him was how lonely and bored she was in Cape Light, how for the last six months she'd felt as if she was in a place where she would never fit in.

Jessica and Paul didn't talk much about personal matters. Paul seemed to prefer lighter topics, current movies or books. And, of course, talking about his business.

Maybe it's just that Paul is a very private person, Jessica thought as he told her about another client. She knew that it took some people time to open up.

"Sounds like you've been working very hard," Jessica said, starting on her fish.

"Nonstop, honestly. But that comes with the territory when you're the boss. Especially for the first few years," Paul said with a sigh. "I may get a break this weekend, though," he added in a happier tone. "A friend of mine invited me out for an overnight sail to Nantucket."

"That sounds great." Jessica loved Nantucket, though she hadn't been there in a while. .

"It should be," Paul replied. "He's just put his new boat in the water, a forty-foot sloop, custom-made. He hasn't tried her on a long trip yet, and he's asked a whole gang of people to come along."

A whole gang of *people*? Did that mean women *people* as well as men *people*? Maybe Paul had invited another woman to join him, instead of her, Jessica realized. After all, she was stuck out here in the country, and he surely dated other women he knew in Boston.

Paul touched her wrist. "I wish you could come along, but my friend said he's full up. He's planning an overnight for July Fourth, though, and promised I could bring you then," he added, looking at her hopefully.

The look in his eyes dispelled her doubts. "Really? That sounds fun. I'll make sure I get some extra time off."

He answered with a smile, looking pleased at her reaction.

Well, at least he was thinking of the future and *almost* considered them a couple, Jessica consoled herself as she took a last bite of the fish. It was better not to ask too many questions. She didn't want Paul to think she was getting too clingy.

"I hope you get good weather," Jessica said brightly as the waiter removed their empty dishes.

"Yes, so do I. I get out on the water so rarely."

When Paul declined coffee and dessert—and discreetly looked at his watch—she declined as well, realizing he must be in a hurry.

"Don't rush on my account. Please," he urged her, covering her hand with his own. "How about that crème brûlée you mentioned? I saw it on the menu. Let me order one for you. . . ."

Jessica smiled and shook her head. "No, thanks. I'm fine," she assured him.

"Are you sure?" he asked again. When she declined once more, he asked for the check, and they were soon on their way back to the bank.

"This is such a pretty place. So peaceful and picturesque," Paul said as they drove down the Beach Road toward town. "You were lucky to grow up here."

"Yes, I guess that's so," she said slowly.

Paul had no idea of what her family had been through, and Jessica didn't feel comfortable enough with him yet to talk about her past.

"Cape Light can be a little too peaceful," she added. "Fortunately, my mother is improving with her new physical therapist. I'm hoping to be back in Boston soon. Definitely by the fall."

"I wouldn't be in any hurry if I were you. You ought to just relax and enjoy it, Jessica. The city will still be there when you get back," Paul gently assured her.

Yes, but will you? she wanted to say.

"It was nice of you to come back and take care of your mother," Paul said. "I'm sure she appreciates it."

"You've never met my mother," Jessica said with a wry grin. "She can be . . . difficult. My sister, Emily, appreciates the help, though," she added.

"Your sister is the mayor here, right?"

Jessica nodded. "For a little more than two years now. She taught English at the high school for a long time and then was on the school board. There's an election coming up in the fall, but she's not sure if she'll run again."

"She sounds like an interesting woman. I'd like to meet her someday."

Jessica glanced at him. "Yes, I hope you do."

She turned away and looked out at the passing scenery. It was pretty here, the Beach Road lush and overgrown with wild roses and tall swaying marsh grass.

"I may take my bike out on this road this weekend," she said suddenly. "I haven't ridden here in years. It could be fun."

"I haven't been cycling for ages, either," Paul admitted. "Maybe next time I come, I could rent a bike someplace and go out with you. Maybe have a picnic on the beach or something?"

"That would be fun," Jessica said. "We could ride to the lighthouse."

"Now, there's a plan." Paul glanced at her and smiled. "And I bet you look very cute in your biking outfit."

"Don't be silly," she replied with a shake of her head. But his compliment made her cheeks grow warm.

They were soon back in the village. Paul pulled up to the bank to let her off. She picked up the bouquet he had brought her, long-stemmed pink roses, tied with a white satin ribbon.

"Thanks for the flowers, Paul. And for lunch, of course," she added. "It was great to see you again."

"A pleasure," he agreed. He stared into her eyes, giving her the feeling he was truly sorry to go. "I'm glad I had the chance to stop and celebrate your big promotion."

Jessica laughed. "You make it sound as if I were made manager of the whole bank."

"I'm giving you a few more months for that. You definitely have the right stuff, Jessica Warwick," he said softly.

He leaned over the car's shift and dropped a quick kiss

on her lips. It was sweet and pleasant. But it was over before Jessica even had time to close her eyes.

"I'll talk to you soon, okay?" He briefly touched her cheek with his hand.

"Sure. Have a good trip back," she said as she slipped out of the soft leather seat. Then she stood on the sidewalk and waved as Paul drove away.

Jessica returned to her office, feeling drained. And she still had a long staff meeting to sit through before she could call it a day.

She suddenly wished she could act more relaxed around Paul. More natural, not always on her guard to say and do just the right thing. She had to admit, she sometimes felt as if he were standing back, judging her, and she just wanted to turn and say, "Okay pal, the audition is over."

But maybe this was more her problem than anything he did? Perhaps it was because she liked him so much and still felt unsure of his feelings. That was to be expected at this stage, wasn't it?

She poured herself a much-needed cup of coffee and found a vase for the roses. They must have cost a fortune, she thought. She hadn't noticed the card stapled to the wrapping before. Now she opened it.

Here's to the start of great things!—Paul

HE REALLY WAS VERY THOUGHTFUL. PERHAPS A LITtle distant or noncommittal, but maybe he was afraid to get involved too quickly because of his divorce. They just needed more time to get to know each other, Jessica assured herself. As she arranged the roses in the vase, she felt almost positive that by "the start of great things" Paul really meant their relationship.

Jessica carried the roses down the hall to her office. Then she remembered the dust and the mess there. And

Sam Morgan. She would have avoided him entirely, but she needed some documents for her meeting.

When she opened her office door, she was surprised to find the room empty. She was even more surprised to see that it was now mostly in order. The drop cloths were gone, the furniture was back in place, and the plaster dust had been vacuumed up. A large double window, its glass still covered by thin brown paper, had been installed in the far wall.

He must have worked through lunch, she thought. Still holding the roses, Jessica drew closer to the window. Then she heard someone enter and turned to see Sam.

"Oh, you're back. How was your lunch?" he greeted her.

A bit presumptuous, wasn't it, to ask her such a question? "It was lovely," she replied crisply. "How was yours?"

"I picked up a *lovely* roast beef hero and sat at the harbor."

That smile again. He was either laughing at her or flirting with her. Or both.

"Good day for it." She watched him walk over to his tool bag and put a hammer and two screwdrivers inside.

"Yes, a very fine day," he replied. She watched him eye the bouquet in her hands again, then he said, "I don't know where you've been . . . but it looks as if you won first prize." He stood up and faced her. "Congratulations," he added, his expression quite serious but his eyes secretly laughing at her again.

She started to answer, then pursed her lips, deciding not to engage him. She turned and placed the vase firmly on her desk.

"Looks like you're almost done here," she said turning back to him.

"Just about. I've been waiting for you, actually. Are you ready?"

"Ready? For what?" He had the most disconcerting manner.

"For the unveiling of your new window."

"Oh, yes. Of course." She didn't have time for this silliness. But still, Jessica felt the edges of her mouth twist up in a reluctant smile as he took a commanding pose by the window and prepared to pull off the brown paper.

"No . . . wait." He came over to her and lightly took hold of her shoulders, leading her to a different spot in the room. "I think you ought to stand right about . . . here," he said.

Before Jessica could resist, she was standing a few feet away, squarely in front of the window.

He went back to the window and grabbed the edges of the paper with both hands. "You may want sunglasses," he warned.

She tried to look impatient. "Let's get on with it, shall we?"

"Okay, here we go. . . ." There was a ripping sound as the paper flew off the top and bottom panes. Then a flood of sunlight poured into the room, and Jessica actually wished she was wearing sunglasses.

"Wow! That looks fantastic!" Jessica hadn't meant to be so enthusiastic about his work, but she couldn't help it. From the second floor of the bank, she not only had a view of Main Street but a scrap of the harbor as well.

"Nice job, if I do say so myself." Sam stepped back to admire his handiwork. "God really knew what he was doing when he invented windows, don't you think? It's a remarkable thing. Now you have sunlight, clouds, blue sky, even most of Main Street," Sam said, removing a few bits of paper that clung to the glass. "Hey . . . look at that," he added, staring at some point in the distance. "You can practically see my shop from here."

She turned to him and laughed. "What a bonus."

"I told you it would get better."

"Yes, it got much better," she had to agree. "And faster than I expected."

"Thanks. Glad you like my work."

"You're welcome," she said simply.

His handsome features relaxed into a warm smile. Not a teasing or mocking grin, but a look that made her feel happy and confused at the same time.

Then she remembered herself. "I . . . uh . . . need to get into a meeting soon. I'd better get ready. Please excuse me."

"Of course." He nodded and picked up a few more of his tools, packing them in a black metal toolbox. "By the way, not that it matters, but I'd never take you for the roses type."

She was already sitting at her desk and looked up, surprised at his comment. "Excuse me?"

He shrugged a broad shoulder. "They're pretty but just so . . . routine. I'd say something more like tiger lilies or sunflowers would suit you."

Jessica was so surprised by his observation, she couldn't even reply.

He closed his toolbox and walked to the door, his wide, supple mouth turned up in a charming grin. "I'll see you around, okay?"

"Bye, Sam," she said slowly.

She watched him leave and close the door. She worked for a few minutes, then looked up.

The roses were beautiful . . . but suddenly they did seem a predictable choice.

She drew her attention back to her work, only to find herself distracted again, this time by the window. It was a perfect day outside—crisp blue skies, a few sailboats skimming lazily into the harbor—suddenly framed for her view like a beautiful painting.

A window really was a remarkable thing.

CHAPTER THREE

⌢

O N SUNDAY MORNING DIGGER HEGMAN WOKE BE- fore daybreak and dressed in the shadows of his attic room. Down in the kitchen he drank a cup of strong tea with a slice of bread and butter, then a slice of bread and jam.

He lifted his pack and left the house, careful of his booted steps on the narrow staircase that led down from the apartment over his daughter's shop. He liked the se- cretive feeling of leaving Grace and Daisy sleeping soundly within while he journeyed out.

Digger would often walk from one end of the village to the other, and back again. He'd take his spot on the dock, pack his pipe, and have a long satisfying smoke. Most mornings groups of fishermen were gathered there, setting out for their workday on the water. He listened to them talk about boats or boast about the size of a catch. He heard them argue and complain, compare prices at the markets, or guess when Maine lobsters would swim down from cold waters.

The talk was the same as it had been in his day. They looked the same, too, dressed in layers of thermal-knit tops, tar-stained sweatshirts, and sweaters unraveling at the neck or cuff, knit caps pulled low. Some of these boys had long beards, like the beard he'd always worn. Except for the time he woke from a nap to find Grace—just half a biscuit then—standing over him, his whiskers in one hand, her mother's sewing shears in the others. She claimed the beard scratched too much when he kissed her so, of course, he had to laugh about it.

Still, the mariner's craft had changed. There were sonar screens on the boats now to help find the fish or hide the lobster pots. No such thing in his day. That didn't seem like fishing to him. No mystery left to it at all. He could teach these fellows a thing or two. Never mind their radar or sonar or satellite dishes; he wasn't out there to watch TV. But Digger never gave advice unless asked, and even then, he kept it short and sharp.

Some days when he found himself at the end of Main Street, he took Hasty Way to the Beach Road and he just kept going—out to the flats or even Durham Point. He kept a shovel in his pack and might dig for clams to work the kinks out. Digger was content when he was digging, arthritis and weak heart and all. Helped him think, to dig awhile. He knew he was blessed that such a simple thing never failed to make him peaceful and content. If he got his wish, the good Lord would take him some day doing just that, just digging.

The weather didn't matter. The rougher the weather, the more Digger enjoyed being out. The raw, damp breezes that swept in from the bay, the icy winds that blew from the northeast and sliced to the bone. The thick, soft fog that settled down over the village, as if the hand of God had dropped an extra blanket on a sleeping child.

He liked to stroll through a feathery snowfall, or press his body full tilt against an icy blast that stung his lips and cheeks. And best of all, he liked standing beneath the full sun that beat down like a golden hammer.

On this particular Sunday morning Digger walked around the village twice, ending up at the town dock, where he settled down on his usual bench at the very end of the structure. He took the Good Book out of his pack and read a few chapters, as was his daily habit.

Today he read from the New Testament, Philippians, Chapter 4: ". . . Not that I speak in respect of want: for I have learned, in whatsoever state I am, therewith to be content. . . ."

When he finished his reading, he put the Bible away and took an apple, a chunk of sharp cheddar, and a paring knife out of his pack to start on his second breakfast.

It was half past seven and the dockside was still quiet, with just one or two weekend sailors riding skiffs out to sleek fancy boats. The harbor was full, a watery parking lot with powerful motorboats tied up beside long, graceful sailboats and the rougher-looking vessels of the baymen.

There were also a few people out jogging and walking. It amazed him to see how people these days had made a science out of walking, with special clothes, hooked up to music and blood-pressure wristwatches. He could remember when walking was just a way to get a person from one place to the other. Now people took it up as if it were some newly invented activity, he thought. Even otherwise levelheaded folks, like Carolyn Lewis.

Digger was not surprised to see her out this early as she strode purposefully down the dock toward him, wearing baggy gray sweatpants, sneakers, and a yellow T-shirt covered with musical notes.

With her arms pumping and legs swinging, she moved with such momentum he almost feared she'd chug right off the edge of the dock and into the water.

He raised his hand in greeting. "Morning, Mrs. Lewis. Taking your exercise, I see."

She nodded and smiled, panting a bit. For Carolyn, a vigorous daily walk was a necessity, to keep both her body and spirit fit.

She sat down on the bench next to Digger and took a drink from her water bottle. "How are you, Digger? How is your new job working out?"

"I've got no complaints so far. And neither does Harry." Digger grinned, displaying a row of large, tobacco-stained teeth through the shaggy opening of his whiskers. "So I guess it's going better than either of us expected."

When Carolyn laughed, he added, "Don't get me wrong. I'm grateful for the work, grateful to Harry and to the Lord for sending it. It's good and right for a man to work if he's able. I like getting my hands dirty, fixing something that's broken. You get a better night's sleep if you put your head down on the pillow knowing you've put your day to good use. And looking to make use of the next day, too."

"I feel exactly the same way," Carolyn said.

"Well, good for you. It didn't sit so well with Grace though," he confided as he sliced an apple. "She came after me that first day, thinking I'd wandered where I wasn't wanted. Even after me and Harry explained it to her, she still tried to get me home. Claimed she needed my help in the shop, when it's really no kind of work at all. Oh, maybe I'll spruce up a little end table or a chair, fix it so it doesn't wobble. I can do that much for her in my spare time," he added.

"Maybe Grace just wants you to take it easy," Carolyn said gently.

"I tried taking it easy," Digger insisted. "It just didn't stick. I really don't understand how you're supposed to do it. Retirement, I mean. Apple?" He offered her a slice of apple from his pocketknife, and Carolyn took it with a nod of thanks.

"It's a challenge for some people. I can see that." Carolyn took a bite of the apple. It was perfect, juicy and tart. "So you've sorted it out with Grace about going to work?"

"You might say. She's not happy about it. But it's going to be so."

Carolyn knew Digger was generally an easygoing person, but at times could be as immovable as the stone memorial in the village square.

This was one of those times, she gathered.

"Grace worries about me too much," he said, shaking his head. "But the Lord's going to take me when He's ready. Whether I'm napping in a chair on the front porch or carrying Harry Reilly piggyback down Main Street."

The image made Carolyn smile. "It's only natural for Grace to worry. Since you had the heart attack, I mean."

"The heart trouble only made it worse. She's scared of losing me—ever since she lost Julie. She's been almost too scared to poke her nose out the door since then. She still blames herself. And God," he added quietly. Digger began to pack his pipe, the scent of sweet tobacco mixing with the sea air.

Carolyn didn't know what to say. Putting herself in Grace's place, she wasn't sure that she could go on after such a loss. Grace's daughter, Julie, was only nine years old when she was hit by a car and killed, right in front of the Bramble Shop. Within a year Grace's marriage had crumbled under the burden of the couple's grief, and she had lost her faith as well. Her husband had left Cape Light. Carolyn thought maybe he'd moved up to Maine or Vermont. It had been five years since the tragedy, and Grace had never seen him again.

Carolyn knew that Ben had done all he could to help Grace and bring her back to the church. Though he hadn't made much progress so far, she knew he was still trying in his quiet but persistent way.

Digger lit his pipe and took a long draw. "My daughter is a good-hearted woman, Mrs. Lewis, and she means well. When I was flailing about on my own, she took me in to live with her, no questions asked. I know I'm not the easiest fellow to live with, either. The gal's going to lose her mind someday, for sure, if I turn up with another bucket of clams."

Carolyn laughed. "Yes, she does have patience with you, Digger. If you don't mind me saying, I've noticed that myself."

But the arrangement had also been beneficial for Grace, Carolyn knew. Except for Digger and Daisy, who had been Julie's dog, Grace had very little in her life.

For a few moments Carolyn and Digger sat side by side, silently gazing out at the harbor.

Carolyn realized she had a question for Digger. "By the way, I meant to stop by the shop and ask Grace about this, but perhaps you know. Is that old piano still sitting out in her barn? I have a new student, Lauren Willoughby, who could really use it. And Molly can't afford much. I thought maybe she and Grace could work something out."

Digger glanced at her, then back out at the water. "The piano is still there. But my daughter is unlikely to part with it, being it was Julie's. I know some have inquired, and she always says no." He glanced at Carolyn, then scratched his ear for a second. "You might ask. Just to test the waters."

Carolyn hadn't realized that the piano had been Julie's. She was glad now she'd asked Digger about it first. "Well, I'll see. There are a few other possibilities. I'll look into those first."

"As you wish." He took a long draw on his pipe. "You know it's hard sometimes for me to see the way Grace is living her life," he confided, "like a crab, scuttling backward on the sand, more worried about where she's been than what's right in front of her. Not making any headway at all. I don't think it's what the Lord intended. But there doesn't seem to be much I can do to help her."

"I'm sure you do your best, Digger," Carolyn said, briefly meeting his pale blue gaze.

Privately, though, she agreed. She, too, was sure that He had something much different in mind for Grace. Like forgiveness. And faith. It had taken years, but Carolyn had finally begun to learn those hard lessons herself. She hoped Grace would eventually get there. More than just hope for it, she would pray for it.

"I'm sorry about Grace." She reached out and lightly touched his arm. "I'll remember her in my prayers."

Digger nodded and puffed his pipe. "Thank you, Mrs. Lewis."

Carolyn smiled at the formality. Although she and Digger had known each other for nearly eighteen years now, he still called her Mrs. Lewis out of respect for the reverend.

Digger picked up a crumb of cheese and tossed it to a fat gull who sat perched on a nearby piling. The bird swooped down with a feathery flap, carrying the scrap away in the blink of an eye.

"There'll be rain by nightfall," he noted, tipping his head back.

Carolyn followed his gaze, but could only see blue sky and large puffy clouds—the kind she'd watched as a child to find faces and animals. "Do you really think so?"

"Absolutely. Heavy, too," he predicted.

Carolyn's brow crinkled. She hadn't heard a word about rain on the radio, but over the years she'd learned that Digger's local forecasts were mostly infallible. "I'll remember to roll up the car windows."

She checked her watch. "Oh, dear. I need to get home and get ready for church."

There was one service on Sundays at Cape Light Bible Community Church, which began at ten-thirty. Her husband usually went to the church much earlier, to look in on the Sunday school and review his sermon. Carolyn liked to walk to the church, which wasn't even two miles across the village from the rectory, but she was short on time today; she'd have to take the car.

"Bye, Digger. I've got to run." Carolyn waved as she headed down the dock again.

Digger nodded and waved back. "See you in church, Mrs. Lewis," he replied. Carolyn knew he meant the phrase literally; Digger Hegman rarely missed a Sunday.

"I HOPE WE DON'T HAVE TROUBLE FINDING PARKING this late. I hate to sit in the back. You can't hear a word." Lillian Warwick checked her slim gold wristwatch again, then removed an invisible speck of lint from her sleeve.

"We're not late, Mother. It's barely ten after," Jessica assured her.

"Your watch must be slow. I have quarter past." Lillian paused and glanced out her window. "Emily always lets me out right over there, near the side-door entrance," she added. "I'll wait here for you."

As they both knew, the side-door entrance was the handicapped ramp, easier for Lillian to navigate with her cane. But she didn't like to admit she needed it. She really still required the walker, but hated to be seen in public using the device and even balked at the cane, a fancy model of polished wood with a mother-of-pearl handle.

Jessica pulled up to the drop-off area and helped her mother out of the car. As she pulled away to find parking, she caught sight of Lillian in the rearview mirror. Standing tall in her navy blue linen dress and patent-leather pumps, her hair fresh from a weekly appointment at the Beauty Spot, Lillian didn't look ill or even infirm.

You could say many things about her mother, but you had to admire her spirit and her nearly unbreakable will, Jessica thought as she parked the car and started toward the church. They just didn't make them like that anymore.

Jessica hadn't been to a service since Easter, when she'd attended with her sister and mother. Emily was a regular churchgoer; she always took Lillian on Sundays. But Emily had called yesterday and asked Jessica if she could take over this week. Emily was attending a conference of local mayors over the weekend and wouldn't be back in the village in time. Naturally, Jessica had agreed.

As usual, Jessica had no sooner walked through her mother's front door than she was bombarded with Lillian's instructions for the seemingly endless tasks required in order to leave the house.

"Draw the shades in the living room and the front bedrooms upstairs. It keeps the house cool. Did you lock the side door and check the bolt on the door to the cellar? And please turn on the sprinkler in the backyard. The grass is absolutely parched. But don't let the water hit the flower beds near the patio. Molly Willoughby gave them too much water yesterday, and I'm sure the plants are going to rot.

"And remember to unplug the coffeemaker, Jessica. Don't just shut it off. I wish you had bought me a better model. I was just reading that this one is a fire hazard. I know I'll forget to unplug it one day and it will burn the house down."

Lillian liked things done a certain way—her way. But Jessica was used to that by now, and like Emily, she rarely bothered to argue.

She soon met her mother at the church's side entrance, and they proceeded inside. Gus Potter, who was an usher, met them as they entered.

"I saved a nice seat for you, Mrs. Warwick," he greeted Lillian. "Just follow me, ladies."

He seemed to know where Lillian preferred to sit, and Jessica was relieved that her mother had no complaints. As she helped her mother move into the pew and get comfortable, she felt someone looking at her.

Jessica glanced up and met Sam Morgan's gaze. He was sitting a few rows back, beside Digger Hegman. He looked so different today—wearing a white shirt, a red tie, and a navy blue sports coat—that she hardly recognized him. Different, she thought ruefully, but just as maddeningly attractive. Something in her eyes must have given her away then, because he smiled at her, and she had the distinct feeling that he knew exactly what she was thinking.

Jessica quickly turned away without smiling back. Sam had been working in other offices on her floor during the week, and she'd purposely avoided him. Well, she would just have to do the same today.

Lillian had put on her reading glasses, her hymnal opened in her lap. Jessica picked up her copy and found the opening hymn. When Reverend Lewis began the service, she did her best to concentrate, even though she wasn't much of a churchgoer.

To her surprise, his sermon caught her interest. He started off talking about bumblebees, how by all engineering calculations, their bodies are too big to be supported by their small wings.

"Yet, off they go, buzzing along. They shouldn't be able to fly . . . but they don't know that," the reverend pointed out.

He went on to talk about believing in yourself, and having faith in God to help you realize your goals.

"It's faith that will help you fly against all odds, like the bumblebees, just one of the many mysterious miracles of creation," the reverend explained. "And after all, aren't we just as mysterious, just as potentially full of miracles?"

Was she full of miracles? Jessica wondered, shifting in

her seat. And what kind of miracles did he mean? To be manager of the bank someday, a corporate vice president or whatever—was that a miracle? Not really, she decided. That was more a matter of hard work and luck.

To be a different kind of person, then . . . a better person? More patient, less judgmental of others, more loving. That was probably what he meant, she decided. She knew she needed improvement in those areas. Who didn't?

Sitting in church made you think about these things, Jessica realized. Whether you really wanted to or not . . .

"Scripture teaches us that, with faith, all things are possible," Reverend Lewis reminded his flock. "Flying against all odds. Unlocking the miracles within. Faith is the key," he counseled.

But as the reverend delved deeper into the issue of faith, Jessica's thoughts drifted. She glanced over at her mother, who was giving the sermon her undivided attention. Her mother didn't speak about it much—and often didn't act in a very Christian manner, Jessica thought—but she had a strong faith and a private relationship with God which had sustained her through hard times.

Jessica remembered when after the scandal Lillian had stopped going to church. Jessica had been a child at the time, and so she wasn't taken to church or Sunday school. Her mother never talked about it, but Jessica was sure that shame had been the reason. Lillian was too proud to appear in public and feel people whispering about her behind her back. Somehow, years later, Reverend Ben had persuaded her to return.

Well, you're an adult now and you can take yourself to church anytime you like, Jessica thought. But for no reason she could really put her finger on, she knew that unless she had to come, like today, she wouldn't.

When the service ended, Jessica was relieved to hear her mother say she wanted to skip the coffee hour. In fact,

Jessica was counting on leaving by the side entrance and completely avoiding Sam Morgan.

Her heart sank as she started for the side entrance only to hear her mother say, "Not that way, Jessica. I want to say a few words to Reverend Lewis before we go."

So Jessica joined the line at the church's front door, where the reverend was receiving his congregation.

"Hello, Lillian . . . Jessica, nice to see you," Reverend Lewis greeted them. Jessica briefly said hello. She'd always liked him. While he spoke with her mother, Jessica glanced around. She spotted Sam standing in front of the church, talking to Harry Reilly. They were right at the bottom of the steps. There was no avoiding him.

As she helped her mother down the steps, Jessica noticed Sam walking toward her. She still found the change in appearance, from his work clothes to Sunday best, remarkable—and very distracting.

"Hello, Jessica. Good to see you," Sam greeted her in his smooth, deep voice. Then he glanced at her mother. "Hello, Mrs. Warwick."

Lillian tilted her head back to look Sam straight in the eye. "I'm sorry . . . do I know you?" she asked curtly.

"Of course you do, Mother," Jessica cut in nervously. "This is Sam Morgan. You know the Morgans."

Sam smiled, looking amused and not at all insulted. "It's true, Mrs. Warwick. We've been coming to this church together for years. But we've never been formally introduced."

Lillian ignored his diplomatic reply. "The Morgans. Yes, of course," she said to Jessica. "He must be the cleaning girl's brother. You know, the new one who just started the other day . . . that Molly," she recalled finally.

Jessica felt her face grow bright red. It never failed to amaze her how her mother prided herself on good manners when, in fact, she could be the rudest person on earth.

"Yes, he's Molly's brother," Jessica confirmed, struggling to keep her voice sounding normal. "We all went to high school together. Molly was in my class," she added, finally daring a glance at Sam.

He smiled at her, still looking calm and mildly amused. If her mother's slight had insulted him, he was too much of a gentleman to show it.

Her mother glanced at her, then blinked. A "so what?" look if Jessica had ever seen one. "How interesting," Lillian said flatly, her tone declaring that it was anything but. "I can walk to the car, Jessica," she added. "I don't know why you have me standing out here in the hot sun."

"Yes, of course." Jessica took her mother's arm. She looked up at Sam. "Well, have a good day. Nice to see you again," she added, though afterward she wondered why. Just trying to be polite, she thought. To make up for my mother.

"Thanks, you have a good day, too," Sam replied.

Had she ever had a more banal conversation in her life? Why in the world did she feel so rattled? She felt his gaze fixed on her as they headed for the parking lot behind the church.

Jessica was troubled as she drove her mother home. She couldn't erase the feeling of complete mortification she'd felt when her mother had been so rude to Sam.

The real problem wasn't her mother, she acknowledged silently. It was that even if she didn't express it as blatantly as her mother did, she was guilty of the same condescending attitude. Because Sam was a workman, some part of her immediately categorized him as less than she was. She knew it wasn't kind or rational. It wasn't even true.

How did I get to be such a snob? she asked herself. Did it come from having been born on the Warwick Estate? Or is it just that I'm not a very good person?

"Jessica, pay attention," her mother snapped, drawing her out of her thoughts. "You've passed the house."

Ten minutes later Lillian was reading the Sunday paper while Jessica set the dining room table for lunch.

"Make sure you use the nice china and silver flatware. And cut some flowers from the garden for the table," her mother called out. "Dr. Elliot is joining us for lunch."

Luckily, Molly Willoughby had left plenty of food in the fridge, in neatly labeled plastic containers. Jessica found a roast chicken, a platter of marinated roast vegetables with orzo and mint, and a green salad, which she transferred to her mother's china platters. There was also some fruit salad and a spice cake with white frosting for dessert. It all looked and smelled delicious. Molly was clearly a fine cook, and cooking was a skill Jessica had never mastered. Looking at the food not only whet her appetite but also disconcertingly reminded her of Sam.

This is ridiculous, Jessica thought as she set the food on the table. Even serving lunch makes me think of Sam Morgan.

Distraction arrived in the form of Dr. Elliot. Ever punctual, he rang the doorbell at one o'clock sharp. A small, wiry man, he was, as usual, smartly dressed in a gray, three-piece suit, button-down collar, and red-and-blue striped bow tie. His steel-rimmed glasses emphasized his narrow face and long nose. Jessica knew he had to be getting on in years, yet he always looked the same to her.

"For you, Lillian," he said, handing Jessica's mother a box of her favorite chocolates.

"Oh, Ezra, you didn't have to," Lillian said, but she was obviously pleased.

Jessica had recently discovered that her mother saved the small blue-and-gold boxes from these chocolates in the bottom drawer of her dresser, though she never seemed to use them for anything.

"I'm not sure if I can have these anymore," Lillian went on. "Not a very health-conscious gift from a doctor."

"Nonsense. Everything in moderation. A little chocolate won't hurt you. Why, they say now it's actually good for your heart. Can you beat that? And it lifts your mood, too. Does something to your brain chemistry," Ezra added with a sharp, affirmative nod.

"I've never heard that," Lillian replied doubtfully.

"You ought to keep up on the medical news, Lillian. It's important at our age."

Jessica loved the way Dr. Elliot cheerfully argued with her mother. No one else ever got away with it. In Dr. Elliot's company, Lillian was actually bright and chatty.

Her mother and their guest sat down while Jessica served. Ezra Elliot was one of the only people in town who was capable of engaging Lillian in a lively conversation. It was relief to Jessica, since she often found it draining to spend time alone with her mother.

"I hear Charlie Bates is up in arms about your property. He's been ranting about it all week," Lillian said as she lifted a crystal goblet of ice water to her lips. She didn't get out much but obviously had her sources, Jessica had noticed.

Dr. Elliot shook his head. "I've heard all about it. I'm sure I don't know where that man gets his nerve. It's none of his business who I sell to. Betty Bowman's already shown it a few times now. She's a sharp gal. She'll have it off my hands in no time. I just want to make a good sale," he added. "I'm ready to retire, to kick back and live the good life. Like you, Lillian," he added.

He winked at Jessica and she smiled.

"Your patients will miss you," Jessica told him sincerely. It was true. She'd already heard quite a few people she knew sounding unhappy about Dr. Elliot's retirement.

"Oh, yes, I'm sure they will. For at least a day or so," he quipped. "I've been making referrals to other physicians in the area, and everyone seems to be very satisfied. People always make a big fuss about change. Then they forget all about it."

"That's not what I've found to be true," Lillian replied in a somber tone. Jessica was fairly certain she was referring to their own family's problems. Sometimes she wondered if people really did remember that part of the past as much as her mother thought they did.

Deciding to change the subject, Jessica said, "These vegetables are delicious. Molly Willoughby is quite a cook."

"Do you think so?" Lillian replied. "I didn't care for the vegetables at all. Too much garlic. The chicken wasn't much better, either. She just about drowned it in rosemary."

Jessica hadn't noticed before, but her mother had hardly touched her lunch. Then again, Lillian liked her food simple and basic. She'd never really approved of spices.

"I thought it was all very tasty. Garlic lowers your blood pressure, you know," Dr. Elliot countered. "Though I think mint leaves are more fitting for a glass of iced tea than pasta salad," he added with a laugh.

"Exactly my point," Lillian cut in. "I prefer plainer food, simply prepared. I'll have to tell that new girl." She pushed her plate away. "They always take offense. But I'm the one who has to eat it, after all."

"Her name is Molly, Mother," Jessica reminded her.

"Yes, Molly, of course. Sam Morgan's sister," she replied, with a quick, sharp glance in Jessica's direction. "Don't worry. I haven't forgotten."

Lillian patted her mouth with the edge of her napkin. "I thought we would have dessert out on the patio," she said wistfully, "but now it looks quite cloudy."

"Yes, it does," Ezra noted, glancing outside. "Well, you know what they say about New England. If you don't like the weather, wait twenty minutes."

*   *   *

A FEW HOURS LATER JESSICA DROVE BACK TO HER apartment in a heavy rain. Even though she didn't have an umbrella, she went around to the back door, looking for the stray cat. She hated to think of the poor thing hungry and soaking wet under the steps. Ever since Monday night she'd been leaving the cat scraps of food in a saucer near the door.

If the cat was nearby, it was hiding. Jessica opened the bag of leftovers from her mother's house and dropped a few pieces of chicken in the dish. The cat, she was sure, would not be nearly as particular as Lillian had been.

Soaked to the skin, Jessica ran inside and headed straight into the bedroom to take off her wet clothes— only to find water pouring in from the wall near the window, right above a built-in bookcase. *What a mess*, Jessica thought, surveying the damage.

She put a bucket beneath the leak and tossed some towels on the floor to soak up the water pooling there. Then she called Warren Oakes, her landlord, and told him about the problem. Warren promised to send a repairman promptly. Still, Jessica hung up feeling annoyed. It was Sunday night. She just wanted to relax, read a book, maybe watch TV. She didn't feel like cleaning up a flood in her bedroom.

When the phone rang, she picked it up quickly, thinking it was Warren calling back. "Yes?" she said abruptly.

"Jessica, glad I caught you in."

Paul's voice surprised her and instantly dispelled her bad mood. They'd exchanged a few short e-mails since their lunch date but hadn't talked since then.

"How was your weekend? How was the sail to Nantucket?" Jessica asked.

"Wonderful. What a boat. I'd love to have a craft like that someday. We had a great time. Great weather all the way, and a really nice group of people."

Those *people* again. Jessica flopped back against her

pillows. His enthusiastic tone sent her into a new bout of worries.

"Sounds like it was a nice break for you," she said carefully.

"Absolutely," he agreed. "Though I did wish you were along," he added in a more endearing tone.

Jessica liked hearing that. But before she could reply, he said, "Listen, talking about nice breaks, I need to see a client in Burlington again next week, and I was hoping we could get together on my way back to Boston."

"Sure. I'd love to." Jessica sat up again. "When will you be in Vermont?"

"I'm going up tomorrow, and I should be coming through your way on Wednesday night. Maybe we could have dinner? If you're free, I mean."

It was hard to imagine an appointment she wouldn't cancel to see Paul, even if she had plans, which she definitely did not.

"Wednesday? . . . I'll just grab my calendar and check." She picked up her date book from her night table and stared at the blank page. She waited a few seconds. "Wednesday looks fine," she said finally.

"I think I can get to Cape Light by six. I'll pick you up at your apartment. How does that sound?"

"Great," Jessica agreed. She would have to leave the office a little early to get ready on time, but that wouldn't be a problem.

"So how was your weekend?" he added. "Did you take that bike ride to the beach?"

"No, I didn't get the chance. I had to catch up on some office work, then chores around the house on Saturday," she reported. "Oh, and I did some gardening at my mother's."

"Oh, that's too bad," he said. "It was such a nice weekend. Well, we'll just have to do that ride together sometime."

"Yes, we will." Heavens, I sound so boring, she thought with alarm. "I had lunch today with . . . with some *people* I know in town. That was fun," she added.

"Oh, that's nice," Paul said. "At least you got out a little."

If Paul was at all curious about her companions, he didn't show it. Of course she didn't want to admit it had been her mother and Dr. Elliot . . . and that Molly Willoughby's spice cake had been the highlight of her weekend.

"And how's the new job going?" he asked with interest.

"Not much different from what I'd been doing before. Just more of it. A lot more," she added with emphasis.

He laughed. "You've got to pay your dues, Jessica," he said knowingly. It was one of those moments when she was subtly reminded of their age difference. "And at least you have a private office with a very nice window now," he pointed out.

"Yes, I do," she replied, her mind suddenly filled with Sam's image. She pushed the thought aside. She really didn't want to be thinking of him at all right now.

They talked a little more until Paul noticed the time and thought he'd better hang up. "I'd better get some sleep. I have a lot of driving ahead of me tomorrow. And then some problems in Burlington to sort out," he confided.

"Oh, that's too bad. I thought it was going well."

"I don't think it's anything too awful. The client is a pain in the neck, but I need to show my face. At least on Wednesday I get to see you. That should keep me going," he said in a mock-brave tone.

Jessica laughed, feeling warmed by his words. "I'm looking forward to it, too," she told him.

They said their good-nights, and Jessica hung up the phone, feeling a good deal happier. Paul really did like her. Things were going well. Three whole days before she saw him. She could barely wait.

Just before she shut out the light on the back porch, she checked to see if the stray cat had come out. It was still raining. The saucer of food was empty, but there was no sign of her mysterious visitor. Little by little, she thought. Just like her and Paul. Things were progressing. Slowly but surely.

THE RAIN BEGAN FALLING HARDER, BUT SARA FRANK- lin barely noticed. She drove slowly down Emerson Street, searching for number thirty-five. When she found the house, she cruised by, then turned her car around at the end of the street and drove back again. She stopped a few doors down, parking on the opposite side of the street, away from the streetlight, careful to be inconspicuous.

It didn't really matter, though. The house was dark without even a light on near the front door. Emily War- wick was not home tonight.

She'd driven by the house a few times since coming to town, curious to see where Emily lived. Tonight was the first time she'd ever stopped and watched it like this. Maybe she was getting more brazen, or maybe she was just taking advantage of the cover of rain and darkness.

Sara felt partly relieved that Emily wasn't home—and partly disappointed. She rubbed some condensation off the inside of her car window and stared out at the house, hoping to learn something about Emily by studying her home.

The small colonial-style house looked quite old— maybe it was even a historic house—with bay windows on the first floor, flanking a covered entry, and a row of small, rectangular-shaped windows upstairs. Sara thought the style might be called an eyebrow colonial, but she wasn't sure.

In the darkness she couldn't really make out colors or details, but from an earlier visit she remembered that the house was a sedate gray-blue, with cream-colored trim, dark blue shutters, and a brick-red door. Window boxes overflowed with flowers and trailing vines, and tall rose-bushes tumbled over a white picket fence.

It was a neat, modest house. The house of a respectable person, for sure. A nice person, Sara concluded.

But what was Emily Warwick really like? Sara knew she couldn't really tell from seeing her house, or even seeing her that one time in the diner on Tuesday morning.

This wasn't going to be over as quickly as she'd first thought, Sara realized. Finding Emily was really just the beginning.

But maybe for tonight I've had enough, she decided. As she reached for the key to start the car again, she suddenly noticed a dark blue Jeep pull up the street and then into the driveway.

Emily jumped out and dashed up the brick walk, carrying a small black suitcase. She stopped at the front door, grabbing a wad of mail from the brass box before she went in.

Coming back from the weekend, Sara surmised. Where did she go? To visit friends, or even a boyfriend perhaps? Did she have a boyfriend? She was certainly attractive enough for her age. Taller than Sara had pictured her, and thin and athletic-looking with her short, tousled hair.

Sara had never expected that Emily Warwick would be the mayor of Cape Light. That put a certain wrinkle in her plan. It could make things hard for Emily later. Then again, that was Emily's problem, Sara reminded herself.

Warm, yellow squares of light soon filled the downstairs windows, and Sara glimpsed Emily passing back and forth, talking on the phone. Then Emily came to the window, pulled back the curtain and glanced out at the rain-swept street. Sara ducked low in the driver's seat, though she knew that there was no way Emily could see her.

Still, the moment made her nervous. She couldn't sit here all night. Sooner or later someone would notice her, she realized. Someone might even call the police.

Sara stared at the house again. The light in the large bay window on the left went out, and then the light in the other window, too. She soon saw another light appear upstairs, but the windows were too narrow to reveal anything inside.

Sara turned her key in the ignition. Watching the house was starting to make her feel creepy. *I'm not here to stalk the woman, for goodness' sake*, she told herself.

Sweet dreams, Emily. You're so different from any of my fantasies, good or bad, Sara thought as she pulled away from the curb. *I could never have imagined you in a million years.*

And I'm sure Emily could never have imagined me.

It was weird to look at Emily's face and see a sort of shadow image of herself. It freaked her out. And it made her wonder: Could Emily ever recognize her and figure it out?

No, Sara decided. *Even if she thinks of it, it's just too unbelievable. She'll never figure it out on her own. I have to tell her. If I can ever go through with it.*

Maybe she ought to just pack up and go back home to Maryland. But she'd come so far and thought about this for so long. Ever since her parents had told her she was adopted, she'd dreamed of, planned, and waited for the day when she'd meet Emily Warwick, her birth mother.

I can't just turn around and go home, she thought. *Not now.*

I have to stay and talk to her, tell her who I am. If I give up now and go home, I'll never forgive myself.

Feeling resolved, Sara drove through the winding lanes

that led away from Emerson Street and soon emerged on Main Street, in the middle of the village.

Driving past the diner, she noticed the Help Wanted sign in the window. Her parents had given her a little money for the trip, but it was quickly dwindling. The diner would be a good place to work, she thought. Emily seemed to be a regular there. Besides, Sara had done some waitressing in college and was pretty sure they'd hire her.

The diner was closed for the night. Sara decided to head over there first thing in the morning. Maybe Lucy Bates would remember her. She hoped so. She seemed a lot easier to talk to than her husband.

JESSICA WOKE TO THE SOUND OF HARD RAIN THE NEXT morning. As she got ready for work, she wondered if she would run into Sam at the office this week. It would be hard to face him after yesterday's encounter at church. Maybe she ought to apologize. Maybe he'd already finished his work there, and she wouldn't have to deal with it at all.

She slipped on her skirt and pulled up the zipper, dismayed to realize that the idea of him having finished at the office disappointed her.

What's wrong with me? she wondered. *I have a date with Paul Wednesday night. Why am I even wasting time thinking about Sam Morgan?*

She found the lavender cardigan that matched her sleeveless top and stepped into her shoes. If she saw him in the office, she'd say a quick hello. But she wouldn't be too friendly and give him the wrong idea—that she liked him, or wanted to go out with him, or anything like that.

Right, Jessica, a little voice replied.

No, really. I don't, she argued back.

The humidity made her hair extra curly, and she pulled

it back in a large, low clip. *He's a nice guy and definitely attractive*, she told herself. *But he's just not my type. Besides, I'm not going to be here very long. There would be no point to it.*

Feeling resolved, she put on her watch and pearl earrings, then picked up her briefcase and headed for the bank.

As she walked down the hallway to her office, she heard the distant but distinct sound of a power drill a few doors down. From the sound she guessed Sam was here. She might see him today, after all. Her stomach knotted. *Just hungry*, she told herself. *I shouldn't skip breakfast.*

Jessica worked in her office awhile, then went down to the customer area to meet with a couple who were applying for a small-business loan to start a nursery and landscaping company. Mark and Nancy Wilson smiled when she came in, but Jessica could tell they were nervous.

"Well, we've reviewed your financial information, and I have good news," she told them, quickly putting the couple at ease. "The loan has been approved for the amount you've requested."

"Really? That's great! Thank you so much," Mark Wilson said.

"This is so wonderful!" his wife agreed. "We've been working for this for years."

Smiling widely, they hugged each other first, then thanked Jessica again so profusely, she thought for a moment they were both going to hug her, too.

"We just need a few more documents to process the loan," Jessica explained, handing them a folder. "Drop these off this week, marked to my attention, and we can draw up the final papers. You can probably come in early next week to sign everything."

The couple asked her a few more questions, thanked her again, and then both husband and wife heartily shook her hand before departing.

This was definitely her favorite part of her job, helping

people start a new enterprise. It was often the realization of a long-held dream, and she liked playing a part in making it happen for them.

Still thinking about the couple, Jessica headed back up to her office. It caught her completely off guard when she stepped into the hallway from the stairwell and found herself facing Sam.

"Hello, Jessica," he said, greeting her with a wide, warm smile.

"Sam. H-hello," she heard herself stammer and felt embarrassed. "So, you're still working here this week," she added, her mind a sudden blank.

What a dumb thing to say. Of course he was. There he was, right in front of her. Why did this guy turn her into a babbling idiot every time he so much as smiled at her?

"I just came back for a few finishing touches. . . . Unless of course someone decides I need to build you a corner office," he teased her.

"Probably not this week." She smiled despite herself. "I'm still getting used to the window."

He laughed. He had straight white teeth and dimples, two deep brackets at the corners of his lean cheeks. She hadn't noticed that before.

"It was nice to see you yesterday. I didn't know you belonged to Bible Community Church," he said after a moment.

"I don't, really," she said quickly. She met his gaze, then looked away. "Emily usually brings my mother. I just did it to help out."

He seemed to take church seriously. Maybe he wouldn't be as interested in her now. Not that it mattered, she reminded herself.

But his expression showed neither approval nor disapproval. "I enjoyed the sermon," he said. "Reverend Ben comes up with some interesting ideas."

Jessica had to agree. "He's a good speaker."

She met his gaze and felt miserably self-conscious. It was as bad as being a gawky thirteen-year-old. Her mind was a blank. She didn't have the first idea of what to say. Still, it was hard to step away.

"Jessica, there you are—" Jessica turned to see Suzanne walking toward her. "I've been looking for you. Ready for lunch?"

"Sure . . . let me just dump this stuff in my office," she said.

She wondered if she should ask Sam to join them. No, that would be sending him the wrong message . . . wouldn't it? Before she could figure it out, Suzanne beat her to it.

"Hi, Sam. Want to have lunch with us?"

Jessica met his gaze and felt herself freeze in place. He looked at her briefly, then back at Suzanne.

"Thanks, but I really need to stick around here and finish up."

Suzanne frowned. "Too bad. Maybe another time?"

"Sure, some other time," he agreed with a friendly nod.

Jessica met his gaze again, and for a moment he seemed to share a private smile with her. As she watched him turn and walk away, she felt a mixture of relief . . . and disappointment.

She walked down to her office and closed the door. Alone inside, she shook her head and said to herself aloud, "Okay, get a grip. He's done with his work today, and that is *that* with Sam Morgan."

JESSICA AND SUZANNE ATE LUNCH AT THE CLAM BOX. Jessica was hoping to run into her sister, Emily, there, realizing she'd meant to call her this morning. She would try to call her later, or maybe tonight. She just wanted to assure Emily that everything had gone all right on Sunday with Lillian. She wasn't sure why she felt obliged to report in to her older sister . . . she just did.

"I wonder if Sam Morgan really had to work, or he just didn't want to have lunch with us," Suzanne said suddenly as their waitress brought their order.

"I haven't got a clue," Jessica replied honestly.

"Oh, well. I tried." Suzanne plunked a straw into her iced tea. "All those women's magazines are always saying guys like it when you make the first move. But I still haven't met one that does."

Jessica didn't know what to say in reply. For one thing, she'd rarely had the nerve to make the first move. And for another, she didn't really want to talk about Sam Morgan.

"He did look busy," she said finally. She felt sorry for her friend, putting herself out like that, then getting rejected. "Hey, maybe it was me he didn't want to have lunch with," she added.

"Nice try, Jessica. But I don't think that was it," Suzanne said with a small, knowing grin.

After lunch Jessica went straight into a meeting. It was nearly five when she finally emerged. She was sure Sam was gone, and it gave her a funny feeling, as if she'd missed out on saying good-bye to him. She caught herself. That was silly. No. It was crazy.

Back in her office she checked her messages and considered the work she still had to do before she went home. Then she looked up to see a small yellow Post-it note on her window. She approached, already knowing who had left it.

His handwriting was bold and straightforward, just like his personality, she thought.

"Jessica, Enjoy the view—Sam," the simple message read. She pulled it off the glass, laughing. She sat down at her desk again and was about to toss it in the trash, when she suddenly changed her mind. She stuck it on the edge of her desk blotter. She wasn't sure why.

CHAPTER FOUR

⌒

THE CLAM BOX WAS PRACTICALLY EMPTY, EMILY noticed as she walked in. Just the way she liked it.

She took a big booth by the window all to herself and spread out her papers from the office. She didn't usually eat dinner early, but at half past five her day was only half over. She needed a break and some refueling before that night's town council meeting. Starting at seven, it could go on until midnight or later.

The big item on tonight's agenda was the new parking meters proposed for Main Street. Most of the council agreed on the need for meters. The shopkeepers, however, were opposed.

Emily glanced around for Charlie Bates. She knew that on meeting nights he usually went home in the afternoon to get ready for his public appearance. He'd be leading the charge against the meters. She only hoped that if he was still around, he'd let her eat her dinner in peace and save his powder for the meeting.

A waitress walked up to the table and put a glass of ice water on the table, then handed Emily a menu. Emily had never seen her before, though she knew Lucy and Charlie had been looking for extra help again.

"Hi, my name is Sara. We have some specials on the board tonight. Can I get you something to drink while you're deciding?"

The young woman seemed nervous, Emily noticed. She could barely meet Emily's eye. Probably her first day on the job. Emily smiled up at her. She didn't bother opening the menu; she knew it by heart. "I think I can order now."

The young woman nodded and took out her pad and pencil. Emily ordered a cup of chowder and a sandwich. "And some coffee," she added, hoping it would wake her up.

"No problem. I'll be right back." Sara looked up from the order pad and stared at her.

Emily smiled again and handed her the menu. "Is this your first day working here?" she asked.

"Uh . . . yes. Yes, it is." The waitress looked down at the menu, then back at Emily. "You're the mayor, right?"

For some reason the question made Emily laugh. Or maybe it was just the way the young woman had asked it. "That's me. But everybody calls me Emily. What's your name?"

"Sara. Sara Franklin." The young woman stared at her again. Her eyes looked full of emotion, as if she had many more questions or something important she wanted to say.

"Where are you from, Sara?" Emily asked after a moment.

"Maryland. A small town called Winston. It's a lot like this one, actually."

Emily felt the girl watching her, as if studying her reaction. But that was silly. The girl is just shy with strangers, Emily told herself. Though, in fact, the mention of

Maryland did elicit a strong, instantaneous reaction in her. One she struggled to repress.

"Maryland is beautiful," Emily said, keeping her voice steady. "I don't know Winston. But I lived down there once, on the Chesapeake Bay."

"Did you really?"

Emily nodded, not sure of how much she wanted to add. She'd never forget that one magical year after high school when she ran away to Maryland to marry Tim Sutton . . . the joy when she became pregnant. And she'd never forget the excruciating way it had all ended.

"A long time ago . . ." she finally said. "I'm sure the area has changed a lot since then."

"Ever go back to visit?" Sara asked.

"No . . . only once. But not for a vacation or anything like that." Emily met Sara's curious gaze and looked away. "I had to take care of some business. I didn't really see very much."

"I'll get your coffee now, okay?" Sara asked suddenly. "It will just be a minute. I think I ought to make a fresh pot."

Emily looked up at the waitress and smiled again. "You don't have to go to any trouble."

"It's no trouble," Sara insisted. She seemed embarrassed as she took the menu and hurried away.

Pushing her papers aside, Emily stared out the window. Talking about Maryland had made her remember. Again. The memories were still sharp and jagged, even after all this time, tearing at her. Tim's death in the car accident . . . having to give up her baby. She struggled to push them aside. She didn't want to go back there now, though not a day passed that she didn't think of her daughter and wonder where she was and how she had turned out.

She glanced over at Sara. Her daughter would be about the same age as this girl, Emily thought. She might even look like her, with her richly colored brown hair and blue eyes. *If she'd taken after me instead of Tim*, Emily thought.

Emily felt a sharp ache and glanced out the window. She didn't even know what her daughter looked like. She didn't know the first thing about her. Had she had a happy life? Were her adoptive parents good to her?

No, it was too hard....

She couldn't think about it. Not here. She felt a sudden pressure in her head and rubbed her brow with her fingertips, trying to compose herself.

You can't sit here crying in full view of Main Street, she told herself. *That won't do.*

She reached for her water glass and took a sip. Her hand trembled a bit, she noticed, as if she were looking at someone else's. She stretched out her fingers and looked down at them, still bare and ring-less after all this time.

She had resumed her life in Cape Light as if that year with Tim had never happened. Or had happened to someone else. But under the surface, that brief chapter was still taking its toll. She sometimes felt as if a part of her had remained stuck and frozen in that place, that time in her life, twenty years ago.

Emily closed her eyes a moment and took a deep breath to clear her head. She couldn't think about this anymore. She'd never be able to go back to work tonight.

When she looked out at Main Street, she saw Jessica passing the diner. She quickly tapped on the window, and her sister looked up and smiled. Emily waved, inviting her in.

The two sisters hugged in greeting, and Jessica sat down.

"I'm just having a quick bite before the town council meeting. Want some dinner?" Emily asked.

"No, thanks. I've got to get home," Jessica replied. The

waitress appeared with Emily's coffee and a menu, but Jessica waved it away.

"This is my sister. She just dropped by to say hello," Emily explained to Sara. She noticed Sara's blue eyes grow wide as she stared at Jessica. Did the girl find it odd that she had a sister?

"Can I bring you something to drink?" Sara asked nervously.

"Okay . . . I guess I'll have an iced tea," Jessica said, sitting back her seat. Once Sara left, she turned back to Emily. "Is she new here?"

"Yes, very new." Emily took a sip of her coffee. "But she makes good coffee. And she seems very sweet," she added. She looked up at her sister. They hardly ever met like this, for no reason at all. She wished Jessica would stay and visit with her awhile, but she didn't want to press it.

"How did it go with Mother on Sunday? I called her this afternoon, but Rachel Anderson was there. They were in the middle of Mother's physical therapy."

"Well, I got her to church and back in one piece, so that was a success," Jessica reported. "And Dr. Elliot came for lunch. So all I had to do was feed and water them. Molly Willoughby is a great cook, by the way. Mother, of course, thinks she uses too much seasoning."

"Any seasoning is too much for Mom," Emily said, shaking her head. "Did they gossip about everyone in town?"

"Everyone but you. But maybe they covered that topic while I left the room, I can't be sure."

"Probably," Emily said. "Thanks for taking over."

"No problem. That's what I'm here for." Jessica shrugged. "I meant to call you this morning, but I got too busy."

"That's okay." Emily glanced at Jessica, then away again. "I just wondered, that's all."

Maybe it was their nine-year age difference. At times Jessica felt Emily didn't realize she was an adult now, too. Especially in regard to taking care of their mother.

Sara brought Emily's dinner and served Jessica's iced tea.

"Are you sure you won't have dinner with me? I have plenty of time," Emily said again.

Jessica seemed tempted, then shook her head. "No, thanks. I have a busy day tomorrow. I have a lot to do at home."

Jessica considered telling her sister about Paul. Then decided not to. She'd never really talked to Emily about dating. She wasn't sure her sister would understand. Emily didn't seem interested in men or romance. She had never had a relationship—not that Jessica knew of, anyway.

They didn't have the kind of close relationship some sisters shared. Jessica wasn't sure why. It wasn't as if they argued. They rarely disagreed. But they'd never had those heartfelt talks or cried in each other's arms, the way Jessica thought sisters should. Moving back to Cape Light hadn't helped. For Jessica, it had only made her more aware of the gap between them.

"So how's the job going?" Emily asked while Jessica sipped her iced tea.

"Good. They gave me a window," Jessica added with a laugh.

Emily arched one eyebrow in interest, and Jessica filled her in. "Sam Morgan put it in," she finished, curious to see what her sister's reaction would be.

"Mmm . . . Sam does excellent work," Emily said. She took another bite of her sandwich. "I need some bookcases in the living room. But he's always so busy."

"Yes, he seems to be," Jessica agreed. She considered asking Emily what she thought of Sam. Then gave herself a mental shake. That would be silly. No point to it.

"So, what's on tonight's agenda at the meeting?" she asked Emily, quickly changing the subject. "Anything interesting?"

"Mostly routine matters. But I am expecting an all-night argument over parking meters. Care to speak in my defense?"

"I think you'll do just fine without backup," Jessica assured her with a smile.

"Thanks for the vote of confidence." Emily grinned. She left money for the check and the two got up to go. Sara was standing behind the counter and looked up as they passed.

"Thanks for the coffee, Sara," Emily said. "A fresh cup of coffee was just what I needed."

"You're welcome. . . . Good night." Sara met Emily's gaze and smiled, then quickly looked away.

As Emily and Jessica left, Lucy came over to the counter and stood next to Sara. She took a stack of menus and started sponging them off one by one.

"There they go, the Warwick girls. Say what you want about that family, but they have class, right down to their fingertips. You could put those two on a desert island. The class would still show."

Sara gave a nervous laugh. "Do you really think that's true?"

"Absolutely. You're either born with it or you're not."

Lucy wiped down the last menu, then straightened out the stack. She seemed very lively and upbeat tonight, Sara noticed. She wondered if Lucy's mood had anything to do with the fact that Charlie wasn't in the diner this evening.

"Hey, I want to show you something. You're going to die laughing," Lucy promised.

She leaned down under the counter and came up again holding a brown cardboard box. "Charlie was just throwing a fit about the Beanery opening up down the street.

Now he wants to do everything around here like they do. He even had these silly T-shirts made up. You know, because the Beans have T-shirts. So look at this. . . ." Lucy opened the box and pulled out a blue T-shirt.

"The Clam Box" was printed across the front in bold white letters, with a small illustration of the diner and a list of specialties. The back had a cartoon of a smiling clam with a cartoon bubble. "Try our famous clam roll. Mmmm, good!" it read.

"Now, is that the silliest thing you've ever seen? Charlie says the drawing was his idea. He never asked me about it, I'll tell you that much," Lucy added, gazing down at the talking clam. "He made them up for the help to wear and thinks he's going to sell them, too. First of all, I'm not wearing a shirt with a silly cartoon clam on it every day, thank you very much. And why would a clam even say that? It just doesn't make any sense."

"It is sort of . . . odd looking," Sara admitted. "Maybe he'll have it changed."

Lucy's warm laughter burst out. "Sure, he'll change it. After we use up the four dozen shirts that are coming tomorrow. Then there's the flavored coffees. Did you see Tucker taste that hazelnut today? He spit it right back into the cup." She folded the T-shirt and put it back in the box. "Let's just hope Charlie gets over this Bean problem quickly."

Lucy sighed and shook her head. She glanced over at Sara. "How do you like it so far? I mean, besides the new T-shirts."

"It's fine." Sara smiled and shrugged. "I know I messed up a few orders this morning, during the rush. But I'll get better once I know where everything is."

"Of course you will," Lucy assured her. "I think you're doing great. Don't pay too much attention to Charlie. Even if he yells, it doesn't necessarily mean he's mad at you." Lucy paused. "Listen, I wanted to ask you something. I was wondering if you could give me some advice."

"Advice? About what?" Sara couldn't imagine what kind of advice she could give the older woman. Though she already felt comfortable with Lucy, as if they could be good friends.

"Well, you went to college and I was wondering if you could take at look at these with me. . . ."

Lucy leaned down again and pulled out something else from another shelf under the counter. Whatever it was, it was buried back there, Sara noticed, and it took Lucy a few moments to wrestle it out. Finally, a bit flushed, Lucy emerged with several college catalogs, which she dropped on the counter in front of Sara.

"Listen, this is just between us, okay? I haven't told Charlie yet, but I've been thinking about going back to school. I had a year or so of college before Charlie and I got married, and I always hoped I'd finish. But you know how it is." Lucy shook her head. "Once the kids come, that's it. Then Charlie took over this place when his father died, and if I have a spare minute to breathe, I'm in here, working."

Sara couldn't imagine Lucy's life, so busy with so many people to take care of. She only had herself to think about, and sometimes even that seemed too much to handle.

"I think that's great," Sara told her. "What do you want to study? Anything in particular?"

Lucy looked almost embarrassed, but finally she said, "Well, I know it's a long haul, but I'd like to be a nurse."

Sara smiled. "I think you'd be a really good one," she said sincerely.

"Oh, thanks, honey. You're sweet. But I'm not sure I can do it. So much studying and memorizing . . . But I really want to try, you know what I mean? Then I can say, well, at least I tried. Right?"

"Sure, I understand." Sara felt a sudden kinship with Lucy. She wanted her to go for it. It went without saying that it wasn't going to be easy.

"Want me to look through the catalogs with you?" Sara offered.

"Would you? That would be terrific."

"The thing is, I don't really know much about the colleges around here." Sara paused and leafed through the book on top. "Maybe the Beans could give you some advice," she suggested. "Weren't they college professors? I'm sure they know a lot about which schools are stronger in arts or sciences. That sort of thing."

"The Beans?" Lucy looked shocked. As if Sara had suggested she call the White House. "Oh, I couldn't do that."

"Why not? They might even know some teachers at the schools who could help you get in when you're ready to apply."

"I guess that's true." Lucy bit her lip. "They probably could help me a lot . . . if I asked, I mean. And they wanted to." She paused and took a deep breath. "Charlie sent me over there on Tuesday. He wanted me to sort of spy around for him," she added, glancing at Sara. "But I couldn't really do it. I told them who I was, and I more or less apologized for Charlie and the way he's going on about their store. They were awfully nice. They even gave me a cappuccino and this little toasted sandwich with goat cheese and tomato. It was scrumptious."

"Maybe you ought to go see them again," Sara urged her with a smile. "You could go right now. I can handle everything here."

"Yes, I guess I could, couldn't I?" Lucy glanced down at her watch. "Charlie should be in that meeting until at least ten or eleven. Sometimes they go all night."

"It's quiet here. I can cover for you."

"If Charlie ever finds out I went over to the enemy,

he'll kill me. . . ." Lucy said, pulling off her apron. "But I suppose you have to live dangerously once in a while." She picked up the catalogs. "If you have any problems or can't find something, just ask Fred, he'll help you out," she said, mentioning the replacement cook. "And promise you won't breathe a word of this to a living soul."

"Your secret's safe with me," Sara promised.

"Thanks, hon. See you later." Lucy gave a little wave and headed out the door.

The diner was quiet for the next few hours, and Sara easily took care of the few tables. When she had nothing to do, she leafed through some back issues of the *Messenger*, looking for articles that mentioned Emily Warwick. A number of articles did, but only in connection with the issues in the town. None of them had any personal information. Sara decided she'd go over to the library on her day off and see if she could find out more about Emily. And the whole Warwick family, for that matter. She knew that the Warwicks had been in this area for a long time and had once owned a big estate with an old mansion. She'd driven past but hadn't gone inside. She would check that out, too, she resolved.

Sara was at the register, ringing up a check, when a new customer entered. He looked to be in his mid-twenties, wearing jeans with a denim jacket and a black T-shirt. His thick brown hair was cut short. He stood at the door and slowly looked around, as if he were unfamiliar with the place.

"You can sit anywhere," Sara greeted him. "I'll be with you in just a moment."

He looked at her but didn't smile. His pale gray eyes were unusual, she thought. Something about them was wary and cold.

As he headed for an empty table, she noticed his slow, halting gait. Not really that obvious, but she always noticed small details about people.

"There are specials on the board," Sara said, handing him a menu. "Can I bring you something to drink while you're deciding?"

"Just coffee, please," he said without looking at her.

At first she thought he might be one of the local workingmen, who seemed to favor the diner. But when she brought the coffee back, she noticed that his hands looked too smooth and clean for outdoor work. For that matter, so did his clothing.

He stared at the menu, seeming not to notice her. Then he said, "What's good here?"

"Gee . . . I'm not sure. It's my first day. Everybody seems to like the clam rolls, though," she added quickly. "And the hamburgers look good."

"Okay, give me a clam roll, then." He closed the menu and handed it to her. "At least you're honest."

Sara wasn't sure how to respond to that. She jotted down the order on her pad.

"So, how do you like your new job?" he asked before she could walk away.

Sara shrugged. "It's okay. I'm just here for the summer and I needed something."

"The summer is nice up here. I used to come here every year with my family when I was a kid. It doesn't look like it's changed much since then."

Sara found herself studying his face while he spoke. A thin white scar ran from the corner of his eye, down his cheek. He still wore that serious look, but when he talked about the past, his expression lightened a bit.

"I haven't been here very long, but I get the feeling they don't like a lot of changes," Sara said.

"I get the feeling you're right." He leaned back, his eyes narrowing as he looked at her. "What's your name?"

"Sara . . . What's yours?"

"Luke," he replied. He continued to look at her but didn't say anything more. Sara suddenly felt self-conscious and eager to end their conversation.

"I'll just go put this order in. I'll be right back with a refill on your coffee," she added.

She turned and walked away without looking at him again. He was just being friendly, she thought. Not bothering her, or anything like that. Still, his gray eyes gave her an odd feeling each time she met his gaze. He was attractive, actually, but not in a typical way. And he hadn't smiled once. There was something about him, something . . . unsettling.

Remembering that she wasn't alone in the diner and Fred was back in the kitchen made her feel a whole lot better.

IT WAS AFTER ELEVEN O'CLOCK WHEN THE TOWN council meeting began to wind down. Emily was bleary-eyed, and her throat felt hoarse, but she forced herself to remain sitting tall in her chair, her back straight and chin high, the way her mother had insisted. Good posture came in handy in her job.

Seated at the center of a long narrow table in the front of the town hall's meeting room, she was flanked by the rest of the council, including the village clerk, treasurer, secretary, police chief, and others. As she'd expected, the debate over parking meters on Main Street had been long and loud. It was now time to call a vote . . . or at least try again.

Emily took a fortifying sip of ice water. She couldn't wilt now, though she certainly felt as if she might.

Charlie Bates, leading the outraged merchants, was once again stating his case. ". . . and I'm telling you, we'll all be out of business in a week if our customers are forced to feed a meter or worried about getting a ticket. And who's going to run in and out of the diner with quarters while their food is getting cold?"

"The meters will take two hours' worth of coins," Harriet DeSoto, the village clerk, reminded everyone. "Maybe you ought to speed up your table service."

"Or you could open a drive-thru window," Warren Oakes remarked.

The suggestion drew a laugh. But the argument continued, heated and bitter at times.

"The town needs more revenue. It's a plain and simple fact," Clark McCormack, the village treasurer, stated flatly. "Look at these figures. The blue line is revenue. The red line, expenses . . ."

Emily shifted restlessly in her seat as Clark referred to his poster-board chart with its color-bar graph. He was losing them.

"I think Clark makes a very sound point," she cut in. "Merchants want more frequent sanitation removal, the storm drains improved, and bigger flowerpots on Main Street. The police station needs new computers and squad cars. . . . As we all know from working on this year's budget, the wish list is endless."

"I agree with Emily," Harriet added. "The money has to come from somewhere. Meters will definitely help fill the till."

Emily saw her moment and moved in to close the deal. "I move that the question be called to a vote," she said loudly into the microphone. "All in favor?"

Five of the six council members raised their hands and said, "Aye."

The secretary recorded their votes in the minutes as Emily asked, "All opposed?"

Police Chief Jim Sanborn raised his hand. "Opposed," he said gruffly. Emily was not surprised. As much as he wanted his new cars, he had balked at seeing his law-enforcement team turned into "a pack of meter maids."

"The motion is carried," Emily declared. "Let it be noted in the minutes that the motion to install parking meters on Main Street has been passed by a vote of five to one."

Grumbles, some louder than others, sounded in the hall. But as Emily had sensed, the opposition recognized that meters were inevitable. The question had come up often over the last few years. It was only a matter of time before it passed. Cape Light still boasted authentic gaslights on Main Street, but the town could not entirely escape the modern age.

"That completes tonight's agenda," the town secretary said.

Thank you, Lord. Emily breathed a silent prayer. She removed her reading glasses and raised her wooden gavel. "I move this meeting is adjourned—"

"Wait just a minute." Charlie Bates rose up as others shifted in their seats, ready to go. "We still have something important to discuss here. Mayor, you'd better call the room back to order."

Everyone looked at Charlie and then at Emily. She knew if she didn't recognize him, there would be a stampede out the door in a matter of seconds. But if she ignored him, there was no telling what kind of scene he would make.

"Please keep your seats a moment more," Emily said wearily. "All right, Charlie. You're recognized."

"This isn't on the official agenda, but that doesn't mean it shouldn't be," he began. "As many of you know, Dr. Ezra Elliot has put a large tract of land up for sale, out on the Beach Road, just northeast of the village. It borders the Warwick estate, and it's visible to anyone coming in or out of town."

Emily shifted restlessly. Charlie had missed his calling, she thought. He should have been on Broadway, he had such a flare for drama.

"Yes, Charlie. We know our geography. Please get to the point," she prodded him.

"My point, Mayor, is that Dr. Elliot just can't up and sell to the highest bidder. He has a responsibility to this town to make sure that no one is going to buy that land and turn it into some ugly eyesore—a bunch of cheap condos or a fast-food place or a tacky motel."

"I hear you, Charlie." Corey Nolan, who owned Nolan's Stationery, stood up. "Like over in Fairfax. A couple came in, bought some land, said they were starting an herb farm. Before you know it, the place turned into a commune. Took years to get them out."

"I heard it was worse than that," Marge Quigley, who taught at the high school, chimed in. "I heard it was a cult kind of thing."

"Ezra can't just cash in and leave us with a mess, while he's enjoying himself down in Florida or something," Corey Nolan complained.

"I heard Dr. Elliot is getting senile. All his patients are leaving him, you know," added Lester Pyle, who owned the barbershop across from the fire station.

"That's not true," Miriam Nelson, who owned the bake shop on Main Street, countered. "Dr. Elliot is about to retire. He's referring his patients to other physicians."

"And he's never said a word about leaving town," Gus Potter added. "I just spoke to Ezra a few days ago. He never mentioned Florida."

Emily wondered if anyone had heard Miriam or Gus. At least half the people in the hall were still in a flurry over the commune comment. If she didn't restore a rational voice, the meeting would go on till dawn.

"There is a system of law in our village, designed to prevent such unhappy outcomes . . . from ugly condos to communal living," she explained. "We have zoning laws and building permits. Permit applications that come up before this very board. Dr. Elliot is a private citizen, who has the right to sell his land without interference."

"Does he have the right to ruin this town? To just ignore and trample on everybody else's rights around here?" Charlie demanded. "It's up to the mayor to protect Cape Light's integrity. We all work hard to keep this village a clean, decent, nice place to live. If the mayor doesn't stand up for that, who will?" he challenged her.

Charlie, I hope you've got a tape recorder hidden somewhere. That was a magnificent campaign speech.

That's what Emily wanted to say. Instead, she took a steadying breath. "When I need you to coach me on my job description, Charlie, I'll let you know," she said lightly. "Now, if some of you agree with Mr. Bates, let me ask you this: How many of you would like me to review and approve—or disapprove—all your private business transactions?"

"Now, wait a minute . . ." Charlie moved down the aisle, closer to the table where Emily sat. "That is not what I said—"

"That's exactly what you said, Charlie," Emily insisted. "It is not my place—or anyone else's—to interfere with Dr. Elliot's transaction. None of us has the legal authority to do so. I don't see that there's need for any further debate on what strikes me as an unreasonable and even absurd proposal." Emily raised the gavel and struck the small wooden block. "I move this meeting is adjourned. All in favor . . ." The council gave immediate, unanimous consent. "Opposed?" She waited a beat, then banged the gavel. "Motion passed. The minutes of this meeting are hereby closed. . . . Good night, everyone."

She clicked off the microphone and began to collect the papers on the table in front of her. The crowd quickly thinned out.

"Good job, Emily," Harriet DeSoto said quietly. The older woman gave her a reassuring pat on the shoulder as she passed.

"Good night, Emily. You earned your pay tonight," Warren Oakes added with a kind smile as he ambled past.

A few others also said good night, adding she'd done well to oppose Charlie.

But as the room emptied, Emily felt deflated. *I'm just tired*, she told herself as she packed her briefcase. Sometimes she wondered why she'd wanted this job in the first place.

As she stood up she suddenly found herself facing Dan Forbes. A reporter usually covered meetings like this one, but since the *Messenger* didn't have a very large staff, Dan sometimes filled in. She'd noticed him sitting in the back of the room, jotting notes, his expression interested but neutral.

"So what did you think?" she asked him point blank.

"Pick up a copy of the paper tomorrow, Mayor, and you'll find out."

"Spoken like a true reporter," Emily replied with a weary grin.

"I'll take that as a compliment." Dan had a talent for remaining objective, but something in his smile suggested he had agreed with her. "Get a good night's rest, Mayor. Tomorrow is another day."

"Tomorrow is today. Didn't you notice?" Emily opened the door at the room's side exit. "This was a long one."

He glanced at his watch and shook his head. "So it was. . . . I'd better get to my computer, or I'll have a blank front page and nobody to yell at."

Was he really going to write for the rest of the night? It was nearly one o'clock. Emily was looking forward to going home and crawling into bed.

"Good night, Dan," she said. With a smile, she slipped out the door.

CHAPTER FIVE

～

THE YELLOW POST-IT NOTE FROM SAM, STILL
stuck to her blotter, was the first thing Jessica noticed
when she sat down at her desk on Wednesday morning.

As she entered the bank that morning, she realized his
work there was done. There was no chance she would run
into him today. Sam Morgan was gone.

*Just as well. I'll concentrate much better without that
distraction*, she told herself as she sorted her work into
priority piles: "Urgent," "Important but can wait," and
"Ignore and maybe it will go away."

She wanted to leave the office early to get ready for
her date with Paul. That meant she had to get through all
of the "Urgent" pile by lunch time or she wouldn't make
it.

Resolved to forget about Sam Morgan, Jessica tossed
his note into the trash basket.

*   *   *

PASSING ON THE OPPOSITE SIDE OF MAIN STREET, Carolyn Lewis waved at Emily Warwick, but did not cross over to talk. For one thing, Emily appeared to be walking even faster and with more determination than usual, which was saying something. Carolyn imagined that she was late for an early-morning meeting, or just needed to get to her office at Village Hall quickly.

The mayor was an unusual woman, Carolyn thought. On the surface at least, Emily Warwick was so sensible and centered, so reliable and straightforward, she was the very definition of the expression "Ask a busy person to do something and it will get done." Along with her demanding job and caring for her mother, she still found time to work on church committees, rummage and bake sales, and even cook for charity dinners. She managed to sail through it all with her calm smile and clear blue eyes, rarely voicing a word of complaint or revealing a downbeat mood.

Yet, Carolyn suspected, the image Emily projected was only part of her story. Though Ben was unerringly discreet, Carolyn knew Emily had come to him often for counsel, and merely from his attitude when he spoke of Emily, Carolyn sensed that there was more to their mayor than her still waters suggested. More secrets. More intensity. Everybody knew Emily. Most everyone liked her. But did anyone really know her all that well?

Do we ultimately ever know each other? Carolyn wondered. Even in the most intimate relationships—parents and children, husbands and wives, lovers and friends—it was a common mistake to think we understood and then to pass judgment. Whatever Emily's private struggles, and Carolyn felt almost sure that she had them, her strong faith surely provided a bulwark.

Unlike Grace Hegman, Carolyn reflected as she approached the Bramble Shop. Grace had such painful memories. How could she bear them without faith?

Grace's marvelous garden in front of her shop must surely be a source of pride and pleasure and solace, Carolyn thought as she walked up the flower-lined walk. Carolyn had always admired the garden with its sheer horticultural audacity, the way Grace grew huge tomatoes and zucchini alongside daisies and roses and hollyhock, mint and basil in the midst of foxglove and tiger lilies.

The porch of the Bramble Shop was stocked with discounted items. Carolyn couldn't stop herself from browsing before going in. As always, it was an eclectic and interesting collection—a dressmaker's dummy, an iron-rimmed wagon wheel missing a few spokes, an antique baby carriage with torn upholstery, half of a salt-and-pepper set, a stained-glass window lacking a few panes of glass.

A bell above the door jangled as Carolyn entered the shop. It was cool and quiet inside. The musty odor of old furniture and the perfume of dried rose petals scented the air. Carolyn already knew what she'd find in each of the small rooms: a mix of antique pieces and garage-sale finds, some beautifully refinished, some needing repair. There were dressers full of linens and a rack of vintage clothes, baskets of antique postcards and shelves of miscellaneous bric-a-brac.

The barn behind the house held larger items, like a marble fireplace mantel, a treadle sewing machine, and a wooden carousel horse. When the barn would periodically become filled to the rafters, Grace would put out her painted wooden placard announcing Barn Sale Today, and the tourists would help her make room for more finds.

That was the Bramble. The scripture "Seek and ye shall find" could hang over the front door, Carolyn thought, reminding her of her morning's mission.

The piano in Grace's barn. Despite Digger's doubts that Grace would ever part with it, Carolyn wanted to give it a try. She'd tried to track down a piano through other sources but had no leads on a suitable instrument. Maybe Grace would be ready to let it go.

Grace usually sat on a stool near the door, next to the jewelry case, with Daisy at her feet. But neither the shop owner nor her faithful companion were in sight. Then Carolyn heard Grace coming down the stairs from the apartment above. She heard her talking to someone but saw only the large yellow dog padding softly behind.

". . . and he knows he has to see the neurologist in Southport today. He should've just stayed home, so we would be on time. Bad enough I need to close up all afternoon. Do you think I can pry him loose from that blasted boatyard *if* I even find him there? Harry Reilly says he'll keep an eye on him, but no telling what that means. . . ."

Carolyn softly coughed into her hand. Grace looked up. Her straight chin-length gray hair swung back from her face. A stack of lace-edged linens, freshly pressed, was cradled like a baby in the crook of her lean arm.

"Carolyn—you startled me."

"Good morning, Grace," Carolyn said.

"I didn't hear you come in. Can I help you with something?"

"Why, yes, Yes, you can." Carolyn had thought many times about how to ask Grace for this favor, but now she suddenly drew a blank. *Dear God, please give me the right words to persuade her,* she silently prayed.

"I came to speak to you about an item in the barn, actually—"

Grace stared at her with a questioning look and blinked her eyes. She carefully put the stack of linens down on the counter.

"That piano. It's way in the back," Carolyn continued, "with a green cover over it—"

"I know what you mean," Grace cut in curtly. "The piano's not for sale."

"Oh . . . are you sure?" Carolyn persisted. Then, before Grace could interrupt her, she added, "The reason I'm asking is that I have a new student, very talented, too. Molly Willoughby's oldest girl, Lauren."

"Yes, I know who you mean." Grace nodded. "She and her little sister both come here to see their uncle, Sam. He has a workshop out back."

"So maybe you know her a little, then," Carolyn rushed on, encouraged by this small connection. "She's a lovely girl and a very promising young musician. I told her mother I'd try to help them find a piano for Lauren. They can't afford much, of course, so it would have to be something secondhand. I was thinking that instrument in your barn would be just right."

Grace was silent for a moment. She smoothed her hand over the pile of linens. Carolyn watched her, consciously holding her tongue. Grace wasn't the kind of person who could be talked into things. Carolyn knew that if she said too much, she'd only end up irritating her.

At last Grace shook her head. "No. I can't do it."

Carolyn didn't know what to say. "Are you sure?" she asked.

Grace glanced at her briefly, then walked around the glass counter. Carolyn watched as she tugged at the edge of her pale green cardigan, examining one of the small pearl buttons. She wore a white cotton blouse underneath, neatly pressed. No matter the weather, Grace could always be counted on to wear a sweater, Carolyn vaguely reflected.

"It's not for sale," Grace said finally, looking up. "Like I said before. You might try that place out on the highway, that furniture warehouse. Some old instruments go through there from time to time."

"I called them last week. They don't have one right now."

Grace did not answer. She reached under the register

and pulled out a plain notebook with a black-and-white marble cover. It said Inventory on the front in block letters. She put on her reading glasses, then opened it and thumbed through the pages.

"Why won't you sell it, Grace . . . if I may ask," Carolyn said softly, though she already knew the answer.

"It was Julie's. She used to play on it." Grace continued looking at her notebook, making notations with a yellow pencil. "I need to hold on to it."

"Yes, I understand," Carolyn said after a moment. "But it's sitting out there, going to waste. Someone could be playing music on it. It's just going to get ruined from the weather, if it isn't already."

"Then that's my problem, I guess," Grace said crisply. She closed her book and looked up at Carolyn.

Carolyn had her answer. She bit down on her lip, wondering if she'd pushed too hard. Maybe she had been wrong to ask about the piano, to force Grace to remember why the neglected piece was so dear to her. Checking her notebook again, Grace suddenly seemed so fragile, so brittle.

Dear God, please forgive me, Carolyn silently prayed. *I didn't mean to hurt her. Please grant Grace a greater measure of peace and consolation.*

Carolyn glanced at the pile of linens and reached out to touch the lace border. "Those are lovely," she said. "So finely made."

"They don't do handwork like this anymore," Grace said. "But nobody has the time to wash and iron. In the old days, if you could afford fancy sheets or tablecloths, there were probably a few maids in the house to do the laundry."

"Yes, that's most likely true." Daisy trotted over and sniffed Carolyn's hand. She patted the dog's soft head. "Good-bye, Grace . . . I'll be seeing you."

"Yes, I'll be seeing you, Carolyn. Have a good day." Grace nodded, looking relieved to see Carolyn go.

Carolyn headed out the door, the jingling bell a contrast to her deflated hopes. A battered black pickup truck was just pulling up to the curb. Digger sat in the passenger's seat, and Harry Reilly was behind the wheel.

Looking his typically disgruntled self, Harry's tall, bulky body emerged from the truck. He walked around to Digger's door and pulled it open. Then he stood aside, as if coaxing a reluctant child to go inside after being caught at some mischief and brought home.

Scowling, Digger emerged and started walking up the path to the shop, his head bowed. Harry followed. They both greeted Carolyn briefly as they passed on the path.

"You have an appointment with the doctor and you're going. Now, stop arguing about it," Carolyn heard Harry say.

"I can at least get myself inside on my own two feet, Harry," Digger muttered in reply.

"It's no trouble, I can walk you to the door," Harry insisted. "Not that I think you might run off the moment I get back in that truck or anything like that," he added.

Then Carolyn heard the shop door open and Grace's surprised greeting.

"Here he is, Grace," Harry said dolefully. "I can run you down to Southport if you like. It's no trouble."

"That's okay, Harry. I can take it from here," Grace assured him. "But thank you for delivering him to me," she added. "That was a big help."

Carolyn was too far away by then to hear Harry's reply, but it seemed clear that Harry was trying to help Grace, and that was good. Grace needed help now and again, even if she was determined to convince everyone—herself, included—that she didn't.

JESSICA'S WORKDAY PASSED QUICKLY. IN THE MORNing she managed to review a huge stack of loan applications and write up the necessary recommendations for her boss, Alfred Fisk. Most of the afternoon was taken up by a staff meeting.

At half past four on the dot, she packed up and left for home. As soon as she got in, she kicked off her pumps, dropped her briefcase near the door, and dumped a stack of unopened mail on the kitchen table.

Shower, dress, do my hair and makeup . . . She made a mental list as she headed through the kitchen to her bedroom. Then she noticed the light on the answering machine and stopped to press the Play button.

The first voice was her landlord's, Warren Oakes. "I'm trying to get a guy over there to fix that leak, Jessica. Will you be home tonight? Call me back, okay?"

Sorry, Warren. I'll be out, she thought happily. *Probably at some very fine restaurant. Maybe there'll be music and dancing. Maybe even a moonlit walk on the beach* . . . Then she heard Paul's voice on the next message. The hesitant, apologetic note in his greeting didn't bode well.

"Hi, Jessica. It's me, Paul. I'm still up in Burlington. I'm so sorry, but I'm not going to be able to make it down to Cape Light tonight. . . ."

Jessica was so stunned, she barely heard the rest of the message. ". . . I feel awful about this, honestly. I was really looking forward to seeing you tonight. But it just can't be helped," he said with a long sigh. "The problem up here is more complicated than I expected. It might take a few days to straighten this mess out. The client is very angry. I have to do some real damage control. It may take the rest of the week, but maybe I can see you on the weekend?" he added hopefully.

"I'll call you back later tonight," he promised. "Talk to you then." Then there was only the beep signaling the message was over.

Jessica felt her eyes fill with tears. A few drops squeezed out and trailed down her cheek. She sniffed hard and whisked her wet eyes with her fingertips. She wouldn't let herself cry over this. That was so . . . silly. She just wouldn't.

She stared down at the rubber trash pail and after a long moment, gave it solid kick. Then, her toe throbbing in pain, she jumped back, hopping on one foot and feeling like an idiot.

The pail had been surprisingly hard and she was barefoot. And she'd spilled trash all over the kitchen floor. Feeling like a dolt for making such a mess and stubbing her toe, to boot, she sat down on a kitchen stool and laughed at herself.

She was disappointed about not seeing Paul. She'd been focused on the date all day and now felt as if the rug had been pulled out from under her. But it wasn't as if Paul didn't want to see her, she consoled herself, or had purposely stood her up. It sounded as if he was really stuck up there, and honestly felt disappointed about canceling.

Well, it couldn't be helped. She was almost glad she hadn't been home to take the call. She might have sounded annoyed or worse yet, burst into tears. At least she had a little time to cool off, and when he called later she would say all the right things and show him what a good sport she could be.

Jessica sighed, wondering what to do with the rest of the evening. It was too early for dinner. She thought about taking a walk in town but didn't really feel like it. Then she opened the door to the back porch and noticed the plants she'd bought last week. She'd potted some bright pink geraniums and expected to put the rest in the ground on Sunday, then didn't get the chance. It was a warm night and the ground was soft from the rain, ideal for planting. So that's what she'd do. The perfect way to work off some steam about Paul.

She quickly changed into her gardening clothes and a pair of old sneakers. The large hole in her left shoe conveniently accommodated her sore toe. This was truly meant to be, she thought, wiggling her toe. Her hair pulled back in a careless ponytail, Jessica went back outside to work.

Some time later, totally engrossed in a battle with a particularly tenacious dandelion, she didn't even hear the back gate open. Kneeling in the dirt, she yanked hard on the weed. When it finally came out, root and all, she felt a surge of accomplishment as she fell backward, clutching her prize in her gloved hands—and landed squarely on her bottom.

That's when she noticed Sam Morgan standing about a foot away, obviously trying hard to keep a straight face.

"That's a beauty," he congratulated her. "Grandma Morgan used to save those and make soup."

She stared up at him, still holding the weed and feeling the fool. "How resourceful of her. I'm just making a garden."

"Obviously." That amused smile again. She was glad she could give him so much entertainment. "How's it going?"

"Well . . ." She stood up and brushed the dirt off her gloved hands. "It's probably going to look worse before it gets better. If you know what I mean."

He laughed. A rich, warm sound that made her pulse quicken. "Yes, I do. Need a hand?"

"No, thanks." In a black polo shirt and new-looking jeans that emphasized his long, lean legs, he wasn't dressed for gardening, she noticed. What was he dressed for?

And what was he doing here? Did she need to have some sort of . . . talk with him?

Then, as if in answer to the look on her face, he said, "Warren asked me come by. To look at that leak in your apartment?"

"Oh, the leak. Right . . ." She pulled off her gloves and

dropped them in the basket she used to hold gardening tools. "Let's go inside and I'll show you."

She led the way to the house, thinking, *So you're not nearly as irresistible as you thought, Jessica. Here you are, working on a gentle, kind brush-off . . . and he's only here to see the leak.*

"You seem surprised to see me. Didn't Warren call?"

"He left a message. But he didn't say for sure when someone would come."

Or who. She would have definitely remembered that.

When they reached the porch, she paused to remove her soggy sneakers. "Just a sec," she said, leaning against the wall.

She yanked off one, then started on the other. Balanced on one leg, she began to tip—then felt Sam's gentle, steadying grip.

"Whoa, there—" he said softly. Reaching out, she automatically grabbed his arm to right herself. His skin felt warm and smooth, the muscles in his arm, very hard. She met his gaze and quickly looked away. She caught her balance and quickly let go.

"Thanks," she said without looking at him.

"No problem." She felt his dark gaze on her as she opened the door and entered the kitchen.

Could I possibly look worse? she wondered. She was streaked with dirt from head to toe and wearing her oldest T-shirt and faded jeans with a rip in the knee. Battling the weeds, most of her hair had sprung loose, and she could feel damp strands hanging in her eyes and curling around her face.

Luckily, Sam seemed more interested in the architectural details of her apartment, glancing around at the walls and moldings. He seemed especially taken by the fireplace, with its carved marble mantel.

"This is a great old house," he said. "I worked in here a while ago, when Warren bought it and turned it into apartments. I like the way you've fixed it up. It suits the space," he added.

"Thanks. It's all right for now. I had to leave a lot of my things in Boston when I sublet my apartment. My mother gave me a few pieces she had in the attic, and I found some other things at Grace Hegman's shop." Jessica glanced around at the eclectic mix. "I guess it works. If you don't look too closely."

"I think it's very nice," he said again. "Very . . . homey."

She heard a note of surprise in his tone. He hadn't taken her for the homey type. Was that good . . . or bad?

Some family photographs stood on the mantel, pictures of herself and Emily as children playing in the gardens at the old estate and opening gifts under the Christmas tree. Another of her parents on their sailboat, captured in a rare carefree moment. She noticed him glance at them with interest. For some reason, she felt uncomfortable having him look at the old photos.

"The water is coming in over there," she said. "Right over the bucket."

"Yes, a bucket. A dead giveaway," Sam replied. She remained on the far side of the room as he went to examine the leak.

She watched him check the wall with his broad hand, and then the ceiling, the fabric of his shirt stretching taut over his back, outlining his broad shoulders and biceps.

When he suddenly turned around, she felt herself blush, as if he could guess she'd been studying him.

"I'm going to get a ladder from my truck and check the roof and gutters."

"Sure." Jessica shrugged. This was going to take longer than she thought. She watched him leave by the back door in the kitchen, then wondered if she should go outside and start gardening again. For some reason, her gardening mood was broken. Without thinking twice about why, she turned and went into the bathroom to make some speedy repairs on her appearance. She nearly screamed when she saw her reflection but, with a stalwart effort, stifled the sound.

UP ON THE LADDER SAM SPOTTED THE PROBABLE cause of the leak in moments but took his time examining the roof. He offered up a silent prayer, thanking the Lord for Warren Oakes and this unexpected but astonishing opportunity.

He'd definitely caught Jessica by surprise tonight, wrestling that dandelion. He thought she was going to scream when she saw him there. He could have watched her all night. He liked the way she looked all scruffy and covered with dirt, her wonderful hair flying in all directions. He was sure he'd never seen her looking more beautiful. Not even that first day, when she'd been dressed to perfection for that guy who brought her the roses.

He tugged off a rotten shingle and tossed it the ground. He didn't think there was anything serious there. Maybe she wanted him to think so. But where was this guy if he was so serious about her?

She has to like me a little, Sam thought, *or at least feel some attraction . . . or why would she get so jumpy when I so much as look at her?*

Still, she'd been careful not to give him any sign she wanted to go out. Just the opposite in fact. Sam ripped off more shingles, then checked the gutter.

Maybe he was crazy. But he still felt he might have a chance with her, given time and a little luck. This job should take a few days. Maybe that would be long enough to find out.

He didn't even know why he liked Jessica Warwick so much. She wasn't really his type. And she didn't make it easy for him. Not like a lot of other women he met. But something about her just got to him. Like the way she looked when she dropped her guard and laughed at his jokes. He liked to make her smile. Maybe that was all he needed to know for sure right now.

JESSICA CAME TO THE BACK DOOR QUICKLY TO ANSWER Sam's knock. She had changed into a blue tank top, shorts, and sandals. Her hair was brushed out and worn loose, parted on the side. He'd never seen it down like that before, and it was more beautiful than he'd even imagined.

"So, what's the diagnosis?" she asked.

"I'll need to fix the leak in the roof, frame out the hole in the ceiling in here, patch it with some wallboard. Then tape and paint."

"Sounds pretty involved," she said.

"Not really . . . but it may take a few days," he warned her.

"That's okay. Warren can give you an extra key if you need to come in while I'm at work. I don't mind."

"That would be helpful," he said thoughtfully. He crossed his arms over his chest. "I do have some other jobs going, so I may have to come by at the end of the day sometimes. Is that okay?"

"Sure." She shrugged. Did that mean he was purposely using this repair project as an excuse to see more of her? *Don't be silly*, she chided herself. *Of course he has other jobs, probably much more involved than this one*.

"I'm just going to check the wall and ceiling again. To see how much wallboard needs to be replaced."

"Help yourself," she replied. She turned back to the counter, where she'd been opening her mail.

Sam went back into the living room and checked the wall again. The water had seeped into a bookcase near the window. He hadn't noticed that before. He pulled out some soggy paperbacks. Some self-help books—*10 Rules of 12 Women at the Top, Lean Legs in 30 Days.* And then, Sam's favorite, *Women Men Run To . . . Women Men Run From.*

As if she needed any improving. He smiled as he found a few more with flowery covers and sentimental titles. *So she does have a romantic side,* he thought. That was encouraging.

Just as she walked in the room he saw something else—a Bible with a dark red cover.

"Your books got wet. The water must have leaked in through the back of the case. Most of them are ruined . . . but you probably want to save this," he said, handing her the Bible.

She took it in both hands and looked down at it. "Thanks . . . I didn't even know it was there," she admitted, looking up at him again.

"I don't think it's ruined. Not like the other stuff."

"I'd save it anyway. It was my father's. He read it every day toward the end," she added.

She glanced at him and he didn't reply, just stood listening, hoping she'd say more.

"When I see it, it makes me remember that despite everything, he had a lot of peace when he died," she said after a while. "That was really amazing to me."

"Was it?" he asked in a gentle but curious tone.

Jessica looked up suddenly and met his gaze. "Of course it was," she admitted, looking down at the Bible again. "You can't imagine what my family went through back then."

He knew it was hard for her to open up to him like this. He paused a moment, hoping he'd say the right thing.

"I'm sure I can't. Nobody can. . . . But I think your father realized that God loved him, no matter what. And that gave him peace."

She placed the Bible very carefully on the mantel without looking at him. "You make it sound so simple."

"It is," he said quietly.

Jessica glanced at him but didn't reply. Then she turned away and started back toward the kitchen. He felt his heart sink. *I blew it*, he thought.

But in the doorway she turned and looked at him again. "I'm making dinner if you want to stay. Have you eaten yet?"

The wet book in his hand nearly slipped to the floor. "Thanks. No . . . I mean, I haven't eaten yet, either. Thanks for asking me."

"Nothing fancy," she warned.

"That's okay."

"And I'm not a very good cook, so don't expect much," she added, starting to smile at her own caveats.

"Do I need to sign a waiver or anything?" he asked innocently.

She laughed and he felt happy. "I'm not that bad," she said, walking out of the room.

"Well, now you've scared me," he called after her in a serious tone. Though he knew he'd gladly chew cardboard and claimed it tasted like soufflé if Jessica Warwick had cooked it.

A few minutes later he found Jessica in the kitchen, surrounded by ingredients, sizzling pans, and pots boiling over . . . and no apparent plan.

"Hmm, smells good," he said encouragingly. "What are you making?"

She glanced at him, pushing back a handful of curls with her hand. "Well, there's some rice in here," she said, pointing to one pot that appeared to be cooking too quickly. "And some chicken in there," she added, pointing to another pan that was definitely cooking too slowly. "And maybe some salad in the fridge. I'm not sure," she added with a sigh.

"I'll check," he offered. In the refrigerator he found an onion, a pepper, a tomato, and some mushrooms, but no lettuce for a salad. He took the items out and placed them on the counter.

Jessica glanced down at the vegetables, then back up at him. "You can make a salad with that?" she asked.

"Well . . . no. But I can probably make the chicken a little more interesting. Mind if I give it a try?" he offered.

She looked surprised at first, then relieved. With a small shrug, she stepped aside, giving him more room in front of the stove. "Not at all. What should I do?"

"Let's see. Why don't you chop this?" he instructed, handing her the onion.

Sam cooked as Jessica chopped, and in a short time he managed to transform her shaky start into a victorious finish.

To escape the warm kitchen, they took their plates outside and sat on the porch steps. Jessica chewed slowly. "Hmmm. This is good. What do you call it?"

He frowned. "How about . . . Chicken Warwick?"

"No, I mean really." When Sam just smiled in reply, she said, "You mean, you just made this up, without a recipe?"

He shrugged. "Morgans are resourceful in the kitchen. You remember Granny, with the dandelions," he reminded her, drawing another smile. "My dad is a commercial chef. He taught all of us a few culinary tricks."

"Well, remind me never to cook for you. Now I'm totally intimidated."

"That's all right. I liked cooking dinner with you," he said. *I could get used to it pretty easily*, he added to himself. "Besides, you chopped. That was important," he teased her.

"Yes, essential. Behind every great chef is a great chopper."

"Exactly," he agreed.

She was quiet for a moment, then she put her dish aside. "I don't have anything for dessert. I can make some coffee for you, though."

"Why don't we walk into town? I'll buy you an ice-cream cone," he offered.

She took a moment to think over his offer. "Okay, but I'm buying since you made dinner."

Taken by surprise again, he tried not to show it. "Fine with me," he said smoothly.

She took his plate and he stood up and stretched. Then he noticed her dropping small pieces of leftover chicken in a saucer by the back door.

"Do you have a cat?" he asked.

"I'm not sure," she answered, glancing over her shoulder. "There's this stray that comes around. It hides under those steps. I've been putting out food, but it won't come out yet. I don't even really know what it looks like."

He put his hands in his pockets, watching her from the bottom of the steps. "Maybe Chicken Warwick will do the trick."

"Maybe." She smiled at him. "I'll just bring these plates inside. Be right back."

He nodded, watching her disappear into the house again. He turned and stared out at her yard—the hopeful, half-finished garden and the pots of pink geraniums. Everything about her seemed . . . remarkable. Even the way she couldn't cook. He hadn't felt like this about anyone in a long time. It was wonderful and terrifying at the same time.

He heard her come out the back door again and turned. She'd combed her hair back and tied it with a thin, blue satin ribbon that matched her shirt . . . and her eyes.

She was carrying a small purse and had put on some lipstick. "Ready?" she asked.

He nodded. When she turned and started walking, he fell into step easily beside her. He had the urge to take her hand, but didn't dare. He had the feeling this was going to get worse—a whole lot worse—before it got better.

IT WAS A SHORT WALK TO THE VILLAGE FROM JESSICA'S house. They stopped at the Creamery for two ice-cream cones—mint chocolate chip for Jessica and Rocky Road for Sam—then continued down Main Street to the harbor. When they reached the Bramble Shop, Sam pointed out his workshop, which was on one side of the barn behind Grace's place. Jessica wondered what it was like inside and almost asked Sam if they could take a look. Then caught herself. She didn't want to seem too interested. He might read too much into it, she thought.

When they reached the dock, they found an empty bench and gazed out at the water as they ate their ice cream. The sun slipped behind a mound of peach-and-lavender-colored clouds, the rippling water in the harbor reflecting the colors of the sky.

"Great ice cream," Sam said between bites. "Thanks."

"You're welcome. The Creamery has the best," she added.

"Absolutely. Always did, always will."

She could tell from the way he said it that he'd been a regular at the Creamery as a child, the same way she had. She suddenly wondered why he'd never left Cape Light. She'd had her own reasons for going, getting away from an unhappy family history. But Sam seemed to have so much going for him. Why did he stay here? Wasn't he curious to see more of the world? "Sam . . . did you ever think of leaving here?" she asked after a moment. "I mean, it must be hard to live in the same place where you grew up, see all the same people all the time."

He was quiet for a moment. She wondered if she'd insulted him. "I did leave New England for a while. A few years after high school, I went down south with a buddy of mine. He talked me into going down to Texas for the winter, to the Gulf, and I just sort of stayed down there and moved around. Savannah, Charleston, the Keys. There was plenty of work wherever I went, plenty of fishing, sunshine, and . . . socializing," he recalled. From his wistful smile she assumed he meant women and partying. Sowing his wild oats, as they used to say.

"Sounds like fun. Why did you come back?"

He shrugged. "I like it here. It suits me." He ate some more ice cream, then added, "I missed my family. I missed the seasons changing. Even the winter. It can get pretty boring, staring out your window at a palm tree."

"I guess so," Jessica said.

"Why do you ask?"

"I just wondered," she said quietly.

"I don't find it dull around here, if that's what you mean. Not too dull anyway. You could live in the biggest city in the world and be bored," he pointed out. "You remember what Thoreau said: 'I've traveled widely in Concord.' " His ability to quote Thoreau surprised her. But the more she learned about him, the more he disproved her assumptions.

Besides, he had a point. She'd often been bored in Boston, even though she was surrounded by things to do, new places to go.

"I like to see the same people every day," Sam went on. Not defensively, she noticed. Just stating a fact. "It makes me feel . . . connected. Like I belong." He shrugged. "Maybe it's just because I grew up in a big family. I don't know. It just feels right to me. I just think this is a great place to live. A great place to raise kids," he added.

"Uh . . . yes. I guess it is." She blinked at him, suddenly feeling tense and uncomfortable. Raising kids? How had they gotten onto that subject? She hadn't been thinking of him that way . . . well, not really. She was, she had to admit, attracted to him. Very attracted.

But all that was totally under control. It really was.

Sam was nice. Nicer than she'd ever expected, actually. Spending the evening with him had been fun, a great diversion from her canceled date with Paul. But Paul was the one who was right for her, Jessica reminded herself. He fit with her future, the kind of life she wanted for herself. Not here in Cape Light, but out there, someplace different, more exciting.

Tonight had been a pleasant way to pass a few hours. Lovely, really. But that's all it was. She was sorry now if she'd given Sam the wrong impression. She looked down at her ice cream and concentrated on finishing.

Sam was quiet, too. He looked up at the sunset. "That's gorgeous, isn't it?" he said. "Same show every night, but I never get tired of watching."

Jessica nodded. It wasn't necessary to answer. She had an urge to reach out and take his hand, but only because he seemed disappointed, and she felt bad for him. He was really such a nice man. With a quick wit and a thoughtful side. More complicated than she expected. And interesting.

But not for her.

The sun dropped below the horizon and the blue sky darkened.

"Time to go," Sam said finally. He stood up and offered her his hand. She took it, holding on lightly as she came to her feet. She met his gaze for a long moment, then let go.

"So what do you actually do at the bank—besides stare out your new window, I mean," Sam asked as they walked back to her house.

She glanced at him and smiled. He never tired of teasing her, did he? She had been staring out the window a lot, too, though she'd never admit it.

"Review loan applications mostly," she said. "Do the number crunching. Make recommendations about which ones should be approved, and structure the terms."

"Give out money, you mean?"

"Well, you could put it that way." She glanced up at him and nodded, his strong, handsome features in profile distracting her for a moment.

"Hmm, that sounds like fun."

She met his eye and laughed. Most people assumed her banking job was serious and dull.

"It is fun sometimes. I really like telling people their loan has been approved, especially when I know they want the money for something special. Like buying a house or starting a business."

"Yes, that must be a good feeling, helping people that way." His quiet smile and the light in his dark eyes made her forget what they were talking about for a moment. "Did you always want to be a banker?"

"Not really. Even in college I didn't really know what I wanted to be," Jessica admitted. Thinking back, she could only recall her mother's pressure that she pursue some career path that would lead to respectability and success. "I liked business courses, though, especially finance. And one thing led to another."

"Well, I'd never guess what you do for a living. . . . I mean that in a nice way, of course," he added. His tone and attractive half smile told her he was teasing her again. But somehow, she didn't mind.

"Well, thanks . . . I think," she said wryly.

He laughed and reached around her to open the front gate at her house. Jessica went around to the back door to let herself in, and Sam followed.

Halfway across the yard she touched his arm. "Wait," she said quietly. He followed her gaze and saw a big, scruffy-looking calico cat sitting on the top step, licking its paws.

"It's the cat I've been feeding," she whispered. "I don't want to scare it."

"Be careful. She might bite."

Jessica called quietly to the cat. It looked up and arched its back, its body stiff. Jessica kept her voice gentle as she slowly moved forward. Then she bent down and held out her hand. Cautiously the cat approached her and took a tentative sniff. Then it circled her, finally rubbing against her legs.

Jessica looked at Sam. "I think she's friendly."

"I think she knows you've been leaving her chicken."

"I'm going inside to get some milk. Just watch her a second," Jessica instructed. "Don't let her get away."

"Okay, I won't," he promised, looking a little unsure.

Jessica reappeared seconds later, with a small bowl of milk. She set it down on the top step, and the cat ran over and began lapping it up. Jessica sat down on the steps and ran her hand along the cat's back.

"What are you going to call her?" Sam asked.

Jessica thought for a moment. "Elsie," she said very decisively.

He laughed. "I thought that name was more in the pet cow category."

Jessica gave him an indignant look. "For your information, I had a cat named Elsie when I was young. Another stray, actually. I found her at our new house when we first moved into town. It took me weeks to get her to come out. I used to work on her every day after school. I didn't have any friends, so I guess I had the time," she added with a rueful laugh. "This Elsie is really a pushover compared to the first one."

"Maybe you've just gotten better at it," he said kindly.

He felt sorry for her, hearing that she hadn't had friends, but thinking back, that was probably the way it had been. He remembered kids talking about Jessica and Emily when they first started school. Their father had created quite a scandal. Sam couldn't remember the details now, only shocked suppositions that Mr. Warwick might go to jail. He never did, but they'd had to give up the estate, and the town had talked about it for years. It must have been awful for Jessica and Emily.

"I'd better get going," Sam said after a moment. "Thanks again for dinner."

"Thank you for cooking it," she said, smiling at him.

"I'm not sure when I'll get back to start the roof. Maybe tomorrow or the day after. Will you be around?"

"I should be. I'm in the phone book. Just give me a call and let me know if I need to move furniture or cover anything."

"All right." He nodded. She thought he would leave, but he didn't. "How about on the weekend . . . can I call you?" he asked.

She felt a curious nervous feeling in the pit of her stomach. "About the ceiling?"

"Well . . . no. Not really. I was wondering if you'd like to get together. Maybe have dinner or see a movie?"

His expression was so serious. Even in the dim light Jessica could see that though he was trying to sound off-hand about it, it was important to him. When she met his gaze, she nearly felt herself saying, Yes. Sure. Why not?

Then she remembered Paul. He'd be calling any minute, if he hadn't already left a message. He said he'd be coming down from Vermont later in the week. That could mean the weekend. She couldn't make a date with Sam, then miss out on seeing Paul. She already had plans. Practically . . .

"I'm sorry . . . I have plans," she said slowly. "But thanks, anyway."

"That's okay." He shrugged. "Maybe some other time."

"Sure, some other time." They both knew he wouldn't ask again. She felt sorry for hurting him. "Good night, Sam."

"See you, Jessica. Thanks again for dinner." Then,

looking down at the cat, he added, "Looks like you found a good deal here. Don't blow it."

He smiled briefly, then left the yard through the back gate.

Jessica sat stroking the cat as she watched Sam disappear into the shadows. Did she make a mistake? It didn't matter anyway. It was too late to change things.

Back inside she found the message light blinking on her machine. "Hi, Jessica. It's Paul again. Are you there? Sorry I keep missing you tonight. Call me back if you can, okay?" He gave the number, and Jessica nearly fell over herself, rushing to get a pad and pencil to write it down.

She called Paul back right away, and he picked up on the first ring.

"Jessica, I'm so glad you called back. I was just sitting here, watching the news, hoping it was you. I thought maybe you were mad at me for canceling our date. I hope not."

"Oh, no . . . I wasn't mad," Jessica quickly assured him. "Disappointed at not getting to see you, though," she admitted.

"Me, too," he agreed.

"But it's okay, really," she continued. "I'm sorry to hear you're having such a tough time up there."

"Well, the situation has improved a lot since this afternoon. A glitch with some software was worked out a lot a faster than I expected. So things are basically under control here now," he explained. "I can probably leave sometime tomorrow."

"Wow, that's good news," Jessica said, feeling a surge of happiness. They'd be able to see each other even sooner than she'd expected.

"The only problem is," Paul went on, his voice suddenly tight, "I have to head straight back to Boston. I'm flying out tomorrow night for Minneapolis. I just found out about it a couple of hours ago, but there's another huge problem out there, with the motel chain account. Looks like I'll have to oversee the entire project, or I'll lose the deal. And it's a big one I don't want to lose," he added emphatically.

"Really? Minneapolis?" she asked. That was halfway across the country. . . .

"I know it sounds terrible. I guess it is," he admitted with a sigh. "Looks like I'll be out in the Heartland for most of the summer. There are at least, oh, a dozen properties. I'll have to visit all of them— Minnesota, Wisconsin, South Dakota. I hear it gets very hot in the summer out there," he added.

"Yes, I've heard that," she said quietly. She was trying not to sound as shell-shocked as she felt. "Will you really be gone the whole summer?"

"Unfortunately . . . yes," he said slowly. "But I'm sure I'll come into Boston every so often, just to check up on things. It will probably be on short notice, but maybe we can get together then," he suggested hopefully. "Maybe you could meet me in the city for dinner or something when I come in?"

"Sure, I could do that," Jessica replied, trying to mask her disappointment. It had been hard enough having a relationship while she was in Cape Light and he was down in Boston. What was going to happen now?

"And there's always a chance I can wrap this up a little faster," he added. "I really hope I can."

"So do I," Jessica admitted. Still, she didn't want to seem too upset. Men hated it when a woman sounded too clingy. "Maybe it won't be so bad."

"I'm starting to think the worst part will be not seeing you," he said.

His admission made her feel a little better. "That's nice of you to say," she said softly.

"I didn't say it just to be nice. It's really true. But the

time will go quickly, I hope. In a couple of months we'll both be back in the city again, right?"

"Right," she agreed. At least he sounded as if they were thinking along the same lines about their future. That was some consolation.

They'd keep in touch with phone calls and e-mails, she had no doubt. After the summer, when they both got back to the city, they'd start seeing each other on a regular, more steady basis. Jessica was almost sure of it.

They talked a bit more and Jessica told him about the stray cat. Paul listened for a while, then seemed tired and distracted. He said he'd call when he got to Minnesota, and Jessica wished him a good trip.

"Great," she said, hanging up the phone. She wished she could get rid of the funny hollow feeling in her chest. Part of what she found so attractive in Paul was his ambition, so what right did she have to feel so upset when he had to put business first?

Jessica got ready for bed, telling herself this was just one of those downs in the usual ups and downs of a relationship. She'd just changed into her nightgown when she noticed the Bible on her small white table next to her bed. She flipped through the old pages, stopping every once in a while to read a few lines that she seemed to remember. Did she hear them at Sunday school? Or did her father read them to her? After more than half an hour passed, she closed the Bible and settled into her pillows.

Sam found the Bible. She wondered if she would see him when he came to repair the leak. She knew she'd feel awkward facing him after tonight.

But then again . . . some part of her looked forward to it. . . .

CHAPTER SIX

❧

ᴇVERY PIANO LESSON HAD A RHYTHM OF ITS OWN,
the Reverend Lewis mused as he entered the parsonage
and trod softly past the music room off the foyer. And
yet they all had a similar progression.

First the sound of halting notes, bravely carrying a melody, speeding up in the easy places, stumbling at the more
difficult passages. Finally the music coming quickly to a
conclusion, as if the player were carrying a large stone
downhill those last few bars. And through it all, the sound
of his wife's voice, low and patient, praising the effort,
however slim.

The student whom Carolyn was working with now was
actually better than most. She struck the keys with crisp
confidence and had a good sense of timing. Not that he
knew very much about music.

The reverend paused in the kitchen, where he peeked
under the lids of the pots on the stove. Carolyn had made
shrimp Creole, one of his favorites, a dish she often made

for company. He wondered if anyone was coming.

He kept himself busy while he waited to find out, glancing through the mail, then washing up the dishes in the sink.

He soon heard the student's mother arrive. It was Molly Willoughby. He recognized her voice, but she was in and gone before he had the chance to step out to say hello.

Molly had come to church regularly as a girl and attended Sunday school with the rest of the Morgan clan, he recalled. But Molly was now among the few in her family who didn't belong to Bible Community Church. A single mother with an ex-husband who didn't support his children financially or emotionally, she probably saw joining the congregation as just another pressure—one more obligation in an already harried life. The irony, Ben thought, was that growing in faith would actually lighten Molly's load, for she'd soon see that the Lord is happy to share the burden with anyone who asks Him for aid. Yet years of ministering had taught Ben that he couldn't push faith on anyone who didn't want it. Molly would come back to the church when she was ready. All he could do was let her know that she would always be welcome.

He glanced over his shoulder, expecting to see his wife come into the kitchen. Instead he heard her begin another piece, one that was bright and quick with pleasing counterpoint. Bach, he thought, the *Goldberg Variations*, though which one exactly, he could never be sure.

Ben smiled as he thought about how Carolyn would gently correct him when he got the name of a piece wrong. He still couldn't understand what she'd seen in him, all those years ago.

He loved to listen to her play, especially when she thought she was alone and was playing just for herself. He was almost sure she didn't know he was in the house right now.

He left the kitchen and walked down the hallway. He stood very still by the half-open door of the music room, watching as his wife's hands danced along the keyboard.

I've been graced with so many gifts, Ben thought.

Carolyn must have finally caught sight of him out of the corner of her eye, for the next sound was a crashing jumble.

"Ben?" She pressed her hand to her throat. "You nearly scared me to death. How long have you been standing there?"

"Not too long. I didn't want to interrupt you. I knew you'd stop playing," he admitted.

She got up from the piano bench and clicked off the brass lamp over the score. "Just as well. If I don't check the rice, it gets stuck to the bottom of the pan."

"I'd rather listen to you play Bach than have perfect rice any day," he said, following her into the kitchen.

"That's sweet of you to say, dear." She smiled and kissed his cheek. "Especially since I know how you feel about shrimp Creole."

She stirred the rice, then checked the other pots on the stove. "Dinner is almost ready. Rachel and Jack are coming over."

"I thought we might be having some company tonight," Ben said. "I was out at the Potters' today. Sophie gave me a pie. We can have it for dessert."

"That was awfully convenient of you. Especially since I didn't have time to pick up anything." Carolyn took four dinner plates out of the cupboard and then counted out some silverware. "Rachel's going to tell us tonight, so make sure you act surprised."

Ben was momentarily confused, then catching the expression on his wife's face, he remembered. The Big News, they had started to call it privately. Ever since Carolyn had spilled the beans on Memorial Day, the two of them had been waiting for Rachel to make it official.

"Ahh . . . so tonight's the night, is it? Well, this is a celebration." He rubbed his hands together happily. "Let's set the table in the dining room. Maybe I should use the good china?"

Carolyn smiled at him and handed him the everyday plates and silverware. Her husband was clearly unaccustomed to even the smallest, most innocent deception.

"The kitchen will be fine, I think. We don't want to overdo it. Besides, you're supposed to be surprised, Ben, remember?"

"Oh, yes. Of course." He touched his forehead with his hand. "I still can't quite believe it. Me, a granddad!" He shook his head in amazement as he set out the dishes. "I remember when you were just pregnant with Rachel. Remember how you used to crave . . . what was it again . . . tapioca?"

"Rice pudding," she corrected him. "The same thing happened with Mark. I don't believe I've eaten it since."

"It doesn't seem that long ago, does it?" Ben remarked, shaking his head. "Where does the time go?"

"Where indeed?" Carolyn replied as she began to make a salad. They were both quiet for a few moments, working together in companionable silence.

Ben noticed a faraway expression in his wife's eyes. "Penny for your thoughts," he said.

Carolyn blinked, as if he'd just brought her back to the present. "That pie you brought made me think of the Potters' orchard. Remember when the kids were small, and we'd take the two of them apple picking? We'd bring home so many apples. . . ." She shook her head. "I'd be baking and putting up applesauce for days."

"Yes, I remember. Mark would race between the trees and make me chase after him."

"And he'd wind up so tired, you'd have to carry him down to the car." She smiled at the memory.

"Well, pretty soon we'll have our new grandchild to

bring up to the Potters. That will be fun," Ben said.

He took out some glasses and filled them with ice water, then set them on the table. "Was that one of Molly Willoughby's girls you had in today?"

"Yes, the older one, Lauren. She's thirteen." Carolyn poured some oil and vinegar on the salad and tossed it. "She only started a few months ago, but she's quite good."

"She sounded considerably better than some of the others," he agreed.

"I think Lauren has real talent," Carolyn told him. "She loves it, too. She's been very diligent about practicing. It's a shame that she only has a keyboard to practice on. I'd love to see a student like that with a real piano." She brought the salad over to the table, where Ben now sat. "I can't imagine how that will happen, though, considering Molly's circumstances. When I first mentioned it to her, she looked at me as if I'd lost my mind." Carolyn gave a small laugh. "You'd think I suggested she buy herself a mink coat and a pair of diamond earrings. But of course, it's enough of a stretch paying for the lessons," Carolyn added in an understanding tone. "I offered to take Lauren for free. She has so much promise. But Molly insisted on paying something."

Ben regarded his wife thoughtfully. "Yes, Molly's very proud, from what I understand. She doesn't like to take help from anyone, though I suspect Sam helps her out a bit. He told me she's working three jobs now—school bus driver, baking for the Clam Box and the Beanery, and doing housework around town."

Carolyn set the salad bowl on the table. "Molly doesn't have it easy," she agreed. "And I guess a piano would be a real luxury. But a few weeks ago she said she'd been thinking about it and really wanted Lauren to have an instrument and asked if I would help her find an inexpensive used one. I started looking. I even asked Grace Hegman about the piano in her barn. But that didn't turn out very well." Carolyn sighed.

"Really? What happened?"

"The piano had been Julie's, and Grace simply won't part with it. I honestly felt bad even for asking her," Carolyn admitted. "She's still so . . . in so much pain."

Ben sighed. "Yes, I know. I wish I could help her in some way, at least persuade her to return to church."

Carolyn glanced at him and lightly touched his shoulder as she passed. "I know how hard you've tried to reach Grace over the years, Ben."

"Yes, I've tried," he said, removing his steel-rimmed glasses and rubbing his eyes. "And I'll keep trying. Five years may seem a long time in some respects. But for Grace, it's been no time at all."

"I can see that now," Carolyn said. "I really shouldn't have even asked her, but I was feeling a bit desperate. I've checked everywhere. I really don't know where else to look. Unless I start calling places in Boston. But the cost of transporting a piano from anyplace far away just doesn't make sense."

" 'Ask and it shall be given you; seek and ye shall find,' " he reminded her.

"I ought to ask for some help on this one? Is that what you're trying to tell me, Reverend?" Carolyn asked with a twinkle in her eye.

" '—Knock and the door shall be opened unto you,' " Ben concluded.

She laughed. "Okay, I will pray on it and I'll try my best. Something might turn up," she added hopefully.

The doorbell rang then. Carolyn leaned toward Ben. "They're here, Grandpa," she said quietly.

"I'll get the door," Ben replied just as softly. "You wait here . . . Grandma," he said, patting her hand.

Rachel looked radiant, Carolyn thought, her long, honey-blond hair framing her face, her blue eyes bright.

Jack seemed equally happy. The opposite of Rachel in coloring, he had thick dark hair and brown eyes. Tall, lean, and athletic, he'd played basketball in college and now helped coach the team at the high school, in addition to being a guidance counselor there.

After sitting down at the table, the family joined hands, and Ben gave a prayer of thanks.

As Carolyn had hoped, it didn't take long for Rachel to announce that she and Jack had some news.

Ben glanced at Carolyn, then, trying not to smile, he turned back to his daughter. "Yes, dear?"

She took her husband's hand. "Jack and I are expecting a baby," she said.

"That's wonderful!" Ben declared. He got up to kiss and hug his daughter, then leaned forward and shook Jack's hand. "I'm thrilled and delighted beyond words."

"So am I," Carolyn said. "When is the little one going to arrive?"

"The baby is due in January," Rachel said, beaming. "But I'll consider it a belated Christmas present. You don't have to get me anything else," she told Carolyn and Ben.

"Me either," Jack added.

"That makes our list very short this year, honey," Ben said with a grin. "We might not even need to go to the mall."

"Yes, we will. We'll all be shopping for the baby," Carolyn predicted.

"They do seem to need a lot of equipment." Rachel sighed. "When you start reading those pregnancy books, it's practically overwhelming."

"Don't worry, dear. I'll help you figure it out," her mother assured her. "The gadgets help the new parents feel better, I think. But babies really don't need much to keep them happy and healthy."

"Just a lot of love," Ben said. "And I know my future

grandchild will get plenty of that in this family." His smile took in everyone around the table in turn: Jack, who now sat with his arm around the back of Rachel's chair, Rachel herself, and then Carolyn. "I'd like to say a brief prayer for you, Rachel, if that's all right," he added.

"Of course it is, Dad. I was hoping you would," she replied.

They all bowed their heads and joined hands again. Then Ben said, "Thank you, Heavenly Father, for this blessed news. Please bless Rachel and help her through the pregnancy, and please send us a healthy, happy baby. And please keep us ever mindful, Lord. Help us not take for granted the ordinary but marvelous moments in life like this one, for which we should always give thanks."

They were all quiet for a moment. "That was lovely, dear," Carolyn said.

"Yes, it was, Dad. Thank you," Rachel agreed. Jack leaned over and kissed Rachel on the cheek.

Carolyn smiled at them. Then her expression clouded. "I wish Mark were here," Carolyn said.

"So do I," Rachel agreed. "Is he still in New Mexico? I sent him a birthday card there, but I'm not sure he ever got it."

"Mark's on the move again," Ben reported with a sigh. "He sent a note a few weeks ago saying he'd be in touch when he had a new address and phone number." Ben glanced at Carolyn, who was looking down at the remains of her supper. "I'll let you know as soon as I hear from him again, honey."

"Maybe he'll come home for Christmas," Rachel said wistfully. "I think we should start working on him now. I'd be so happy if he were here when the baby comes."

"Yes, that would be wonderful," Carolyn said hopefully.

Ben reached over and covered Carolyn's hand with his own. "I think he'll come home soon, at least for a visit.

A new baby is very tempting bait," he joked to lighten the mood. "It just might do the trick."

While Carolyn served coffee and the pie from the Potters' orchard the conversation moved on to other subjects, including Jack's job at the high school.

"You know how I love working with the kids," Jack said, "but at this time of year, I don't mind saying I'm counting down the days until summer vacation begins."

"Will you be working at your father's lumberyard again this summer?" Ben asked.

Jack nodded. "It's pretty dull down there, to tell you the truth. But driving a forklift around a warehouse for a few weeks will be a nice change from teenage angst."

Rachel tried to hide her yawning as the conversation continued, but Jack picked up on it.

"We'd better go, honey, before I have to carry you out to the car." Turning to his in-laws, he added, "Rachel falls asleep at the drop of a hat these days. She'd topple right into her dinner plate if I wasn't there to prop her up."

"Oh, Jack, now you're exaggerating," she protested. "I'm not that bad!"

"You need to take care of yourself now, Rachel," her mother said with a laugh. "Don't overdo. Especially in the beginning."

"Don't worry. I'll take good care of her," Jack assured them.

Carolyn smiled, thinking her daughter had chosen a very fine husband. She patted Jack on the arm and said, "Yes, I know you will."

After Rachel and Jack left, Ben and Carolyn worked together to clean up the kitchen. "We have a lot to look forward to," Ben said. "This baby will be a big change for everyone."

"I can hardly wait," Carolyn admitted as she loaded the dishwasher. "I think I have a few of Rachel's special baby things put away up in the attic. I know I saved her first Christmas dress. Do you remember that little red velvet dress with the lace collar? She has it on in that picture in the living room."

"Yes, I remember," Ben said thoughtfully. "But what if the baby is a boy?"

"I've saved some of Mark's things, too. That blue sweater with the bear on the pocket, the one your mother made. He was such a beautiful little boy," she reminisced. "So sweet."

Ben heard Carolyn's voice grow thick and falter. He stepped toward her and laid a hand on her shoulder. "There, now," he said softly.

She looked up at him, her eyes wet with tears. "Rachel misses him. We all miss him. He'll barely speak to us. And it's all my fault."

"Carolyn, darling. You must believe that isn't so."

She looked into her husband's eyes a moment, then down again. She didn't always feel this way. In her best moments she held on to the perspective of her faith. But tonight had been so emotional, all the talk of babies stirring up so many memories. Her own babies were now both adults, one loving and close to her, the other, far away.

"I don't mean to start feeling sorry for myself," she said firmly. "But I know the way Mark sees it, the reason he has all this anger bottled up inside. You can't deny it's because he thinks I failed him."

"You were sick, dear. You couldn't help that, and Mark shouldn't have held it against you. But I was the one who lost my temper and pushed him away when I should have helped him. If there's blame here, it should be mine."

Carolyn put a hand on her husband's shoulder. "Blame isn't terribly useful, is it?"

Ben sighed deeply. "No one is perfect. Not on this side

of heaven. Still, it's difficult when you wish you'd done things differently."

Man's imperfection was not an accident of this mortal life, Ben knew, it was a necessity, essential to His plan. It was our imperfections that created our opportunity to grow in faith, to know and love God, and experience His vast, unconditional love for us. But at times, Ben thought, our all-too-human feelings overwhelmed us, making it hard to see the truth.

"I'm still sorry and sad for all those difficult years," Carolyn admitted. "It was so hard for you and the children. I never imagined my life would be that way."

"No, of course not," her husband agreed. "We can never imagine how the story will unfold. We make our plans and think we know, but that's just our worldly egos, foolish enough to believe they have control when, in fact, every moment is a mystery."

"And every person," Carolyn said.

Would Mark ever really return to them? Ben wondered. Would he ever let go of this anger and find peace within himself? Mark had spent three years in college studying philosophy. Yet he could not find it in his well-informed epistemology, or his young heart, to forgive his parents for their mistakes. For their human frailties, as Ben saw it. They had tried to talk to him, with counselors and without. They'd asked for his understanding and done all they could to assure him of their love. To his credit, Mark had heard them out, and even said the right words at times. But clearly, he still felt isolated and angry, short-changed and unloved.

Ben's own part in the problem was the irony of his life and faith, this knotty tangle under his own roof, a desperate, painful frustration for him, which, in his darkest moments, had caused him to question and doubt his own faith. Here he was, dispensing advice to his congregation, and his own son wouldn't even talk to him.

Ben took Carolyn's hand. "We can't change the past," he told her. "We tried do what we thought was best at the time."

Carolyn gave him a brave smile. "Maybe if Mark ever has children, he'll understand."

"In the meantime," Ben said, "we mustn't fill our hearts with regret or worries about what will be. You did your best. You've always loved your children with all your heart. You were always a good mother to them both, and I have treasured you as my wife," he assured her as he took her gently into his arms.

"Let's be thankful for what we have, and trust the Lord to work this problem out in His own time," he counseled.

Carolyn nodded into his shoulder, taking comfort from his loving words and insight.

She pulled back and touched the end of his beard with her fingertips. "You'd better go work on your sermon," she reminded him. She knew that he always liked to look over his notes on Saturday night. "I'll finish up here."

"All right, dear." He released her and kissed her on the cheek. "I won't be long," he promised.

There were only a few pots left to wash, and Carolyn was glad for some physical task to distract her. Ben had been right, that the course of one's life was a mystery that we generally took for granted. Carefully curled within each moment was the potential for some unforeseen, startling experience, taking our lives on a sudden detour around an unanticipated corner.

Her depression had been a mystery, a puzzle that took years to unravel. It had moved in on her like a large dark cloud, shortly after Mark was born. At first she and Ben had thought she just felt overwhelmed with two small children and the busy life of a minister's wife. But soon they had to face that it was something more, an affliction too complex and insidious to be cast off by a weekend away from the children or some help with the housework.

It had abated for a while, then when Rachel was about nine and Mark five or so, it returned. There had been a time when she could barely get out of bed in the morning. Dark days full of dread and a feeling of total helplessness, when Ben would come home to find the house in a shambles, the children left largely to their own devices, the simplest task overwhelming to her. A time when even her music seemed meaningless.

Carolyn had seen doctor after doctor, but the condition was not as easily diagnosed back then. The medications were hit or miss, working for a while, then failing and leaving them back at square one.

Finally, with a combination of new drugs, therapy, exercise, and her own determination to get better, she felt her life come under control again. It was not a steady, straight ascent, but a jagged, often frustrating course, with countless setbacks.

Carolyn knew she never would have made it without Ben's love and patience. He'd never lost faith in her, never treated her as less than a whole person. Even when she felt like an empty shell, he made her feel that she was still talented and beloved, the center of their family.

No one's life is free of challenges, Carolyn had learned. Everyone gets knocked down. The trick of it is, how you get up. God is always there, stretching down a hand to grab onto. Once she had truly come to accept that, she couldn't be afraid again. Not even on the days she woke feeling the familiar uneasiness, the dread. *Is it coming back again?* Then she'd catch herself and close her eyes to see God's hand stretch down to her. She would reach for her Bible. Or simply recall a verse that she knew by heart, "Be strong and of a good courage, fear not, nor be afraid of them, for the Lord thy God, He it is that doth go with thee; He will not fail thee, nor forsake thee."

The fear would ebb and her strength rise up again.

How ironic that, just as she seemed to get her bearings,

Mark's rebellion had begun. He'd never gotten enough from her, enough love and nurturing. Would she ever be able to make it up to him? Would he even let her try?

Dear God, she prayed as she scoured out the rice pot, *please bring Mark back to us. Help him feel our love and find forgiveness in his heart. Help him find your love, heavenly Father. And your peace.*

JESSICA GLANCED AT HER WATCH, WONDERING HOW long it would be before the movie was over. She'd been trying to lose herself in the film, a suspense story about a woman on the run, but her thoughts kept drifting. Maybe it was because the sight of so many couples out on Saturday night dates kept reminding her that she was alone. Her friend Suzanne from work was supposed to be at the movie with her, but at the last minute Suzanne had begged off with a bad cold. Jessica had been determined not to stay home, curled up in her bathrobe with a video. *I don't need a boyfriend to have a life*, she reminded herself, so even without Suzanne she'd dressed up and gone ahead with their plans.

Finally the movie ended, but it seemed too early to go home. Jessica walked down Main Street toward the harbor and decided to stop into the Beanery. She hadn't tried it yet and was curious. The small café had drawn a crowd, and she had to wait by the door for a seat.

She looked around, remembering the rather nondescript stationery store that used to occupy the space. The Beanery was definitely an improvement, she decided. The pleasant aroma of freshly ground coffee beans filled the air, and the walls were now painted a muted coral color with a hand-rubbed sepia glaze. Ceiling tile had been pulled away to reveal the original tin ceiling, painted high-gloss black and rimmed by a thick mustard-colored border on the upper part of the walls. Black stools were lined up against a long black lacquer counter, where customers sat sipping their coffee and eating delicious-looking desserts.

Behind the counter a huge brass cappuccino machine was the center of the action. Jessica spotted an older man filling orders and giving direction to the young staff. He was a bit bald on top but still had long white hair tied back in a short ponytail and a full but neatly trimmed beard. He wore a black apron over a black T-shirt and jeans. From his manner, Jessica assumed he had to be Jonathan Bean. He seemed quite comfortable working the hissing coffee machine, and not at all out of his element away from a college classroom.

In counterpoint to the sound of the cappuccino machine, jazz played on the sound system. Jessica recognized one of her favorites, Billie Holiday, singing, "Come Rain or Come Shine."

Small black bistro tables filled the rest of the floor space, except for one corner where a curved purple couch and two armchairs with print upholstery were arranged like a cozy living room.

She spotted Felicity Bean moving easily among her customers. The former college professor was slim and petite and looked quite fit. She wore no makeup, but her thick gray hair was cut in a short, spiky sort of hairdo that Jessica knew was very high-style. Jessica liked Felicity's outfit, too, a loose-fitting top in a rough, wine-colored cotton, a long gray muslin skirt, and a necklace of large amber beads. Felicity had the arty, natural look typical of Cambridge but somewhat unusual in Cape Light.

More customers came in, and Jessica moved up to make room. Hearing a familiar voice behind her, she turned around and felt a sudden jolt. Sam Morgan had just come in with a woman, clearly on a date. The woman was attractive, Jessica had to concede. Most men would think so, anyway, though to Jessica her hot-pink T-shirt and black pants were a little . . . obvious. The woman took no notice of Jessica, flipping her long blond hair away from her face, her gaze glued to Sam.

Sam noticed Jessica almost the second she noticed him. Her breath caught in her throat as their eyes met, and she felt her cheeks grow red. He was too far away to say hello, but he smiled and nodded at her. She forced herself to smile back. Then his date drew his attention once more, talking to him.

Jessica turned away sharply. She decided not to wait for a seat any longer. What if she was seated right next to Sam and his . . . blonde? She'd feel much too awkward and self-conscious.

She walked up to the take-out space at the counter and ordered a cappuccino. She couldn't help a backward glance at Sam. It was a mistake. Jessica felt a hot stab of jealousy as the blonde put her hand on Sam's arm and he smiled at her.

A teenage boy behind the counter handed Jessica her coffee, and she left, relieved that she wouldn't have to see any more of Sam and his date.

It wasn't very late and the harbor front was crowded, more couples and families strolling together, reminding Jessica yet again that she was spending the evening alone. She found a bench near the water and drank her cappuccino. She had told Sam she had plans for tonight, and then he'd seen her by herself. That was embarrassing. It hadn't taken him very long to recover from her rejection, she noticed. The woman he was with was very pretty, too. When Jessica remembered seeing Sam smile down at her, she felt . . . jealous. Then she got mad at herself for letting him get under her skin. She was just lonely tonight and feeling down about Paul being away all summer. It didn't mean anything, she told herself.

She dumped her empty cup in the trash and headed home. She planned to get up early tomorrow and work on the flower beds before it got too hot. Thinking of the garden reminded Jessica again of Sam. *This is nuts,* she told herself. *What's wrong with me? Why is my every thought leading to Sam?*

SARA WAS BONE TIRED BUT COULDN'T SLEEP. SHE'D worked at the diner until closing tonight, then stayed to help Lucy set up for the Sunday-morning breakfast rush. Now she sat up against the pillows in the long T-shirt she wore for bed, her hair still wet from the shower. She stared at the TV and didn't even know what she was watching, a lot of noise and talking that made no sense to her. She picked up the remote and clicked it off. The silence in the motel room was instantly soothing.

She had to be up by six for work. The small digital clock on the nightstand read 12:33. Still, Sara didn't feel ready to sleep. Maybe it was this room. It was getting on her nerves, tonight more than ever. The motel was run-down, the bed lumpy and the room musty, even on the sunniest day. Sara had tried not to let it bother her. She knew it was only short-term. Besides, she didn't think she could afford anything better.

Lucy did, though. "That place is a dump. You can definitely find something nicer for the summer," she told her.

"I don't know. I can't afford much. It is a dump, but a dump in my price range," Sara answered.

"Don't be silly. It isn't expensive around here, like Cape Cod. We get some summer people, but we're sort of off the beaten track. There are plenty of nice guest-houses and cottages closer to the village than that old motel."

"Really?" The idea of leaving the motel had caught Sara's interest. "Do you really think I can find something?"

"Hey, I know just the place for you," Lucy said suddenly. "Dr. Elliot owns some cottages on the Beach Road, right near the Warwick Estate. He rents them out cheap, too. I bet it might be even less than the motel. It's pretty there, and you can walk right down the beach."

"Sounds great." Sara felt encouraged. Her own cottage would be nice, she thought. She could do some cooking and be much more comfortable than she was at the motel.

"Let me call him for you," Lucy offered. "We can run over there later if he's free. Since you'd be renting for the season, maybe he'll give you a break."

Sara was usually a very private person, a real loner at times, and she barely knew Lucy. But for some reason, she didn't mind Lucy's friendly interference. Lucy was such a sweet person, always looking out for others. Sara was sure her husband didn't really appreciate her.

Later that day, during the break between lunch and dinner service, Lucy drove Sara over to the cottages. Despite Lucy's assurances, the small faded sign on the road that read Cranberry Cottages didn't look very promising. A pitted, gravel-covered drive led to the property. But the cottages—five in all—appeared to be in good repair, each with a wood-burning stove for the cool weather. The cottages were set at decent intervals apart, and the tall old trees between them gave each cottage an air of seclusion and privacy that Sara liked.

Sara already knew Dr. Elliot by sight from the diner. He met them at the property, and he and Sara soon struck a deal. Lucy came up with idea of Sara moving in the next afternoon, when things at the diner would be slow.

Now that Sara had found the cottage, she was eager to move out of the motel. Maybe that was why she couldn't settle down to sleep tonight. She thought about packing. It wouldn't take long. She hadn't brought much with her; she'd never thought that she would be away for the entire summer.

It was funny how this had all worked out, deciding to

live here and even taking a job. Now another commitment, renting a cottage. She felt herself getting in deeper every day, deeper into a life that felt so false in some way, so deceptive. The friendlier she became with Lucy, the guiltier she felt about not being totally up front with her. But she couldn't confide in Lucy, or anybody, about Emily.

Seated on the edge of her bed, Sara picked up her journal and flipped it open. She came to a passage she wrote a few months ago, before graduation.

> *. . . I talked to my parents tonight. They know I'm ready to start looking for her. They tell me they're worried about me, how it will turn out. I know it must hurt them, too, to see me so hung up on this. Even though they try not to show it.*
>
> *I'm sorry, but I can't help it. It's just something I have to do. I told them that I've already contacted the adoption agency and found out that Emily Warwick was there, about ten years ago. She left information in case I ever wanted to try to find her. That has given me hope. Maybe she wants to find me, too.*

EMILY HAD ADMITTED AS MUCH HERSELF THAT FIRST time they talked in the diner. She said she had gone down to Maryland about ten years ago. On business. The statement had given Sara goose bumps. She turned the page and read some more. . . .

> *I remember, after my parents first told me I was adopted, I used to have this fantasy about my "real" mother. She looked like a fairy princess, of course. I'd imagine that she would hug me and cry and tell me how much she loved me and how happy she was that we were finally together. Then she would take*

me away with her, and she'd be the perfect mommy—
we'd play together, whatever I liked. She'd never say
she was too busy, and she'd never scold me or tell
me to clean up my room or do my homework. Some-
times in the daydream I'd hurt myself or get sick,
and she would take care of me.

I remember telling Mom about my fantasy once. I
guess I was mad at her for something and yelled that
my real mother was coming to take me away from
her because she wasn't my real mother. Mom didn't
get angry or anything. She hugged me close. Then
she told me that would never happen. My birth
mother didn't even know where I lived now. She
didn't know anything about me.

At first I thought Mom was lying, but she looked
so sad, I knew it was true. I started crying then.
Didn't my first mother care about me at all? Didn't
she love me? Why did she just give me away? She
must have not loved me at all if she was able to do
that. I asked my mom all those questions. She said it
meant my birth mother loved me even more, because
she wanted me to have a happy life, even if she was
going to miss me. But I guess I just never really be-
lieved that. Not deep down inside. Where the hole is.

That's when the hole started. The cold, black hole
inside me. There is sadness there. And anger. And so
much confusion. I don't want to dislike my birth
mother, whoever she is. But sometimes it feels good
to be angry at her. Then I feel angry at myself. In
some strange way I also love her. Blindly and hope-
lessly.

It's funny how months, even years would go by,
and I wouldn't think about it so much. Then I'd see
a show on TV about children finding their birth
mothers, or read a letter in "Dear Abby," and it

*would start me thinking again. I'd pass women on
the street, or in a grocery store, and I would think
that could be her. That tall, tired-looking one, or
that short, well-dressed one. She could be anyone, anywhere, I always say to myself. But now it's time to
really find out.*

WELL, HERE I AM, SARA THOUGHT. *I'VE BEEN HERE
almost two weeks now. I've found Emily—my mother. I've
seen her face-to-face and even spoken to her a few times.
But I still don't feel very much closer to telling her who
I am.*

Sara thought back to the phone conversation she had
with her parents a few days ago. She told them that she
had a job and was going to stay in Cape Light awhile.
She could tell that they didn't like the idea and didn't
really want her to stay. Their questions almost made her
doubt the plan herself. But she dug in and didn't waiver.
At least they hadn't argued with her very much.

"How long do you think you'll be up there, honey?"
her mother asked quietly.

"I don't know," Sara replied. "Not too much longer, I
hope." Still, she wasn't sure if that had been the truth.
Maybe she'd only said it to make her mother feel better.

Sara turned to a clean page in her journal and began
to write:

*Why didn't Emily ever look for me? That's what I
wonder now. Why did I have to look for her? If she
loved me so much, like my mother always says, and
felt forced to do it, why didn't she ever try to find
me?*

*I can see now that she's smart. She has enough
money. She doesn't even have a husband or kids to
worry about. Though being a politician, she does*

have bad publicity to consider. But she wasn't always mayor. What about before that?

What if I just go and confront her? Tomorrow, first thing, I could go to her house and knock on her door. "Remember that baby you gave up for adoption about twenty-two years ago? Well, guess what? Here I am."

Maybe she'd totally freak out. She might hate me for messing up her life. She might even deny it.

That would hurt so much. I don't know if I could take it. I don't know if I could even go to her and tell her the truth.

Still, even if Emily took the news well, having an abandoned daughter pop back into her life would cause her some major trouble. Charlie Bates would find a way to use it to make her life miserable. I've only been here a few days, and I can already see that.

But that's not my problem, right? Maybe a little bad publicity is the price she has to pay.

This is going to be hard, but I guess I have to stay and confront her. I owe it to myself. I need to answer these questions about Emily.

I need to get to know her. What kind of person she is. Then, maybe, I can tell her who I am.

Yes, that was it, Sara thought, closing the book. She leaned back on the bed and closed her eyes, resting the book on her chest, the touch of the worn leather cover comforting to her somehow.

She'd come this far and had to stay. She needed to answer these questions about her birth mother. To fill this gaping hole inside. Emily Warwick was the only one who could make it go away.

CHAPTER SEVEN

ⵥLSIE HAD NO TROUBLE MAKING HERSELF AT HOME. In a matter of days the large, multicolored feline had staked out her favorite napping spots, curling in a fluffy ball in the exact middle of the bed, or on the antique ballroom chair in the living room. The satin upholstery seemed to hold her fur like Velcro, Jessica realized woefully. And when the cat craved diversion, the wide windowsill near Jessica's desk afforded an unobstructed view of the birdbath.

Elsie sat there on Wednesday morning as Jessica worked, her tail twitching and a low, guttural meow occasionally distracting Jessica from her calculations.

Jessica would have been in the office, but her boss had given her permission to work at home in order to complete a report on the first-quarter loan activity for the branch. It had to be done by Friday and sent to the main branch in Boston. And it had to be good.

Or they might try to take back my window, Jessica

joked to herself as she leafed through a large binder of computer printouts.

She heard a scratchy sound near the door and at first assumed it was the cat. But then the sound grew a bit louder, and she suddenly realized it was the sound of a key in her front-door lock. She jumped up from her seat, knocking the binder and papers to the floor as the door slowly opened.

Someone was standing there, just out of view, and she jumped behind her chair. "Who is it? Who's there?" she shouted out.

Frightened by her quick movements, the cat jumped back and arched its back, releasing a long, low hiss.

Sam Morgan stepped through the doorway and stared at both of them. "Call off your cat. I'm not here to rob the place."

"Very funny, Sam." She stepped out from behind the chair and straightened out her blouse.

"Sorry, I didn't mean to scare you," he apologized as he came in. "I had a chance to do some work here this morning, so I picked up the key from Warren. You said it was okay, remember?"

"Sure, I remember," she said, still recovering from her surprise at seeing him. "I just didn't expect you, that's all."

"I would have called. But I thought you were at the bank by now. What are you doing here anyway?" he added curiously. "Feeling okay?"

"I'm fine. I just needed to work at home today." She pushed her hair back with her hand. She hadn't bothered to tie it back today. Or put on any makeup, she realized unhappily. "I have to finish this report, and there are too many interruptions in the office."

He glanced at her computer and the binders of printouts. He leaned over and picked up the one that had fallen off her lap.

"Maybe it's not a good day for me to start in here." He handed her the binder. "I don't want to distract you from your work."

He'd be distracting her whether he was knocking a hole in her ceiling or turned around and went halfway across town.

"That's okay." She glanced at him, then down at her desk. "I'll just work in the kitchen." She closed her notebook computer and piled up some of the papers. Moving to another room wouldn't be a problem. Besides, now that he was here, she didn't want him to leave so quickly.

He picked up her stack of folders to help. "I keep chasing you out of office space. I really don't mean to keep doing that."

She briefly met his dark gaze. "I'm starting to get used it, actually."

Sam laughed and followed her into the kitchen, where she set up her computer and papers on the kitchen table. He wore a denim shirt with a dark blue T-shirt underneath, painter's overalls and worn work boots. He looked very tan today, she noticed. Or maybe he'd just been outdoors lately. At the beach with the blonde? Jessica brushed the thought aside. What difference did it make? she asked herself.

She set up her work on the kitchen table, and Sam left to bring in his supplies and tools. Although she returned her attention to her numbers, she couldn't help noticing him passing back and forth through the doorway. The crazy thing was, though the sight was distracting, she didn't close the door.

A short time later, when the phone rang Jessica let the machine pick it up. Her mother came on the line, sounding weak and quavering. "Jessica? Are you there? I called you at the office . . . but they said you were home. . . ."

Alarmed by the odd sound of Lillian's voice, Jessica

quickly picked up the phone. "Hello? Mother? Are you all right?"

"I'm not at all sure. I'm feeling . . . odd this morning. Dizzy or something. I may have mixed up my pills," she said slowly, her words slurred. "I'm not sure. . . ."

Jessica's pulse raced with alarm. "Have you called the doctor?"

"I called Dr. Breitfeller, my cardiologist. He's out of the office. Some associate is supposed to call me back. But he hasn't . . . Let me see, what was his name? I wrote it down on a piece of paper here somewhere. . . ."

Her voice trailed off. It sounded as if she'd put down the receiver without realizing it. "Mother? Can you hear me?" Jessica called to her.

There was a long silence. Then Lillian said, "Yes, yes. I'm here. No need to raise your voice, Jessica."

"Do you need to go to a hospital? Should I call for an ambulance?" Jessica asked anxiously.

"An ambulance? Don't you dare," her mother warned. "I won't be carted away like a sack of potatoes, thank you very much. I've just confused my pills or something," she repeated in her quavering tone.

"I'll be right over. Just stay right where you are, okay?"

"Don't be absurd. Where would I go?" Lillian argued.

"I mean, don't start walking around the house. Just stay in one place until I get there."

"Yes, I understand. But you can't get here through the phone line, you know."

"Yes, I know," Jessica replied evenly. "I'm on my way."

Her mother sounded as if she still had her wits about her, dizzy or not, Jessica thought as she hung up the phone. She hoped her mother wouldn't start wandering around the house in her weakened state, looking for phone numbers or scraps of paper. She might have a fall. Or worse, Jessica thought with alarm.

She got ready to leave the house but first dialed Dr. Elliot's number. She breathed a sigh of relief when he answered right away. Quickly she described her mother's situation.

"I wanted to call 911, but she insists that she won't go to the hospital."

"Could be her medication," Dr. Elliot said. "I'll take a look at her if you like. I'll meet you there in a few minutes." Jessica thanked him and hung up. On the way out she stopped in the living room, where Sam was up on a ladder, looking into a large hole in the ceiling.

"I have to get over to my mother's place right away," she explained. "You can just lock up here when you're done."

Sam looked down at her, his dark eyes filled with concern. "Is she sick?"

"She says she feels dizzy. She doesn't sound like herself, either. She may have mixed up her pills. Dr. Elliot is going to take a look at her."

Sam climbed down from the ladder and wiped off his hands. "I could take you there, if you like. You might need some help."

Jessica met his warm gaze. It was kind of him to offer. Especially since her mother had been so rude to him. Most people wouldn't want to get involved.

"Thanks . . . but I think I can manage. Dr. Elliot will be there. And I can call my sister," she added.

He seemed about to persist with the offer, then stopped. "All right." He nodded. "If you need me, just call. I'll be here."

"Thanks." Jessica glanced up at him again, then headed out the door. Outside, rain had begun to fall. She slipped behind the steering wheel of her car and turned the key in the ignition. The engine sputtered but wouldn't turn over.

Just what she feared. Lately, she'd been having trouble with her car in damp weather, but she'd been too busy to get it to a mechanic.

"Come on, just start, will you," she coaxed, trying again. And then a third time.

The sputtering sounded once more. Then a dull click. "Oh, blast—" She slammed her hand on the steering wheel.

Then Jessica realized that Sam was standing next to the car. He leaned over and looked at her through the window.

"My car won't start," she said breathlessly.

"I was watching from the window. You probably flooded it. Come on, I'll drive you there." He opened the door for her, and she got out.

"Thanks. I appreciate it," she said.

"It's no trouble. I'd feel better taking you."

She felt his hand lightly on her shoulder as they walked over to his truck. His touch was gentle and comforting. She didn't mind it at all. He helped her into the truck, and they were quickly on their way.

It was a short drive to her mother's house on Providence Lane. Although the wide avenue, lined with tall trees and gracious, well-kept homes, was one of the nicest streets in town, her mother's modest colonial was still a far cry from the family's former surroundings at Lilac Hall. Jessica knew that in some ways her mother had never recovered from their exile.

Sam had barely parked the truck when Jessica flew out and ran up to the front door, noticing Dr. Elliot's car in the driveway. *Thank goodness!* she thought as she used her own key to get in.

As Jessica and Sam entered the foyer, she heard voices in the living room—her mother and Dr. Elliot. She started toward the living room, then glanced back at Sam, who stood near the long oak bench and coat tree, not following her any farther.

When she gave him a questioning look, he said, "You go ahead. I'll wait here. It's okay."

She hesitated, thinking she should encourage him to come with her. But they both knew her mother disliked him, and he probably thought it best not to cause more waves in this domestic drama. Feeling pulled by the sound of her mother's voice as she argued with the doctor, Jessica finally turned away and continued on.

The rooms were shrouded in darkness, as usual; it was particularly obvious on such a rainy day. Her mother seemed to prefer it that way.

In the living room her mother sat in an armchair by the window. Jessica rushed to her side. "Mother? How are you?"

"I'm not sure. Ask him," Lillian replied, glancing at Dr. Elliot.

The doctor stood with his stethoscope around his neck. It looked as if he had just taken Lillian's blood pressure.

Jessica kissed her mother's dry cheek and took hold of her hand. Her icy touch was alarming. "What do you think, Doctor?"

"Her pulse and blood pressure are normal. There are no other signs of a stroke or heart attack, far as I can see," he added. "You could bring her into the emergency room. We may need to tie her up and gag her, of course, in order to get her there. And knowing how impatient she can be, waiting around for tests and what have you might bring on a real problem."

"I detest being talked about as if I were not in the room," Lillian protested. "Or unconscious perhaps . . . or a complete idiot."

"Now, now, Lillian. You don't want to get your pressure up," Dr. Elliot warned her.

"Don't 'now, now' me. I'm feeling quite ill. Can't you be any nicer?" Lillian complained. "It's the pills. Those new yellow ones. I felt odd the moment I swallowed them."

"Did you start on a new medication today? You didn't tell me that," Ezra said.

"I didn't . . . ? But of course I did, when you came in," Lillian countered, sounding confused. "Or maybe I told Jessica," she added, glancing at her daughter.

Jessica didn't recall her mother mentioning a new medicine, only that she had perhaps confused her regular dosage. She didn't make an issue of it, however.

"Where are the pills, Mother? We'll call your doctor and ask about it."

"In the kitchen, on the counter near the phone. The yellow ones. I can't remember the name right now. So many names to remember, you know," Lillian added with a sigh.

"I'll go take a look at them," Dr. Elliot said. "Jessica, you stay with your mother."

Jessica glanced at her mother, wondering what to do. Just then Sam entered the room. He stood near the doorway, his arms crossed loosely over his chest. Lillian's eyes widened as she noticed him.

"What in the world is he doing here?" she asked Jessica.

Jessica flushed, embarrassed by her mother's shocked tone. "My car wouldn't start, and Sam was kind enough to drive me over," she explained.

Lillian glanced at him, then back at Jessica. "Well, the favor is done. I hardly see the need for him to remain. I'm not dead yet. It's still my house, you know."

Jessica felt her breath catch at her mother's response. She only hoped that Sam hadn't heard all of it.

"Sam has gone out of his way to bring me here, Mother, and there's no need to be rude," Jessica replied in a hushed tone. "He will stay as long as he likes."

She knew her mother didn't feel well. But if she felt well enough to insult Sam, then she could be spoken to in a firm manner, Jessica reasoned.

Lillian shifted restlessly, avoiding Jessica's gaze. Jessica glanced at Sam. Their eyes met and she saw the corner of his mouth lift in a small smile. Maybe her sticking up for him had taken the sting out of her mother's comment.

Sam came a few steps closer. "Hello, Mrs. Warwick. Feeling any better?"

"Somewhat," she replied quietly, without looking directly at him. "Bring me a glass of water, will you?" Lillian said to Jessica. "I'm very thirsty."

"I'll get it." Sam lightly touched Jessica's shoulder, then went off to the kitchen.

Although she didn't say anything, Lillian gave Jessica a disapproving look, making it clear that Sam's familiarity had not escaped her sharp eyes.

"I think I'll call Emily," Jessica said to her mother. "She ought to know you're feeling sick."

While Jessica felt perfectly capable of handling the situation herself, she knew that her mother deferred to Emily's opinion, especially in an emergency.

"I tried her office before I called you," Lillian said, making Jessica feel a bit hurt. "She's out somewhere, at a meeting in the county seat. They weren't sure when she'd be back."

"Did you call her cell phone?"

"No . . . I didn't want to alarm her. I just left a message with the secretary to call me. It might not be anything at all." Lillian smoothed her dress out over her knees. Her hand was trembling a bit, Jessica noticed. "Besides, you're here. And Ezra . . ." She had omitted Sam, Jessica noticed.

Sam returned with a tall glass of water. "Here you are,"

he said, carefully handing it down to Lillian.

"Thank you." She took it in two hands, sparing him a brief glance. After a long sip she said, "What happened to Ezra? How long does it take to find a bottle of pills?"

"I'm right here, Lillian. Have no fear." Dr. Elliot walked into the room carrying two pill bottles. "I took the liberty of calling your doctors while I was investigating. We've concluded that one of your other medications, the blood-pressure pill, may not mix well with this new one. He's going to prescribe something else for you. The pharmacy will bring it over later.

"This reaction you're having, the dizziness, disorientation, et cetera, should wear off in a few hours," he added. "The doctor said he'll call later to check in with you. He also said that you'll need to see him soon."

Jessica felt greatly relieved. She'd hated the idea of running her mother to the hospital and watching her endure a lot of difficult tests. For today at least, they had dodged that bullet.

"Can the medication hurt her?" Jessica asked.

"Not this one time," Dr. Elliot replied. "Of course, she shouldn't do any highway driving or operate heavy machinery today," he added in a dry tone.

Sam laughed quietly, and Jessica had to struggle not to.

"Very droll, Ezra," Lillian scoffed. "You ought to consider stand-up comedy as a new career in your retirement."

"Excellent suggestion. I'll look into it," he replied.

She turned her face away from him and smoothed out her dress again. "It's no picnic getting old, I'll tell you that."

"Oh, lighten up, Lillian. You're going to outlast all of us, I don't doubt it."

"That's what you all say," Lillian retorted, a sour expression on her face. Jessica and Sam exchanged a secret smile.

"Your doctor said to skip the rest of your medication for today. What you need now is a good long nap," Dr. Elliot advised. "You'll feel better when you wake up, I almost guarantee it. Why don't you take your mother into the bedroom, Jessica?" he suggested.

"I can rest right here, on the couch," Lillian said. "I suppose I do feel a bit sleepy," she admitted.

"Here, let me help you," Jessica said, taking her mother's arm as she rose off the chair. Sam stepped over to help lead Lillian to the couch, but she pulled away from his touch without looking at him. She stretched out on the sofa with a long sigh, and Jessica spread an afghan over her.

"All right. That will do," Lillian said to no one in particular. Moments later her eyes closed and she dozed off.

Jessica watched her, wondering how fragile she really was. She heard the phone ring, but it didn't wake her mother. Dr. Elliot came out of the kitchen carrying the phone and handed it to her. "It's your sister," he said quietly. "She wants to speak with you."

"Jessica?" Emily had a nervous edge to her voice. "I just checked my messages, and my secretary said Mother called. Is everything all right?" Jessica could tell from the sound of the connection that she was calling from her cell phone, probably in her car.

"Well, she had a bit of a scare," Jessica reported, carrying the phone to the far side of the room. "But it's okay now. She started a new drug today and had a bad reaction. It didn't mix well with her other medication. Dr. Elliot is here. He's spoken to Mother's doctor about it, and they don't think she needs to go to the hospital or anything like that."

"Thank God," Emily prayed aloud. "Thank goodness you got over there in time."

"I was working at home today actually." She glanced across the room at Sam, who was talking quietly with Dr. Elliot. He met her gaze and smiled. "My car didn't start, and Sam Morgan gave me a lift," she added.

"That was lucky," Emily replied. If she thought there was anything unusual about Jessica being friendly with Sam, she didn't mention it.

"I'm on my way into town," Emily said. "I can be there in five minutes."

"It's all right, Emily. Honestly. You don't have to rush. You can stop at the office if you need to. Everything's under control," Jessica assured her older sister again. It was almost as if Emily didn't believe the emergency could be managed without her, Jessica reflected, feeling a bit insulted.

"How is Mother now? Can I speak to her?"

"She's having a rest. Fast asleep, in fact." Jessica glanced at their mother, who looked peaceful and comfortable in her sleep. "She looks as if she'll sleep for a while. Dr. Elliot said the reaction should wear off in a few hours."

"I'll come over and stay with her. You've done your share," Emily said. "She'll need someone there when she wakes up, and you probably have to get back to work."

"Well, Sam does, I'm sure," Jessica said, realizing how long she'd kept him. Aside from working on the ceiling in her apartment, she was sure he had other things to do today. She'd already imposed upon him, using up his entire morning with her family crisis.

But she already guessed that when she mentioned it to him, he wouldn't complain, or act as if helping her had been an inconvenience to him. Probably the opposite, as if he'd been happy to do it.

"Listen, I'll check in at the office a minute and come over right after that. Then you and Sam can go," Emily said.

"That's fine," Jessica agreed. "I don't think Sam will mind hanging around a bit more."

"I won't be long," Emily promised. "And thank you again for getting over there and taking care of Mother, Jessica. When I got the message, I just didn't know what to do. I feel so relieved now, knowing you were there."

"Well, it didn't turn out to be much. A false alarm, I guess," Jessica said, downplaying her part. "When Mother threatened to disown me if I called an ambulance, I knew she wasn't feeling too badly."

"Yes, that's always a good sign," Emily agreed with a laugh. "Good work," she said again, and Jessica felt closer to her sister and quietly gratified to be the one to put Emily at ease.

"Emily is on her way," Jessica said to Dr. Elliot and Sam as she hung up. "She should be here in a few minutes."

"Why don't you two go along?" Dr. Elliot said to Jessica. "There's nothing more you can do here. I'll stay with your mother until Emily arrives. I need to stay awhile longer anyway, to check on her while she's sleeping. I'll bring Emily up to speed," he added.

"All right, if you don't mind," Jessica said to Dr. Elliot. She glanced at Sam. He'd been very patient so far, but she was sure he was eager to go by now. "Tell Emily I'll call her here later."

"Will do," Dr. Elliot said. "Don't worry. Your mother will be fine," he assured her.

Outside, Jessica and Sam found that the rain had stopped, and the sun was breaking through the clouds. Once they were back in the truck, Jessica said, "I just want to thank you for helping me out this morning. It was really good of you."

"That's okay. I'm glad that your mother will be all right. And I was glad I could help you," he added, looking into her eyes.

She met his gaze for a long moment, unable to look away. Why was he so nice to her? She wasn't nearly as nice to him. Looking down, she said, "My mother isn't very polite to you. She's rude, actually. I'm sorry about that."

Sam stared straight ahead, his mouth forming a tight line as he appeared to consider his reply. She was sure then that her mother's insults hurt him and even made him angry, more than he would let show.

"Don't worry, I don't take it personally," Sam said finally. He glanced at Jessica, then looked away again. "She's not nice to anybody, as far as I can see."

Jessica looked up at him, not knowing what to say in reply. She bit back a smile. "She's never been easy," she agreed. "That's just the way Lillian is."

"I think your mother is unhappy. Disappointed in her life," Sam offered quietly. "I guess I even feel a little sorry for her," he added.

Sam Morgan feels sorry for my mother? If my mother ever hears that, she'll really have a stroke, Jessica thought.

Still, she was surprised at Sam's insight. How did he get to be so wise about people? she wondered.

"I think what you said is probably true," she admitted. "Most people . . . most people just don't like her. They think she's a snob."

And sometimes I am, too, Jessica realized with a sudden pang of conscience.

Sam didn't say anything. He glanced at her, a soft, enveloping light in his dark eyes that made her feel good again. He started up the truck, glanced at his watch, and said, "I have an appointment to give an estimate in an hour, but first . . . I have this old house I'm fixing up. Out on Crab Meadow, near the pond there. Whenever it rains I need to check on it, the land is so low. Want to come with me? It won't take very long."

Jessica thought about it, taking in his hopeful expression. There was that report to write, but that could wait, she told herself. After the stress of dealing with her mother this morning, she needed a break. A ride out on the Beach Road would be just the thing. Besides, she owed it to Sam since he'd been so nice to her. And, if she was going to be perfectly honest with herself, she'd like another hour of Sam's company.

"Sure . . . I'd love to see it," she said.

Sam drove out of the village and turned onto the Beach Road. After a few miles he veered off on a narrow dirt lane, barely wide enough for his truck. The path was twisting and downhill, covered with puddles and mud from the rain. She noticed Sam's concentration as he navigated the course, and unconsciously gripped the door handle.

"You wouldn't want to do this at night," she said.

"Not if you didn't have to," he added with a laugh. "I know sooner or later I'll get stuck in the mud out here and need a tow, but it hasn't happened yet. When I'm finished with the house, I'll have this widened and paved. Just haven't gotten to it yet."

She glanced out her window at the muddy banks of their narrow road and hoped they wouldn't get stuck today. Suddenly the narrow passage opened. After the sheltering tunnel of trees, Jessica was nearly blinded by the light.

She looked out and saw the house. It was absolutely charming, even in its disheveled, half-finished state. Like a house from a fairy tale, she thought, with large wooden shutters, window boxes, and loads of gingerbread trim. There was a balcony on the second floor and a wrap-around porch below.

It needed work. No question about that. It was the kind of house that would be described by real estate agents as a "handyman special." But it could definitely be a jewel one day, and it appeared that the right handyman for the job had come along to save it.

"Well, here it is," Sam said, turning off the truck. "It's not much to look at yet. But I'm getting there."

"I think it's great," Jessica said, turning toward him as she opened her door.

She climbed out of the truck and took a better look. "How long have you owned it?"

"Almost two years now. I got a pretty good deal on it since it needed so much work. No one has lived here for a long time."

"Yes, I can see that," Jessica said, walking closer.

She remembered this house from years ago. There was a pond in back that she used to love when she was a kid. Sometimes in the summer she and Emily would swim there, and in the winter they'd ice-skate on it. An older couple had owned the place, she recalled. But that was so long ago. They must have moved away, or even passed on, by now.

"Honestly, it's really a beautiful little house," she said, turning back to look at him. "It will be worth a fortune once you've renovated. Is that why you bought it—to turn it over?"

"Uh . . . no." Sam shook his head. "I'm going to live here." He glanced at her, then back at the house. "I'm just thinking ahead, I guess. Plenty of room and it's pretty out here—still wild looking—but not so far from town."

Jessica nodded. Here they were again, talking about the future, marriage, and family. He was, at least. But she wasn't about to go there.

"Yes, it's a very pretty setting. Very private."

Sam gazed at the house intently, hands on his hips, his expression unreadable. What was he thinking about? she wondered. Was he picturing coming home to his future wife and a houseful of children? They'd be very good-looking children, she imagined, if they took after their father. Or was he thinking about the sagging roof and crooked shutters, calculating the work left to do here . . . ?

"Come on," he said suddenly. "I'll show you around inside."

Jessica followed him through the front door, into a foyer where colored beams of light filtered through stained glass.

"That wall was boarded over and the window covered up," Sam said. "Can you believe someone would do that?"

"That's almost criminal," Jessica said, taking a closer look at the intricate pattern of the glass. "But it must have been a nice surprise when you found it."

"Definitely," he agreed, glancing at her. "You get a lot of surprises, fixing up a house like this. Some good . . . some not so good," he said with an easy laugh.

He showed her around the first floor, starting with the front parlor, which had a fireplace and a pressed-tin ceiling. "This room was mainly used for guests," Sam explained. He led her to a smaller room beside it, saying, "This is the side parlor, which they used as a sitting room, or sometimes a music room or library."

Jessica followed him toward the back of the house to a room with another beautiful mantel and fireplace and a large bay window with a window seat.

"The dining room," he explained. "Look at this wood paneling. It's walnut," he said, smoothing his hand over the dark wood. "And it was covered with plasterboard—"

"But you found it," Jessica cut in with a smile.

He looked up at her and smiled. "I suspected something interesting under there from the start."

He led her to the next room, a large kitchen with a hearth almost large enough to stand in and fixtures that dated back to the turn of the century, including a deep porcelain sink on metal legs complete with an authentic wringer for laundry. Jessica gave the handle a turn as they passed by. "You could build some real muscles doing this," she noted. "I guess women back then didn't need to go to a gym to work out."

Sam laughed. "I like a woman with a few muscles." He smiled at her, his eyes sparkling.

"Check this out," he said, showing her a back stairway that led from the kitchen to the second floor.

"I love a house with a back stairway," Jessica said as she followed him up. "It's so . . . mysterious or something."

Sam only laughed in reply. At the top of the stairs, she found a center hall leading to four rooms and a bath. As they peered in the first room, Jessica saw that it was almost completely refinished. He'd restored the old-fashioned moldings and floors perfectly, she realized.

"Now, this will be the master bedroom," Sam said as they came to a large room in the front of the house. "Those French doors open to a little porch. But don't go out there. I haven't fixed it yet," he warned.

"I won't," she promised.

On the other side of the room she was drawn by a beautiful rocking chair and matching table, both partially covered by a white sheet. The furniture looked brand-new . . . or newly refinished, she thought. From what she could see they weren't antiques, but their design was definitely influenced by period elements.

"What's this?" she asked Sam. "Did you start buying furniture already?"

"Oh, the chair and table, you mean," he said, walking toward her. "Just a few pieces I made. I thought they'd go well in the house, so I brought them up here." He leaned over and pulled off the sheet.

Jessica studied them. The furniture was absolutely beautiful, like the pricey, one-of-a-kind pieces you might see in some exclusive shop on Beacon Hill.

"They're beautiful," she said sincerely. She reached out and ran her hand over the satiny finish on the tabletop. "Did you design them, too?"

"From start to finish. It takes me a while to make them, though. I only work on the furniture in my spare time. And I have to have a good idea. The sketches take me forever," he added.

"You're an artist," she said, glancing at him. "I had no idea."

He didn't reply, but his slow, wide smile showed her how much he appreciated her compliment. Then he said, "Try the rocker. It's pretty comfortable." When she looked at him hesitantly, he added, "Go ahead, it won't fall apart."

Jessica sat down in the rocking chair, her hands on the arms. "Very comfortable," she said. "Just right."

She didn't know why, but she suddenly felt self-conscious, sitting in the chair while Sam watched her. She briefly imagined that he'd made this chair with some special woman in mind, the woman who would live with him in this house, have children with him, rock them in her arms at night in this very room. . . .

She got up quickly and took a few steps toward the window.

"Have you ever thought of going into business, making furniture like this? I'm sure you could do well if you connected with the decorators and specialty shops in Boston."

Sam looked surprised by the question. He leaned back and folded his arms over his chest. "I've thought about it, I guess. But I'm not quite ready for that yet."

Then he turned away from her abruptly, unfolded the sheet and started covering the pieces again. She wondered if something she said had offended him. She certainly meant her question as a compliment.

"Well, the furniture is beautiful," she said. "I'm sure

when you're ready to market it, you'll be overwhelmed with interest."

"We'll see," he said modestly. Still, she thought he was pleased by her compliment. Everything she said was sincere; she wasn't trying to flatter him.

Down in the kitchen again, he led her outside, through a back door. The yard behind the house was overgrown but full of flowering bushes and hardy perennials—floribunda roses, daisies, and clumps of tiger lilies that struggled through the weeds, surviving through years of neglect.

"The pond is just down past those trees. There's a path that goes all around if you want to try it. . . . Or I could take you back to town," he added, glancing at her.

Jessica checked her watch. She had lost all track of time. The day was passing, but she didn't want to go home yet, back to her stuffy apartment and her endless calculations. . . .

"I'd like to see the pond," she said, falling into step beside him. "I haven't been down here in ages. The last time, I think, was in the sixth grade, on some kind of nature walk with the science teacher, Mr. Ludlow."

"I remember him. I think he made all the classes do that. You had to get a jar of pond water and look at it under a microscope later." Sam chuckled. "This kid in my class pushed me in."

Jessica laughed, picturing him at that age. "Did he get in trouble?"

"I pulled him down after me, so we both ended up in the principal's office," he recalled. "I wasn't the most serious student," he admitted, glancing at her. "I don't think I ever got to see those little bugs in the water."

Jessica smiled at him. "You didn't miss much," she said lightly.

Now that she knew Sam better, how he'd done in school, or the fact that he probably hadn't gone to college, didn't seem that important to her. She wondered if he thought it did.

When Sam met her eye, she could tell she had said the right thing.

They came to the start of the path. It was thick and overgrown. Sam reached around her to pull a branch with sharp stickers out of the way, and his face came close to hers. She felt his warm breath on her cheek for a moment when he spoke.

"Be careful. I haven't had a chance to cut it back lately."

Jessica kept walking without a reply. The path was narrow and they walked side by side, his body occasionally brushing hers. Her pulse quickened at his nearness.

Then to their left the foliage thinned out and the pond came into view. The water was deep blue, smooth and serene. Mallards and a graceful, long-legged heron nested nearby in the tall rushes.

They walked on without saying much, but it was a comfortable silence between them. The path was mysterious and magical—and very beautiful, Jessica thought, with wildflowers and thick vines, and on the water, stretches of water lilies.

She felt very far from the real world, from her apartment and the work waiting there. From her office at the bank, and even from Boston and her interrupted life. How could she really miss the city? she suddenly wondered. This place had so much to offer, beauty and tranquillity around every corner. These last five months living in Cape Light, she hadn't really noticed, hadn't opened her eyes and taken it in—taken it to heart.

But now she thought she saw it clearly, maybe for the very first time in her adult life. She could understand why Sam had returned and why he wanted to stay. He wasn't limited or timid, as she had first thought, but fortunate and sensible. He had found a place he loved and had the good sense to stay there. He would be happy here with his future family. He certainly deserved to be.

They were more than halfway around, and the sun was still shining, when fat raindrops fell on Jessica's skin and hair. She turned to Sam. "It's raining again. We'd better run for it."

"It's just a sun shower. It will stop in a minute," he said, showing no inclination to dash off for the house. He looked down at her. "Haven't you ever taken a walk in the rain, Jessica?"

"Not on purpose, I haven't," she admitted.

He tugged her hand, pulling her out from under the sheltering branches. "Come on, try it. It feels great."

"Sam—what are you doing?" A needless question. She knew what he was doing, making her get drenched.

He opened his arms and lifted his face into the rain, which was coming down harder now. "This is great. Don't you like it?"

Jessica stood with her arms stiffly at her sides, her head bowed a bit. Then she finally relaxed, giving in to the sensation. She felt the cool rain seeping into her hair and clothes, soaking her skin. It felt wonderful. She wiped her face with her hand and opened her eyes to find Sam watching her. She smiled at him.

"Okay, you win . . . I'm drenched," she complained, but she was laughing at the same time.

He smiled back. "I guess we are getting a little wet out here."

She touched her hand to her wet hair. It was plastered to her head. "I look awful, right?"

"Not at all." He brushed her wet hair off her face with both his hands. His palms lingered, cupping her face in his hands. "More like beautiful, I'd say."

Before she could answer, his head dipped lower, and their lips met in a soft, gentle kiss. The touch of his mouth on hers was hesitant at first, testing, as if he half-expected her to pull away. But with her palm pressed against his soft cotton shirt, she felt his heart beating under her hand, and she kissed him back without thinking. His arm moved around her waist, and he pulled her closer. The pressure of his mouth grew more intense for one tantalizing moment, and then he stepped back and let her go.

When she opened her eyes, he was looking down at her, a soft smile curving his wide mouth. "I think we can go back now."

Too overwhelmed to speak, she only nodded. Sam took her hand in his and led her through the tunnel of branches and vines, back to his house.

Once inside, he found some dry clothes for them both. Jessica ended up in a sweatshirt several sizes too big. "I look ridiculous," she said, working hard to roll up the sleeves, though they kept slipping down. "Don't you have anything smaller?"

Sam stood nearby changing into a dry T-shirt. She tried not to stare at his muscular chest and well-defined biceps as he pulled off one shirt and pulled on another.

"Sorry, I don't keep a lot of clothes out here," he said, catching her eye. She could feel her cheeks grow red as she averted her gaze.

"Besides," he added as he tugged his shirt into place, "you look really good in yellow."

"Um . . . thanks," she replied, hoping he hadn't caught her staring.

As they drove back to the village, Jessica glanced at Sam's strong profile. She felt as if something had subtly shifted between them, but she couldn't say exactly what or why.

Of course, he had kissed her . . . and she had kissed him back. That changed everything. But it didn't have to, she reminded herself. It didn't have to mean a thing or create new expectations. You could kiss someone, and nothing more would ever come of it.

But that wouldn't be the case here. She was almost sure of that.

Suddenly Jessica thought of Paul. When he kissed her, it was pleasant but . . . not memorable.

Sam's kiss was different, in another league altogether. For one thing, Sam seemed so sure of himself, not at all tentative or questioning. When he'd taken her in his arms, she felt not only his strength but his emotional intensity. And the way she responded to him had honestly shocked her. His kiss was sort of . . . overwhelming. For her, at least, she thought, glancing over at him.

She was almost sure he'd ask her out again—and then what would she say? How could she refuse after kissing him back that way? Did she even want to refuse?

She looked at him again, and this time he turned his head and met her gaze. As if in answer to her rambling thoughts, he said, "Can I see you this weekend?"

She couldn't help asking, "What about the woman you were out with Saturday night?"

Sam shrugged. "She's a nice person, but we didn't click. So what about this weekend?"

"T-this weekend?" Jessica heard herself stammer. Why was she having so much trouble answering such a simple question? Then, without thinking, she said, "Um . . . I don't have any plans."

His dark eyes glowed. Despite her misgivings, she felt undeniably warm inside to see Sam so happy at the mere thought of spending time with her.

"How about Saturday? We could go out to dinner. Someplace special."

"I'd like that," she said. He had turned down her street and was pulling up to her house.

"Good, then I'll call you and we can figure it out, okay?"

"Okay," Jessica nodded and opened her door. "Good-bye, Sam," she said, suddenly feeling self-conscious.

"Thanks again for your help," she added. She jumped down to the sidewalk and slammed the truck door.

"You're very welcome. I'll see you soon. And I'll come finish that repair tomorrow," he said, then waved good-bye.

As she watched his truck pull away, she wondered if she would regret going out with him. But somehow, she couldn't say no. Paul would be out of the picture for weeks, maybe the entire summer. It wouldn't hurt to go out with Sam one time, Jessica reasoned. Or even more than once. It wouldn't mean anything.

When she got back to the city in the fall, she would return to her real life again. If there was one thing she learned today, it was that this summer in Cape Light was definitely not her real life.

CHAPTER EIGHT

❧

"MAYOR WARWICK, I'D LIKE A WORD WITH YOU."

Emily cringed as Charlie Bates charged toward her, practically vaulting over the counter the moment he spotted her at the diner.

Sara stood by with a menu, about to seat Emily at a table. Emily waved her away. "Never put your hand between two snarling dogs, dear," she advised quietly.

Sara laughed, then stepped aside for Charlie, who stood inches from Emily's face.

"I have some news for you, Mayor," he began. "It's happening, just like I knew it would. I told all of you at the meeting, but you wouldn't listen."

"What is that?" Emily asked blandly, though she knew Charlie's news had to involve Dr. Elliot's real-estate deal. Charlie had lasted an entire three days without drawing her into another public debate. A record for him, she thought.

"Fran Tulley, Tucker's wife, is working for Betty Bow-

man now. She told me Betty has a buyer for Elliot's property, and it looks like they're coming to terms."

"Hmmm, that was fast. Betty is quite a saleswoman,
isn't she?"

"For pity's sake—don't you even want to know who
the buyer is?" Charlie turned his head a moment, expel-
ling a long breath of frustration.

He had to calm down. He was going make himself sick
at this rate, Emily thought. But it wasn't her place to say
anything of the sort to him, not now anyway.

"Okay, I'll bite. Who is the buyer, Charlie?"

"North Bay Development." He grimaced as he said the
name, as if the very sound were distasteful to him. "Ever
hear of them?" Then, without waiting for her reply, he
said, "Let me tell you about North Bay Development.
Their specialty is putting up these big, ugly eyesore-type
modern houses. Some of them look like an alien spaceship
just landed on your neighbor's lawn. They could probably
pack a whole development of them onto Elliot's land. Of
course, he'll have to tear down all the trees up to the road
to do it. Maybe right up to that nice sign on the Beach
Road that says 'Welcome to Cape Light. A nice place to
visit, a great place to live.' You know that sign, don't
you, Mayor?" he taunted her.

"Yes, Charlie. Of course I do." It did sound bad. But
Charlie was an alarmist and a highly unreliable source of
information. "But I don't know anything about this company. I really need some facts."

"I'm giving you the facts. Plain as the nose on my
face," Charlie insisted. "Haven't you been listening to a
word I just said?"

The door opened, and as if on cue, Dr. Elliot entered.
"Hello, Emily," he greeted her. "Charlie," he added with
a curt nod.

"Hello, Doctor," Emily replied.

"Coming in or out?" Dr. Elliot asked her.

♥

"In . . . I think," she said, glancing at Charlie. Charlie's mouth was set in a hard, grim line as he scowled at Dr. Elliot.

The doctor didn't seem to notice. "Join me, if you like," he said to Emily. "I see an empty booth in the back. I think I'll take it."

"Perfect timing, Mayor. Perfect!" Charlie murmured as the doctor started for the back of the diner. "Here's your chance. Have a nice lunch with Dr. Elliot. On the house," he added. "Talk a little sense into the old man. Not for me, not because I'm asking. I know how you feel about me."

"Charlie—" She shook her head, about to refute him.

"Elliot respects you," Charlie went on. "He's a friend of your family's. He'll listen to you. Think of the village, what we've built here and tried to preserve, your grandfather and mine, too. Once we let something like those houses in, it's the beginning of the end. It will change everything."

While Emily still believed it was not her place to interfere with Dr. Elliot's deal, Charlie's impassioned plea did persuade her to join the doctor for lunch. Maybe she could find out more about North Bay Development, if he wanted to share the information with her, she thought.

"All right, I will have lunch with him," she agreed with a smile, "and we'll give you the bill, too."

Charlie laughed and grabbed two menus. "Specials are on the board," he noted as he seated her at Dr. Elliot's table. "Lobster roll is pretty good today. I'm not even sure if we have any left."

Dr. Elliot peered at Charlie over the edge of his wire-rimmed glasses. "Then why recommend it?"

"The waitress will come round for your order in a minute." Charlie shot Emily a meaningful glance as he left.

"That man is close to insufferable," Dr. Elliot murmured. "Unfortunately, his food is the best in town.

Which presents a dilemma for an old bachelor like me."

Emily smiled. "I know what you mean. But I hear Charlie is starting a new delivery service. I, for one, will be using it frequently."

Sara Franklin came by and took their order. After she left, Dr. Elliot said, "I know Charlie's still hot under the collar about my property. I probably shouldn't even come in here at all. But I wanted some fried clams for lunch, blast it. And why should I be cowering in front of Charlie Bates?"

"No reason at all," Emily replied.

"Exactly," Ezra declared. "Betty thinks she's found a buyer for the land. We're dickering about the price, but I think it will all work out," he added happily.

"Yes, Charlie just told me, when I came in," she admitted. "I heard it was a builder, North Bay Development."

The doctor gave a low whistle. "News travels fast in this town, doesn't it? I bet Charlie already knows what I'm having for dessert. I ought to ask him," Dr. Elliot said, peering around.

"Charlie's worried that this developer will put some unattractive houses on the land," Emily said gently. "Big, modern monstrosities, he calls them." She looked across at Dr. Elliot and held his gaze. "I told him I would speak to you about it."

"Go ahead," the doctor said with a curt nod.

"He's afraid they'll put up buildings that will ruin the town," she related.

"Are you afraid of that as well, Emily?"

"I don't know anything about North Bay Development. I trust that our zoning laws and permit process will hold the line against 'big, modern monstrosities'—wherever and whenever they might storm our pristine shores." She paused to return his small smile. "I do know that this is your call, Ezra. Yours and yours alone."

"I hear you, Mayor . . . and I thank you," he replied with a slight nod of his head. He sniffed and pushed his spectacles up on the bridge of nose. "Now, where's our food? My blood sugar is dropping down to my toes."

Sara soon appeared with their lunch orders, and they put real estate aside and talked over other matters. Dr. Elliot asked after Emily's mother, and Emily asked him more about his retirement plans.

Dr. Elliot admitted he didn't have any clear plan in mind. "I just want to stop practicing medicine. See what that feels like for a change. Get up late, read the newspaper, stroll around town without a care in the world, like a man my age should. I want to live like a regular lazybones for a while. Think anyone will lead a protest in Village Hall about that?"

Emily laughed. "I've learned that in this town, you can't assume they won't."

When they were done with their meal, they walked out together, only to find Charlie hovering near the door. *He's like income taxes,* Emily thought with a sigh; *he can't be avoided.*

"Well, so long," Dr. Elliot said, making a quick exit. Emily, however, could not run the gauntlet as quickly.

"How was lunch?" Charlie asked pointedly.

"The lobster roll was very good today. Thanks for the suggestion."

"Did you talk with him?"

"Yes." She nodded. "But I don't believe it will make any difference. This is his decision, Charlie. Can't you see that?"

Charlie's expression instantly changed from expectant and hopeful to total exasperation. "I should have known. 'Never send a woman to do a man's job.' "

"Really? I thought the punch line was, 'There's no such thing as a free lunch.' "

Smiling, Emily slipped their table check into his shirt pocket and sailed past him through the doorway.

WHEN GRACE HEARD THE MUSIC, SHE THOUGHT AT first she left the radio on upstairs. Then she realized the notes were too scattered and uneven to be coming from the radio. The source of the tinkling melody was closer, more distinct.

She'd been working at the back of the shop. Now she stepped to the window. Sure enough, the music was coming from the barn. She could barely believe it.

She went out the back door and walked across the yard. Her hands were trembling as she pushed open the barn door. The scattered notes stopped. Could she be imagining this? Had she finally lost her mind?

At the back of the long, dark space she saw the shadowy outline of a girl, her head bowed. She couldn't see her face, but the slight build and long dark hair, falling across her cheek, looked so much like Julie. . . .

Grace tried to walk forward, then felt blood pounding in her head, the space around her spinning.

The girl looked up, a guilty, surprised expression on her face.

Grace took a full breath. It wasn't Julie. Of course not. She would never see Julie again. Not in this lifetime.

It was Lauren Willoughby, Sam Morgan's niece. And for some uncontrollable, unaccountable reason Grace felt the anger well up inside of her. This child was not, and could never be, her Julie.

"What are you doing in here?" Grace scolded her. "You're not allowed in here, touching things." Grace's eyes narrowed. "Did Carolyn Lewis tell you to come in here and play this piano?" she demanded.

"Mrs. Lewis?" The girl looked confused. She flinched

and stepped away from the piano. "No . . . Mrs. Lewis never said anything about it. Not at all."

"You're sure?" Grace pressed her.

"I'm sorry . . . I mean, nobody said I could. I was waiting for my uncle and the door was open, so I thought I could come in."

"You're not allowed in here, touching everything, breaking things. You have no business in here," Grace added roughly.

She reached out and shut the cover on the piano keys. It slammed down with a harsh sound. "Especially this piano. Didn't you see the sign here? It says, 'Do Not Touch.' Didn't you see it? Can't you read?"

The girl backed up against the wall. Grace could see her eyes large with fear, her lip trembling. She could see that the girl wanted to run but was afraid to pass her.

"Yes . . . I saw it. I told you I was sorry. I didn't break anything," she insisted, nearly crying now.

"Grace?" Sam's deep voice called from the doorway. "What's going on? Lauren? Is something wrong?"

"Uncle Sam . . . I was just looking around. I didn't do anything, honest," she called back to him.

The girl glanced at Grace, then dashed past her with a quick motion. Grace didn't turn around right away. She felt an awful ache in the pit of her stomach and pressed her hands to the spot.

When she turned, she saw that Lauren had run into Sam's arms and buried her head in his chest, against his shop apron. She was crying, and Sam was patting her back. Grace's father stood there as well, next to Sam, puffing silently on his pipe.

Sam looked over Lauren's head at Grace. "Did she break something? I'll pay you for it."

"I caught her fooling with the piano."

Grace walked to the other side of the piano and snapped down the heavy green canvas cover again, then she picked up the cardboard sign and placed it back on top.

"I don't mind your nieces coming to visit here, Sam. But I don't want them playing in this barn, getting into everything."

Sam looked at her for a long moment. "All right, I understand. I'll make sure it doesn't happen again."

He leaned down and put his arm around Lauren. "I think you need to apologize to Ms. Hegman, honey," he instructed softly.

Grace noticed the stubborn set of the girl's chin, tucked against her chest. But under her uncle's gaze, she finally gave in. She turned just her head toward Grace.

"I'm sorry. I won't come in here again. I promise."

From the tone of her quavering voice, Grace suspected the girl would cross the street to avoid her from now on. Just as well, Grace reflected with a deep sigh.

"All right. That's that, then," she said to Sam.

Sam led Lauren away, and Grace was left alone with her father. When she came to the doorway, Digger looked at her a long time but didn't say anything.

"What? The girl shouldn't have been in here. She ought to know that by now."

"And she's not likely to forget it now. No, sir." Digger nodded and shifted the pipe stem in his mouth. He glanced at Grace, the smoke curling out of his mouth as he considered the situation.

"You needn't look at me that way. I don't feel the least bit sorry." Grace sniffed and wrapped her arms around her middle. "The girl has no respect for other people's property. She needed to be taught a lesson."

"That you did. Put a real scare into her, I'd say. That's one way to do it, I guess." Digger briefly met her gaze, then looked away. "She might even have a nightmare tonight. But don't worry, kids get over these things in time."

"A nightmare? I wasn't that horrible," she insisted.

"The sign was right there. 'Do Not Touch.' Why didn't she pay attention?"

"Oh, yes. The sign. She just ignored that sign, didn't she," Digger agreed. He paused. "Never expected that old piano to make such a nice sound. I would have thought it was rotted out by now, you know, with the dampness back in there. I figured the days when anyone could make nice music on it were gone. But I guess you'll have to wait a few more years before it's that far gone. Then you won't have to worry anymore," he added.

"Why would I want the piano to rot? I never said that," Grace insisted.

"You didn't?" He took the pipe out of his mouth, looked at her, then tapped it on the side of his flat palm. "Well, excuse me. I guess I misunderstood. I thought that was the point of leaving it out here all this time."

"Of course not," Grace said quietly. "Of course that wasn't the point."

Her father could be so difficult sometimes. He got everything twisted around, so that she didn't know what she thought anymore about anything. It was talking in circles, that's what it was. She felt her head begin to pound again.

"I just want to . . . to save it. That's all."

"Oh, I see." He nodded and put the pipe stem back in his mouth, holding it there, unlit. "Well, it's saved, then." He looked up at Grace, his gaze softening. "You save your piano, if that's what you need to do. It's really okay, dear."

Grace stared at him. "I know that, Dad," she said a bit more sharply than she intended.

She turned and pulled the big doors of the barn closed, then fastened the padlock. "Supper will be ready in half an hour. Don't go gallivanting on me," she warned.

"I'm not going any place," he insisted, shaking his

head. "But maybe you ought to take Daisy here for a walk down to the harbor, clear your head."

Grace glanced at him, then at Daisy, who appeared to understand Digger's suggestion completely and now fixed Grace with a hopeful stare.

"Oh . . . all right. I suppose she could use a walk," Grace said quietly, gazing down at the dog.

"You go along now." Digger nodded at her. "I won't get into any trouble. I dug us up some little necks this morning and thought I'd cook up a little chowder tonight. How does that sound?"

"Fine, Dad," Grace replied in a tired voice. "Just . . . fine. Come, Daisy." She turned away, and the dog immediately fell into step beside her.

Then, without looking back at him again, she walked down the drive out to the street.

EMILY AVOIDED THE CLAM BOX FOR THE NEXT FEW days. She didn't need to be drawn into the same debate daily. What else was there to say? Instead, she stopped at the Beanery for a large cup of their French roast and a fluffy brioche or some banana bread baked by the town's own Molly Willoughby.

Felicity and Jonathan Bean were charming people and doing well with their new business, she thought. It wasn't an atmosphere that suited everyone in Cape Light, but she found the café a welcome, refreshing change, and the Beans a valuable addition to the village.

On Friday morning she was especially relieved to be anywhere but the Clam Box when she opened the *Messenger* and saw a full-page editorial, supporting her side of the argument.

Dan Forbes seemed to agree that citizens had the right to privacy and to carry on their private business matters without interference from their neighbors or the mayor's office.

Emily could easily imagine the look on Charlie's face when he read this and his reaction. He'd probably ignore the rush of breakfast orders and immediately sit down to write an outraged letter to the editor. Dan would print it, too, she had no doubt. Not only was he amazingly fair-minded, but he knew controversy sold newspapers, and this one was just starting to heat up.

As Emily headed up Main Street toward the Village Hall, she nearly turned and took a back route to avoid passing the Clam Box altogether. Then she decided she was being silly. She wasn't afraid of Charlie Bates, though he was at times a gigantic pain in the neck. Still, God had sent Charlie into her life for a reason, she knew. Charlie not only gave her the daily opportunity to practice patience, tolerance, and understanding, but his opposing opinions reminded her why she wanted to be mayor of Cape Light in the first place. Which was, in a strange way, something to be thankful for.

THE VILLAGE HALL WAS DESERTED, ALL THE OFFICES dark and empty except for the light at the end of the hall. The door stood open, but Sara knocked anyway, right below the brass plaque that read Mayor Emily Warwick.

Emily was typing something into her keyboard. "Come in," she called out. Then she looked up and saw Sara. She smiled. "Hello, Sara. I didn't know they had you out delivering orders now, too."

"We all have our turn at the take-out," Sara explained with a shrug. "It was mine tonight." She handed Emily her order and the bill.

"Just a second, I need to get my wallet." Emily rose and walked over to a coat closet. "I'm not sure where I put it. . . ."

Sara looked around. She had been curious to see Emily's office; when the mayor had called the diner for take-out, Sara had volunteered to bring it over. It was a fairly nondescript office, she thought. There were some plaques and framed certificates on the wall, awards to the village mainly, and some photographs of town events. Emily was in a few of them, Sara noticed. A framed page from the *Messenger* also caught her eye, a picture of Emily with her arms raised triumphantly as she stood on a podium. "Village Elects First Woman Mayor," the caption read.

On Emily's desk, Sara noticed what appeared to be an old family photograph of a mother and father with two little girls, everyone conservatively and expensively dressed. The mother's smile was strained and forced. The father looked happier, more relaxed, his arm around the older girl, who was all elbows and knees, with long shiny braids and freckles. The younger girl, a toddler, sat on her mother's lap, a small bow in her curly hair. Emily and her sister, Jessica? Sara wondered. Her own grandparents with her mother and aunt?

"Here you are, Sara," Emily said, handing her some bills. "I don't need any change."

Sara stuffed the money in her pocket, noticing the generous tip. "Thank you," she said. "Enjoy your dinner."

"Thanks, I will." Emily gazed at her. "How have you been? Enjoying your job?"

"It's okay." Sara shrugged. "I mean, I'm not exactly going to make a career out of the Clam Box."

Emily laughed. "What do you want to do for a career, then?"

Sara looked away. She felt self-conscious talking about personal things with Emily. Part of her wanted to, very much. And part of her held back.

"I have a degree in English. I could teach if I wanted to, I suppose. Or maybe go to law school. That's what my parents think I should do." She paused and pushed a strand of hair behind her ear. "All my friends from school have real jobs. I guess I should know by now."

Emily gazed at her. "Do you want to be a teacher or a lawyer?" she asked gently.

Sara shook her head. "Teaching seems okay. But I really like to write," she said finally. "I'd like to be a writer if I could earn a living that way."

Emily leaned back in her chair. "I studied English, too, in college. And I liked to write when I was younger. I pursued it for a while, but I didn't get very far," Emily admitted regretfully.

She remembered being hopeful and positive about her talent when she was in high school and later, married to Tim. He had been so encouraging. She remembered writing pages and pages after his death and after giving up their baby. The words had just flowed, along with her tears. But once she returned to New England, she never did that kind of writing again. It seemed as if a giant door had slammed shut on that part of herself.

Sara was surprised at Emily's wistful expression. "I heard that you were a teacher, before you became mayor, I mean. My parents say I should teach and then write in my spare time."

"Some people do lots of things in their spare time . . . but it didn't work for me," Emily confided. "I think if you want to write, you need to give it a wholehearted effort. You know, when people get older they usually say they don't regret the things they tried or even failed at. But they do regret not having taken more chances in their lives."

Sara considered her words for moment. "So you think I should try to write and forget about the other stuff—if that's what I really want to do?"

"Not that I have any right to contradict your parents," Emily said with a small smile, "but teaching is hard work. So is being a lawyer. So is being a writer. Every job takes effort if you want to be good at it. But if you love it, then it will be worth the trouble. If I had a daughter, I think I'd tell her to just find something she loves doing."

"That makes sense. I do love writing." Sara liked Emily's answer. She felt as if Emily took her seriously. While Sara knew her parents loved her, this was something they didn't seem to understand.

"What kind of writing are you interested in?"

"Fiction, short stories mostly. I had one published in a literary journal when I was in college."

Emily looked impressed. "That's wonderful. You must be talented to have your work published already. See, you're already on your way," she said encouragingly. "Maybe I could read it sometime?"

Sara felt her pulse quicken. Could she really give Emily her writing? That was too wild to even think about. "Uh . . . sure. I don't know if I have a copy with me. I'll look around." She paused, then said, "Do you like being mayor?"

"Yes," Emily answered. "I do. Most of the time at least," she added with a wry smile.

"Not when guys like Charlie Bates are hounding you, though," Sara observed. "I noticed you haven't been at the diner much this week. That's why, right?"

Emily leaned back in her chair and grinned. "The problem with Charlie is that, irritating as he may be, sometimes he actually does have a valid point. So I can't just totally ignore him. It can be hard at times, trying to see everybody's point of view and satisfy so many different interests."

"Everybody's watching you, all the time," Sara commented. "That must be hard. I wouldn't like it."

"Just part of living in a small town. Worse for me, of course. But my life is *so-o-o* boring, Sara. You wouldn't believe it," she insisted. "There's not much to gossip about," she added with a small laugh.

There will be if everyone finds out that I'm your daughter, Sara thought. She took a deep breath. "Well, I don't want to keep you from your work. I didn't mean to take up so much of your time."

"Don't be silly. I was glad for the break," Emily said with a smile.

Sara smiled back. "I'd better get back to the diner—before Charlie sends Tucker Tulley after me in a squad car."

Emily grinned. "If it comes to that, let me know. I'll speak to Officer Tulley for you."

"Sure, thanks." Sara laughed. "See you."

"See you, Sara," Emily said warmly.

Sara felt odd as she left the Village Hall, disturbed and definitely confused. It was a balmy, starry night, and she took her time walking back to the diner.

So Emily had wanted to be a writer. *I have something important in common with my mother,* Sara thought. It made her feel closer to her. She wondered why Emily had given up on writing, but hadn't had the nerve to ask. *Maybe I'll ask another time,* she thought.

It was hard to stay angry at Emily, Sara realized. She was just too nice. *She's been especially nice to me, for no apparent reason,* Sara reflected. Still, she couldn't let Emily off the hook that easily. No amount of pleasant conversation was going to make up for the fact that Emily had abandoned her.

Why should I worry what happens to her once people find out? Why should I even care? Why do I have to be stuck with all these questions and hurtful feelings while she gets to go on living her life? So what if people talk about her? I can't help that. Aren't I the one who's been wronged here?

It makes it harder that Emily's so nice, Sara realized as she neared the diner's red and blue neon sign. *But that doesn't change things. I still have to find out why she gave me up. I can't leave here without her knowing who I am.*

"IT'S JUST SAM. I DON'T HAVE TO GO TO ANY TROU-ble," Jessica kept telling herself as she got ready for their date on Saturday night. Sam did mention that he'd made reservations at a new restaurant, a few towns away in Hamilton, one that Jessica knew was quite expensive and fancy. She would have to dress up, she reasoned. He would probably be wearing a tie and sports jacket.

Jessica had a feeling that dinner out at a formal restaurant was not Sam's favorite kind of outing, but that he was going the limit to impress her, to give her the type of evening he thought she liked. It was thoughtful of him, she had to admit.

She took out a beige suit, then pushed it aside and pulled out a blue print silk dress with a halter neckline instead. She had a white crocheted shawl that would work if it got cooler out.

As for her hair, she wasn't sure what to do. She could tell Sam liked it down; she remembered how he'd looked at her the other day. She started brushing it out, intending to wear it down to please him. Then, just to be perverse, she twisted it back and pinned it up. She didn't want Sam Morgan to think she cared what he liked, one way or the other. It was bad enough that she was actually going out with him. She didn't have to dress to please him besides.

She would see him just this once, Jessica told herself. It would be pleasant, fun. But that would be that. She wasn't going to get herself entangled in something too complicated. Some men could just date you and date you, until . . . until forever, without it ever adding up to any-thing. *Like Paul?* she wondered.

No, she was sure her dates with Paul were adding up to something meaningful, though she had only heard from him once, a brief e-mail when he arrived in Minneapolis. He left the phone number of his hotel, but Jessica didn't want to call him first. He was probably swamped with work and the crisis out there. She would just have to wait to hear from him.

Sam arrived promptly at seven. She opened the door and found him holding a beautiful bouquet—daisies, snapdragons, dusky pink lilies, chrysanthemums, and large lavender flowers with trumpet-shaped blossoms that she couldn't identify.

"These are for you," he said.

"Thanks, they're lovely." Jessica bent her head to catch the fragrance, and became more conscious instead of Sam's aftershave, a pleasant spicy scent.

"They're so unusual. Did you get them in a flower shop?" she asked curiously. No "routine" pink roses, she noticed. Was that on purpose?

"Uh, no. I drove up to the Potters' orchard. Sophie helped me pick them out."

"They're beautiful," she said, wondering if he made a special trip to the orchard just for that purpose. "I'll just put them in water before we go."

Sam followed her into the kitchen, watching as she took a vase from the cupboard. "How's the garden coming?"

"Pretty good; I worked on it all day."

He glanced out the kitchen window. "I can see," he said, sounding impressed at her efforts. "Nice work. Maybe I'll hire you to do some landscaping for me. If you ever get tired of your job at the bank, I mean."

"I'll keep it in mind," Jessica said lightly. She set the vase on the table and arranged the flowers, feeling self-conscious as he watched her.

"By the way, you look great. I love that dress."

She felt warmed by his compliment and the admiring

look in his eyes. She smiled despite herself. "Thanks, you look nice, too."

Actually, Sam looked devastatingly handsome. He was wearing a black linen jacket with tan slacks. A slate-blue linen shirt and matching silk tie completed the outfit. She'd seen him dressed up before at church. But he looked different tonight, more . . . stylish or something. In fact, he looked so good she felt a little intimidated.

His hair, still wet from a shower, was combed back against his head, emphasizing his strong features. She was reminded of the way he looked that afternoon they'd stood out in the rain. The afternoon when he kissed her . . .

She caught herself staring at him, then looked away. She picked up the vase and carried it out to the living room, where she set it on the fireplace mantel.

"Shall we go?" she asked.

"Whenever you're ready," Sam replied.

She gathered up her purse and shawl and met him at the door. "How's Elsie?" he said, glancing around for the cat.

"She's okay. Getting fatter and lazier by the day."

Sam laughed. "Sounds like you're spoiling her rotten."

"I am not," Jessica insisted, though when she caught his eye she had to smile. "Well, not that much."

They drove toward Hamilton, talking about the places they passed and how this part of the coast was changing. It was easy talking to Sam, Jessica realized. It had been that way since the first time they met. She felt as if she could say anything to him. But that was probably because she didn't care so much what he thought, she reminded herself. He was just, well . . . Sam.

They were about halfway there when Jessica noticed a car parked up ahead on the shoulder of the road, its hood raised.

Sam frowned and slowed his truck. "Looks like Harry Reilly. I'd better stop. He must need help."

"Sure," Jessica said, though she had a feeling that if they missed their reservation at this restaurant, they'd probably be turned away.

Sam pulled up behind Harry's truck. "Wait here. I'll be right back," Sam told her.

Jessica soon saw Harry walk around the side of his vehicle. He definitely looked happy to see Sam. His hands were covered with grease, and so was the front of his T-shirt.

The two spoke for a minute, then Sam returned to Jessica. "Nothing serious," he reported. "Harry's muffler is hanging and he can't seem to tie it up. I'm just going to help him out. It won't take long," he promised as he slipped off his jacket and put it down carefully on the driver's seat.

Then he opened the buttons on his shirt cuffs and rolled up his sleeves. Jessica watched, knowing Sam would soon look like Harry no matter how carefully he rolled his sleeves.

Sam leaned over and pulled out a toolbox from the narrow bench behind the front seats. He opened it and started rummaging inside.

"Maybe we just should call a tow truck for him," Jessica suggested. "I think there's a gas station up ahead."

"No, that's okay. It will take hours for a tow truck to get here. Especially on a Saturday night. Besides, Harry is hauling a load of fish down to the market in Boston as a favor to some buddy, and he's got a ticket for the Sox tomorrow. He won't wait around here all night; he's got to get back on the road."

"Oh . . . I see," Jessica said quietly.

Sam glanced at his watch. "Don't worry, we have plenty of time," he promised her.

When Jessica didn't answer, he said, "Listen, Jessica, some things are more important than a restaurant reservation. I'm not going to just leave him here. He's my friend."

His stern tone surprised her. "Of course. I didn't say you should," Jessica said quickly, but she avoided his gaze. Although she hadn't said to leave Harry, she had implied it, and they both knew that.

Sam glanced at her again, his expression softening a bit. "Okay, I'll be right back," he said, and left again, this time holding some tools, a flashlight, and a spool of wire.

Jessica watched him walk away, then got out of the truck and followed. The heels on her sandals made her steps wobbly in the gravel and soft dirt, but she soon made it to Harry's truck. She saw only Sam's legs and feet sticking out but noticed that Harry had spread out a blanket for Sam to lie on while he worked underneath the truck. Harry was crouched down, holding a flashlight for him. It was dusk and growing darker.

Harry looked up and smiled at her, his Red Sox cap pushed back on his forehead. "Hey, Jessica. Thanks for stopping. I don't know what I would have done if you folks hadn't come along."

"That's okay, Harry," Jessica replied. She pulled her shawl around her bare shoulders. She guessed Harry didn't have a cell phone. Not too many people seemed to have them out here.

Sam called to Harry to hand him something, and Harry crouched down to hear him. "Oh, sure. I have one in back. I'll go get it for you, Sam," Harry said. Then he turned to Jessica. "Could you hold this light for Sam? I need to get him another pair of pliers."

"Sure," Jessica said, taking the flashlight. She leaned over and tried to point the light to the right spot. "Is that okay?" she asked Sam.

"Harry, I never noticed those great legs before," Sam teased her. "Better step back a little. You're distracting me."

"Just speed it up down there, will you?" she urged him with a laugh. He certainly sounded as if he was in a better mood, she thought. She was glad their tense moment back in the car was over.

"Don't worry, it's coming along," Sam promised.

Harry returned and handed Sam the pliers; then he took over with the light. A few moments later, Sam slid out from under the car, looking triumphant. "Got it, Harry. It should hold for a while. At least until you get to the city."

"Thanks, Sam. You're a pal," Harry said. He patted Sam on the back, unmindful of his grimy hands. Jessica nearly gasped when Harry took his hand away, leaving a complete print, with all five fingers distinctly outlined in black grime. She felt her hopes for the evening plummet.

"I'll tell you, even if I managed to get myself under there, I'm not sure I would have ever gotten out," Harry admitted, patting his large, low stomach.

"Drive safely. Better go slow," Sam advised.

"Always do," Harry promised. "You two have a nice night out. And thanks again," he repeated, glancing at Jessica this time.

"That's okay," she said slowly. Though at the moment she felt anything but. Harry jumped in his truck and drove off.

Sam watched him go, then turned to Jessica. "I think we can still make it. Let's go."

Jessica didn't move. "Look at your shoulder. Harry left a handprint."

He turned to check out the smudge. "Oh, no! I just got this shirt this morning."

His admission was touching to her, dispelling her anger. Had he really gone out and bought new clothes for their date?

"I'll keep my jacket on. No one will ever know."

"Good idea," she said, feeling agreeable again. She turned and started walking back to the truck beside him.

"We can stop at a gas station and wash up. My hands are grimy, too," she added, looking down at her hands.

Suddenly Jessica's feet flew out from under her. She felt herself falling.

Sam reached out quickly and grabbed her by the shoulders. She held on to him and finally righted herself. Their faces were very close, and even in the falling darkness she could see a telltale flash of longing in his eyes. She swallowed hard and stepped away, but not before pressing her hands to his chest.

"It's hard to walk in these sandals on the stone," she said. "I need to watch where I'm going." Then she caught sight of his shirt, streaked with oily grime on the arms and front—everywhere she'd touched him. "Oh, Sam . . . look what I did to you. I'm so sorry."

She nearly reached out to touch the dirty spots, then realized she'd only make it worse. "I'll have to buy you a new one."

"Oh . . . that's okay." Sam looked up at her, his gaze falling on her shawl. "It's no worse than your shawl," he said, and Jessica saw the black handprints on the white wool. "I'm sorry. I just didn't want you to fall down."

"I'm the one who grabbed you. . . . I even got some on your tie," she noticed.

"So you did," he agreed. "Well, I hate wearing a tie, so please don't get me another one," he said, yanking it off cheerfully. "I do want to replace the shawl, though. It's so pretty."

Jessica shook her head, laughing. "Listen, I ruined your shirt and tie. Let's call it even."

He smiled at her, meeting her gaze and holding it. Then he leaned over quickly and, without touching her, dropped a soft kiss on her mouth.

"It's a deal," he said. "Now, let's go eat, I'm starved. I know the perfect place, too. It's sort of relaxed. Nobody dresses up there and the lighting is so low, no one will notice our dirty clothes."

"Sounds charming," Jessica replied wryly, taking his arm as they walked the rest of the way to the truck.

Sam glanced at her and grinned, then helped her up into the truck again. "Trust me, you're going to love this place."

She sighed and closed the door on him. She didn't have an answer. The funny thing was, she did trust Sam Morgan. It wasn't the evening she expected, but she had a feeling it would all turn out okay.

They soon found a gas station where they both washed up, then drove a short time on the highway until Sam turned off onto a tree-lined road that led down to the water. Jessica spotted a secluded dock with a few weather-beaten, clapboard buildings.

"Where are we?" she asked as they got out of the truck.

"Spoon Harbor. You've never been here before?"

She shook her head. "No, I don't think so," she said. "I've heard it's nice." It was a pretty place, quiet and peaceful—plain but welcoming.

A small building close to the water had lights outside and umbrella tables on the nearby dock. Inside, they found a few more small tables and an open kitchen, emitting clouds of steam and appetizing smells. The walls were unfinished aged wood, decorated with fishing tackle and brass lanterns and colorful floats.

They chose a table out on the dock and were quickly served their dinners and some cold beer. Sam persuaded Jessica to order lobster with him, and she finally agreed. Jessica didn't like to order the most expensive item on the menu on a date, especially a first date. But Sam had somehow divined that she loved lobster and insisted. Besides, he pointed out, eating a whole lobster could be messy business, and they could hardly get any dirtier— so she really had nothing to lose.

The night was clear and warm with a full moon hanging low over the water. The lobster was delicious, and Sam saved Jessica the work of cracking it open by reaching over and quickly doing the job with his strong hands.

They talked about their pasts and got to know each other better. Jessica was curious about Sam's family and asked him questions about growing up with so many sisters and brothers.

He appeared to have only happy memories of his childhood, and she felt wistfully envious. After dinner they walked on a nearby beach. Jessica took off her shoes. The damp sand felt cool, and Sam put his arm around her shoulders when she shivered. They walked for a while, talking a bit, but mainly enjoying the comfortable silence.

Sam stopped and turned to her, circling her loosely with his arms. "I'm sorry about tonight. I was really planning on a special night out. I didn't mean to stick you out on a dock with paper plates," he said regretfully.

"I know it wasn't what you planned," she replied. "But it was special anyway. I loved eating out here. Honestly."

"You're being a good sport." He smiled and she felt pleased to see him cheered up. "It was fun," he agreed. "But I will take you to that place in Hamilton next time."

Jessica was caught off guard. Would there be a next time? She met his gaze, then looked out at the water. A cool breeze blew in from the sea, but Sam's body sheltered her. Without thinking, she turned her cheek against his broad shoulder.

Of course there would be a next time. Who was she kidding? He was the sweetest, loveliest, most caring man she had met in a long time. The very reason she shouldn't encourage anything serious, perhaps. But standing here like this, in the warm circle of his arms, it was hard to be so reasonable.

It was hard to think at all, really. So she didn't even

try. The wind grew stronger, and they walked back to Sam's truck.

An hour later, when they reached the outskirts of Cape Light, Sam suggested they stop at the Beanery for coffee.

"Sounds good," Jessica agreed. It wasn't that late, and she wasn't ready for the evening to end.

They took a table near the door and were soon served their coffee. Jessica noticed Lucy Bates sitting at a back table with Felicity Bean. "Look, there's Lucy," she mentioned to Sam. "I wonder what she's doing here. I heard Charlie Bates hates this place."

"Looks as if she's filling out some forms. Maybe she got tired of working for Charlie and is trying to get a job here," he joked.

"Who could blame her?" Jessica replied.

Then the door opened and Sam's gaze was suddenly fixed on the woman walking in. Jessica turned. At first she didn't recognize the woman, who was carrying a long metal tray covered with a sheet of plastic wrap. Beneath the plastic the tray held dozens of muffins. Was this another one of Sam's girlfriends? *If she is, she looks as if she's a better cook than I am,* Jessica thought.

"Hey, Molly, let me help you." As Sam rose from his chair, Jessica recognized Molly, Sam's younger sister.

Molly hadn't changed very much since high school. She still had curly dark hair like Sam's and striking light hazel eyes. Although she was never slim as a teenager and had put on a bit of weight since then, Molly was still very attractive. Beautiful, in fact, Jessica concluded.

Sam took the box and tray from Molly and set it on the counter. He brought Molly over to their table. "Jessica, this is my sister Molly," he said, his hand resting lightly on Molly's shoulder.

"Hi, how are you?" Jessica smiled up at her.

Molly didn't smile. In fact, Jessica got the distinct impression that Molly was sizing her up. "Can't complain,"

Molly said at last. "So you two are out on the town to-night?"

"We had dinner at Spoon Harbor, at the lobster-in-the-rough place," Sam replied easily.

"Sure. I know that place," Molly said, still studying Jessica. "How did you like that, Jessica?" she asked.

Jessica sensed a faint taunting edge in her tone, but ignored it. "It was great," she answered.

"Really? Something different for you, I guess," Molly said. "Nice dress, by the way."

"Thanks," Jessica said, unsure of whether she was being complimented or mocked.

Felicity Bean walked by and waved to Molly.

"Looks like I need to take care of some business now," Molly said.

"Come back and have coffee with us when you're done," Sam suggested. Jessica smiled but secretly hoped Molly would refuse. Being with Sam was easy, but Molly made her uncomfortable.

Molly glanced at both of them. "No, thanks. I've got my neighbor looking in on the girls. I just came by to make a delivery." She gave Sam the trademark Morgan grin. "I may need to get a second oven. The one I have is going to be on all weekend."

"Don't work too hard," Sam said sympathetically. "I can pick up the girls tomorrow morning and take them to the beach, if that helps."

"You're the best." Molly patted her brother's shoulder. "Just fire a warning shot, and I'll get them ready. You know how girls are," she added, rolling her eyes.

"Yes, I know," he said with a laugh. "See you tomorrow."

"Nice seeing you again," Jessica added.

Molly nodded but didn't reply.

Later that evening, as they drove back to Jessica's house, Sam talked about Lauren and Jill, his nieces. Jessica noticed that he didn't talk much about Molly.

Finally she couldn't help but say, "I don't think your sister likes me very much."

Sam looked surprised. "What makes you say that?"

Jessica shrugged. "I just get this feeling. Didn't you notice? I don't know . . . maybe she's like that with everyone."

Sam stared out at the road. "Molly can be a little . . . defensive sometimes," he admitted. "She's had a hard time lately, raising the girls on her own. Phil was supposed to send child support, but he sort of just disappeared. Half the time I think she's just tired and worn out."

Jessica considered this. She was sure that there was truth in what Sam said. As much as she wanted children, she couldn't imagine shouldering the kind of responsibility that Molly dealt with twenty-four hours a day. But Jessica also had a feeling that Molly was still working off the old high school script, with Jessica cast in the role of Miss Prim and Proper, the haughty, formerly rich girl and honor-roll student. Molly had been one of the wild ones, rebellious and a poor student. She'd gotten pregnant their senior year, Jessica recalled, and was married a few days after graduation.

Okay, so maybe Molly still had an automatic dislike for her. Or maybe Molly didn't think Jessica was right for her older brother, whom she clearly adored. It was the same attitude that Sam faced with her mother, Jessica realized.

But Sam handled it differently. Her mother was far ruder to him, and he hadn't even mentioned it. She would follow his example, Jessica decided as Sam pulled up in front of her house. She would be gracious to Molly and not complain about her again, she decided as she and Sam walked to the door.

"Thanks for a great evening," Jessica said. "I had a lot of fun."

"Even fixing Harry's muffler?" he asked, his dark brows raised.

"Especially that part," she assured him. She thought back to her selfish attitude and how Sam reminded her of the right thing to do. She looked up to find him smiling at her. He didn't seem to be thinking about that at all.

"Well, it wasn't at all what I had planned," he admitted. "But I think it turned out all right."

"Just perfect," Jessica assured him, her voice suddenly failing her as she stared into his eyes.

His strong arms rose up and surrounded her, and she moved toward him willingly. He kissed her deeply, the touch of his lips slow and savoring. Jessica kissed him back, realizing that she had wanted this to happen again, ever since that day out in the rain. It felt good to be in his arms. Easy and right and exciting all at the same time.

Finally Sam pulled away, looking as if it wasn't all that easy for him. *At least I'm not the only one feeling swept away here*, she thought.

"I have Molly's kids tomorrow, but I'll call you," Sam said. "Maybe we can get together next week."

"Okay." Jessica nodded, feeling a bit dazed. "I'd like that," she said honestly. Smiling, he kissed her on the cheek and said good night again.

She watched Sam's truck pull away. He would call her, she knew, unlike Paul, who promised to stay in touch but so far had only e-mailed her once. Paul seemed so far away now—not just far away in miles but so far away emotionally.

Inside the house Jessica saw the flowers Sam had brought her. Elsie was sitting beside the vase, and it appeared she had been nibbling them.

"Elsie, get away," Jessica scolded the cat. She picked up the flowers and carried them into her bedroom, where they would be safely out of the cat's reach.

The bouquet seemed precious to her now, and she hoped it would last awhile.

DIGGER CAME DOWN THE STEPS SLOWLY AND FOUND Grace sitting at the kitchen table. Wearing her pale blue robe tightly belted at her waist, she sat with both hands wrapped around a large mug on the table.

He walked over and stood beside her, resting a hand on her shoulder. Hot milk with a dash of cinnamon, he noticed. The same drink her mother used to fix for the girls when they couldn't sleep. Digger missed his wife. He needed her. She would know what to do for Grace right now, what to say. He didn't know where to begin and said a swift silent prayer, asking for help.

"What's the matter, dear? Can't sleep again?" he asked quietly.

Grace shook her head. "I wish I could. I'm so tired," she said wearily.

"You work too hard, Grace dear. You ought to take a day off now and then. Close the shop tomorrow. We'll go out to the beach," he suggested.

"I don't think so. I really can't, Dad. Sunday's a big day in the summer. You know that."

She glanced up at him. Her face looked drawn, thin. She had been such a lively little girl, so happy and bright. Like a new penny. It used to lift his spirits just to see her smile. Where was that girl now? he wondered. Where had she gone? When Grace lost Julie, he lost Grace, too, he thought sadly.

"You need some peace, dear. Some peace from your own thoughts," he said, reaching out to cover her hand with his own. "Why don't you come to church with me tomorrow?"

"Oh, Dad . . . no, I don't think so," she said with a

weak smile, but she didn't pull her hand away.

With his gaze fixed on her, Digger's grip grew firmer. There were other times like this, when her sadness welled up like a tide, overwhelming her. Digger felt as if he had to hold on for dear life, or she would surely go under.

"You've been thinking about Julie," he said simply.

She nodded, her head bowed. He could see she was crying, soundlessly. "Yes, of course. I always do, you know."

"Yes, I know. I know how hard it is for you, dear." His gaze searched her face. He waited for her to say more. When she didn't, he said, "Is that what woke you? Did you dream of her again?"

Grace nodded. She reached into the pocket of her robe and took out a tissue. "It was so real, Dad," she said, wiping her eyes. "I put my arms around her. The way her skin felt against my cheek, the smell of her hair . . ." Grace paused, unable to say more. "Then I woke up," she added finally.

"Oh, my dear girl." Digger leaned over and put his arms around her. "What can I say?" he asked her quietly.

"Nothing," she answered. "Nothing at all."

After a long moment Digger stood up and gazed down at her. "It doesn't really get any easier, does it?" he asked.

"No," Grace said, her voice barely audible. "I-I was thinking about that Willoughby girl, too. Sam Morgan's niece." She met her father's gaze and looked away. "I shouldn't have been so hard on her."

"Well, she caught you by surprise, I guess," Digger said sympathetically. He patted Grace's shoulder. "Next time you see her, tell her you're sorry. She's a big girl, she'll understand."

"I don't know what to do about that piano now," Grace admitted.

"What to do?" Digger echoed. He sat down again, in

the chair next to Grace this time. "I didn't think there was anything you wanted to do."

"Well, I didn't really give it much thought, even when Carolyn came to ask me about it. Then, when I saw the girl playing Julie's piano, something in me just snapped. But I feel badly about the way I treated her." Grace sighed and took a sip of her milk. "Now it seems like I just can't stop thinking about that piano."

Digger just watched his daughter, unsure of what to say. At last he said, "Well, I think the answer will come to you, Grace. You needn't force these matters. It will just sort of drift up, and you'll look down and see it there."

"Like a shell on the shoreline," Grace said simply.

Digger smiled. He had given her that advice many times when she was a young girl. It pleased him to see that she had not forgotten.

"Exactly. And you'll bend over and pick it up and say, 'Ah. That's the one,' and put it in your pocket."

The corner of Grace's mouth lifted slightly. Not really a smile, he thought, but a heartening sign nonetheless.

"All right, Dad. I'll watch for it." She nodded and picked up her mug again.

"Good. You tell me when you find it," he said, patting her hand again. "I love you very much, Grace. You know that, don't you?"

She nodded, her eyes looking glassy again. "I love you, too, Dad."

"Maybe we should take Julie some flowers from the garden tomorrow," he added. Grace visited the grave at least once a week, and while he didn't care much for the cemetery, he liked to join her in that task from time to time.

"Yes, I was planning to," Grace said, her expression relaxing a bit, he thought, into something more peaceful. More resigned. "I'll be glad for your company."

CHAPTER NINE

~

E MILY AVOIDED THE CLAM BOX FOR MORE THAN A
week after her run-in with Charlie. But on the morning
she returned, she discovered her sabbatical hadn't been
long enough.

She was quietly eating her breakfast at the counter
when Dr. Elliot came in. He barely noticed her greeting.
He walked straight over to Charlie, who stood chatting
with some customers at a booth near the window, and
tapped him on the shoulder.

Emily watched Charlie turn, his expression changing
from a questioning look to a nervous smile.

"You think you're so clever, don't you, Charlie
Bates?" Ezra began angrily. "Well, let me just tell you,
you're the same now as you were when you were a boy—
playing spiteful pranks and thinking you're too smart to
get caught. Well, you're not. Not this time."

"What are you talking about?" Charlie faced the older
man with his hands on his hips. He was still smiling, but

Emily thought his smile seemed forced. "I have no idea what your problem is, Dr. Elliot." He glanced around. "Can anybody understand him?" he asked the onlookers.

Dr. Elliot's body grew even more rigid, his face pale and gray as his suit.

"Spare me your theatrics, Bates. You don't fool me. I know you scared off my buyer. Told him he'd never get the permits to build, never get his plans past the town board, never make good on his investment . . . an anonymous call besides." His voice rose on a shrill note. "You're not only a liar and a meddler, you're a coward!"

Emily saw Ezra take a breath, struggling for control, and she wondered if she ought to interfere.

"I did no such thing. You're crazy!" Charlie huffed. "Coming in here, calling me names. You're a crazy old man. That's what you are, Elliot." He turned and started to walk away.

"Don't you dare turn your back on me." Dr. Elliot moved quickly behind Charlie, grabbed him by the collar with surprising strength, and turned him around again.

Charlie looked shocked, then red-faced with anger. He was considering taking a swing at Dr. Elliot, Emily was sure of it. She stood up quickly. She had to put a stop to this.

Just as she got up from her stool, Reverend Lewis entered the diner. He took in the scene with a surprised glance, then quickly approached the two men.

"There, there . . . what's all this?" he asked, his voice soothing.

Emily saw Charlie back away, raising his hands in a sign of surrender. "Nothing, Reverend. Just a big misunderstanding is all." Then he turned to the doctor and said, "Listen, I don't know what made you think I fouled your deal, but it wasn't me. Honest."

"You have the audacity to ask me to take your word?" Dr. Elliot asked, his voice trembling with rage. "Your word? When you've sat here, day after day, making speeches against me? I know you did it. The only problem now is trying to prove it. There's something unlawful in what you did, Bates, and if you try it again, I'll ruin you. No matter how chummy you are with the police."

The doctor strode out of the diner, slamming the door behind him. The restaurant was completely silent for a long moment. Lucy stood next to her husband, her eyes questioning him with a worried look.

Charlie waved his hand in a dismissive motion at the door. "I don't know what got into him. Sounds like he lost his big deal and now he's looking for someone to blame. Sounds like he's losing his mind in the bargain, if you ask me."

A few nervous laughs sounded, then the customers began talking among themselves again. Emily saw Charlie nudge Lucy to bring around more coffee before he made his way back behind the counter.

Emily left some bills under the edge of her plate and started back to her office. There she called Police Chief Jim Sanborn and related the strange story.

"Dr. Elliot came into the station a few minutes ago, and he's sitting down right now, filing a formal complaint," Chief Sanborn reported.

"Well, that's the first step," Emily said. "You'll look into it right away, of course?"

"Of course. I'm going to assign Officer Tulley."

Emily wondered if that was wise. But she didn't voice her concerns. She didn't want to raise any doubts about Tulley's integrity. Tulley was a good man and a dedicated officer, the heir apparent to the title of police chief if Jim ever stepped down. But he was also Charlie's oldest friend.

"Well, keep me posted, Jim," she said.

"I'll let you know right away if we uncover anything interesting, Mayor," Jim promised.

*   *   *

"EASY NOW. EASY . . . WAIT JUST A MINUTE. YOU'RE going too fast for me. . . ."

"Hold your end up higher, will you? Oh, blast . . . it's slipping. . . ."

"Keep your shirt on, Harry. I've got it."

"Let's put her down a minute. Here, on the grass."

"Slowly boys, easy does it."

"Do be careful, you'll ruin the action."

"Not in my garden! You're trampling the dahlias!"

Jessica was walking home from work when she heard them, a cacophony of voices, all shouting excitedly. Then she realized that Sam's truck was backed up in the Bramble Shop's drive, and a small crowd of people was trying to lift something large and cumbersome into the truck bed.

She recognized Sam, Digger, and Harry Reilly, holding up various ends of the odd-shaped piece. She also recognized Carolyn Lewis and Grace Hegman, standing together on the sidewalk, calling out even more directions. Molly Willoughby stood in the truck bed, spreading out blankets as two young girls danced around the crew. Unmistakably Morgans, even from a distance, Jessica thought. They had to be Molly's daughters, Lauren and Jill.

Jessica crossed the street and approached the chaotic scene. Nobody even noticed her. She could see now that they were moving an upright piano in several large pieces. The group was struggling with the harp-shaped piece inside that held the strings.

"Up on the count of three," Sam said. "One, two, three . . . In you go . . ." he gasped.

The piano innards went up and into the truck with Harry and Molly guiding each side.

"Very good!" Carolyn shouted encouragingly. "You

don't want to put anything on top of that, of course, you'll ruin the strings."

"Did you hear that?" Grace asked, approaching the men with concern.

Carolyn suddenly noticed Jessica. "Hello, Jessica. Come to see the circus . . . or joining up?"

"I'm not sure," Jessica answered with a smile. "Need any help?"

"Ask Sam, he's in charge," Carolyn said.

Sam was up in the truck now, pulling the piece to one side to make room for the rest. He wore heavy gloves and looked hot and sweaty. His eyes lit up when he saw Jessica. "Just what we need, fresh recruits. Want to help?" he asked.

"Sure. What can I do?"

She noticed Molly glance at her brother, and shake her head, as if to say, "What in the world can she do?"

Wearing a business suit and pumps, Jessica suddenly realized she wasn't quite dressed for this project. But Sam had a job in mind for her anyway. "She can drive one of the trucks. Molly, you'll drive the other. The rest of us need to stay in the beds, holding this stuff down so it doesn't slide all over the place."

Molly glanced down at Jessica. "He wants you to drive his truck," she said with a challenging edge to her tone.

Jessica swallowed hard and squinted up at Molly and Sam. "I can do that. No problem."

"That's my girl," Sam said, flashing her a grin.

Was she his girl? Jessica noticed Carolyn's small knowing smile. No, that's just an expression, Jessica told herself. Sam probably used that expression with every woman he met, from age eight to eighty.

While the moving crew continued their efforts and arguments, Jessica took off her suit jacket and left it on the grass alongside her briefcase.

Lauren walked over to Jessica. "Hi," she said in a

friendly tone. "That's my piano. Well, Grace Hegman is going to loan it to me for as long as I need it."

"That's wonderful," Jessica said sincerely. Sam had told her about the incident with Lauren in Grace's barn. She was surprised to hear it had all turned out so well.

"It's a beauty, too," she said to Lauren, glancing at a segment of the outer wooden structure as it was loaded into Harry Reilly's truck. "I never saw one painted like that before."

"Grace did it. She said the wood was a little funny in spots, so she painted it yellow and did the flowers. The inside is still good though," Lauren added. "Mrs. Lewis checked it for us. She says it only needs a few strings and some work on the pedals."

"I think it will be perfect. I'd love to hear you play sometime. Sam says you're pretty good."

Jessica saw Lauren flush, suddenly shy. "I'm okay."

"Lauren." Molly came up to them. "We're ready to go. You and Jill ride with Mrs. Lewis, in her car."

Lauren found her sister and took her hand. Jessica saw them leave with Carolyn Lewis. As she walked over to Sam, she heard Molly thanking Grace sincerely.

"I told you before, I won't take any payment for it," Grace said, shaking her head. "I'm loaning it to you—to your girls. You just take care of it. And make sure Lauren practices every day."

"I will," Lauren promised. She glanced at her mother, then back at Grace. "I'm not doing much this summer. Maybe I can come by here sometime and see if you need any help. You know, dusting and straightening up for you?"

Jessica noticed Grace's look of surprise. Before she could say anything, Molly added, "She's old enough and she knows how. It was all her idea, too," Molly added proudly.

"Well, I don't know. . . ." Grace said slowly. Daisy,

who had been lying on the porch, now trotted down the path and sat at Grace's feet. She absentmindedly reached down and stroked the dog's head. Then she added, "Lauren can come if she likes, I suppose. We can see how it works out."

"I'll come tomorrow," Lauren said eagerly.

"After you practice," her mother reminded her, smiling. It was the first time Jessica could recall seeing Molly so openly happy. "Thank you again, Grace. I'm going to bake you a cake. Do you like chocolate?"

Grace waved her hand. "Heavens, no. No cake for me."

"I like cake," Digger said firmly, walking up to them. "I like that carrot cake you make. With the frosting."

Grace gave him a look. "That's loaded with cholesterol, Dad. You know that."

"Just leave out the raisins, please," he told Molly, ignoring his daughter completely.

"Hey, come on now. Let's get this show on the road," Sam said, clapping his hands. "We still have to get that sucker up two flights of stairs."

The group let out a moan.

"You there." Sam pointed at Jessica. "Up in the truck. Here's the keys." He tossed the ring to her, and she reached out with both hands to catch them.

"You're being very bossy tonight," she muttered as she passed him.

"It's a dirty job, but somebody's got to do it," he replied, a half smile lifting the corner of his mouth.

As he shouted more instructions to the others, Jessica stashed her briefcase and jacket in the cab. Then she got behind the wheel and took a deep breath. This was the first time she had driven a truck, and it was a little scary. The truck seemed huge. But she couldn't quit. She would manage somehow. She had to drive super slow anyway, to protect the precious cargo.

She put on her seat belt and started the engine. When

Sam slapped the side of the truck, she put it in drive.

The truck lurched at first as Jessica got accustomed to the feel of the gas pedal and brake. She heard moans from the back, which made it even worse. She had never driven such a heavy vehicle before, and it was harder to handle than she expected. Up ahead of her, Harry's black truck turned and Jessica cringed.

"Here goes nothing," she murmured under her breath. She eased her foot down on the brake, but not quite soon enough for a totally smooth maneuver. She winced as she took the turn too sharply.

"Watch it, will you?" somebody called out.

"For pity's sake, you nearly killed me," another voice protested.

"Easy does it, pal!" Sam yelled at her, slapping the side of the truck with his hand.

Ten minutes later Jessica breathed a long sigh of relief when she saw Harry's truck slow to a stop and park. At least they made it without a major mishap, she thought.

Molly lived near the Village Green in the second story of an old house converted to apartments, much like Jessica's. The narrow stairwells made the move all the more challenging, but eventually all the pieces of the piano made it up the two flights of stairs without major incident.

In Molly's apartment Harry, Digger, and Sam helped themselves to cold drinks while Carolyn directed the three men as they reassembled the instrument. It didn't take nearly as long as Jessica thought it would. The piano was soon in one piece, looking perfectly suited to the wide wall of Molly's living room.

Carolyn sat down to test it out and played a quick classical piece with a Slavic flavor. She missed a few notes here and there, Jessica noticed, but when she played the final chord, everyone applauded enthusiastically.

Then Lauren sat down and did a quick scale. She

looked up at her mother, her face beaming. "Isn't it great?" she said.

Molly nodded and patted her shoulder. "It's really great, honey." She turned to Carolyn. "Thanks again, Mrs. Lewis. I don't know how you did it."

Carolyn laughed and shrugged. "Grace was really the one who did it, though some prayers helped, I think." She lightly touched Lauren's shoulder. "See you on Saturday, sweetheart. I can't wait to hear your lesson."

Harry and Digger said good night after Carolyn left. Finally Sam and Jessica were the only members of the crew remaining.

After thanking Sam for his help and giving him a hug, Molly turned to Jessica. "Nice driving," she said. "Good thing you stopped by."

"I wasn't sure I could drive Sam's truck," Jessica admitted. "Good thing you don't live very far from Grace."

Sam turned to her, looking surprised. "You never drove a truck before?" She shook her head. "Why didn't you tell me?"

"You didn't ask," she replied.

He turned to his sister. " 'Night, Molly. You owe me for this."

She grinned at him. "Yeah, I know. Big time."

Outside, Jessica pulled out the keys to Sam's truck. "You look tired, want me to drive?" she offered innocently.

"No way." He shook his head, grinning. "I can drive."

Jessica laughed and climbed in the passenger's side. Sam did look tired. They had gotten together a few times since their Saturday night date, but she knew he was working hard on a house extension and his own house at the pond. She didn't know where he found the energy or the time to move Molly's piano tonight. But that was Sam. He never seemed too busy when someone asked him for a favor.

"Want to stop at the Clam Box for a bite? My treat," she offered.

"That's sweet," he said. "But to tell you the truth, I'm really beat. And grubby, too. Why don't we go to my place? We can order a pizza or something."

Jessica had never been to Sam's apartment. She wasn't even sure where he lived. But she didn't see any real harm in it. She was glad she had run into him tonight. She had been thinking of him all day.

"Okay, that sounds fine," she said.

Sam lived near the harbor in an old building that had a marine supply store on the first floor and an apartment above. His front rooms had a view of the harbor with glass doors that opened to a small deck. The view drew Jessica as soon as she stepped inside. "This is beautiful. What a great place."

"It's nice," he agreed. "But I'm looking forward to having a real house soon. Make yourself at home. I'm just going to get cleaned up."

He left Jessica alone in the living room, and she soon heard water running. She looked around, curious about his surroundings. She liked his taste. It was masculine but not too spare and cold, like the places of some men she knew. There was a brown leather couch, covered with kilim pillows, and a brick-red area rug. The rest of the furniture was a mix of new pieces and old, many in the Mission style. All of the old ones were beautifully refinished.

She saw a small writing desk near the window, with photographs of Sam's family and friends. There were some books stacked neatly on top, a Bible the most prominent of them. Above his desk hung a framed black-and-white photo of a baseball player, leaping to make a catch. Jessica recognized Fenway Park's notorious Green Monster, but didn't recognize the player, one of the Red Sox, she had no doubt.

She turned as she heard Sam enter the room. He had showered and changed to a white T-shirt and jeans. He was barefoot, she noticed, which was somehow touching to her. He looked even more worn out than before, and she wondered if she should go.

"Ready for that pizza?" he asked, picking up the phone. "What do you like on it?"

"Just plain is fine for me," Jessica answered.

A moment later she heard him order the pizza, one side plain, the other with everything but anchovies.

"It will take about half an hour," Sam said after he hung up. "Let me get you something to drink."

He poured some cold drinks in the kitchen and brought them into the living room where they sat together on the couch.

Sam put his feet up on the coffee table and sighed. "That shower sure felt good."

"I'll bet. I never saw anyone move a piano before. You must be exhausted."

"It was a group effort. I was mostly the foreman."

"So I noticed. I never knew you were so bossy," she teased.

"Yeah, well, there are still a few things you don't know about me," he countered with a smile.

Jessica was sure that was true. Just when she felt she had Sam figured out, he would show her some new, surprising aspect of himself.

"How did Grace ever decide to give Molly the piano?" she asked. "Last I heard, she scared poor Lauren out of her wits."

Sam shrugged. "I guess she thought it over and had a change of heart. Digger told me she felt bad about yelling at Lauren. Kept mentioning it, mulling it over. Maybe she finally realized that the piano was just going to waste out there. She told Molly she thought that some other child should use it to make music, that that's what Julie would have wanted. Carolyn Lewis said she had been praying for Grace."

Jessica sat back. Whenever Sam talked about religion, it made her nervous. That was one subject that made her feel far from him. "Do you think Carolyn's prayers really helped?" she asked after a long pause.

"I'm sure of it," he replied, meeting her gaze. Jessica was the first to look away, taking a long sip of her iced tea.

The sun had dropped down to the horizon, sinking in a blaze of color. The view was breathtaking. Jessica took Sam's hand. "Let's go out on the deck and watch the sunset."

Sam smiled and leaned back into the couch. "You can go. I'm too tired to move," he said, but he didn't let go of her hand.

Jessica looked at him with concern. For Sam not to get up for a sunset, it had to be serious.

"I'll sit here with you. Maybe you ought to lie down until the pizza comes."

"Good idea. My back is killing me," he confessed. "I must have lifted something funny."

Jessica got up so he could stretch out on the couch. "Did you take some aspirin?"

He shook his head. "No, not yet. I guess I ought to."

"I'll get it for you."

He told her where to look in the medicine cabinet, and she soon returned with the aspirin and a glass of water. The room was almost completely dark now, but she didn't bother to turn on a light. Sam sat up halfway to swallow the tablets.

"Thanks. That should help. I'll be okay by tomorrow. It's just a pulled muscle or something." He rolled over onto his stomach and put his head down on his folded arms. "It feels better on my stomach."

Jessica sat down next to him on the floor. She'd never

seen him so wiped out before. He seemed drained, physically and emotionally, not at all himself. He was really such a giving person, caring and hardworking. But he had some low moments, too, she realized, when he needed someone to look out for him.

She rested her hand on his back and rubbed it lightly, with a circular motion. His T-shirt felt soft, his skin warm underneath.

"How does that feel?"

"Good," he said with a sigh. He glanced at her, moving his head to one side. "That's good, Jessie. Thanks . . ."

No one except Sam ever called her Jessie. He had only used it a few times, but it was clear that it was his private nickname for her. At first that felt strange, but now Jessica secretly liked it.

"Up near my shoulders more. That's where it hurts," he said.

She moved her hand up to his shoulders. His muscles felt tense and hard. Gradually they started to relax under her hand.

Sam's eyes closed completely, his thick black eyelashes curving against his cheek. Was he asleep already? Jessica wasn't quite sure. She didn't want to say anything and risk waking him.

It is funny, she thought, *how it doesn't feel strange at all to be with him here like this.* She felt so close to him in such a short time. *This is what it would be like to be his wife,* a small voice suggested, *to take care of him and be his partner.*

Then her mind backed away from the image. No, that's not what she wanted. Sam was a nice guy, a wonderful person. She couldn't deny that. She cared about him and respected him. But this was just a summer thing. She probably shouldn't have even come here.

There was a knock on the door, and Jessica rose to answer it. The pizza, at long last, she realized. She paid the delivery man and put the box in the refrigerator. Then she wrote Sam a short note and placed it on the coffee table, where he would be sure to see it.

She glanced at him one more time. He was on his side now, sleeping soundly. She reached down and touched his hair and then his cheek. Then she found her jacket and briefcase, and slipped out the door.

It was a reasonable walk home, not much farther than her walk to the bank and back each day. The night was mild, the tang of the salt air refreshing. Jessica was glad for the exercise to clear her head.

At home she found a message from Paul on her answering machine.

"Jessica, are you there? No? Well, then I'm sorry I missed you. I know I've barely been in touch, but it's been an absolute zoo here. I've been thinking about you, though. Listen, I'll call you again soon. 'Night."

Jessica felt a small jolt of surprise and even some guilt at hearing Paul's voice. She was pleased that he'd called her—finally. He even sounded as if he'd missed her a bit. Or maybe he was just feeling lonely on his prolonged business trip. In any case, it was good to hear his voice. It made him more real somehow, reminding her of her "real life." The world she belonged to.

Paul was "right" for her, Jessica told herself, a much smarter choice than Sam would ever be. Sam would never leave Cape Light, and she would never have the heart to tear him away. He belonged here, with his half-finished house on the pond and his friends and his family. But Jessica didn't want to stay. It was not the life she imagined for herself.

She glanced at the clock. It wasn't too late to call Paul back, but for some reason, she didn't want to. It seemed like too much effort. She decided she would try him tomorrow night.

She sighed and stared into the refrigerator. She wasn't

very hungry, but she could use a snack. Elsie came out of nowhere and twined herself around Jessica's ankles.

"Why is life so confusing?" she asked the cat.

Elsie meowed in response.

Jessica bent down and ran her hand along the cat's back. "That's a philosophical answer if I ever heard one," she said, grinning. "Let's have some tuna salad and go to bed."

AN HOUR OR TWO AFTER CLOSING THE CLAM BOX FOR the night, Charlie Bates was just finishing cleaning up the diner. He normally had a cleaning crew in to do the job, but they canceled on him today, and he was stuck with the dirty work of wiping down, sweeping, and mopping up. That's what it was like when you had your own business. You couldn't rely on anyone. You had to be able to do it all.

Once he was mayor, of course, he wouldn't be caught dead mopping up this place. It was hard for a man to better himself, expand his horizons. You needed support. He wished Lucy would take more interest. She would have to, once he won the election. . . .

He heard a tapping on the big plate-glass window and was about to shout, "We're closed!" when he spotted his buddy Tucker Tulley.

Charlie unlocked the door. "Hey, Tucker," he greeted him. "Did you pull the night shift? I thought you were beyond that now."

"Just doing a guy a favor," Tucker answered as he walked into the empty diner. "I don't mind night duty once in a while. It's nice and quiet. Gives you a chance to think."

"Sounds like fun. Let me know how it goes," Charlie joked.

Tucker sat on a stool at the counter and pushed his hat

back on his head. Something in his serious expression made Charlie feel nervous.

"Can I get you some coffee?"

"Sure, thanks," Tucker said.

"Got a nice fresh pot here. I just made if for myself a little while ago."

He poured Tucker a mug and then one for himself. Tucker looked down at the coffee but didn't drink it.

"So what's up?" Charlie asked.

Tucker cleared his throat. "I'm investigating this harassment claim from Dr. Elliot. Did you scare off Elliot's buyer?" he asked point blank.

Charlie reeled back, as if his friend had struck him. "Of course I didn't do it. Why is everyone blaming me? There's a heck of a lot of people in this town that feel the same way I do about the situation. You were at the meeting. You saw how many people agreed with me. It could have been anyone."

Tucker did not reply. He just sat, looking at Charlie, his mouth pursed in a tight line. "All right, I'll grant you that much. But you have been the most outspoken about it. Someone told me you and Elliot nearly came to blows in here the other day."

"Well, that's just the way I am. I can't help that. Besides, he started it," Charlie argued. "First Elliot, then Lucy, now you, too. It's insulting that you don't believe me," he said in a quieter tone. "My best friend."

"You can add Betty Bowman to the list. She came into the station and wanted to give a statement. She says it was you."

"On what grounds?" Charlie demanded loudly.

"She's got no proof, if that's what you're asking."

"Betty Bowman's just mad because her deal fell through," Charlie said. "I'd rather step between a Rottweiler and a roast beef than that woman and her commission."

Tucker didn't smile, as Charlie expected him to. He picked up his coffee and took a sip. When he put it down, he stood up and righted his hat. "I want your word, Charlie. Look me in the eye and tell me again you had no part in this."

Charlie's mouth twitched. He rubbed his ear with a large calloused hand. "Why don't you just believe me? Don't we go back to kindergarten together?"

"What are you saying, Charlie? That you won't swear to it?"

"I swear to it," Charlie insisted. "But it's a shame to see you press me like this, I'll tell you that much."

"Yeah, it's a shame." Tucker looked down a moment. "I hate to say this, Charlie, but I'm warning you, as a friend—if you're a party to this mess, I can't protect you."

"Your best friend forever and you wouldn't help me out?" Charlie chided him, smiling nervously. "You surprise me, Tucker. You disappoint me."

"I hope I don't have to, my friend," Tucker said solemnly. "I really do."

Tucker nodded good night and left Charlie alone again in the diner. Out on Main Street, Tucker adjusted his hat and the heavy radio hanging off his belt, then walked on, grateful for the cool breeze blowing in off the harbor. He still didn't know what to think about Charlie. He hated to think the worst, but he had to admit he suspected it.

The shops on Main Street were closed. Everything looked quiet and sound. As he approached Bible Community Church, Tucker saw a single light burning in a window, the Reverend Lewis's office. He paused as he saw the reverend pass the window, then sit at his desk. Tucker wondered if he should stop in and check, just to see if he needed help of any kind. Maybe Reverend Ben was writing a sermon or whatever preachers worked on late into the night. Tucker didn't want to interrupt. He decided he would pass by again later and check up.

*   *   *

Reverend Ben Lewis sat at his desk, a pile of blank stationery before him, his favorite pen in hand. He knew it was late. Carolyn would be waiting for him, even if she was in bed already. She never really let herself fall all the way asleep until he was home. He had been at the church tonight for a meeting of—something, then decided to stay, knowing there was something he had to do, better done perhaps away from his home, in a quiet place where he could gather his thoughts.

He had thought about it and prayed about it and come to the decision that he needed to write a letter to his son, Mark. Not a chatty letter, updating him on family and village news, or even telling him about Rachel's pregnancy. No, Ben needed to send a different kind of letter, one that would reach across the giant rift between Mark and his family.

But it was very hard to know how to start, to really know if he should do this at all. What if he did more harm than good, by making Mark feel pressured and driving him even further away? Was the boy ready to listen—to reconnect, to forgive?

Ben had not told Carolyn of his intention. He worried about her reaction, too. But he would tell her once he sent the letter off. Secrets were not good; they were not an option for him and Carolyn.

He frowned at the return address on the last letter they had received from Mark. Mark wasn't there any longer, but it was the only address they had. Ben hoped that his letter would be forwarded to wherever Mark was now. He could, of course, wait for Mark to send him a new address. He always did, eventually. But Ben felt a certain urgency to get the deed done. He felt a strong intuition this was the right thing to do. And the right time to do it.

He closed his eyes and clasped his hands. "Dear Heavenly Father," he prayed, "please give me the right words. Words that will heal and help, not do more harm."

He opened his eyes and sighed aloud. "Oh, Lord. I must be a poor minister, indeed, if I can't even heal this rift in my own family."

Yes, poor old Ben, he admonished himself for giving over to the wave of self-pity. That would not get the job done.

He took a deep breath and began writing.

Dear Mark:

　I am not sure if this letter will even reach you, but I feel the need to speak to you, son, from my heart. The first and most important thing I have to say is that I love you. We all do.

　I sit here and hope and pray that no matter where you go, or what you do—or what you feel toward us, your family—you will believe this simple truth.

　And feel our love with you, always. . . .

CHAPTER TEN

$\mathscr{S}$ARA WAS SETTLED IN COMFORTABLY AT THE
Cranberry Cottages. She had a pot of flowers from a farm
stand on her front steps and a poster tacked up over her
kitchen table. Since renting the cottage, she'd seen very
little of Dr. Elliot around the property, but as the summer
wore on, vacationing families would come and go in the
neighboring buildings, arriving with their carloads of lug-
gage, bicycles, kayaks, golf clubs, and other vacation ne-
cessities.

She would see them slamming screen doors, lighting
barbecue grills, hanging out wet bathing suits, or taking
them in. The children ran free, chasing butterflies or each
other from early in the morning. Sara didn't mind the
noise too much. The other tenants helped her feel less
isolated, though she rarely spoke to any of them.

She had been living in sight of the Warwick Estate for
a month now, passing it every day on her way in and out
of town. But so far, she hadn't driven through the gates

or entered the mansion. The funny thing was, the longer she lived at Cranberry Cottages, the more she thought about the estate, wondering what her birth mother's childhood was like. Sara had heard stories about the Warwicks and the scandal that drove them out of Lilac Hall. She even spent a day in the village library, looking up old newspapers articles to help fill in the blanks.

According to the newspaper stories, her grandfather, Oliver Warwick, was the sole heir to a small fortune that included two canneries, one in Cape Light and the other in Newburyport. He was also part owner of a lumberyard and had various other business interests. But he was a poor businessman. The newspaper articles didn't say as much, but Sara surmised it. When his canneries began to lose money in the late 1960s, he took large loans to keep them running. To pay back the loans, he borrowed even more money and then tried to build up his capital by gambling with the borrowed funds. Somewhere along the way he reached into accounts that were off limits to him.

He was caught red-handed, embezzling funds from his corporation, mainly out of the retirement account for his employees. He gambled away the money at the racetrack and in high-stakes card games for society gentlemen. His debts mounted, and he couldn't recoup his losses. He ended up owing money all over New England.

In the reports of his trial Oliver Warwick professed that he always planned to pay the money back. Looking at his picture—a handsome man with a stunned expression and a mournful gaze—Sara could believe his testimony was sincere.

But by then the situation was hopeless. The family was ruined and the townspeople outraged when the cannery that employed so many was forced to shut its doors.

Sara had used the library's copy machine to copy some photos of her grandfather. Now she pulled them out of an envelope and spread them out on her kitchen table. In the pictures taken before the trial, Oliver Warwick appeared to be dignified and intelligent, with a thin, neat mustache and wire-rimmed glasses. He also seemed surprisingly friendly; nearly all the photos showed him smiling widely, which made Sara wish she had had a chance to meet him.

Her grandmother was another story. Even in the early photos Lillian looked disapproving and severe. Sara had seen her around town once or twice. The old woman always wore a sour expression. Then again, Sara thought, Lillian had had a hard time of it. Oliver died only a year after his trial, leaving Lillian to pick up the pieces. Lillian liquidated the businesses, cashed in the investments, sold the antique furniture, paintings, even jewelry in order to repay as much money as she could. She arranged with the town to take over the estate and mansion, Lilac Hall, and turn it into a historic house and park. Sara guessed that time must have been very difficult, not just for Lillian but also for Emily and her sister.

Sara stuffed the photographs back in their envelope. It was the Fourth of July weekend, and she had two full days off—Thursday and Friday—and nothing to do. She wasn't in the mood to write in her journal. The day was wearing on and the cottage was growing stuffy.

Maybe I'll hit the beach, she thought. *But it will be so crowded this weekend. I guess I could go to the Warwick Estate. I've been meaning to go up there.*

She showered quickly and dressed in a long cotton skirt and a brown tank top, her wet hair pulled back in a braid. She wore small silver hoop earrings and a necklace made of a leather strip with a small polished chunk of turquoise bound with a silver thread in the middle. Her leather knapsack was cumbersome to carry, especially in the hot weather. But she rarely went anywhere without it and sometimes thought of the jumble inside, including her journal, as the perfect reflection of her subconscious.

The estate was so close, Sara decided to walk. She was

glad that the long drive leading to the hou
gate was shady.

The tour of Lilac Hall was self-guided. S
a pamphlet at the entrance, describing the esta   ory.

The Warwick family had helped found the village back in the mid-1600s and had earned their first fortune as the leading shipbuilders along the nearby stretch of coast. Several generations had lived in a large house in town, near the harbor. Soon after World War I, Oliver's father, Harrison, bought the property outside of town and planned the building of Lilac Hall, in the style of great houses he had seen on a grand tour of Europe. The stone, along with the stone masons, had been imported from Europe. Intricate carvings surrounded the windows and entrances.

The house had over forty rooms in all, but only the first floor was open for viewing. Sara strolled through the rooms slowly, most impressed by the portico, with its vine-covered stone columns that framed a view of the marshland and not-too-distant sea. Most of the original furnishings were gone, but Sara could easily imagine the Gilded Age splendor.

What she couldn't imagine was what it must have been like to be a child here. It seemed so grand and extravagant, yet it was Emily's and Jessica's everyday reality—and then it was all suddenly taken away.

Sara toured the house for more than an hour, lingering in the many rooms. Finally returning to the main entrance, she stopped to look at some portraits of Warwick ancestors that hung in a long gallery near the vast foyer.

She turned as she heard voices coming from the staircase—and felt her heart begin to hammer as she saw Emily leading Lillian down the stairs. She felt almost as if she had been caught spying—except that Emily and her mother weren't aware she was there.

"And not one of them listens to a word of common sense," Lillian was complaining. "Some board of direcırs. Empty-headed fools, the lot of them. I don't know why I make the effort to come here at all. Just to waste my breath on a hot summer day, apparently."

"Committees need to discuss things thoroughly, Mother. You know that. They never come to a quick decision about anything," Emily said calmly.

"The house will fall to pieces before they'll actually agree that it needs repairs," Lillian snapped as she reached the bottom of the steps.

Sara considered ducking into the shadows, but at that moment Emily saw her and called out her name.

"Sara . . . hello. How are you?"

"Fine," Sara said, feeling terribly awkward.

"Taking a tour of the house?" Emily asked.

"Yes, I just finished, actually. I have the day off, and it's a little too hot for the beach."

"My mother and I were just here for a meeting. Mother is on the museum board," she explained. "Mother, this is Sara Franklin. She's visiting town for the summer. She's a writer," Emily added with a twinkle in her eye as she glanced at Sara.

"And a waitress at the Clam Box," Sara added with a smile.

Lillian had been concentrating on getting down the last step with her cane, but now paused and extended her hand. "Nice to meet you," she said briefly. "The Clam Box," she murmured to herself. "I haven't been in there for years."

"You haven't missed much," Sara said.

Lillian looked up. "What an endorsement . . . but that's probably true." She turned to Emily. "Will you stay for lunch after you take me home? Molly has fixed something, I think."

Sara felt then that Lillian must be lonely, just from the way she asked her daughter the question and the expectant expression on her face.

"Yes, I think I can stay. For a few minutes anyway." Emily glanced at her watch, then looked at Sara. "Would you like to have lunch with us at my mother's house?"

Sara noticed that Lillian looked shocked, but she fixed her lips in a tight line and stared straight ahead.

Sara debated silently. Lillian's attitude made it clear she wasn't welcome, and yet what a chance to see the Warwicks up close and personal. She felt a little sneaky accepting the offer but couldn't resist.

"Yes, thank you. I'd like that," Sara said evenly. "If it's not too much trouble."

"No, not at all. We'd love to have you," Emily insisted. Lillian was silent but looked more resigned to the idea, as Emily helped her through the foyer.

The ride to the house was brief. Sara sat up front with Emily while Lillian sat in the back and made disparaging comments about the other houses in town. "You would think they'd have that house repainted," she said about a colonial that looked fine to Sara. "And I don't understand people who can't be bothered to weed their gardens," she commented on another.

At her house Lillian insisted she didn't need help and started up the path with her cane. "Don't forget those plants in the trunk, Emily," she called. "They'll smother in there before long."

"Oh, yes. The plants. I nearly forgot," Emily admitted quietly to Sara. She opened the back, and Sara helped her carry several pots and flats of bedding plants around to the backyard.

A table on the small patio was already set for two. Sara waited outside while Emily went in. She soon returned with a tray, holding another place setting, as well as cold cuts, lettuce, tomatoes, and cheese for sandwiches and a basket of rolls.

Lillian joined them outside and sat down at the table. "Hmmm, that doesn't look too exciting, does it?" she asked, glaring at the spread. "For the money I'm paying her, you'd think she could come up with something a bit more original for lunch."

"You've also told her that you prefer plain foods, Mother," Emily reminded Lillian. "She can't be original and plain at the same time."

"Of course she can," Lillian insisted. "But that would require a little thought, I suppose. Too much to ask from help these days."

Ignoring her mother, Emily turned to Sara. "Have a seat, Sara, and fix yourself a sandwich. What do you like?"

Emily sounded like her mom back in Maryland, Sara thought suddenly.

"Young women diet far too much these days," Lillian observed. "It makes them sick. I've seen it on TV. Some sort of epidemic." She looked at Sara. "You're not on a diet, are you?"

"Uh, no. Not at all." As if to prove her point, Sara reached for the basket and put a large roll on her plate.

"So, you're a writer. What have you written?" Lillian asked, a challenging edge to her tone. Sara noticed Emily give her mother a quelling look, but Lillian ignored it.

"I write fiction mainly," Sara replied. "I had a short story published in a literary magazine this spring. And I worked on the college newspaper."

Lillian had been fixing a small sandwich for herself, a slice of ham and some lettuce, Sara noticed. She carefully cut it in half. "Do you read?"

"Yes. Too much I think, sometimes."

"You can never read too many books," Lillian replied. "Just the wrong kind, I think."

"I think it's important to read, no matter what kind of books you like," Emily said. "Sometimes I'm in the mood for a biography or something serious. And other times I just want a mystery or something entertaining."

"Beach reading, I think they call it now," Lillian said disapprovingly. "You can take a nap in the middle of it, or even get sunstroke, and you won't miss much."

Sara shared an amused glance with Emily. Lillian was the very definition of a curmudgeon, but Sara found her pronouncements oddly refreshing. At least you didn't have to worry about Lillian being two-faced; she told you exactly what she thought. Whereas Emily . . . what *was* the truth about Emily?

"To each his own, Mother," Emily said.

"To each numbskull, you mean," Lillian replied. She dabbed her mouth with the edge of her napkin. "I like a book that expands your mind. That's the point of literature and the point of art."

"I think art is about self-expression. Authentic thoughts and feelings. An artist's personal vision," Sara said. "I don't think real artists consciously set out to edify or educate. If they do, it's by accident. If they do it on purpose, it's not really art to me."

Lillian turned and looked at her, as if truly noticing her for the first time. "Interesting point," she conceded. She looked over at Emily. "The girl does have a mind. She's so pretty, I didn't suspect it."

"Of course she does," Emily agreed, sounding as if she had full confidence in Sara to hold her own in any conversation.

"Of course, self-expression, the glorification of the individual, is a very modern notion," Lillian went on. "The French probably invented it."

"Though in New England we always take full credit," Emily pointed out.

"Yes, we do. Shamelessly at this time of year," Lillian remarked. "But getting back to my original point," she continued, "some very great works of art have been informed by—and conformed to—strict doctrines of belief. The religious art of the Renaissance, for instance."

"Yes, of course," Sara agreed. "But I still think that even the great artists of that period were expressing a personal vision."

The older woman frowned as she took a sip of her iced tea. Maybe she disliked being challenged, Sara thought, or maybe she was just surprised that anyone would dare. Emily never seemed to.

"Well, I suppose you have a point," Lillian conceded at last. "I'm reading an interesting book right now that I would recommend to you if you like fiction. It presents intriguing questions about art as it's shaped by society, though the author doesn't necessarily answer them," Lillian clarified. "Very interesting writer . . ."

She named a book that Sara had already read, a new novel by an Asian author that received good reviews but was somewhat obscure. Sara was not only surprised that Lillian was aware of the book but sounded as if she was enjoying it.

"I read that," Sara said. "I really liked it, but I think I need to read it again. It had so many levels of meaning. And I'm not sure I understood the ending," she confessed.

"I'm only halfway through. Don't spoil it for me," Lillian warned her. "With my eyesight these days, it's slow going. Even if I can find the large-print edition."

"That's too bad," Sara sympathized. She had never thought there might be a time in her life when it would be hard to read. That would be awful.

"What about Molly?" Emily asked. "I thought she was going to read to you a bit when she comes."

"Oh, well, she tried. But she doesn't have the time really. Nor the interest. You can't force that type of thing, you know."

"I can read to you," Sara offered, surprising herself.

Emily glanced at her. "You must be very busy with your job, Sara. And tired from being on your feet all day."

Sara knew she was just trying to give her an easy way

out if she wanted one. But then she looked at Lillian, staring straight ahead, her chin lifted high. She could sense that Lillian was pleased by the offer but too proud to show it.

Lillian is interesting, Sara thought. *She is every bit as difficult as people claim, but once you get past her prickly temperament, she is more intellectual and stimulating than her reputation suggests*. Besides, Lillian was her grandmother, and Sara was very curious to get to know her better.

"Of course I can do it," Sara insisted. "I have plenty of time off during the day. Lucy mainly likes me there at night, so she can be with home with her children. I can come in the mornings or around lunchtime."

"That would be nice," Lillian said finally. "You have a nice strong voice, too. Good diction."

Sara smiled. No one had ever complimented her pronunciation before. Not since elementary school anyway.

"Where are you from?" Lillian asked.

"Maryland," Sara answered.

"Yes, of course. I noticed your accent."

"That's funny, I thought everyone around here had an accent," Sara replied with a grin. Lillian didn't quite laugh, but she did smile.

"Would you like to start today after lunch?" Sara offered.

"Yes, let's start today. I have a day off from my physical therapist. I don't have anything to do, really, once Emily leaves."

"Neither do I," Sara said.

Emily caught Sara's gaze again. She looked very grateful for Sara's kindness to her mother, and Sara felt a wave of warmth for her.

"We'll see how it works out," Emily advised. "It's very nice of you to offer, Sara. Honestly." She glanced at her watch. "Oh, dear, I have to run. I'm sorry, Sara," she apologized as she rose from her seat. "How will you get home without your car?" she asked with concern.

"No problem. I'll walk down to the diner, and Lucy will give me a ride later. She always has to pass the cottages on her way home anyway."

"Okay then. I'll see you. Thanks for coming over," she added. "This was a nice break for me." She leaned down and kissed her mother on the cheek. "I'll stop by later or tomorrow morning and put those plants in for you."

"Maybe Jessica will come and do it. She likes to garden," Lillian said.

"Yes, I'll call her and see if she's free this weekend."

"I hope she's stopped seeing that Sam Morgan," Lillian said.

I hope she still is, Emily nearly countered. She liked Sam, and though he and her sister were an unlikely match, she thought her sister seemed happier since she'd started going out with him. But she didn't have the time or energy to get into that debate. She simply waved and left.

As she walked around to the front of the house, she heard Sara compliment the garden.

"A good garden requires persistence and the ability to learn from your mistakes," Emily heard Lillian reply. "A lot like life . . ."

Emily could not hear Sara's answer. She was sure when the young woman had volunteered to read to her mother, she didn't expect to sign up for a philosophy course as well. Emily hoped it would work out. She liked Sara Franklin very much. Something about her was very . . . endearing. She hoped they'd be seeing more of her.

THE DINER SEEMED LONELY WITHOUT SARA, LUCY thought. She was used to the young woman's company. There had been a rush during lunch hour, a lot of tourists in for the weekend, taking a break from the beach, or just getting into town. She must have served over a hundred crab rolls.

The place was empty now, though. Lucy passed the time refilling the empty ketchup bottles and wiping them down with a damp cloth. She glanced up from time to time, to see if her two lone customers needed anything. One of them was Tucker, taking a coffee break at the counter, and the other was Luke McAllister. Lucy didn't know Luke well but recognized him. He had been coming into the diner fairly regularly since the summer started.

When Luke waved for his check, she brought it over to him and set it down on the table beside his plate. "There you are. Need more coffee?"

"No, thanks," he said, putting some bills on the table. "By the way, where's Sara today?"

"She's off," Lucy said, picking up the check and the money.

Luke rose from his seat and put on his sunglasses. "Tell her I said hello," he said as he started toward the door.

"Sure, I'll tell her," Lucy promised, though she wasn't at all sure that she would pass on the message. Something about Luke bothered her. Maybe it wasn't any of her business, but she didn't like the idea of Sara's getting involved with him.

She walked back to the counter and stood by Tucker, who was reading the newspaper. "That guy Luke McAllister is an odd one," she said.

"Hmmm, I know what you mean," Tucker agreed. "He's been hanging around town all summer. Doing a lot of nothing, far as I can tell."

"I heard he spent summers in the village as a kid, so he wanted to stay here again," Lucy said.

Luke still knew a few people in town, old friends of his family's, so whatever he told them sort of got around.

Tucker looked around, then leaned a bit closer. "I heard from a cop I know down in Boston that McAllister was a police officer there. So were his dad and older brother—he comes from a family of Boston cops." Tucker's voice dropped to a whisper. "I heard Luke was hurt in a shooting and nearly died."

"Is that so?" Lucy replied with interest. "I would have never taken him for a policeman."

"He worked undercover, drug cases mostly," Tucker told her. "This fellow I know who told me the story says McAllister's partner was killed, and it might have been Luke's fault—if things like that can ever be anyone's fault. So he left the force—quit or got fired, I don't know which. Then it seems he had some other problems. Trouble with his family, his fiancée dumping him, and then maybe some drinking."

"Hmmm, that's too bad," Lucy said, revising her opinion. If Luke was strange, maybe it was just because he'd been through a rough patch. Lucy was always sympathetic to another person's troubles. "He seems to be straightened out now," she said. "Sort of a loner, though."

"Yup, I'd say that for sure," Tucker agreed. "I guess he's got a lot on his mind."

Tucker went back to his newspaper, and Lucy began the task of replacing the ketchup bottles that she had refilled.

Sara had never mentioned a boyfriend, she realized. Did she have someone back in Maryland? Was Sara attracted to Luke? Some women liked that angry, loner type. It seemed romantic at first. *Then you get stuck with a piece of work like Charlie*, she thought, shaking her head.

She decided that she would tell Sara that Luke had asked about her. But she would also pass on what Tucker said.

Ruth Harvey, the mail carrier, came in with the Clam Box mail and handed it to Lucy. Lucy glanced over her shoulder, looking for Charlie. He was safely out of sight in the kitchen, so she quickly riffled through the envelopes.

Felicity Bean had secretly helped her fill out some college applications, and though Lucy knew it was probably too early to hear anything, she checked nervously each day. She couldn't risk having Charlie find anything from the colleges. He would start asking a lot of questions before she was ready to talk to him about it.

Which might be never, she thought woefully. She knew it was wrong to keep the secret from her husband, but she also knew how he would react once she told him. Flip his lid was a good prediction. Lucy figured that she would wait to see if she even got accepted to any of the schools, then tell him. If she didn't get in, she wouldn't even bother.

Finding nothing incriminating in the mail, Lucy stacked the pile neatly and left it for Charlie on the shelf under the register. She was feeling momentarily at peace, about to start refilling the salt and pepper shakers, when an unholy roar sounded from the kitchen.

Charlie burst through the swinging doors, waving two paperback books at her. Lucy's heart sank. She recognized them as the two college catalogs that had arrived the day before. Lucy had been looking them over with Felicity; she hadn't had a chance to bring them home and hide them in the attic with the rest of her collection.

"What is this?" Charlie asked, pushing the catalogs toward her. "I pulled open the cupboard up on top of the stove, and these things hit me in the head."

Lucy made a show of looking at his partially bald scalp. "I don't see anything. Want some ice?" she asked.

Charlie remained focused on the books. "These are college bulletins. What are they doing up in that cupboard? Who put them there?"

He was frowning, but just confused, not really angry yet, she thought. She twisted her hands together. Should she tell him? Just come right out and say, *Charlie, I want to go back to school. I really, really want this. I've been looking into it, and I think—*

"Look at this—" His voice cut into her wandering thoughts. "They're addressed to Sara Franklin, care of the diner. I thought that girl already went to college. Didn't she tell you she just graduated?"

Lucy felt her body go slack with relief. Of course, she'd had those two sent under Sara's name, just in case. Well, just in case had come, and she was, for the moment, saved from confessing.

"Maybe she's thinking of going back to school in the fall to study something else," Lucy offered.

Charlie looked back at the books again, mulling over her explanation. "I don't know. It seems queer to me. Nearly gave me a concussion, for Pete's sake," he muttered. Shaking his head, he turned back to the swinging doors.

Lucy breathed a deep sigh of relief. "Yes, I'll talk to her about it," she called after her husband.

It wasn't entirely a lie, either. She would certainly tell this whole story to Sara.

HAVING INVENTED INDEPENDENCE DAY, NEW ENglanders could not be faulted for the way they revered the Fourth of July. Happy to don garb of the Revolutionary era, they cheerfully dusted off their muskets and tricorn hats and took to the streets. All morning they would turn back the clock with mock battles and marches, only to carry off the wounded later in the day to baseball games, clambakes, and barbecues.

The village of Cape Light was no different. At dawn a band of counterfeit redcoats marched down the Beach Road, starting off from their landing at Durham Point, to meet the plucky, ragtag village militia in the village square.

The reenactment was always well attended, but the highlight of the day was the parade, a grand affair with marching bands, floats, the county's award-winning bagpipe corps, veterans of foreign wars, Girl Scouts, Boy Scouts, the Coast Guard, and the Visiting Nurses Society, not to mention police chiefs, fire chiefs, and the entire town council on a float, trailing the village crest on a long banner. There was even the complete inventory of the town's fire-fighting and emergency vehicles, all highly polished.

Jessica didn't care much about parades down Main Street. She had seen enough in her childhood to last a lifetime. But on the Fourth of July she was obliged to take her mother into town to watch the parade and see Emily, first waving from the back of a convertible, then up on the reviewing stand to give a speech.

Jessica brought her mother into town early enough to find a parking space near the reviewing stand. Because Emily was mayor, they had special seats under an awning, which made Jessica feel a bit self-conscious. Her mother, however, had no such problems. Dressed in an outfit normally reserved for Sundays, Lillian seemed quite comfortable in her privileged position.

"Now, if the show is half as good as these seats, it won't be a wasted morning," Lillian said as the parade began.

The parade was actually a lot more fun than Jessica expected. It was colorful and silly and completely goodnatured. And then it was time for Emily to climb to the podium to make her speech.

"Good morning, fellow Patriots," she began, and was answered by a loud cheer. "Have you heard? The British are coming. . . ."

As always, Emily made a good speech, starting off

with a touch of humor and eventually stirring patriotic and community spirit.

Lillian clapped vigorously, her gaze fixed on her eldest daughter. She was so proud of Mayor Warwick. Jessica knew that, but today it seemed especially poignant. She didn't think about it much, but she was very proud of Emily, too. She realized now she had never even told her.

Emily met up with them when the presentation was over. "That was a very nice speech, Emily," Lillian said, bestowing a rare, unqualified compliment.

"Thank you, Mother. Just the usual for the occasion, I thought." She glanced at Jessica and smiled. "At least you had good seats, out of the sun."

"Well, we happen to know the mayor," Jessica teased.

Emily laughed. "What are you doing today, Jessica? Would you like to come to Betty's with us?" she asked.

"Uh, no, thanks," Jessica replied finally. "I'm going out. With Sam. His parents are having a party," she admitted, hoping her mother wouldn't start an argument when she heard that. "I'm supposed to meet him out on the green in a few minutes," she added, glancing at her watch.

Lillian seemed distracted by all the activity around them and made no comment.

Emily smiled. "Well, have a good time," she said. "I'll call you tomorrow, okay?"

"Sure." Jessica nodded and watched as Emily led their mother away.

She had almost hoped her mother would refuse to go to Betty Bowman's barbecue at the last minute, giving her an acceptable excuse to get out of her plans with Sam. He had invited her to a party at his parents' house and had somehow persuaded her to come.

Most of his family would be there. Jessica didn't know why she'd ever agreed to this. A weak moment, she decided. He must have been staring into her eyes, or holding her hand. From the moment they first met, Sam had a way of throwing her off balance.

Jessica walked to the Village Green, searching for Sam in the crowd. She knew when he asked that it was important to him, and she didn't want to hurt his feelings by refusing.

It didn't take long to spot him. He was standing under a large oak tree, dressed in jeans and a simple white T-shirt that showed off his dark good looks. In fact, he looked maddeningly handsome.

"Jessica," he called out as he saw her approach. Someone had given him a three-cornered hat, and he waved it at her.

She waved back and walked toward him, smiling as their eyes met. Sam leaned over and put his arm around her.

"Not here," Jessica murmured, feeling embarrassed about being hugged in the middle of the Village Green, but Sam just laughed and held on.

"I'm home from the war, woman. Doesn't that even rate a kiss?"

"Give me a break. You weren't even in the enactment," she said with a laugh. But finally she couldn't resist melting into his arms and closing her eyes to kiss him hello.

Okay, so she was going to meet his family. No big deal. He met her mother and knew Emily. It didn't have to mean anything, she reassured herself. It's a small town. Everyone knows everyone.

A SHORT TIME LATER SHE AND SAM ARRIVED AT THE Morgans' modest Cape. She heard music and laughter coming from the backyard. She smelled the scent of Joe Morgan's grill heavy in the air. Jessica froze . . . she didn't want to get out of Sam's truck.

Sam seemed to read her thoughts. "Don't be nervous,"

he said, and took her hand. "They really want to meet you. This is going to be okay."

Jessica sincerely doubted that, but knew she had no choice now. With a firm grip on her hand, Sam led the way into the gathering. She felt him holding her hand a little more tightly than usual. Was he merely offering emotional support or did he fear she'd make a run for it?

The first person he introduced was his mother, Marie, who greeted Jessica warmly. Jessica could see where Sam had gotten his dark good looks and high energy. Marie was busily setting out platters of food while directing her daughters as they prepared the rest of the meal, so their conversation was brief.

Sam's father, Joe, watched over the long, professional-looking grill with a serious expression. A barrel-chested man of medium height, he wore a white chef's apron over jeans and a red, white, and blue shirt. A Red Sox cap topped off his attire. When he saw his son, his round face broke into a wide sunny smile. He had dimples and a cleft chin just like Sam. "Glad you could come. We've heard a lot about you," he said, taking off his oven mitt to shake Jessica's hand.

Jessica smiled, though his words struck a wary note in her. She was sure that Sam's family talked about her—as an unlikely match for their son.

Though she tried to relax and enjoy herself, she felt a vague uneasiness throughout the rest of the party. Sam had two other sisters besides Molly, and two brothers. Most were married with children. While the entire Morgan family was not there, it was still a challenge for Jessica to remember all the names and relationships. Sam rarely left her side, which she appreciated. Yet his attentiveness also made her feel self-conscious. She was sure his family assumed that their relationship was getting serious, which was not the case at all. At least, not from Jessica's perspective.

After everyone ate, grown-ups and kids alike gathered for games in the Morgans' large yard. There was volleyball, horseshoes, and croquet. At first Jessica just watched Sam play volleyball, then she joined in, too, on the opposite team. She used to play in college and surprised Sam with a wicked spike that flew right past him. She would have given a lot for a photo of the look on his face.

"Way to go, Jessica!" Sam's nephew Rory yelled out. She smiled shyly, concentrating on the game, but finally started to relax and have fun.

But later, as dessert was served, Jessica's doubts were confirmed. She was in the house, washing her hands in the small powder room near the kitchen, when she heard two women talking about her in the hallway. It sounded like Sam's sister Molly and his sister-in-law Lisa.

"I don't know. She's not so bad. Besides, Sam seems to be crazy about her."

"He's crazy if he thinks she'll ever marry him," Molly countered. "The Warwicks are all the same, believe me. I deal with the old lady every week now. Princess Jessica is mingling with common folks today, but she's still a snob. Sam's too good for her, if you ask me."

"I don't know what they have to be so proud about. Her father nearly wound up in jail—"

The voices grew less distinct as the two women moved toward the kitchen. Jessica waited, hoping they would go back outside. She also needed a minute to compose herself. Their words had stung.

She wasn't sure what upset her more—the fact that they thought she considered the Morgans beneath her, or the fact that they thought she and Sam were a serious couple.

Who was I kidding? Jessica asked herself. *Did I really think I could come here today and meet Sam's family and it wouldn't matter?* It did, she realized. His whole family seemed to think that their relationship was serious. And most likely, so did Sam, despite everything she had said to warn him otherwise.

Jessica finally joined the party again, but the harsh words continued to trouble her. She and Sam hardly spoke on the drive back.

It was dark when he pulled up in front of her house, the streetlamps giving off a soft glow. He turned to her and took her hand. "You look beat. My family must have worn you out."

"I'm okay. It was fun. Thanks for inviting me," she said politely, though she avoided meeting his gaze.

Sam didn't reply right away, and she knew he sensed something was wrong. "I'm sure it was overwhelming, meeting all of them at once like that," he said. "It must have felt like I was dropping you straight into the deep end. But it won't be so bad the next time."

Jessica had a sick feeling in the pit of her stomach. There he was, talking about the future again, as if they really had one together. It wasn't fair to keep seeing him if he was counting on something serious.

"Listen, Sam," she said, "I think we need to talk."

"What's wrong?" he asked gently.

Jessica withdrew her hand from his. "I'm just not sure about this relationship, where it's going," she began awkwardly. "I love spending time with you, really. You're a great person. But I don't plan on staying in Cape Light. I've told you that from the start. . . ."

Sam sat very still, staring straight ahead, his large hands resting on the steering wheel. She leaned over and tried to see his face, but in the dim light she couldn't really gauge his reaction.

"A great person," he said, echoing her words sarcastically. "Thanks a lot."

"I just feel as if you have more serious expectations about us than I do," Jessica forged on, trying to ignore his anger. "And I want to be fair to you."

Finally Sam turned to face her. "I know you don't plan on staying here, Jessica. But you know, life isn't always so cut-and-dried. Sometimes a person's plans change."

"Mine won't," she said more sharply than she intended. She saw Sam's expression harden. She had hurt him. She didn't mean to, but she had to be honest with him. Now, before things went any further, before she was pulled in even deeper.

She tried to soften the blow. "I think we just have different ideas about life, about what we each want for ourselves."

"Like what, for instance?" he challenged her.

"Like, I can't see myself living here for the rest of my life. I love the city, the excitement there, the opportunities . . ."

Sam shook his head, nearly laughing at her, but not pleasantly. "Maybe you want to be president of the bank, is that it? I guess it would be tough to be with a guy who drives you around in a pickup truck."

Jessica pulled back from him, feeling her eyes well up with tears. It sounded so awful when he put it that way. "That's not what I mean at all."

"Well, what do you mean? If you don't want to see me anymore, just say it."

She glanced over at him. Although his face was shadowed by the streetlight, she could read his emotions in the rigid set of his body. Jessica had never seen him so grim, so cold toward her. She hated hurting him so badly. If she wanted to break this off, now was the time, she realized. She ought to get it over with now, make a clean break so they could both get on with their lives and find whatever it was that might make them truly happy.

But she couldn't. She couldn't stand the idea of not seeing Sam again.

"I'm not saying that either," she said finally, staring

straight ahead. "I'm just . . . worried. I don't want to disappoint you."

"You've already said that," he pointed out. "I think it's more like you don't want to disappoint yourself."

She frowned at him. "What do you mean by that?"

"Well, what are you afraid of, really? Are you afraid of a serious relationship? Afraid you might fall for me and get stuck here? Is that it?"

His comment upset her, confused her. Was it true?

"No . . . not at all," she insisted. "That's not it at all."

He shrugged, looking as if he didn't really believe her. "Well, then, you don't have anything to worry about, do you?"

"No, I don't," she insisted. Still, his questions irked her. "Do you want to stop seeing me?" she asked suddenly.

He took a slow breath and stared straight ahead for an endless moment, then said, "You let me worry about my expectations, Jessica. Whatever is going to happen here, is going to happen. You don't have as much control over your life as you think."

Jessica didn't entirely agree with that. She knew life took unexpected turns now and again. But not when it came to matters as serious as marriage. Not for her anyway. She sighed and turned to him.

"If that's what you want, okay," she agreed. "As long you know how I feel."

"I think I do," he said quietly, gazing down at her.

He moved closer and put his arms around her. Jessica closed her eyes and pressed her head into his shoulder, feeling more relieved than she would have ever admitted.

She had been honest with him about her feelings, and he still wanted to see her. That was his choice. She didn't need to feel as though she was misleading him anymore.

I could have lost him tonight, she realized. *And I wasn't ready to, yet.*

*   *   *

"REVEREND BEN? I NEED TO SPEAK TO YOU ABOUT something. Is this a bad time?"

Seated on a bench in the Village Green, the reverend looked up from his newspaper to find Lucy Bates standing in front of him. "Lucy . . . not at all," he said with a smile. "Here, sit down." He slid over on the bench to make room for her.

"You looked like you were having a little private time for yourself," Lucy said apologetically. "I don't want to bother you."

"Just reading the newspaper. It can wait," he assured her. Lucy rarely sought him out for counsel. He hoped it wasn't anything too serious. She did look nervous, though, literally sitting on the edge of her seat, rubbing her palms together.

"It's a beautiful day," she said.

"Yes, absolutely." He gazed around the Village Green, shady now in the midafternoon, then looked back at Lucy with a gentle, encouraging expression.

"Well, this is hard to talk about . . . but I'll try. You see, the thing is, I have this secret from Charlie. And it's really bothering me. I've never kept anything secret from my husband before, and I'm just nearly sick from it." She glanced at the reverend apprehensively. "It's nothing terrible, not like I'm having an affair or anything like that," she assured him.

Ben was glad to hear that, though he willed himself not to show any reaction at all as she continued to speak.

"I want to go back to school. To college, I mean," she explained. "I guess it's been on my mind a long time, but I just never really told Charlie. Once I mentioned it to him, a year or so ago, and he told me flat-out to forget it, so I never brought it up again."

Ben nodded sympathetically. "I can see why," he said.

"But then I started thinking about it and sent away for some catalogs, and I realized I really wanted to get into a nursing program. So I said to myself, why not? The kids are getting older. They really don't need me so much. And I'm not getting any younger. If I don't start now, it's never going to happen. I think I could manage it and still work at the Box."

Ben found her positive spirit very admirable. He loved to see adults still interested in expanding their knowledge and experience, living out the gift of God's limitless potential.

"I think your aspirations are wonderful, Lucy. I hope you can find some way to fulfill them."

"Thank you, Reverend," Lucy said with emotion. He could see how much his simple affirmation helped her. "Sometimes, I don't know. I'm not really sure I can do it. . . ." She touched her hand to her hair. "I'm not even sure I *should* do it."

"Of course you should. Have you spoken to anyone else about it?"

She nodded. "Sara Franklin, the new waitress, knows. She's been very good to talk to. And—you're not going to believe this—Felicity Bean, over at the Beanery, she's been helping me pick out the schools and do the applications."

Ben's eyes widened. He did find that hard to believe, considering Charlie's negative attitude toward the Beans and their new business. He could see now why Lucy felt such pressure to keep her plans secret from him.

"I don't know," Lucy went on. "At first I thought I'd just wait and see if I got accepted anywhere before I sprang the news on Charlie. But it's so hard not to say anything. I want to tell him," she added. "Even if these applications don't work out, I think I'll try some more. I keep looking for a good time to talk to him about it. Then I chicken out." She sighed and looked at the harbor.

Ben chose his words carefully. "I know Charlie can be difficult. And I can see you have a lot of patience with him, Lucy. He should be grateful for that."

"Sometimes he is." She turned to him and smiled. "Sometimes he even has to laugh at himself."

"We all do, sooner or later," Ben answered. "Secrets are not good, you know, especially in a marriage. We need to be open with our life partners. Do you remember what the Bible tells us about love? Love is patient and kind," he said. "Love believes all things, hopes all things. . . . "

"Yes, I know, Reverend. You hear it enough at weddings," Lucy said wryly. "It's just that when I try to talk to Charlie, I'm afraid of how angry he gets. He can be so unreasonable. He just doesn't listen to me sometimes."

Ben felt that must be true. The Bateses' marriage did not seem entirely balanced to him. Charlie had such a strong personality that Lucy often bent to his will. Still, marriage was like a seesaw, with one side having the upper seat for a while, then the other. And Ben was certain that both Lucy and Charlie loved each other very much.

"I think you're ready to be open with him, Lucy," he said. "You need to tell your husband how important this is to you, help him to understand. He can't meet your needs if you don't tell them what they are."

"I suppose that's true," she said, but she sounded doubtful.

"I know Charlie is very emotional. But give him a chance to be the best he can be. Don't just assume he will be the worst. He may not get it right away," Ben added, "but give him a chance. And give him time."

Lucy gave him a rueful smile. "I understand what you're saying. I'm not giving him a chance. I haven't even brought it up, and already I'm practically mad at him for refusing to let me do it. Charlie can be understanding," she assured the reverend. "I just have to work up my nerve to talk to him. It just never seems to be the right time."

"Once you've made up your mind to do it, I think you'll find the right time. God will see to that," Ben told her. "Have faith that God will help you talk to Charlie. Have faith in yourself and your plans. They are admirable and worthy, Lucy. Don't give up on this." .

"I'll try not to," she promised. She got up off the bench, looking more resolved. "Thanks again, Reverend. I'm glad I stopped to talk to you."

"So am I. I'm glad I could help. Let me know how it works out, okay?"

"Yes, I will," she said, and headed back to the village.

Ben watched her for a moment, then looked out at the harbor. A stiff breeze stirred the treetops and made the canvas sails of nearby boats give off sharp snapping sounds.

He sent up a short prayer for Lucy and Charlie Bates, and got to his feet, troubled. The talk with Lucy reminded him of his own secret. He still hadn't told Carolyn about his letter to Mark. He would have to tell her right away, he decided. Tonight, when he got home. He sent up another small prayer asking for God's help in that conversation.

CAROLYN WAS IN THE KITCHEN, COOKING SUPPER, when Ben got home that evening. He kissed her hello.

"I made some pork chops for dinner," she told him. "There's local corn and some tomatoes Digger dropped off from Grace's garden. Aren't they gorgeous?" she said, pointing to the basket on the countertop.

As summer gardens in town reached their bountiful peak, the parishioners kept Ben and Carolyn supplied with a variety of home-grown vegetables. He picked up one of the tomatoes and sniffed. It was as large as a softball and smelled fresh and flavorful, not like one of those bland, spongy things the grocery stores passed off as tomatoes these days.

"Grace grows the best," he said, setting the tomato on the top of the pile. "She ought to win a prize."

"I think she has," Carolyn noted.

He gazed at her back as she stood at the cutting board, slicing a carrot. This is as good a time as any, he thought, taking a seat in one of the kitchen chairs. He just had to come out with it, as he'd counseled Lucy Bates.

"I wrote a letter to Mark," he said quietly.

He heard the chopping stop. Carolyn's body stiffened, but she didn't turn to him. "You did? When?"

"I wrote it about two weeks ago. I sent it to the last address. Maybe it will be forwarded to him."

"Maybe," she said. She finally turned and wiped her hands on her apron. For once he couldn't read the expression in her eyes. "What did you say to him?"

"That we love him. That we want him to come home and work things out. That I think it's time."

"Did you tell him Rachel's expecting a baby?"

Ben nodded. "Yes, of course I did. Mark would want to know about that, no matter what."

Carolyn sighed and turned her back to him. "I don't know, Ben," she said, shaking her head. She was upset. He felt a tightness in his chest. Maybe he should have asked her opinion first. It was a hard call. Mark was her son, too.

"What don't you know, dear?" he asked quietly. He rose and touched her shoulder, turning her to face him. "Talk to me. Tell me what you're thinking," he urged her.

"Oh, you know . . . the same old thing," she said. She tried to smile at him but couldn't. Her eyes were glassy with unshed tears. "I'm just afraid of doing anything, I guess. I'm afraid that if we say anything at all to Mark, it will make things even worse."

"Yes, I know. I thought you might feel that way." He paused and gently rubbed her shoulders. "But after Rachel told us about the baby, I felt it was time to do something. I've thought a lot about this, Carolyn. I've prayed about it, too. I think it was the right thing to do. I really do."

He met her gaze and watched her consider his words. She looked as if she was struggling with the idea, then her expression relaxed and she seemed resolved. When she looked up at him again, her eyes held a trusting light that made him feel worlds better.

"I know I don't see this situation very clearly," she admitted. "I try . . . but I just can't." She raised her chin a bit. "I do so want him to forgive me for not being a perfect mother, for not being there when he needed me. Then again, sometimes I feel he's being unfair. Not just to me, but to you and Rachel, too."

"I was the one who drove him away," Ben said, his voice filled with pain. "I couldn't bear seeing him so angry with you. I couldn't see past his anger to the pain behind it."

"I know." Carolyn cupped his cheek with one hand. "There were times when neither one of us did the right thing by Mark. Perhaps we even failed him. But hopefully he'll see that we're trying to heal that now. How did you even know what to say?"

He shrugged and sighed. "I wrote from the heart. I asked the Spirit to give me the right words. I said what I had to say, I suppose. . . . Do you want to see the letter? I think I saved a copy."

She considered it for a moment, then shook her head. "No, that's okay. I'm sure that whatever you wrote was right, Ben. Now if only he answers it."

"Yes, if only," he repeated. "But that part is up to our heavenly mail carrier, who has to put it in his hands first. Mark might get the letter but not be ready to receive my message. Remember this verse from Romans? 'But if we hope for that we see not, then do we with patience wait for it,' " he gently recited. "Mark will get the letter when it's time."

Ben searched his wife's eyes, looking for some assurance that she believed that as well.

"I pray he does," she replied quietly.

She turned back to her cooking, checking something in a pot on the stove, and Ben realized they had said all there was to say, for now.

CHAPTER ELEVEN

"SO, THEY FINALLY LET YOU OUT OF THAT DINER? Or did you just make a run for it?"

Sara was startled by the voice behind her. She turned to see Luke McAllister standing in the late-day shadows, not far from her cottage. She'd been writing in her journal and hadn't even heard him walk up to her. She closed the book and stood up.

"It's time off for good behavior," she replied.

Her quick return almost made him smile. But not quite, she noticed as he walked closer. "What were you writing?" he asked. "A letter home?"

She shook her head. "Just my journal."

He glanced down at the leather-bound book. "It looks pretty thick. Do you write in it every day?"

Sara nodded. "Just about. Sometimes I'm too tired after work. But I try to keep up."

"Why? Are you keeping a record for some reason?"

"Uh, no. Not really. I might want to remember things

that have happened to me someday. But mainly it helps me figure out my life better. Things that are happening to me, I mean."

Luke looked down at the book again and stuck his hands into the front pockets of his jeans. "Maybe I ought to try it. I usually can't write anything longer than a grocery list."

"It's easier than you think, once you start."

She wondered if he was going to ask her even more personal questions. She didn't really know him very well—definitely not well enough to confide any secrets.

From what Lucy told her, Sara gathered that Luke had his own secrets. But Sara knew better than to believe everything she heard about a person. If Luke didn't want to tell the world his life story, that was his choice. She respected his privacy.

"So, do you live here?" Luke asked, turning to look at her cottage.

She felt wary for a moment, telling him where she lived. But he could find that out easily enough if he really wanted to, she realized. Besides, while there was something unsettling about Luke, she didn't honestly feel he was dangerous.

"Just for the summer. It's not so bad inside. Are you thinking of renting one?" she asked, still wondering why he was here at all.

"No . . . just looking around," he said vaguely. "I used to stay here when I came up with my family. Good old Cranberry Cottages," he said dryly.

His tone made Sara wonder if maybe his memories of the place weren't very happy ones. Or maybe it was just what had happened since that made him sound so cynical.

"Well, I'm keeping you from your writing, I guess," he said, seeming suddenly uncomfortable.

"Not really. I'd just finished when you came," she said honestly.

He glanced around and looked at the cottage again. Then, looking back at Sara, he said, "I'm going into town. I thought I'd check out the Beanery. Want to come?"

His invitation caught her off guard. "No, thanks," she said abruptly. "It's my only day off this week, and I have a lot to do around here."

"Sure," he replied curtly. "Well, I need to get going. See you."

"See you, Luke," Sara replied as she watched him walk away.

The sun was setting, and the air suddenly turned cool. Sara went inside and put on a pot of coffee, her mind on Luke McAllister. Something about him was mysterious, interesting. She did like talking to him, though at the same time she felt some intuition warning her away. Or maybe it was just Lucy who had planted a seed of distrust with her rumors.

Luke was different, an outsider, drifting around the edges, trying to figure something out. She could see that in him and even empathize. But she still didn't want to get involved with him, not even for a ride to town. Besides, her life was just too complicated right now.

Although she had gotten to know Emily much better over the past few weeks, and was even spending time with her grandmother, Sara still didn't feel any closer to figuring out when—or if—she should tell Emily about her true connection.

The only thing Sara knew for certain was that revealing her identity would deeply distress Lillian as well. The other day she asked Lillian if she had ever been to Maryland, and the old woman started trembling so violently that Sara was terrified she had given her a heart attack. Fortunately, Lillian calmed down as soon as Sara changed the subject, but the incident proved to Sara that the secret she carried within her had to be handled very carefully. She didn't want to hurt anyone with it.

But I feel like such a faker sometimes, Sara thought, *sitting there, sipping tea from Lillian's china cups and reading the newspaper to her. And a fraud with Emily, too. That feels even worse. She's not a bad person. She must have had some reason for giving me up.*

Should she tell Emily who she was? Now that she actually knew Emily and had a relationship with her, it seemed harder than when Sara was a complete stranger. The summer was half over, and she still had no idea what to do. She hoped that something would happen to help her figure this all out.

JESSICA WAS WORKING IN THE GARDEN WHEN SHE heard the phone ring. She went in to answer it, pulling off one dirt-covered glove before picking up the receiver.

It was Sam. She could tell just by the way he said hello that something was not quite right. "I'm sorry but I can't make it to the beach today," he said. "Something came up."

"What is it? Is something wrong?"

"I really need to go up to the Potters' place today," Sam explained. "Gus fell off a ladder this week and cracked some ribs. He's back now from the hospital, but he needs help. A few of us are going up there to do some work for him and Sophie."

"Oh, I see. That's okay," Jessica said. She'd heard about Gus Potter's accident. It was good of Sam to help him. While she really did understand, the idea of not seeing him disappointed her. "Can I come with you?" she asked.

"Sure . . . that would be great." He sounded surprised at her offer but definitely pleased.

Sam picked her up right away, and they were standing on the Potters' porch within the hour. Harry Reilly, Digger Hegman, and a few other men from Bible Community

Church had come as well. Gus came out of the house with his arm in a sling. He didn't look his usual robust self, and Jessica felt bad for him.

"How are you feeling, Gus?" Jessica asked him.

"I've been better," he admitted. "But it could have been worse, I guess."

"He's a darn fool to be climbing up on the roof at his age," Sophie chimed in. "He forgets he's not as young as he used to be."

"Somebody's got to do it," Gus replied to his wife.

Sophie didn't have an answer to that comment and started serving pie and coffee while the men discussed the work to be done. When the work group set off for the orchard, Jessica helped Sophie clear up. She carried a tray of dishes into the kitchen.

"You can set that tray right on the counter, dear," Sophie said. "I'll get to it later."

Jessica tried to do as she'd been asked, but it was hard to find an empty space for the tray in the large old kitchen. Nearly every inch of the counters and tabletop was covered with an eclectic mix of pottery, cooking utensils, flower-filled vases, stacks of dishes, and piles of mail. Sophie's kitchen, it seemed, remained in a perpetual state of clutter.

"Is there anything I can help you do around the house, Sophie?" Jessica asked.

Sophie moved around the room, putting things away and taking other things out. "Well, let me think a minute. I'm not sure. . ." she said in a way that made Jessica certain she was reluctant to ask for assistance.

"Really, Sophie. I'm here to help," Jessica said kindly.

If she stopped long enough to think about it, she wasn't quite sure how that had happened. She didn't exactly belong to Bible Community Church, and she barely knew the Potters. But nevertheless, here she was. *Might as well make myself useful*, Jessica thought. Besides, she had always liked Sophie and Gus. They had been unfailingly kind and fair-minded about her family, especially when her father died, Jessica recalled.

"I was about to put up some peach preserves when Gus had his accident," Sophie admitted. "I had all the jars cleaned and ready. The peaches are ready, too. More than ready," she added. "Think you'd like to try it?"

Jessica had never made preserves. She wasn't quite sure of what she was getting into. "Sure, I can do that," she said gamely.

Sophie glanced at her, a half-smile curving her mouth. Jessica guessed the older woman knew she didn't spend much time in the kitchen. But Sophie didn't say a word, only reached into a drawer and pulled out a big apron. She handed it to Jessica and put on one of her own.

"You'll be doing me a big favor by helping with this job," Sophie said. Then she fixed Jessica with a surprisingly stern look. "Now, as you might know, my recipes are strictly confidential, so I have to ask you not to give away any of my secrets."

Jessica raised her right hand solemnly. "Absolutely not," she promised. She smiled, deciding this might be fun.

Sophie led her into the pantry and showed her the jars. There were dozens of them, sparkling clear glass with gold screw-top lids. Sophie didn't really plan on filling them all . . . did she? Then Jessica saw the peaches in large bushels on the floor. Enough to fill the back of Sam's truck . . . and then some.

"We can bring the stuff in little by little," Sophie said.

Jessica certainly hoped so. She soon found herself set up at the kitchen table with a paring knife and a chopping block.

Sophie quickly blanched a batch of peaches in a large pot of boiling water, cooled them off under running water, then gave them to Jessica.

"All you have to do is peel off the skin, cut out any brown spots, and slice the peaches into wedges," Sophie said.

It seemed easy enough when Sophie did one, peeling off the skin in one long ribbon.

But the peaches were remarkably slippery. Jessica could barely peel a strip an inch long before the knife would slip and she would have to start again. She was glad that Sophie's back was turned so that she couldn't see her struggle.

Unaware of the fierce Woman versus Peach battle going on behind her back, Sophie chatted happily, mixing things in big bowls and checking the huge boiling pots of water.

"If you do this right and you've got a nice, sweet batch of peaches, you've really got something in these jars," Sophie promised. "When you're in the thick of winter and feel like the cold will never end, it's a wonderful thing to take out a peach and hold a little bite in your mouth. Even just the smell of them brings the whole summer back to you. Like sunshine in a jar."

Yes, it was like that when you ate good preserves, Jessica thought. This was a summer she would enjoy looking back on. So far, anyway.

"I'm going to give you some of these to take home, of course," Sophie promised. "For your sister and your mother. And some for Sam, naturally," she added, nodding to herself.

"Sure," Jessica said calmly, but the peach she was trying to slice flew out of her hand and bounced across the table.

"So, what's up with you and Sam?" Sophie asked her point-blank.

Jessica froze in surprise. "What do you mean?"

"I believe we used to call it keeping company when I was young."

"Well . . . we're dating," Jessica admitted. "You know, nothing serious."

Sophie glanced at her over her shoulder. "Maybe you ought to get more serious. Sam is a catch. I'd hang on to him if I were you."

Jessica didn't know what to say to that. Sophie certainly was entitled to her opinions. And she knew the Potters thought well of Sam.

"I was twenty-nine years old when I met Gus," Sophie went on. "That was old for a woman to still be single back then. Not like today. I envy you girls. You can do what you please. We were all expected to catch a husband and have kids. I had a boyfriend, but he died in Korea. I thought maybe I'd never get married."

"Then Gus invited you over to his orchard?" Jessica guessed.

Sophie snorted. "The orchard was in my family, not Gus's. By the time we met, I had inherited the whole place, and I was trying to run it on my own. I figured I would just live up here all by my lonesome. But I was still praying every night for a husband. I don't mind admitting it," Sophie added with a shrug. "Then my half-brother Albert came back from the army, and he brought Gus around. You should have seen my husband back then. He was quite good-looking. Had wavy dark hair. He was very vain about it, too. He looked just like Cary Grant. Maybe you don't know who that was?"

"Yes I do." Jessica bit back a smile recalling the suave, gorgeous leading man. How anyone could think that Gus Potter resembled him was a mystery. Well, they always said love was blind. . . .

"So it was love at first sight?" Jessica asked, genuinely curious.

"Not at all," Sophie said, surprising her. "I never once thought, well, this is the one, the one I was praying for. I nearly missed my chance with him entirely. Gus is quite a few years younger than me, and I thought, well, I'm too old for him. He isn't going to want an old lady like me. And then when he asked me out, I still wasn't happy." She gave a rueful smile. "I wouldn't even see him. I thought, he's fresh out of the army, no prospects at all. He probably just wants me for my orchard."

Jessica laughed. Seeing the Potters now, who seemed so close they barely had to talk, it was hard to imagine that they ever had the slightest bit of romantic trouble. It was hard to picture Sophie as a disappointed spinster . . . or Gus as a dashing would-be gigolo.

Sophie picked up a bowl of sliced peaches and carried them over to the counter. "It all worked out somehow, with God's help. When we announced our engagement, we thought everyone would be surprised. But they knew way before we did. Sometimes you don't think it's the right one, and it really is," Sophie added. "Sometimes a person just gets in their own way. Know what I mean?" she asked kindly.

Jessica felt too self-conscious to really answer. "I guess," she murmured, and kept slicing peaches.

To Jessica's relief Sophie then changed the topic to less personal matters—Emily's speech at the parade and this year's wildflowers.

It was late afternoon by the time Sam and the others returned to the house. Sam's eyes met Jessica's when he came in, and he gave her his special smile. She felt herself melting a bit under his gaze, then caught Sophie's knowing glance and felt herself blush.

"Someone's been working hard." Sam walked up beside her and put his arm around her shoulders.

"We made some peach preserves," Jessica said.

"So I see." But he wasn't looking at the glass jars of preserves at all. He was looking only at her.

"You ought to ask Sophie for the recipe," he teased. "I like what it does to your hair." The steamy kitchen had made small curls spring out around her face, and he reached out and gently tugged on one.

"All of Sophie's recipes are secret," Jessica replied softly. "Everyone knows that."

Sam smiled at her, his face moving so close that she was almost sure he was going to kiss her.

Then Sophie interrupted with an offer of cold drinks out on the porch, exchanging a smile with Jessica as she walked by.

They left the Potters' a short time later, with the back of Sam's truck nearly filled with jars of preserves, Sophie's pies, honey, and fresh fruit. Jessica insisted it was far too much, but Sophie told her to pass along what she couldn't use.

"You were a big help to me today, dear," Sophie said as Jessica left. "I hope I was to you, too."

Sophie's story had been touching. But did it really apply to her? Jessica wondered, glancing over at Sam. Was she getting in her own way or just being prudent?

As they pulled away from the orchard, Sam thanked her for coming with him. "I never thought you'd get stuck in that hot kitchen all day. I really didn't think we'd be there that long."

She glanced at him. She had the window on her side of the truck completely open and was enjoying the fresh breeze on her face and in her hair.

"It's all right. I know how to make preserves now. That should come in handy at the bank," she joked.

"As Granny Morgan used to say, 'It's a dull day that passes when you don't learn something.' "

"The same granny with the dandelion soup?"

He nodded. "That's right."

They were coming up to a roadside stand, famous for its fish sandwiches and fried clams. "Want to stop and get something to eat?" Sam asked. "I'm pretty hungry."

"I am, too," Jessica said. "Why don't we take it out to the beach?"

"Great idea," Sam said, pulling the truck up to the food stand. "The beach will be practically empty now, and we still have a few hours before sunset."

They picked up some sandwiches and cold drinks, then drove out to Durham Point. The food was messy and Jessica's sandwich fell apart in her hands after a bite or two. But she didn't mind. It tasted extra good out in the ocean air. Or maybe just because she was hungry? Sam laughed at her and wiped a glob of mayonnaise off her chin.

"There, now you're perfect again."

"Absolutely," she agreed.

They took a long walk on the beach, out to the jetty near the lighthouse. There they sat on the rocks, watching the sun go down. The air was much cooler, the breeze off the rocks wet with spray.

Sam sat behind her and circled her with his arms. Jessica leaned back against his strong solid chest, and he pressed his lips to her hair. They sat together for a long time, even after darkness fell and the nearby lighthouse found them with its gentle, sweeping light.

Jessica felt good with Sam today. And right with the world. A rare sense of harmony and peace filled her, and she decided, for once, not to dissect it.

Later, when they got back to her house, Sam helped her carry in the bounty from Sophie's kitchen. Jessica glanced around for the cat, noticing her food dish was still full.

"I wonder where Elsie is," she said. "She didn't touch her food. Maybe I locked her outside by mistake."

She went to the back door, looked out on the porch and in the yard.

"Jessica." She heard Sam calling from the kitchen. "I found her. She's in here."

He stood holding open the broom closet in the kitchen,

a funny smile on his face. Jessica followed his gaze and looked inside. "There, right next to the hot water heater," he said.

Jessica saw her cat, stretched out at the back of the closet, surrounded by tiny kittens. "Oh, my goodness!" She crouched down to get a better look.

Sam stood next to her, laughing. "I thought you were just feeding her too much."

"So did I," Jessica confessed. "She's been acting a little odd lately. I thought maybe she just had a hairball or something."

"Looks like six of them," Sam said.

"The vet never mentioned she was pregnant," Jessica said, still shocked.

Sam crouched down next to her, grinning. "I think you need to find a new vet."

"What do we do?" Jessica asked him.

"You can give her a towel or something soft to lie on. I don't think you should touch the kittens yet, though. She'll come out when she's ready."

"Poor Elsie, you must be exhausted," Jessica said. Then she turned to Sam. "I'm going to have seven cats running around here pretty soon."

"That should be interesting." He stood up. "I think you can give them away when they're six weeks old. Maybe I can help you find homes for them. I'll ask around."

"Thanks, I'll ask people I know, too." Jessica stood up next to him. "Six weeks should be enough time."

She felt badly talking about giving away the kittens when they were just born. She would probably get pretty attached to them in six weeks. But the summer would be over by then. And she would be moving back to the city.

Jessica glanced up at Sam and realized that she didn't really want to think about that. She no longer felt the same eagerness to leave Cape Light that she felt a few weeks ago.

Sam slipped his arms around her, still looking highly amused. "Think I can leave you on your own with seven cats—or do you need reinforcements?"

"I'll be fine," she assured him. "After umpteen jars of preserves, I can handle anything."

They kissed good night. Smiling, Jessica watched through the windows as Sam walked out to his truck. She was so tired she thought she might drop into bed with her clothes on. But once she showered and put on her night-gown, she felt too restless to fall asleep right away.

She picked up her father's old Bible from her night-stand. Ever since Sam found it in the bookcase, she'd read a little each night before she went to sleep. She didn't always understand what she read, but she usually came across one or two verses that struck a chord. She opened the Bible to a random page and glanced down to see what she found:

". . . And the peace of God, which passeth all under-standing, shall keep your hearts and minds. . . ."

A few minutes later Jessica turned off the light and lay in bed, thinking about the verse. She had felt peace today, unquestioning and secure. It would be wonderful to feel that way all the time. Was that how you felt if you really believed—so settled and safe?

But faith seemed to be something you had to accept without doubts or questions, and Jessica knew she just didn't think that way. Her mind was always picking things apart, analyzing them, wanting everything to be clear and defined, rational and linear. It was why she was so good with numbers.

She didn't have a very strong faith, she realized. She didn't have much faith at all. How did you get to be like Sam, or Emily even? she wondered. What happened in-side a person to make them like that?

She remembered then that she'd agreed to go to church with Sam the next morning. Should she try to get out of it? No, she decided, that would be a rude thing to do to Sam.

Then again, she would probably run into her mother and Emily there. She hoped that her mother wouldn't insult Sam again. Each time Jessica had seen her mother lately, Lillian asked about Sam, then made some cutting comment about him. It was completely unfair, and it made Jessica angry. But at the same time the comments encouraged her own doubts. She knew that if she ever decided to stay with Sam, she would have to face her mother's harsh censure.

The next morning Jessica met Sam in front of Cape Light Bible Community Church before the service. She was late, so late that she was sure he must have thought she wasn't coming. Sam was standing alone on the steps when she arrived.

"Sorry. I lost track of time," she greeted him breathlessly.

"I don't think it's started yet. Let's go in." He took her hand and they went inside.

They quickly found seats at the rear of the church, on the far left side. Jessica looked around for her mother and Emily and was relieved to see that they were up front in her mother's usual spot. She actually had a chance to avoid Lillian. Sitting in the back, she and Sam would be among the first ones out. Maybe her mother wouldn't even see her here.

Suddenly Jessica felt ridiculous, like a high school girl sneaking out on a forbidden date. She was in church, for goodness' sake, with a man she respected and enjoyed seeing. She wasn't going to skulk around, as if she were doing something to be ashamed of.

When the congregation stood for the first hymn, Jessica was surprised to hear Sam sing. He sang with a strong, rich baritone and didn't falter on the notes.

At the end of the service they walked out toward the

front of the church and waited their turn to greet Reverend Ben.

"Jessica, nice to see you this morning," the reverend said, shaking her hand.

The look in his eyes said more, though. Jessica was certain that what he meant was that he hoped he would be seeing her back in church again. She wasn't sure. She enjoyed the service. It gave her a good feeling to take a break from her ordinary, hectic routine and think about the bigger questions. But going to church still felt like something that other people did. Maybe she would come back again, she thought. And maybe she wouldn't.

Warren Oakes walked over to speak to Sam about a repair he wanted Sam to do on one of his properties. Jessica stood by as the two men spoke, waiting for her mother and Emily to emerge from the church. When she saw them she caught Emily's eye first and waved. Emily waved back, looking surprised to see her. Then her mother finished speaking with Reverend Ben and saw her, too. She started to smile—then spotted Sam.

"There's my mother and Emily. I want to say hello to them," Jessica told Sam, deciding to run interference.

To her dismay he said, "Of course," and fell into step beside her.

They met at the bottom of the steps. "Good morning, Mother," Jessica said.

"Good morning to you," her mother returned. She glanced at Sam, then sharply looked away.

"Hello, Mrs. Warwick," Sam said calmly, unfazed by Lillian's snub.

Lillian turned to face him, her eyes sharp and angry. "I don't have anything to say to you, young man. And I've told my daughter that I think she's very foolish and headstrong to waste her time in a relationship with you. Very foolish."

"Mother, how dare you?" Jessica said quietly.

Sam put his hand on her shoulder, a steadying touch that helped her regain control. "I know you don't like me, Mrs. Warwick," he said evenly. "But Jessica seems to. And she's the one who has to decide if I'm wasting her time."

Jessica saw her mother's eyes widen and feared what she might say next. Then Emily took their mother's arm and leaned toward her. "Let me take you to the car now, Mother," she said in a low, firm voice. "People are watching. You don't want to make a scene."

Jessica quickly met Emily's glance. They both knew that Emily had pushed the one button that would control Lillian's temper. Their mother abhorred the idea of making a public spectacle of herself—though she seemed to do it almost every time she left her house, Jessica reflected wryly.

Lillian glanced up at Emily, then back at Jessica and Sam.

"Yes, I need to get home," she said to Emily. Then to Jessica she added, "I'll call you tonight, Jessica. And I don't want to speak to a machine."

As they watched Emily lead Lillian away, Jessica felt Sam take her hand. She held on and returned his grip, appreciating his quiet strength. She really didn't know what would come of this relationship. But Sam had been right. It was up to her to decide.

"Want to go get some coffee?" Sam asked.

"Sure," Jessica nodded, thinking this was as good a plan as any.

They picked up some coffee at the Beanery and walked down to the harbor. Jessica felt as if all the good feelings from the service had been dispelled by her mother's harsh words.

Sam must have sensed she was feeling down. He didn't say much, and when they sat down he reached out and rubbed her shoulder.

"I apologize for my mother . . . again," she said wearily.

He met her gaze and she could see from his tight expression that the run-in with her mother had made him angry. With good reason, she thought.

But finally he looked out at the water and just shook his head. "Let's just forget it," he said. "Besides, I've got a little surprise for you. How would you like to waste this beautiful day with me and go sailing?"

"Sailing?" Jessica sat up, her spirits instantly lifted. "How? You don't have a boat."

"Harry's got one in his yard he's been fixing up to sell. Somebody just left it there, didn't want to pay the storage. A Piper Ensign," Sam said, naming a small, well-balanced boat that could easily be handled by two. "He said I could take it out any time I like. Sort of a test-drive. I think he's trying to sell it to me. What do you think, want to try it?"

"I'd love to. I hope I remember what to do, though. It's been a while."

Jessica hadn't been sailing in several years. Though Paul sometimes suggested they rent a boat, somehow they never did. Actually, she hadn't heard much from Paul since he went to the Midwest. Their few phone calls had been stiff and awkward. She wondered if whatever spark they had in the spring had been worn down by the long distance now between them. She honestly didn't think of him much, and at times, like today, he seemed very far away.

"I haven't been out in a long time, either," Sam said, putting his arm around her shoulder. "Luckily, it doesn't look too windy. Don't worry. I've seen you at the beach—you're a strong swimmer. If anything goes wrong, I'm trusting you to rescue us."

She saw the light in his eyes and knew he was teasing her. She was eager to go out, though. They had talked about it a few times, and he knew she loved to sail but rarely got the chance.

An hour later they were out on the water. Working together to maneuver the boat out of the harbor, they fell into an easy partnership. Despite Sam's modesty, he was an able sailor, and Jessica's feel for handling the boat quickly came back to her.

As the shoreline receded from view, Jessica didn't think at all about her mother's remarks or her confusion about Sam. She felt far away from everything, surrounded by water, sky, and wind.

When it was Jessica's turn to take the tiller, the mainsail caught a strong, steady breeze, and the boat skimmed along quickly, heeling gently to one side. Sam glanced back at her with admiration. "You're good at this," he said.

"Thanks." She smiled back. "I really do love being out here. I guess I forgot how much."

Sam came back and sat next to her. "Maybe you should buy the boat. I could talk to Harry for you, get you a good deal."

The boat was in good shape but old. Jessica was certain she could afford it, but the notion wasn't very . . . practical.

"I can't have a boat. Where would I keep it?"

"Right here, in the harbor," Sam said. "There's plenty of room."

"But I'd never get to use it, living in Boston."

"Oh, that's right." Sam touched his forehead, as if he'd forgotten. Jessica felt nervous for a moment. She didn't want to get into that conversation again. But Sam just smiled, leaned back, and stretched out his legs. "Well, maybe you'd have to stay here, then. For the boat, I mean."

She gave him a rueful grin. "Right, for a run-down, used sailboat. Tell Harry I'll think about it."

They spent the entire day on the water, sailing all the way to Southport, where they tied up at the village dock and went into town for a bite to eat. They started back to Cape Light before dusk, watching a crimson sunset from the water. By the time they approached the village it was dark.

"Oh, look," Jessica said as they motored into the harbor. "Main Street is lit up like a miniature village under a Christmas tree. It's so pretty from the water."

"It's a beautiful world, don't you think?" Sam asked.

"Yes, it is," she agreed softly.

It was a beautiful day that she was sorry to see end. When she got back home she didn't find a message on her machine from her mother, as she had expected. It was late, so she decided she would call her the next day from the office.

But Monday morning passed in a whirlwind of activity, and Jessica didn't get a chance to call. She was not surprised when she picked up the phone at lunchtime and heard Lillian's voice.

"Jessica, did you take your lunch break yet? You need to come over here right away," Lillian said without any greeting.

Jessica felt her heart begin to beat faster. "What is it? Are you all right?" she asked anxiously.

"I'm fine, fine and dandy. But that cleaning girl Molly Willoughby walked out in a snit and left this place a complete disaster. The vacuum cleaner is all in pieces. The furniture is rearranged every which way. There's a bucket of suds in the middle of the kitchen floor and the mop, dripping wet, right where she dropped it."

"She walked out in the middle of mopping the floor?" Jessica didn't quite understand the story. Maybe Molly had an emergency with one of her children. "Why?"

"Why? Why does someone like that do anything?" her mother railed. "Because she's ignorant and disrespectful, that's why. Though I can't say I'm the least bit surprised, when you consider the woman's background. . . ."

Jessica gritted her teeth in an effort to ignore the last comment. "There must have been some reason," Jessica said. "Did you make some comment about her work?"

"I made a comment about her brother," Lillian said pointedly. "But you already know my feelings on that subject."

"Yes, I do," Jessica said curtly. "I guess I'm getting the full picture now."

"The full picture is my home in complete disorder. Are you able to come or not?"

"Yes, I can come. I didn't take lunch yet, so I'll be right over." She glanced at her watch. "Don't go into the kitchen. You might slip."

"It's a regular obstacle course around here. I don't dare get out of the chair."

Jessica could tell that it wasn't so much the house as her mother's equilibrium that had been turned upside down. She was undoubtedly going to get a full catalog of the Morgan family's shortcomings.

Well, if it gets too bad, I'll make some excuse to return to the office, Jessica told herself.

THE NEXT DAY JESSICA MET EMILY FOR LUNCH AT THE Beanery, where they compared notes about their mother's run-in with Molly.

Jessica had also heard another version of the story from Sam, who held Molly and Lillian equally responsible.

"Molly's got a hot temper," he told her. "She shouldn't have let Lillian get under her skin."

Easier said than done, Jessica thought ruefully. She really couldn't blame Molly for taking offense.

"So what do you think really happened?" Emily asked after a waiter brought their iced lattes and salads.

"It seems Mother told Molly that Sam wasn't good enough for me, or some such outrageous comment. And, of course, Molly got angry and told her what she thought of our family." Jessica rolled her eyes. "You can imagine the rest."

"Yes, well, to tell you the truth, I was expecting a meltdown, especially after Sunday," Emily admitted. "Mother can be so impossible."

"How do you do it?" Jessica asked. "I mean, how do you remain so patient with her day in and day out? I've only had six months of it, and sometimes I think I'm going to scream."

"Practice," Emily said with a grin, but then her expression became more serious. "I've come close to losing my temper a few times," she admitted. "But I pray for patience and compassion. And I remind myself that after Father died and our world was falling apart, Mother was the one who held it all together for us."

"I think about that, too," Jessica admitted. "I know how hard it was for her to stay in Cape Light after the trial—when everyone treated us like outcasts."

"Lillian Warwick has never lacked either pride or courage," Emily said. "It must have been dreadful for her when Father was found guilty. Imagine being raised in a wealthy Boston Brahmin family, marrying for love, and then watching your husband gamble away his fortune and be convicted for embezzlement."

"Mother married for love?" Jessica asked. "*Our* mother?"

"You never knew that?" Emily replied, sounding surprised.

"Well, I knew that there had been some falling-out between Mother and her family, and that was why we never saw any of them," Jessica recalled. "But I guess I never really knew why. Because they didn't like Father?"

"They didn't think he was good enough for her. Despite all of the Warwicks' money. When she met Father she was already engaged to a man from her family's social set back in Boston. But she went against her parents' wishes and married Dad anyway. People say it was love at first sight."

"Really?" Jessica asked, astounded.

"Yes, really," Emily replied with a laugh. "Hard to imagine, I know. But that's why she couldn't leave Cape Light. After Father died, she was too proud to make amends with her family. Of course, they must have heard about the scandal. But as far as I know, they never offered to help, or even tried to contact her."

"How do you know all this? Did Mother tell you?" Jessica asked curiously.

"Of course not." Emily shook her head. "It's not the kind of story she'd share with us. You know that. Sophie Potter told me."

"How sad," Jessica said, trying to take it all in. Once she married against her family's wishes, she was too proud to return to them later when it all fell apart.

It was so strange, she thought. Here was Lillian disapproving of Sam when she had defied her own parents to follow her heart. You would think she would understand.

Jessica met her sister's thoughtful gaze. "Thanks for helping me out yesterday," she said.

"Oh, I didn't do anything, just dragged her off to the car," Emily said.

"I don't know why I even let it bother me so much," Jessica said. "Sam seems to handle these situations much better than I do."

"Yes, he's really very . . . centered," Emily said with a nod. "He's very dignified."

Jessica was surprised by her comment, though when she thought about it, she felt the same way. "I wasn't sure what you thought of him," she admitted.

Emily smiled. "I like Sam very much. I've always liked him. But I am surprised to see you two together."

"We're not that different," Jessica heard herself say. "Not as much as you'd think."

Her observation surprised her, but once she said it aloud, she knew it was true.

"So it's getting serious, then?"

Why was everyone asking her that question? Was it something in the water around here?

"No . . . I mean, I don't know. I don't think so," Jessica said, twisting the straw in her drink. "Sam and I are just going out. For the summer." She paused, then added, "There's this other man I've been dating. His name is Paul. We went out a little in the spring, but he's in the Midwest on business for the summer. We've stayed in touch, though. When I get back to Boston, I'm sure I'll start seeing him again."

Emily looked down and took a bite of her salad. "So you like this Paul more than Sam?"

"Well . . . not better, really." Jessica sat back, trying to find the right words. "It's just . . . different. Paul and I have a lot in common. We talk about our work. He has his own consulting firm, financial analysis, reorganizations. That sort of thing. He's very successful."

"Oh, I see." Emily pushed aside her plate. "Well, maybe that's just as well, then. If things were more serious with Sam, I think one of you would need to make some serious compromises for it to work out. I can't really see Sam leaving here to live in the city."

"Yes, I know that," Jessica said quietly. Emily had just offered the exact line of reasoning Jessica had given Sam. But for some reason that Jessica didn't quite understand, she felt disappointed by it—as if her sister didn't understand her feelings.

"I might be wrong," Emily went on, "but I think

you've set a course for a certain kind of life. And I don't think it's the same life Sam wants."

"You don't think we'd be happy together?"

"I'm not sure. . . ." Emily glanced at her. "Who can really predict these things? I think Sam is great. But you seem to have doubts, and then there's this other man in the picture," she added. From her expression, Jessica thought her sister was really trying to understand. At least that was some consolation.

Then Emily reached across the table and patted her sister's hand. "Oh, don't pay any attention to me. What do I know?"

What *did* Emily know? Jessica asked herself. Her sister had very little romantic experience, as far as Jessica could tell, at least lately. It seemed all of Emily's romantic impulses were played out when she was much younger.

Jessica knew that when Emily was due to leave for college, she had run off to Maryland and eloped with a young man Lillian disapproved of, a fisherman from a nearby town who was in his early twenties. About a year later Emily's young husband died in a car accident. Her mother had gone right away when Emily had called for help and soon after brought her home. Far more sedate and dutiful than when she left, Emily went on with her life in Cape Light, almost as if her marriage had never happened. As far as Jessica knew, there had been no serious relationships for her sister ever since.

So how could Emily really understand how she felt about Sam? Or Paul? Jessica wondered. Then again, Jessica had to admit that she didn't really understand herself, so how could anyone else?

As Jessica finished her salad, the two sisters briefly discussed finding new household help for Lillian. "We can take turns helping her until we find a replacement for Molly," Jessica suggested.

"I'll ask Sara Franklin if she can help out," Emily said.

"She's been coming over to read to Mother a few times a week, and they seem to get along well. Maybe she'll pitch in temporarily. We'll pay her, of course."

The waiter brought the check and Emily snagged it. "It's my treat," she insisted. "You deserve a treat after yesterday. Besides, we don't get together much. I hope I'll see more of you before the summer ends. I'll miss you when you go back to Boston."

Jessica was touched by her sister's admission. Maybe they didn't understand each other completely, but she did love Emily and felt that Emily loved her.

"I'll see you," Jessica promised. "Don't worry."

SAM FOUGHT BACK A STAB OF IMPATIENCE. HE WAS AT Molly's house, sitting on the living room floor with Lauren and Jill. They were all watching a nature show on TV while they waited for Molly to return from her errands. Sam couldn't help it. He simply was not in the mood for watching peregrine falcons build their nests. Besides, he had somewhere he had to be.

He had just checked his watch for the third time when he heard Molly at the front door.

"Mom's home," he said, jumping up. He went into the kitchen and helped his sister unpack groceries.

"Want to stay for dinner?" Molly offered. "We're having tacos."

"Not tonight, thanks," Sam said, grabbing his jacket off the chair. "I'm already late to meet Jessica."

"Oh, that again." Molly turned her back on him as she put a carton of milk in the refrigerator. "You know what they say, if you want to see how a woman is going to turn out, just take a look at her mother. . . ."

Sam didn't want to get into an argument, but maybe it was time he did.

"You're being unfair," he said carefully. "Jessica is nothing like her mother."

"Oh, really? I think they have the same nose. It's up in the air," she mocked. "Way up."

Sam felt another stab of impatience. "Oh, come on, you're being silly now."

"Am I?" his sister asked. "Look, I'm sure it's a thrill to date a Warwick. But you can't be serious about her, Sam."

"What if I am?"

"You're an idiot, that's what. I can't imagine what you're thinking. She's not for you, can't you see that?"

"You keep saying that, but you never say why."

"I'm worried about you," Molly told him. "With all the women you could end up with, why her? She'll never make you happy. Jessica Warwick will always act like she's above you, too good for you. Too good for anybody, just the way she was in high school."

Sam sighed and rubbed his forehead. "Look, I appreciate your concern. But you have no idea of what actually goes on between me and Jessica. You don't even know her. Except for high school, which was a very long time ago. Are you the same person you were back then?" he asked quietly. He saw his sister's expression change and knew he'd made a point. "You don't like it much when people judge you by your past, but you're doing the same thing to her."

"I'm just worried about you," Molly said, but more gently this time. "I don't want to see you get hurt."

"I know that," Sam said, touching his sister's shoulder. "But can't you see I'm happy with Jessica? All I'm asking is that you give her a chance."

He watched her take a deep breath. "If you say so," she said reluctantly. "But I'm sure glad I'm not working for that dragon lady mother of hers anymore."

Sam laughed. "I'm glad, too," he said. From the beginning he thought that the combination of Lillian and Molly spelled trouble. "See you later."

Just as he started to leave, his nieces ran into the kitchen. "Did you ask Mom about the . . . you know what?" Lauren asked eagerly.

"Oh, I almost forgot."

Molly crossed her arms over her chest. "Go ahead, spill it. You know how I love surprises."

"Jessica's cat just had kittens. I told the girls I'd ask if you wanted one."

"Me? Why would I want a cat? I hate cats."

"Please, Mom? *Please?* We'll take care of it totally," Lauren promised.

"We'll do everything," Jill added. "Honest. It can even sleep in our room."

"Let's talk about it later, girls," Molly said, rolling her eyes. "Thanks, pal," she said to Sam.

As Sam went down the stairs, he heard his nieces begin a new wave of begging. He had a feeling they were going to win this one.

THE CLEANING CREW HAD CANCELED AGAIN, AND Charlie was stuck at the Clam Box, mopping up. It was after midnight when he finally got home. He expected to find Lucy asleep, but she was sitting up in bed, reading a book.

He sat on the edge of the bed, pulled off his shoes, then unbuttoned his shirt. He couldn't wait to shut his eyes.

"How are you doing?" Lucy closed her book and put it on the nightstand.

"I'm beat, that's how. I should have slept there. It would have added some time in the sack tomorrow morning."

"Why don't you ask Fred to open up?"

"Fred can't do breakfast. He'll mess up everything."

Charlie stood up and rubbed his back with both hands, thinking about a hot shower.

"Listen, Charlie," Lucy began, "I know you're tired, but I really need to talk to you about something."

He looked down at her. She had that little crease between her eyebrows that came when she got worried or lost her patience with the kids. "Charlie Junior's teacher call again?"

"No, nothing like that," she said. She got up and reached for her robe. "You know those college catalogs you found? Well . . . they don't belong to Sara. They're mine."

"Yours?" He didn't get it. "What are you talking about?"

"I want to go back to school, Charlie. I want to finish my degree and be a nurse."

He blinked, wondering if he heard her right. Lucy couldn't go back to college. What would she do in a college? "Are you crazy?" he finally asked.

"Now, Charlie, don't just brush me off like that. I'm serious," she insisted.

He could tell by the look in her eyes that she was. But she was kidding herself if she thought *he* would take this loony idea seriously.

"What kind of dreamland are you living in, Lucy?" he asked tiredly. "How are you going to go back to school? Did you win the lottery and forget to tell me that, too?"

"I know it will cost money—"

"You're darned right, it will."

"—I've looked into that, Charlie," she said calmly. "I can take loans. I'll pay them back once I'm working."

Charlie stared at her and rubbed his face with his hands. Why in heaven's name did she have to pull this on him tonight? Couldn't she see the kind of pressure he was under? The police investigating him. His best friend, no less. The diner losing money every day since those blasted Beans came to town. The election coming up, and he had hardly done a thing about it yet.

"Money is tight now, Lucy. You know that. We can't take loans for you to go fooling around in college. You'll never finish, and the whole thing will be a waste of my money," he said harshly. "If we're going to take a loan for anything, it will be to pay for my campaign. I have support and I know I can win. *That* will be doing something for us."

"Something for you, you mean." Lucy folded her arms over her chest, her face red and angry looking.

She was going to cry any minute, he could tell. He felt sorry for her even, but he couldn't let on. Not now. The message hadn't sunk in yet.

"When I'm mayor, it's going to be good for our whole family," he argued. "For pity's sake, haven't we been talking about this for years now? It's my time. I'm going for it. That means I'll need you to pick up the slack at the diner. And what about the kids? What are they going to do while you're in college? You have responsibilities here, Lucy. Did you forget that?"

"Of course, I haven't forgotten. I wouldn't be at school every minute. Just for classes," she explained. "The kids are big now. They can practically take care of themselves. I sent in an application and I was accepted, Charlie. At the community college in Southport. I could start in Sept—"

"That's enough!" He put his hands over his ears, feeling fury well up inside. "I don't want to hear another word about this. No college. You're not going to college! Understand me?"

Lucy's mouth trembled. Tears ran down her cheeks, but she didn't seem aware that she was crying. "Sometimes I just . . ." She shook her head, then put her hand over her mouth. "I can't talk to you. I don't know why I even try," she said, shaking her head.

Charlie stared at her, his hands on his hips. Was she giving up now? He hoped he wasn't going to hear any more about this college nonsense. It was the most insane idea she'd come up with in a long time. She had to see that, didn't she?

"Mom? Mommy? . . ." He heard their youngest son calling.

"It's Jamie," Charlie said. "You'd better check on him."

Without answering, Lucy turned and walked away from him. She reached into her robe pocket for a tissue and wiped her eyes before entering Jamie's room.

"What is it, honey?" She leaned over her son's bed and put her hand on his forehead. "Do you feel okay?"

Half-asleep and dressed in his train pajamas, Jamie looked much younger than eight. Out in the world, he was a little man. Right now, he looked almost like a toddler again.

"I had a bad dream. About a vampire. He was chasing me with his claws." He lifted his hands in the air to show her.

"Oh, my, that is scary." Lucy sat on the edge of the bed and hugged him. She didn't know why, but she felt like crying again. *He probably heard us arguing,* she thought. *That's what woke him up.*

"Do you think you could fall back to sleep now?"

He looked up at her hopefully. "Can you stay with me a minute?"

"Sure, I can." She sat up again and fixed his covers. "I'll sit right here. You go to sleep now, okay?"

He rolled over onto his side and curled up in his favorite sleeping position. Lucy knew he'd drop off again in a minute or two.

She loved her children, more than anything on God's green earth. She loved being a mother. She was good at it, too. But she felt so bad now—empty and cheated.

Lucy felt tears welling again and blinked them back. She wanted to do something more with her life than bringing up kids and working at the diner. Charlie was so selfish sometimes. He could only see her a certain way. It just wasn't fair.

BLUEFISH WERE RUNNING, AND THE BOSTON RED SOX were only one game behind the first-place New York Yankees. Steadfast fans, like Harry Reilly, woke up knowing that when the day was done, the Sox could be sitting in the number one slot. If they grabbed an early lead and hung on tight, they could make it this year, all the way. He was praying on it, too, as he drove down to the harbor to meet his fishing party—Sam, Digger, and the Reverend Ben.

The group met at half-past five, soft-spoken and unshaven, ready to fish. They loaded Harry's boat with their supplies for the day, including three thermoses of coffee, a bag of fried-egg sandwiches, a box of doughnuts, tackle boxes, rods, reels, and buckets of bait. When Sam carried on not one but three foam coolers, Harry looked up at him with a challenging gaze. "What's that for—in case we wash up on a desert island?"

"Ice for the catch," Sam said simply, jumping aboard.

Harry shook his head and tugged on his cap as he turned toward the stern. "A boatload of optimists," he muttered to himself.

"True fisherman always are," Digger assured him with a wink.

Harry's Boston Whaler was outfitted with twin outboard motors, a small cabin with two bunks, and an open cockpit above. It notably didn't have a fish finder, but Digger vowed he'd find plenty.

"Your arms will get sore from pulling them in," he promised.

"We'll see," Harry replied evenly. "The guy who lands the biggest fish buys dinner, right?" he asked as he took the wheel.

They all nodded in agreement. It was their tradition. Like most men, they found a bit of competition made the fishing more exciting.

Harry started up the engines, and Sam and the reverend pushed off. With his Sox cap pulled down tight, his fishing vest flapping in the wind, Harry drove the boat at full throttle due east, until the shoreline disappeared from view.

Nearly forty minutes later they reached what Harry considered to be the right spot. He dropped anchor, and the three friends assembled their rods and quickly cast off.

Carolyn had given the reverend a MacGregor double-reel pole for his birthday. He hadn't tried it yet in open water, only sand-casting from the beach at Durham Point.

Sam and Harry liked to joke that they did it all wrong down in Gloucester, the fishing village just south of Cape Light, where the reverend had grown up. Ben would give them a tolerant smile, then cock his arm back and with a flick of his wrist show off his stuff. His father was a professional fisherman, who taught his son the trick of it when the boy could barely reach over the edge of the boat.

Sam usually spent Saturday with Jessica but didn't mind getting out on the water with his pals today. They were only able to get away together for these fishing trips a few times each summer.

He would see Jessica tomorrow night. They planned to have dinner and go to a movie. He hadn't asked her to meet him at church in the morning. He had asked her the week before, and she had given him some plausible excuse. But he knew she just didn't want to go, and he didn't push it. After the run-in with her mother, he didn't blame her. At least their day out sailing had been just about perfect. But something changed after that; he couldn't quite put his finger on it. Maybe his argument with Molly had thrown him off, stirred up doubts.

Sam was in love with Jessica. He knew that by now. He had been involved with women before, and he knew what was real and what was not. But sometimes he thought if it was right, it ought to be easier than this. There seemed so much they still had to work through.

Sam expected the fishing to be a distraction from his Jessica problem, but as the sun rose higher, he found that casting about for a bite—elusive so far—gave him too much time to think. When the group decided to pull up the anchor and try another spot, Sam moved up front to the cockpit and took the wheel.

As they cruised north of the Point, the reverend joined him, holding a soft drink.

"Hot out here today," the reverend observed. "It must be too hot for the fish. I'm beginning to think they've all gone down to the bottom, trying to get out of the sun."

"We'll find a few that like to sunbathe," Sam promised. "Digger can always find them. He says he's got a fool-proof spot."

"How about Jessica, does she like to fish?"

Sam glanced at him. "I don't think so. She likes to sail, though. We went out about two weeks ago. Harry lent us a boat."

"I'd love to have a sailboat. You know, something small. But it's a great deal of work," Reverend Ben said. "And I don't really have the time for it."

"I know what you mean," Sam replied. He saw a land-mark Digger had mentioned and steered to the right. "When I'm not so busy maybe."

"Maybe you'll have one with Jessica someday . . . or am I assuming too much now?"

"Hard to say, Reverend," Sam answered carefully. "You can't call a ball game in the sixth inning."

"Oh." Ben fixed his cap, which had been lifted by a

gust of wind. "I'm sorry. I thought maybe it was further along than that."

Sam laughed to himself. "I thought it was, too. But some things happened. We had a talk. It wasn't exactly what I wanted to hear." He paused to lower the throttle. "I love her," he said simply. "No doubt in my heart about that. But I'm not half sure this is going to work out. And I don't know what I'll do if it doesn't."

He felt Ben watching him but didn't turn his head. Then he felt the reverend's hand on his shoulder, and something in his touch made Sam feel as though Reverend Ben understood what he was going through.

"I'd like to say something bright and optimistic to you, Sam. But no one can say what God has in store for us. You and Jessica may or may not stay together, but I believe God always gives the best to those who leave the choice with Him," Ben said quietly. "And no matter what happens, think of Jessica and how her faith has grown."

Sam raised one dark eyebrow. "Do you really think it has?"

"I watched her face when she was at Sunday service two weeks ago," the reverend told him. "I truly believe she felt the peace of the church, and that alone could be a good thing." He looked at Sam approvingly. "I think you played some part in that."

Sam was quiet for a moment, thinking about what the reverend said. "I'm glad for Jessica. I think she's happier, too. Sometimes I think if we just had some time, it could happen for us. Then I get frustrated and I just want to know the answer. Even if it's going to hurt, I just want to know and get it over with."

"Be patient, Sam. Let events unfold," the reverend counseled. "To feel real love for someone is a miracle. It's as close as we come to the Divine in this lifetime and truly its own reward. Love wholeheartedly, without fear, and you'll find it's the most powerful force we know on this earth. Love can work to wear away many differences. But I believe it works best like water on stone," he added with a small smile. "Not like dynamite."

Sam smiled broadly and nodded. "All right, Reverend. I understand—no dynamite."

"Is the radio up here?" Harry Reilly suddenly pushed his big body into the small cabin. "Doubleheader at Fenway," he explained anxiously. "First pitch is at one-fifteen."

While Harry worked on the radio, Digger gave Sam directions for the exact location of his foolproof spot. A short time later they dropped anchor, baited their hooks, and cast off.

There was no action at all through two scoreless innings. Harry groused, saying they ought to move again.

Then the fish began to bite, everyone's line tugging at once. The school was so thick, the slick curved bodies could be seen breaking through the water, jumping all around the boat.

The men swung their lines in the water and out again, pulling in fish after fish. The empty coolers were filled, then Sam dumped out the food and drinks to fill the others, as well.

The four friends stayed out on the water until sunset. They returned to the harbor cheered by the Red Sox's double victory and their coolers full of fish. It was impossible to say who had hauled in the largest of the lot, which didn't stop them from debating the question, long and loudly.

Sam settled the matter of who would buy dinner by having them all up to his place, where he cooked a simple but fine meal of grilled bluefish with all the trimmings.

"I HAVE SOMETHING SPECIAL FOR YOUR BIRTHDAY, Jessica," Emily had said over the phone, "but I'm afraid you have to come here and pick it up. Can you stop by my house, oh . . . say one o'clock on Saturday? I'm sorry, but that's the only time I can do it."

Jessica found herself both touched and surprised. Her sister and mother always sent cards, but neither had given her a birthday gift since she was a child. "Of course I'll come," she had told Emily and promised to be there at one.

ON SATURDAY EMILY GREETED HER AT THE DOOR with a kiss and a hug. "Your gift is in there," she said, pointing to the living room.

What could it be? Jessica wondered as she walked ahead to the living room. All this mystery was very unlike her usually straightforward sister.

Jessica's eyes widened as she noticed a balloon drifting up toward the ceiling. Then a group of familiar voices called out, "Surprise!"

"No!" She jumped back, smiling, laughing, and even crying a little all at once. She looked back at her sister, who smiled but looked teary-eyed as well.

"Happy Birthday, Jessica." Emily walked over and gave her another hug.

"Why did you do this? You didn't have to go to all this trouble for me. It's not a special birthday or anything."

"Every birthday should be special, I think," Emily countered. "And it was no trouble at all. Just some lunch and cake. I really wanted to. Besides, I never got the chance before."

Sam came over to her and kissed her. "Happy birthday, Jess," he whispered, smiling into her eyes. "You were really surprised, weren't you?"

"Totally," she said, shaking her head.

Emily had also invited two of Jessica's friends from work, Suzanne and Dana. She quietly mentioned that she invited their mother, too, but Lillian didn't want to come.

"Oh," Jessica said, feeling badly about that. *Maybe it's just as well, since Sam is here,* she realized a moment later.

Jessica enjoyed every minute of the celebration, including blowing out her candles. When she made her silent wish, it came out more like a little prayer: *Let me find the right resolution and peace in my heart about Sam.*

"Good job," Sam said as she blew out the candles in one breath. "What did you wish for?"

She met his gaze. "It doesn't come true if you tell."

Sam smiled at her, but she noticed that the smile didn't quite reach his eyes.

While everyone ate birthday cake, Jessica opened her gifts—a CD from Suzanne, perfume from Dana, and an antique sequined purse from Emily that they had admired one day when they were in Grace's shop together.

"Oh, Emily . . . this is so beautiful," Jessica said, lifting the purse to admire it. "It's too fragile to use. I'm going to have it framed in one of those display boxes."

"I knew you liked it." Emily smiled at her, looking satisfied. "I was so relieved when I went back to the Bramble and it was still there."

Sam leaned over her chair and whispered in her ear. "I need to give you my gift in private," he told her. "How about afterward, down at the dock?"

"Okay," Jessica agreed, but Sam's request set off a chain of anxious thoughts in her mind.

She had an awful feeling that it was going to be jewelry—an expensive bracelet or even a ring—something that would imply a commitment if she accepted it. If he gave her a ring, then what would she do? They would have to have another heavy conversation, and she dreaded that. And she hated the idea that she might hurt him.

Jessica and Sam were the last to leave the party. Jessica hugged her sister at the door. "This was so sweet of you, Emily. Really." Jessica gazed at her sister, feeling overwhelmed with emotion. She had rarely felt closer to Emily and was sad that the afternoon had to end. "I can't remember ever having such a nice birthday," she said.

"I'm glad," Emily replied sincerely. She smiled and patted Jessica's shoulder. "I just wanted to do something special for you."

"You did," Jessica assured her as they hugged again.

"Nice party," Sam said as he and Jessica walked toward her car.

"It was perfect," Jessica agreed, feeling another twinge of apprehension. She just hoped that the rest of the afternoon wasn't about to slide into disaster.

Jessica drove, acutely aware of the way Sam sat back, looking at her with that secret smile on his face. She wished he'd look out the window or something.

"Where shall we go?" she asked when they reached the village.

"Park down by the harbor," he said. "We can sit out on the dock, and I'll give you my present."

They walked out on the town dock, hand in hand. Jessica thought back to the first time they came here together, the night he stopped by to look at the hole in her ceiling. That seemed so long ago now.

Though it really wasn't, she reminded herself. They had come a long way in a short time. *Would they go much further together?* was the question.

They sat on a bench at the end of the dock. Sam took a small box out of a bag he'd been holding.

"Here you are," he said softly. "Happy birthday."

She glanced up at him, then down at the box in her hands. It was carefully wrapped in fancy paper with a thick satin bow. It appeared to be from some expensive store—a jewelry store probably—and Jessica felt nervous all over again. It was heavier than she expected, though. Definitely not a ring. That was some relief. Now she had no idea what it could be and tore off the wrapping.

She opened it slowly and saw a glint of gold through the tissue. It was jewelry. Oh, dear. . . . Then she folded the tissue back.

And couldn't figure out what it was.

She picked it up and stared at it. Some kind of brass handle? A fancy paperweight?

Sam watched her, his hand on his chin, nearly covering his mouth so he wouldn't speak.

"It's a winch," he said finally.

"Oh . . . right." She nodded and glanced at him. She still didn't understand.

"It has an inscription on the handle. See it?"

She checked the handle for the writing and found it. *Wishing you smooth seas and a steady breeze, wherever you may roam. With love, S.M.*

Smooth seas? She looked up at him. No . . . he didn't. She met his gaze, his dark eyes shining, his wide smile answering her unspoken question.

"This is a handle . . . to a winch. On a sailboat," she finally pieced together.

"That's right." He nodded and pointed out in the water. Jessica looked and saw it tied up a short way down the dock, the sailboat they'd borrowed from Harry.

"I bought it from Harry for you," Sam said.

"You didn't really—" she said, still staring at it bobbing gently in the water. It had a big plastic bow tied to the jib, the kind people put on houses at Christmastime.

"Yes, I did." He nodded again. "I wanted to get you something I knew you really wanted. . . . I can refinish the wood inside for you and get some new brass fittings. I had Digger repaint the hull," he added. "But you have to choose a new name."

Jessica stood up. She didn't know whether to scream at him or throw her arms around him. He was impossible, infuriating, totally . . . beyond belief sometimes. How could he have done this when she had been so clear with him?

"I can't believe you," was all she managed to say.

Sam got to his feet and put his hands on her shoulders. He looked into her eyes, almost smiling but not quite.

"I can't believe how I feel about you," he said quietly. "I just want to make you happy, Jessica. Don't you like the boat? I thought you loved it."

When he looked at her like that, with his heart in his eyes, her head felt overruled, and her own heart, overwhelmed. She looked down and swallowed.

"I love the boat," she said quietly. *And I probably love you, too,* she nearly added. "But I can't accept it from you, Sam. You must realize that."

"Why not? Why can't you?"

She glanced at him and then away. "I just can't. You know why. . . . Why do you have to make it so hard for me?"

"Why do you have to make it so hard for yourself?" he asked in a low, quiet voice that held just an edge of anger. When she looked up at him, she saw the emotion in his dark eyes, his anger and frustration. His disappointment. And his love.

She didn't know how to answer.

"Just keep it and enjoy it, Jessica," he said. "It makes me happy to give it to you. I'm not asking you to make any promises here."

She sighed and touched his cheek. "I know you're not . . . but it's still the same. Whether you ask or not, I can't accept a gift like this from you. I can't let you keep hoping I might stay here when I won't."

His hopeful look hardened, and his eyes looked glassy with anger . . . or maybe even tears. Her heart ached for him. He stepped closer to her.

"Think about it a little. You don't have to decide now."

She moved away from him and folded her arms across her chest. Clouds slid across the sun, and Jessica felt chilled.

"Give it back to Harry, Sam. He'll understand."

She felt him staring at her for a long moment, but she didn't dare look up at him again.

"Sure, I can give it back to him," he said finally. "That part's easy."

He turned and looked out at the water. The breeze tugged on his shirt. She felt the impulse to put her arms around him and hide her face against his strong back.

She'd never known anyone like Sam. Most likely, she never would again.

He glanced back at her. "I'll do it now," he said angrily, and started walking toward the boat.

"Right now?" Jessica stood a short distance away, watching him untie the lines.

He nodded, not even looking at her. He untied the lines from the dock, tossed them on the deck, and jumped onboard.

Jessica watched, feeling sick. She wished desperately that she could say something that would make things better, erase all the hurt. Her hair blew across her face and she pushed it away.

Sam yanked the pull cord on the motor, and it started right up. "I better get this over with. Before I make an even bigger fool of myself."

He put the gear in forward and turned the boat away from the pier. Jessica moved to the end of the dock. "Sam, don't go like this, please. We really need to talk. Please?" she called out.

At first she wasn't sure if he heard her over the sound of the motor. Then he glanced at her over his shoulder. He lifted his arm and waved, but she didn't wave back. Was this good-bye? Was it over now between them? Sam watched her for a moment as he turned the boat around toward Harry's yard. Then he looked away, out at the open water.

CHAPTER TWELVE

"THE PROBLEM IS THERE'S NO HARD EVIDENCE," Chief Sanborn explained to Emily. "Phone records show the call was made from a pay phone out on the turnpike. That's all we could come up with. George Godwin, the owner of North Bay Development, received the call. He couldn't even describe the voice very well, except to say that he thought the caller was a man."

Chief Sanborn's voice held an edge of frustration. He liked to get to the bottom of things, Emily knew. "We know someone called North Bay and told them if they bought Dr. Elliot's land, they wouldn't get permits to build. But we don't know who it was."

"I finally tracked down the guy who was working at the gas station that night," Tucker Tulley added. "I interviewed him twice. He thought he saw someone using the phone near the air pumps. But he couldn't say for sure."

"Yes, I read the report." Emily leaned back in her

chair. A brown police folder sat open on her desk. "What do we do now?"

"Not much we can do," Jim Sanborn admitted. "None of the parties involved wants to file a suit. Mainly because they just don't know whom to sue," he added. "That phone call wrecked Dr. Elliot's sale, but they all seem ready to forget it."

Emily tapped her pen on the desktop. She'd made a few notes in the margin of the report and glanced at them before closing the cover. "As much as I'm reluctant to let this go, I guess we have no choice." She looked straight at Tucker. "You've done a good job here, Tucker. A thorough job, it appears to me."

Tucker nodded. "Thank you, Mayor."

They all knew what she meant. With Charlie Bates as the most likely suspect in this scenario, the assignment couldn't have been easy for Tucker. He looked soft as cheese, but the man really did have grit and integrity, Emily reflected.

"I suppose we'll just to have to wait and see what happens when Betty finds a new buyer," she said.

"Nothing, I hope," Jim said. "I hope the caller got scared off when he or she saw how we followed up on it."

"Yes, let's hope so," Emily agreed. "Has anyone told Dr. Elliot that you've finished the investigation?"

"We were waiting to meet with you first, Emily," Jim said. "I can call him this afternoon."

Emily paused. "Would you mind if I did?"

Jim looked surprised but shook his head. "No, not at all. Tell him to call me if he has any questions you can't answer."

Emily thanked the men as they left her office. When she was alone, she dialed Dr. Elliot but only got his answering machine. She left a brief message and hung up.

She was worried about him. Ever since he openly accused Charlie, she hadn't seen him around town as much. Lately, his house seemed almost deserted, with the shades nearly always drawn. He had come to visit her mother once in the last few weeks, but had since declined her invitations to their usual Sunday lunches.

Although Dr. Elliot seemed the quintessential tough old Yankee, Emily suspected he was more fragile than he let on. As unreasonable as it seemed, many people in town sided with Charlie on this issue and had made harsh, even untrue comments about the doctor. Emily only hoped that his land sale would move along smoothly now, and the issue would die down. And that Dr. Elliot would feel free to come out of hiding, if that was what was going on.

JESSICA STARED OUT THE WINDOW IN HER OFFICE, IR-rationally wishing she could board it over. Every time she looked at it, it reminded her of Sam. But everything did these days. She hadn't heard a word from him since he'd motored off on the sailboat.

It had been just over a week and felt much longer. Her feelings seesawed between believing it was all for the best and wishing she could just pick up the phone and call him. More than once she found herself in tears. She had talked to a friend in Boston about it, written in a journal. She even read a self-help book about how to move on from a breakup. Nothing seemed to resolve her conflicting emotions.

But maybe things would change soon. This morning she received an e-mail about a job opening at the Boston branch that she was qualified to fill. It was a good opportunity for her, and the transfer was just about guaranteed. She picked up the necessary papers from the Personnel Department and started filling them out.

She glanced down at the forms on her desk. It was slow-going. The questions were simple. The problem was more in the questions she read between the lines.

If she applied and it all went through, she could be back in the city in a few weeks. Her mother didn't really need her here anymore, not the way she had in the winter, and Emily would be very understanding, Jessica was sure.

But did she really want to leave Cape Light now? It all seemed so . . . abrupt. Maybe she just felt that way because of the way things were with Sam. They had just walked away from each other without really settling anything.

Sometimes Jessica found herself giving in to habit—picking up the phone, about to call Sam's shop or apartment. Then she would remember they weren't speaking to each other. While she knew that everything she said on the dock was true, she missed him. It hurt so much to think their relationship might really be over for good.

When Jessica got home that evening, she kicked off her shoes at the door and dropped her briefcase. She felt beat, too tired even to work in the garden. Her flowers were thriving in the last wave of summer heat. Elsie's kittens were thriving, too, and had basically taken over the apartment, either dashing about madly or sleeping in the most unexpected places. Last night, as she was making a cup of tea, she found one curled up on a shelf in the cupboard.

But she didn't have anyone to share the story with.

Maybe I'll feel better after a shower, she told herself, though she didn't really believe it. Still, when the phone rang minutes after she got out of the shower, she rushed toward it. Her mother or Emily, probably. Sam, hopefully?

Jessica forced herself to wait while the machine picked up. Her pulse jumped when she heard a male voice, then she recognized the speaker. It was Paul.

"I just got back a few days ago. It's been a real madhouse around here, of course, or I would have called you sooner. But I wanted to touch base and let you know I was back. . . ."

She picked up the receiver before he could hang up. "Paul? Hi, how are you?"

"I'm crazy, stressed, still running on Central Time and suffering from culture shock. Don't ever order pizza in Dudley, South Dakota, by the way. How are you?"

"I'm . . . good," she replied, sitting down in a kitchen chair. Elsie jumped up on the table, looking to be petted, and Jessica obliged.

"How has your summer been?"

"Busy," she said, "but fun. I've planted a garden here. Everything's in bloom now."

"Hmmm, I turn my back for a few weeks and you turn into Martha Stewart on me. You can get help for that, you know," he teased her.

She laughed but had the old feeling again—that she needed to be on her guard, to live up to Paul's expectations. Or what she thought they were. "I like to garden," she said simply. "Besides, there isn't much else to do out here."

She suddenly felt guilty, realizing she was being unfair to Sam. She was making it sound as though the time she spent with him was nothing. But it had felt like something. It had felt like something great most of the time.

"Sounds like I returned just in time to save you from your humdrum country life. I'm driving up to Vermont tomorrow, and I thought we could get together on my way back, on Thursday."

"Thursday?" Jessica's voice trailed off on a vague note. Not because she thought she had something to do. But because the idea of seeing Paul, going out on a date with him, was suddenly strange to her.

The strange thing was that even though she hadn't spoken to Sam in over a week and didn't have any idea of where they stood, dating Paul seemed terribly disloyal.

"Are you busy?" Paul asked, interrupting her thoughts. "Maybe you could come down to the city on the weekend."

"I-I'm not sure about the weekend. But Thursday night sounds fine," she said.

"Great." He sounded genuinely pleased, and they set a time to meet.

Jessica hung up, wondering if she'd done the right thing in agreeing to see Paul. All of a sudden it felt as if she were being pulled away from Cape Light. And from Sam. First the news about the job opening, now Paul. Maybe God was trying to send her a message. She'd never really thought that way before, but maybe there was something to this.

But when she was really honest with herself, she wasn't sure she wanted to leave here, after all.

Jessica closed her eyes and tried to pray. *Dear God, I'm new at this stuff. Sorry if I'm not doing it right. If you're trying to tell me something, could you please make the message a little more obvious? Thank you.*

ON THURSDAY NIGHT PAUL PICKED UP JESSICA AT SIX o'clock sharp. She didn't have much time after work to fuss with her appearance. She just pulled on a beige linen shift and wore it with low sandals and her hair down loose. At the last minute she added silver earrings and a few thin silver bracelets.

When she opened the door Paul's eyes lit with pleasure. "Either I forgot how pretty you are, or you're looking especially wonderful, Jessica."

He leaned over and kissed her cheek. Jessica felt her body stiffen; she couldn't respond in kind. Even though it was just a friendly kiss hello, suddenly all she could think of was Sam.

Paul stepped inside and looked around. "Cute place,"

he said. "I didn't know you liked antique furniture."

"Yes, I do. My mother loaned me some of these things. The rest of my furniture is back in Boston."

"Oh, that makes sense." He gazed around in a way that made her feel self-conscious.

"I just need to do something in the kitchen, then we can go," she said quickly.

"I'll come with you," Paul offered, following her.

Elsie and her kittens were nowhere to be seen. Jessica suspected that they were scattered about in various sleeping spots. But the minute she set down their dishes, they all rushed into the kitchen, mewing loudly.

"Yikes, it's a stampede," Paul joked as he stepped aside to let the cats pass by. One of the kittens started playing with his shoelace, and he knelt down and scratched it behind the ears.

"I didn't know you liked cats so much," he said, glancing up at her.

"I took in a stray, the mother," Jessica said, pointing out Elsie. "The rest are sort of an accident. I need to find homes for them pretty soon. You don't want a cat, do you? That one seems to like you."

"Me? No thanks." He shook his head and stood up. "I travel so much, it would be hard to have a pet. It's a big commitment," he added, gazing down at the kittens. "They are awfully cute, though."

"Absolutely," Jessica agreed.

Taking in a cat *was* a commitment. So was having a girlfriend . . . or a wife. Was Paul leery of all commitments? Jessica wondered. He was a nice man, and when they were together he seemed considerate and thoughtful. But she hadn't heard much from him while he'd been away. Maybe he just wasn't ready to make a commitment to anyone.

"Shall we go?" he asked.

"Yes, of course," Jessica agreed. She grabbed her

sweater and purse and headed for the door.

Paul had reservations at an expensive waterfront restaurant in nearby Newburyport. All the way there and straight through appetizers, Paul gave Jessica a detailed account of the business problems he encountered on his trip.

She was actually feeling a bit bored by the time the main course was served, even though Paul asked her advice on several matters and seemed impressed with her suggestions.

"You're very sharp," he said. "Want to come work for me?"

Jessica laughed. "Don't be silly."

"I'm perfectly serious," he insisted. "We'd make a good team. Your looks and brains. And my wheeling and dealing."

As her mother might say, he could talk a dog off a meat wagon. Still she laughed, flattered by his compliments.

"Paul, be serious. What would I do there?"

"Oh, I don't know. We could think of something. Calculate this and that. Money is money, Jessica, makes the world go round. What do you do at the bank? I'm sure they're wasting you there. How's the new job going, by the way?"

"Not so new anymore," she pointed out. "It's going fine."

The truth was, she had been cruising this summer at work. She did her job responsibly, of course, but she wasn't nearly as focused on it as she had been in the city.

Or had been before she met Sam, she corrected herself.

"I've put in for a transfer to the main branch in Boston," Jessica admitted. "It's a lateral move, same title, but there's much more going on there. I'm sure it will be more challenging for me. Better experience."

"Sounds good." Paul poured them each a glass of wine

from the expensive bottle he had ordered. "I hope it comes through. I'm glad to hear you're coming back to the city. I was wondering about that. It would be nice to be closer."

He smiled and met her gaze. The warm look in his eyes made Jessica uneasy. She looked away and took a sip of her water.

"It's not certain yet. I might not even get it."

"Oh, you'll get it," he said encouragingly. He lifted his glass. "Let's have a toast, to your victorious return from exile."

Jessica lifted her glass. He made it sound as if she had been banished to a desert island. And she was the one who had given him that impression, she realized.

The rest of the dinner passed slowly for Jessica. Paul did most of the talking. If he noticed that she wasn't contributing much to the conversation, he didn't let it show.

"So how's your mother doing?" he asked at last. "I guess she must be better if you're ready to come back to the city."

"She's still having physical therapy, but she's improved a lot this summer."

"I bet she'll be disappointed to see you go, though. And your sister, too," he added.

"Well, I haven't told either of them about the transfer yet," Jessica admitted. "I thought I would just wait and see what happens."

Paul nodded. "That sounds logical. From what you've told me, sounds like they both know you weren't going to stay here forever. Besides, Boston's not a very long drive. You can get back here in less than two hours if you're really needed again."

"Yes, that's right," she said. "I really won't be that far."

Jessica smiled in agreement, but the talk of leaving Cape Light was making her feel unbearably sad. She would be leaving Emily, whom she was just growing close to, and her mother, who might not have that many years left. Most of all, she would be leaving Sam, whom she already missed.

Jessica didn't realize that her feelings were so evident until Paul reached across the table and took her hand.

"Something wrong?" he asked kindly.

"No, not at all," she lied. "I'm just a bit tired, I guess. It's been a long week."

"I'm sure. Making a job change is stressful, even within the same organization. Then you'll have all the hassles of moving again," he said with a sigh. "If there's anything I can do to help you, I hope you'll let me know. I really want to speed along this process," he added with a smile.

"Thanks . . . I will," Jessica said hesitantly. The warm look in Paul's eyes made her uneasy . . . when once it would have made her so happy.

She wondered if she really could call on Paul for help. She knew he meant the offer sincerely, yet she didn't really see him as someone she could rely on. Somehow it seemed more likely that if she called Paul, he'd have some important business to attend to.

Unlike Sam, she couldn't help thinking, who would drop everything for a friend.

That didn't make Paul a bad person. He meant well, but his business was his real priority.

". . . but unfortunately, the world is a fiercely competitive place," he was saying. She hadn't even noticed that he had changed the subject. "A man's got to do what he has to in order to succeed—before the other guy does it to him. I can't help it, Jessica. I like fine things—good food and wine, nice clothes, tickets to the shows, an expensive car. I work hard and I want the very best."

He gave her a boyish grin. "I know people say money can't buy happiness, but it sure can buy an awful lot of stuff to distract you while you're waiting."

Jessica smiled. He hadn't said anything about true happiness, she noticed. What did all these trappings of success really add up to? Would Paul ever meet his goals—or would there always be something else just out of reach? She once thought she would be perfectly happy sharing a life with him, but now she wondered.

Again her thoughts returned to Sam, who was genuinely happy in his own skin, marching to his own drummer, not measuring his wealth by anyone else's standard. If Sam inherited a million dollars overnight, she doubted that would change him or his values. And if Paul suddenly decided to be a waiter, or dig clams for a living, he'd still be Paul. Sam would still really see and appreciate his surroundings, sharing himself with the person he was with. He would still value more than dollars and cents. Would Paul?

What am I doing here? Jessica asked herself. She had an urge to bolt from her chair, drive straight to Sam's house, and tell him about her revelation. She didn't want a relationship with Paul.

She tried to look interested as Paul talked on about a financial analyst he was working with. Paul thought she was sharp. Maybe with numbers. When it came to men, Jessica felt like an idiot. She had been so focused on Paul, she hardly noticed that Sam had come into her life and changed everything. She finally understood Sophie Potter's advice, about getting out of her own way.

"This waiter is awful." Paul frowned and pushed back his plate. "I'll just ask for the check. Let's go somewhere else for dessert."

"Uh . . . okay," Jessica agreed. The waiter seemed fine to her. The restaurant was quite crowded, and all of the staff were clearly working hard. Maybe it was just as well, though. She wanted to make this an early evening.

Unfortunately, when they reached Main Street in Cape

Light, the Beanery caught Paul's eye. "That place looks cute, sort of hip for this town," he said.

"It's nice inside," Jessica said. "They have good coffee."

"Who would have thought? Let's give it a try." He pulled into a nearby parking space.

A quick coffee wouldn't hurt, Jessica decided. And that would be that; she didn't expect to see Paul again.

To her surprise, Paul took her hand as she stepped out of the car. She felt uncomfortable with the gesture, but it was awkward to pull away.

As they turned to walk to the Beanery she saw two women coming out—Molly and a friend. Jessica met Molly's gaze and froze, like a deer caught in the headlights of an oncoming car.

Molly stared at her a moment. Then she glanced at Paul and the silver sports car behind him. She didn't look at all surprised. Molly's lips pressed together in what Jessica could only describe as a self-satisfied smile.

She thought I would treat Sam badly, and now she's gloating because she thinks she's right, Jessica realized.

"Hi, Jessica," Molly called, then she and her friend walked in the other direction, toward the harbor.

Jessica felt her heart sink. She was sure that Molly would give Sam a full report by morning.

I'll call him first and explain, Jessica resolved as she and Paul entered the Beanery. She would go to Sam's house right after Paul dropped her off. Even though it was late, she was almost sure Sam would talk to her.

No, I can't do that, she realized, her courage wavering. Once Sam heard that she was out with Paul, he would be hurt and probably furious. He might not even listen to the rest. Jessica didn't think she could face that now.

They were soon seated. Paul stared at her across the small table, his expression concerned. "Are you all right, Jessica?"

"Uh, sure . . . I'm fine," she answered. She sat up and studied her menu, though she knew that she was anything but fine. And maybe never would be again.

"IT'S A HOT DAY FOR CHOWDER," LUCY COMMENTED as she served the reverend his bowl of soup. "Good thing I gave you this seat under the air conditioner."

It was hot outside, over ninety, the air uncommonly still. The deep, heavy days of summer had set in.

"Yes, I know," he said. "But I was really in the mood for chowder." He spread a napkin over his lap. "My mother used to make this kind, Rhode Island. You don't see it on many menus."

Lucy smiled. "I think that's the same menu from Charlie's dad. I don't think we ever changed it."

Ben was taking a late lunch, enjoying the fact that the diner was in one of its rare, quiet lulls. "Where's Charlie this afternoon?" he asked, tearing open a packet of oyster crackers. "Is he ill?"

Lucy shrugged and put her tray under her arm. "Just out and about. Starting to get his campaign for mayor together," she added. "There's a lot to do."

"Oh, I'm sure." Ben nodded, tasting a spoonful of the flavorful broth. "Do you have a minute to sit with me, Lucy? I'd love the company," he encouraged her.

Lucy looked surprised but glanced around for the other waitress, who was making a fresh pot of coffee. "Sara, watch my tables a minute, will you?" she called. Then she slipped into the booth across from him.

"How are things, Lucy?" Ben asked.

She shrugged. "The same, I guess." She was silent for a moment, then said, "I know what you're asking. I told Charlie I wanted to go back to school. But it didn't go over so well."

"No? That's too bad," the reverend sympathized. "You must be disappointed."

Lucy nodded, playing with a pack of crackers. "He said we don't have the money right now, and he doesn't want to take loans."

"I see." Ben put down his spoon and wiped his mouth. "Is that so?"

"Charlie handles the money in our house, so it's so if he says it is." She sighed and sat back in her chair. "I think we could afford it if I did it a few credits at a time. I'm looking at going back to college as sort of an investment."

"It will be an investment, Lucy. In many more ways than one," Ben assured her.

"My husband doesn't agree. So that's that."

Ben felt moved by her disappointment. He could see it in her eyes. Dreams were important, no matter how distant or implausible they seemed to others. Dreams weren't about being rational or practical, he knew. If that was the case, civilization would have barely progressed; people would still be living in caves. There would be no inventions or vaccines or quantum theory. It was the dreamers who pushed us ahead.

"Don't give up, Lucy," Ben said simply. He reached across the table and patted her chapped hand. "Don't give up on your plans—or on Charlie. I'm sure this idea was a shock to him."

"That's putting it mildly," Lucy returned, smiling for the first time. "You should have seen the look on his face. He hardly understood what I was saying at first."

"Charlie may need some time for this news to sink in. He's used to the status quo, having you on hand to help him around here and take care of the household. Some of us don't like change very much. It makes us afraid."

He watched Lucy consider this theory. "I understand

what you're saying, Reverend. I think that's probably true about him."

"Did you ever hear the expression, God answers our prayers three ways—yes, no, and wait? Maybe you just pulled wait this time."

"I can wait," Lucy said patiently, "but I don't see how I can get Charlie used to the idea if he blows up every time I mention it."

"Whisper it, then," Ben advised, making her laugh. "Just don't forget to keep communicating. If you both shut down, you're stuck at square one."

"I suppose that's true." She shook her head. "Marriage is hard work sometimes. Know what I mean?"

"Yes, it is, but well worth it. The hardest part is changing ourselves, not the other person. It's a lifelong self-improvement course, you know."

Lucy laughed. "That's one way to look at it." She stood up and straightened out her apron. "I'll do what you said, Reverend. Thanks."

"You're very welcome. Hold on to your dreams, Lucy. And pray."

"I will," she promised, a certain look in her eye telling him she meant it sincerely. "Can I get anything else for you?" she added.

He paused. "Maybe you could turn up the air a notch? It is a warm day for chowder," he conceded. "I don't know what I was thinking."

"Sounds to me like you were thinking about your mom, Reverend," she said kindly. She smiled and turned away. "No problem. And I'll bring you a big glass of ice water."

WALKING HOME FROM WORK ON FRIDAY EVENING, Jessica wondered if Molly had spoken to Sam yet. She hated imagining that conversation but couldn't help herself. She had slept badly the night before and just about dragged herself through the day. Her boss had found a huge error in a loan application she handed in, and she had to stay late to correct the error.

But even that embarrassing event hadn't focused her. She could only think about Sam.

Again, Jessica thought about going to his house to talk to him. Right now. She wouldn't wait. She couldn't be timid about this. It was too important. Even if Sam refused to hear her out, she would feel better knowing that she had tried.

Then, as if in answer to her thoughts, as Jessica reached her apartment, she spotted Sam's truck across the street, parked near the barn behind the Bramble. It was after six. Sam usually wasn't at his shop that late. But he was there now.

Jessica's heart hammered. She forced her feet to step off the curb and cross the street. She nearly lost her nerve when she reached the Bramble but forced herself to walk down the gravel drive.

The shop door was open. Taking up half of the barn, the shop was cool and dark. Jessica inhaled the scent of fresh wood and varnish. She looked up at the ceiling that stretched up to the rafters. There was something peaceful yet purposeful about the place. She had only been here a few times, but somehow it always reminded her of entering a church.

Just like the first time they met, Sam was working with a noisy piece of equipment—a power saw—and didn't hear her come in. She stood near the doorway, not wanting to break his concentration. His face looked so intent.

Finally he turned the machine off. The piece of wood he had been cutting dropped heavily to the floor.

"Hello, Sam," Jessica said quietly.

He looked up at her and stepped back. "Hello," he said gruffly.

This was going to be harder than she thought. She took a breath. "I ran into Molly last night. I guess she told you by now."

"Yes, she told me." He put down the saw on the workbench. "How was your date? Did you have a nice time?"

"Sam—don't do that," she said quietly. "I really want to talk to you. I want to explain."

He shrugged. "You don't have to explain anything to me. I think I get the picture, Jessica."

He was acting so cold. She had never seen him like this, and it scared her. What if Sam really didn't care about her anymore?

"I did go out with Paul. The date was terrible. I never want to see him again." Jessica paused, trying to gauge his reaction. He stood over the worktable, lining up pieces of wood cut to the same length. She couldn't see his face.

"I thought about you," she went on. Her voice was trembling, and she took a breath to steady it. "I missed you the whole time, and I kept telling myself I was an idiot to go out with him."

Sam gave a careless shrug. "Maybe you should have figured that out before you went out with him," he said.

She felt her heart drop. This was hopeless. Sam wasn't going to give her another chance. She had ruined everything beyond repair.

"I wish I had," she said quietly. "But I didn't. Sometimes I'm really dumb about these things." Jessica sniffed and brushed away a tear.

Sam looked at her with regret. "That makes two of us, I guess. I didn't listen to you when you told me you had your doubts and wanted to go back to Boston. I know now, you were right. I thought we could share a good life here. But I wasn't listening to you. You wouldn't be happy staying in this town. With me. If it's not Paul, then sooner or later you'd find some other guy with a briefcase and a Mercedes."

"That's not true!"

"Isn't it? You kept saying it was fun going out with me, but it couldn't be more than that. Now I think what you meant was that it was fun to hang out with a guy like me, but I'm just not good enough for the long term."

"That's completely untrue!" Jessica protested. "That is not how I think of you." Even as she spoke, though, she knew his accusations held a kernel of truth.

She *had* felt that way about him in the beginning. But her feelings were so different now. Couldn't he see that?

Jessica dropped her head and wiped away her tears. When she looked up at him again, Sam said, "Listen, I'm sorry. But it's nobody's fault. All I'm trying to say is, I think you were right. This isn't going to work out. Let's not drag it out."

His hard, certain words chilled her. She had lost him. It was over.

"All right." Jessica straightened her spine and lifted her chin, determined to leave with dignity if nothing else. "We won't drag it out." She paused, wondering if she say should more, then added, "I applied for a transfer back to Boston. I should hear soon if they want me."

Dear God, please let him say he doesn't want me to go. Please let him give us another chance.

Sam turned away from her, measuring a board with a metal straightedge, making quick marks with a pencil.

"Sounds like it's settled for you, then," he said. "Congratulations. I guess I'll see you around before you go."

Jessica felt stunned, aching with loss. It hurt to breathe. She could hardly will her feet to move away but somehow managed to walk to the door. "Yes, I'll see you around, then. Bye, Sam," she said.

She slipped out the big door, into the thick, airless evening.

*   *   *

CAROLYN WAS MEETING AN OLD FRIEND FOR A DINNER in Newburyport and would be home quite late. Ben had no meetings, no wedding services to plan, no bereaved families to visit, no troubled parishioners seeking counsel. Though there was plenty of paperwork to catch up on, none of it was terribly pressing. It was so unusual, Ben double- and then triple-checked his date book.

With a rare free night Ben decided to drive to Durham Point and do some surf casting until the sun set. He knew he needed to get out of his office for a few hours, away from the church, as well. Earlier that day he found his letter to Mark in the mail, marked, "Return to Sender. No forwarding address."

For the longest time he just sat with the envelope in his hands and stared at it. Finally he had opened his top desk drawer and slipped it inside. It was not the right time yet for Mark to hear him. God had some other plan in mind. Ben had to believe that.

But out on the shoreline, not far from the rocky jetty and lighthouse, it felt good to work off his disappointment with the rod and reel. Timing his throw to the rise and fall of the waves required a kind of concentration that quieted his restless thoughts. It was a kind of physical meditation that sometimes made Ben feel as though the motion of his body and the motion of the sea became one. For Ben these were true moments of grace when the boundaries between mind and body and spirit blurred and dissolved, the way the line of the horizon and the edge of the sea seemed one vast blue continuum.

Surf casting always reminded him that God created a beautiful world for people to live in. And yet Ben often got so caught up with the little, worrisome matters that he often didn't see the beauty and the wonder—the ordinary, everyday miracle of the natural world that the Lord had provided to replenish the spirit.

He worked the line for a time, caught a few, kept one,

and threw the rest back. He put the pole aside and sat and watched the waves. The beach was empty, growing misty as clouds gathered on the horizon.

A young man walked toward him on the sand with a slow, uneven gait. Something about him seemed familiar, though Ben didn't really recognize him. He certainly didn't know him by name, though the stranger seemed to know Ben and smiled once he drew closer. He walked up and stood a short distance away on the smooth wet sand.

"Hello, Reverend. Catch anything?"

"To tell you the truth, I'm not really out here to fish. Just tossing the line out for exercise," Ben admitted with a smile.

"I get it." The young man smiled and looked out at the waves.

Ben picked up the rod and cast again, then glanced over at him. "I don't believe we've met. What's your name?"

"Luke McAllister." He met the reverend's gaze, then leaned over and offered Ben his hand.

"Nice to meet you," Ben replied. "I don't believe I've seen you at Bible Community Church," he added. "But maybe around town?"

"I sort of landed in the village for the summer. An unscheduled vacation." Luke shoved his hands into his pockets. "I stopped in the church a few weeks ago and heard your sermon. It made a lot of sense to me. Made me think about . . . important things, I guess. I wanted to say thanks."

"That's good. Glad to hear it helped. But there's no need to thank me. I'm just the instrument."

"The instrument?" Luke frowned and tipped his head.

"It's like thanking the telephone for good news," Ben explained with a smile. "I'm just the instrument for the Heavenly Spirit that speaks through me."

"Oh . . . sure. Yeah, of course." Luke nodded. "You'll

have to excuse me. I'm not a churchgoer. Haven't been in years, actually, except for dropping in on you."

Ben gazed at him, intrigued. "Why *did* you come? Not that I mean to pry, of course. You really needn't answer if you prefer not to," the reverend hastened to assure him. "I do get curious, though, when people tell me that sort of thing. I would like to understand, so maybe I can figure out how to have it happen more often," he explained. He shook his head ruefully. "I must sound like those bothersome calls, asking you to do a product survey."

Luke's smile grew wider. A pleasant smile, though Ben sensed the man didn't use it much.

"I was walking through town on Sunday morning, and when I passed the church, I just decided to go in for old time's sake. My family used to come up here every summer, when I was a kid. I just wanted to come in and look around, I guess."

Ben tried to picture what Luke's family might have looked like. "Let's see, I came to Bible Community Church eighteen years ago. Does that time frame overlap with your family's visits?"

Luke thought a moment, then shook his head. "No, not quite. We stopped coming to Cape Light just about that time. Besides, I think I would have remembered you."

"That's kind of you to say," Ben said. "What Sunday was this that you came?"

"Two or three weeks ago, I think. You were talking about guilt and worry, and how they rob you of today. Living in the past and worrying about the future, instead of living in the present." Luke paused and squinted for a moment, focusing his thoughts. "You said something about people who walk through life like a crab, looking backward instead of forward, missing what was right in front of them. Then you talked about accepting God's plan for your life. . . . I wanted to remember the verse you quoted, but I don't know the Bible."

"Oh, yes . . . I remember now," Ben said. He had borrowed the crab image from good old Digger. Not entirely original, but his old friend had seemed pleased when he noticed that Ben had woven it in. "I believe the verse was, 'And we know that all things work together for good to them that love God. . . . ' "

"Yes, that's it." Luke nodded.

"Romans, Chapter Eight, verse twenty-eight."

"I don't know. It just pushed a button or something," Luke admitted. "It was like a light went on in my head."

Ben smiled gently and smoothed his beard. He felt gratified to hear Luke say that. If he could truly touch even one person in his lifetime, his ministry would not be in vain.

For a moment the sound of the waves beating on the shore filled the silence between them. "You've been dwelling on the past," the reverend said finally.

"More like wallowing in it. Feeling sorry for myself—and feeling guilty about something that, I see now, I probably couldn't have changed, no matter what I did differently." Luke glanced away, at the white line of foam on the sand.

"We have less control over our lives than we think," Ben said.

"I didn't think that way before," Luke told him. "But maybe I do now." He shrugged. "I've been hanging around here, trying to sort things out. I wasn't getting too far, though. Then what you said, it just all hit home. It made me see I should be grateful for my life, not wasting it. Not angry and down on myself and making everyone around me miserable." Luke hesitated, then went on. "Something terrible happened, but I was spared. I was spared so I could live on. But I haven't been living."

Luke had shared enough for Ben to understand what he was going through. The details really didn't matter. The young man's life seemed to be taking a positive new turn. Ben said a silent prayer of thanks for allowing him to help Luke McAllister.

"Do you ever pray, Luke?"

"Not really . . . not since I was a kid," he replied. "I did that night, when I was scared out of my skin about what was happening to me. I prayed my—" He caught himself and flashed a quick grin. "I prayed really hard," he amended.

"Perhaps God answered your prayers," Ben said.

"Maybe," Luke conceded. "I guess I thought so at the time, when I woke up in the hospital. But then my life turned into such a mess, I guess I lost track."

"Maybe you're back on track now."

"I might be," Luke agreed. "I don't know, I think part of it is coming up here again. It just feels right to me. I've been thinking of staying here permanently."

"Have you? It's a great place to live," Ben assured him.

"I have some money now, from this accident I was in. I might buy a piece of property that's for sale outside of town, the Cranberry Cottages. That's where we used to stay. I heard it's for sale, and I had this sort of intuition when I was looking around for a more permanent place to live."

"It must bring back good memories."

"Yes, very good memories." Luke nodded. "I was just a kid then, but I felt very sure of myself, the way kids do sometimes. Like I knew who I was and exactly what I wanted to do with my life. Life was simpler then, of course. But I have to say back then I felt . . . invincible."

Empowered with faith, you could feel that way again, Ben wanted to say. But he kept his silence. The young man had been through a lot, a rough ride he had only hinted at. Luke needed to find his own way. Ben knew better than to push him.

This mention of Dr. Elliot's land was surprising, though, especially after all the controversy in town about who the buyer would be. Maybe God has some real-estate plans of his own, Ben reflected, amused.

Luke traced a circle in the sand with his toe. "I'm not sure about buying the land. I'm going to see the real estate broker tomorrow."

"Betty Bowman." The reverend nodded. "She's very professional, very knowledgeable about the area."

"Well so far, it's just a thought."

"Talk to Betty about it . . . and to God," Ben suggested. "Give it time. See if your intuition remains strong. Maybe it's not clear now what you should do with the property. But one step leads to another. Once you start, things have a way of falling into place."

"Yes, I can see that. Like running into you down here. I hope I didn't impose on you, Reverend. I appreciate you taking the time to talk to me like this."

"No need to thank me. I think we did have an appointment tonight. It just wasn't in my book," he said with a smile. "That happens to me fairly often."

Ben brushed off some sand. Out on the rocky jetty the Durham Light had just become visible in the gathering darkness.

"There used to be four whale-oil lamps up there," Ben noted. "Now it's an electric bulb, of course. With a light that can be seen more than twenty-five miles away, someone told me."

"Did the town build it, do you know?"

"It was the Durham family, actually. They owned this neck of land. They bought it from the Wampanoag Indians in the late sixteen hundreds. Joshua Durham built the light just after the Revolution. He even had the lens brought over from France. It's still the same one, too."

Luke continued to watch the light. "So it's more than two hundred years old, then? That's remarkable."

"Yes, it is, isn't it? Sometimes I wonder how many boats that light has guided safely past the harbor. A countless number, I'd imagine," he said as he bent to gather his belongings.

"Let me help you with your gear," Luke said, lending him a hand.

When Ben turned, carrying his fishing gear, Luke stood smiling at him. "I like your T-shirt, Reverend. 'God Answers Knee-mail,' " he read aloud.

Ben returned Luke's grin. "I got it at a conference last summer. Truth in jest. He does, you know," he promised Luke as they walked up toward the parking area together.

CHAPTER THIRTEEN

～

*If I know, then Charlie must know by now,
too,* Emily decided, snapping open her newspaper. He always had a way of ferreting these things out before her.
*But I won't bring it up and I won't gloat. That wouldn't
be either dignified or Christian,* she concluded.

Yet, as she sat in her usual morning spot at the Clam
Box, sipping coffee and scanning the *Messenger,* the
temptation was nearly overwhelming. For once she was
actually looking forward to seeing Charlie Bates.

Tucker came in and sat down next to her. "Good morning, Mayor."

Emily looked up. "How are you today, Tucker?"

"Above average, I'd say." He nodded to himself with
a cheerful air that did seem above average.

Sara came by and poured him a mug of coffee. "I have
some news for Charlie. But you might as well listen in. I
think you'll both be interested," Emily said.

"About Dr. Elliot's land, you mean?"

Tucker's cheerful expression dropped like a deflated balloon, and Emily regretted trumping him. "How did you know?"

"Dr. Elliot. He told my mother and she told me."

"And here I thought I had the inside line with Fran," he said, mentioning his wife, who worked for Betty Bowman. "Of course, she's not allowed to say anything until it's a done deal. But this one seems to be."

"Yes, it does—if the closing goes through without any problems," Emily said.

"I hear there won't be," Tucker offered, sounding pleased to have some authority on the subject.

Charlie came out of the kitchen and walked toward them.

"So did you hear?" Tucker asked him. "That guy from Boston, the ex-cop who's been hanging around town lately, he bought Elliot's land. Says he just wants it as an investment. He may not even rent out the cottages anymore."

"I heard," Charlie said grimly. He barely glanced at Emily.

Now that he was an official candidate in the election, he seemed to think that it was inappropriate to carry on any personal conversation with the current mayor. Which was fine with Emily.

He suddenly surprised her when he met her gaze. "Go on, say it. I know you must be busting to say something."

"Me?" She put down her mug and managed to keep a straight face. "I don't have anything to say about it, one way or the other. I never really did," she reminded him. "Of course, I'm glad Dr. Elliot found a buyer that no one seems to object to."

Emily was sure that Charlie felt foolish now for over-reacting. There was also the fact that the new deal with a nondeveloper dissolved one of Charlie's main campaign issues. That couldn't be improving his disposition, either.

"Well, we still don't know much about this McAllister guy," he pointed out. "Except that he seems to have an awful lot of money for an ex-cop. He says he's just going to hold on to the land, but who knows what he might have up his sleeve."

Tucker glanced at Emily. Charlie was reaching now, and they both knew it.

"It sounds as if he's had his problems, but he seems like a stand-up guy to me," Tucker said with a shrug. He gave Charlie a shrewd look and smoothly changed the subject. "So how's the speech coming, Charlie? Still working on it?"

The candidates were scheduled to speak at the upcoming Blueberry Festival, which was the unofficial start of the campaign. As the incumbent, Emily knew she had the advantage. The mayor always appeared at a number of the weekend's events, which gave her automatic visibility. But Charlie had his supporters and would draw a curious crowd, she was sure.

"I'm working on it," Charlie grumbled. "I like to speak in my own words, you know. I don't have anyone else writing these things for me."

He glared pointedly at Emily, as if she had a team of professional speechwriters hidden in her attic.

"I'll be interested to hear what you say, Charlie," Emily said. She didn't mean it as a joke, either. She had never heard Charlie give a real speech. So far she had only heard him hold forth from behind the counter of his diner.

"You'll get a run for your money, Mayor," he assured her. "Don't worry."

Emily grabbed her briefcase and left some money for the check. "I'm not the worrying type," she reminded him. "Good luck with your speech, Charlie," she added as she left the diner.

On the way out she passed Sara Franklin, who was

busy waiting on her tables. Emily smiled a greeting and left.

WHEN LUKE MCALLISTER CAME INTO THE DINER later that day, Sara was the only waitress on duty. She'd overheard talk all morning about his real-estate deal and knew that he was now her new landlord. She wondered what this would mean. Would he want her to move out or raise her rent? If he didn't bring it up, she would have to.

"Hi, Sara. What's good today?" he asked, glancing at his menu.

"There's a barbecued-chicken special. You can have a sandwich or a platter. It's pretty spicy, though."

"I'll go for the platter. I'm celebrating today."

"About buying the cottages, right?" she asked as she jotted down the order.

"You know!" He sounded disappointed. "I thought I'd surprise you."

Sara shrugged. "It's a small town. News gets around quickly."

"Very quickly. We just came to terms last night. So I guess this makes you my new tenant—and future neighbor."

Sara felt a small shock of surprise. She also felt Luke watching her, gauging her reaction. "You're taking one of the cottages, then?"

"I think so. I'm going to make some improvements, too. So just tell me if you need any repairs."

"That's okay. I don't know how much longer I'll be staying around here."

She saw a flash of surprise in Luke's eyes. He hadn't expected that.

"Oh . . . I thought you'd mentioned staying through the summer. But maybe I misunderstood."

"I may have said that. I'm sort of scattered these days.
I don't really know if I'm coming or going." She shrugged
and pushed her pad into the pocket of her apron. "I should
go and put in your order, though."

"Sure." He nodded, handing her back his menu. "See
you later."

Sara was sure that Luke thought she was a flake.
Maybe that was good—it might make him less interested.
Luke was definitely attractive, and that was the problem.
She wasn't ready for another layer of complication in her
decision.

She honestly didn't know whether to stay or to go. Her
mission was accomplished, she realized. She had gotten
to know Emily and even Lillian. But lately she felt more
and more like a fraud. She had even begun avoiding Emily, feeling the pressure of her secret every time they
spoke.

Sara was thinking she might just leave Cape Light
without telling Emily about their true relationship—without causing any problems for her. That meant she really
should go before the election campaigning started up.

Sometimes that seemed like the right thing to do.

HELD ON THE SECOND WEEKEND OF AUGUST, THE
annual Blueberry Festival marked the beginning of the
end of summer. Perhaps that was why the village went
all out in their celebration of the small but formidable
berry.

The festival started on Saturday morning, with a ten-
kilometer race through town that attracted runners from
all over the country. Emily ran in it every year, just for
fun, since she was the slow-but-steady type of jogger. Lillian, of course, disapproved, thinking it terribly unfitting
for the mayor to gallop all over town in her track shorts,
getting all sweaty and red-faced. None of that bothered

Emily. She didn't want her office to set her apart. She enjoyed being out there, taking part. People in the town seemed to like it, too.

In the gazebo on the Village Green, musicians, a magician, a juggler, and Mr. Lucky and His Amazing Dogs performed. There was also a crafts fair with a row of long tables where cakes and concoctions—all containing blueberries, of course—were offered for free by local restaurants, bakeries, and ice-cream shops. Of course, there was a prize for the best blueberry pie, and another for the fastest blueberry pie eater.

Though Emily had been attending the festivals since she was a girl, she was still amazed by the sheer number of blueberry-connected events that the program committee came up with. Probably the most popular was the ceremonial crowning of Miss Blueberry and her glide down Main Street on a float that looked like a giant blueberry sundae. Least popular was the inevitable speech by the official representative from the National Blueberry Foundation, relating more information about blueberries than most people ever wanted to know. Emily had the facts practically memorized by now, including the scientific proof that the modest blueberry contained more antioxidants than almost any other readily available fruit.

For Emily it was a demanding two days. Her schedule called for introducing a number of events, giving several speeches, and doing her best to meet as many of the voters as possible. The most dangerous part was that restaurant chefs and amateurs alike all wanted the mayor to sample their blueberry creations. The last time she campaigned, she gained ten pounds, then quickly had to work off fifteen.

On Saturday afternoon, after yet more blueberry concoctions were forced on her, Emily started toward an empty table, balancing several paper plates. She stopped as she caught sight of Sara Franklin standing nearby.

"Hello, Sara. Want to join me? I have enough dessert here for a family of five, I think." She glanced down at the plates in her hand. "You've got your choice of pie, cheesecake, ice cream, sorbet, and—cooked up by the health-food store—a blueberry-tofu muffin."

Sara glanced at the dishes and smiled. "You never order dessert at the diner. I guess you're making up for it now."

"Come on, help me out here," Emily coaxed her. "There are two seats, right over there."

Sara seemed tempted, but she shook her head, her long, straight hair falling against her face. "Thanks, but I'd better not. . . . I'm on my way to meet someone at the crafts fair."

"Oh, sure," Emily replied, but Sara's reason struck her as strange. She had never seen Sara with any friends in town, she realized. *Not that it's any of your business*, Emily chided herself. Maybe the girl was just shy.

"Well, feel free to bring your friend over," she suggested to Sara. "Everything looks really yummy . . . except maybe the muffin," she added.

"Maybe I will . . ." Sara met Emily's gaze, then stared down at the ground. Emily thought Sara looked as if she wanted to say something more—something hard for her to put into words, she sensed.

"I'm probably leaving town soon. I'm not sure yet," Sara said finally. "I just wanted you to know . . . because of Lillian and all."

"Oh . . . I'm not sure what to say," Emily said honestly. She finally set down her dishes on a nearby table. "My mother will be sorry to hear that. So am I. . . . When are you leaving?"

"I'm not sure. I thought I would speak to Lucy about it this week. I don't want to leave her shorthanded. It's hard enough for her lately, with Charlie campaigning."

"Yes, I'm sure." Emily still felt surprised at the news,

though she knew Sara never meant to stay. "Well, that's nice of you to think of her. I hope you won't go without saying good-bye?"

"Of course not. Don't worry, I'll let you know."

"Thank you." Emily reached out and touched Sara's bare arm. She was really such a pretty young woman, seemingly without any awareness of it. Emily smiled at her gently. "Have fun."

"I will, thanks." Sara grinned. "Don't eat too many blueberries." Pushing the strap of her backpack a bit higher on her shoulder, Sara turned and walked away.

Emily watched her until her slim figure disappeared into the crowd. With a sigh, she sat down at a table with her dishes of blue desserts. They all looked rather unappetizing now. She took a halfhearted taste of the pie with her plastic spoon and gazed around at the milling crowd. The festival had drawn a record number this year. She would get the official numbers tomorrow, but Sunday afternoon was usually the height of it.

She didn't know why, in the midst of so many people, she suddenly felt so alone. So . . . invisible. She was probably just tired; low energy always lowered her spirits. But Sara's news had unexpectedly made her feel sad. She didn't know the girl well, and yet she was going to miss her. Jessica would be leaving soon, too. Just when they were starting to grow closer. It didn't seem fair.

Maybe it was just the start of another election, Emily reflected. All that chatting up of acquaintances and strangers somehow made it so much more acute that she had no strong ties in her life. So many friends, acquaintances, supporters, connections . . . but no husband. No child.

She liked being mayor, doing a job that she felt made a difference. But she knew she struggled daily not to lose her authentic self. It was easy to get caught up in the vivacious, hand-shaking role of mayor, to the point where she started to believe that role was her real personality . . . or more accurately, all there was to her.

And if she didn't get elected again, what then? Of course, she'd find some other way of earning a living, return to teaching maybe. But what would be the point of her solitary life, really? What was the point right now?

This turn of her thoughts surprised her. *Maybe blue food brings on a blue mood*, she joked to herself. The man from the Blueberry Association never mentioned that.

"Can we have a picture, Mayor? Maybe tasting a bite of that pie?"

Emily usually obliged such requests automatically, but this time she raised her hand in front of her face, waving Dan Forbes and his roving photographer aside. "Not right now, if you don't mind."

"Sure," Dan said, glancing at her. She saw him tell the photographer to take some photos of another table, then he turned back to her. "Are you okay?" he asked.

"I can refuse a photo once in a while." She forced a smile but knew it wasn't convincing.

"Of course you can. We have a few of you already— a great one of you crossing the finish line at the race." Dan sat down in an empty chair. "I've already got the caption—'Mayor Warwick Runs Again.' Or maybe just 'See Emily Run.' "

Emily smiled and this time it wasn't forced. "Cute. I might have that framed for my office."

"Are you sure I can't get you something?" Dan sounded concerned. "Some cold water maybe?"

She considered his offer a moment, then shook her head. "Time to announce First Prize on the bake-off. I'd better get back to the stage."

"Sophie Potter, right?" Dan prodded.

"Who else could it be?" Emily replied.

"I wish, just for one year, I could run the winner's

photo with the recipe alongside it. Just once," Dan said in a mock frustration. "But we ask and ask and she never gives it to us. I've even resorted to bribes—a free lifetime subscription to the paper, delivered to her doorstep."

"Tempting bait, indeed. The woman has willpower, doesn't she?" Emily joked. She rose from her chair and raked her short tousled hair with her fingers. "Sophie's writing a cookbook. Haven't you heard?"

"She's been writing that book since I was in grade school. I'm starting to get suspicious."

It was a slight exaggeration. But not by very much. His observation made Emily smile.

"You're a writer. You know how these things take time." Emily lifted her hand briefly, waving good-bye. "See you later."

"Of course. The show must go on, Mayor," he said, watching her easy stride as she walked away.

JESSICA STROLLED THROUGH THE THICK CROWD IN the Village Green, and looked up at the stage in the distance to see Emily front and center. She was about to give someone an award for . . . something. Something having to do with blueberries, of course.

Jessica had seen Emily once or twice over the weekend, but her sister was so busy, they barely said hello. *I'll call her tomorrow,* she thought. *Maybe we can get together for dinner.*

She was very aware of the fact that she wouldn't be in town much longer, and she would miss Emily.

Jessica came to the festival that afternoon with Suzanne. They headed for the crafts fair first. Suzanne stopped to talk with another friend, and Jessica wandered on, looking at everything but unable to focus on any of it. As she strolled from booth to booth, she wondered if she would run into Sam, and what she would do if she did.

They hadn't spoken since that awful night in his shop. She saw him around town a few times and in church when she joined Emily and Lillian for Sunday services. That was difficult, too. Jessica went to church twice and couldn't concentrate on the sermon either time. She was totally distracted by Sam's presence and the possibility of facing him afterward. But each time he slipped out, disappearing before she even left her pew.

Obviously, Sam didn't want to see or speak to her. And obviously she couldn't spend her life hoping he would change his mind. She couldn't stay in Cape Light any longer. It was too painful.

By now her transfer to Boston should have come through. From what Jessica could tell, though, if you really want something to happen, it always takes longer than you expect. She had driven up to the main branch in Boston twice, so far, for interviews.

Each time she diplomatically avoided seeing Paul. He had called a few times since their last date and sent a couple of e-mails. Jessica was sure he was getting the message that she was no longer interested.

She had a feeling she would get the job at the main branch. But it was hard to stay in Cape Light and wait. It felt as though part of her was still waiting to hear from Sam, though she knew she would never get that call.

Lately Jessica wondered if she should just move back to Boston without a job. But it wasn't like her to take that kind of leap—to quit one job without having another lined up. She felt stuck, forced to wait out the transfer approval, forced to endure daily—sometimes hourly—reminders of Sam.

She picked up a large ceramic bowl with a fluted edge and put it down again. The glaze was interesting, but the bowl was quite expensive and not really her taste. She had to be careful. In this state of mind she was liable to come home with just about anything.

She looked around, wondering where Suzanne had disappeared to. Her friend was a dedicated shopper and hard to keep up with at a place like this. Jessica spotted Suzanne's orange T-shirt a few booths down and quickly went to nab her before she disappeared again.

"There you are—" Jessica lightly touched her friend's arm to get her attention. "Find anything good?"

Suzanne turned to her with a funny look on her face, and Jessica followed her gaze. It was Sam, standing just a few feet away, talking with two women, showing them a piece of furniture. It was a piece that he built; Jessica could tell instantly by the classic, clean lines and perfect finish.

She had nearly walked into his booth without realizing it. Fortunately, it wasn't too late to get away without his noticing her, she thought. But just as she turned to go, he looked up and caught her eye.

Jessica swallowed hard, willing herself to look away. And walk away. But she couldn't. Did he still care? Didn't he know that this separation was tearing her apart?

Sam's expression was strange, unreadable. He looked shocked or angry—or maybe just confused. Jessica couldn't be sure.

He was the first to look away, responding to a question from one of the women. Jessica looked away, too, feeling almost sick to her stomach. Without even remembering Suzanne, she quickly turned and left the booth.

What did she expect? That Sam would run over to her and beg her forgiveness? If she still had doubts, this ought to convince her. He hadn't even said hello.

Sam would never call or try to see her again. Her hopes were all in vain. She had to leave here, the sooner the better. It just didn't get any easier for her. In fact, Jessica had a feeling it was going to get a lot worse before it got any better.

And that vague but poignant reminder of Sam made her even sadder. . . .

ON MONDAY MORNING JESSICA RECEIVED A CALL from the Human Resources Manager in Boston and was offered the job at their branch. Her title would be the same, but the salary was a substantial increase. It seemed an answer to her prayers at first. But ten minutes after the phone call a vague sense of unease set in—as if she were being forced to go when she still wasn't sure she wanted to.

But there was no help for it. Jessica really had no choice but to accept the offer. She had no real reason to stay in Cape Light anymore. Leaving would be hard, but ultimately it would help her get over Sam faster. Though at times she doubted that she would ever get over him. How did you get over someone who was so deep in your heart?

Taking a breath, Jessica dialed Emily's number at work and told her the news. "I told them I would call back tomorrow. I guess I'll accept," she finished.

Emily was quiet for a moment. "I thought you wanted this very much. But you don't sound that sure about it, Jessica."

"I'm sure," Jessica insisted. "It's just that I was getting used to it around here. Now it will feel like a big change again to go back."

"I'm happy about the job—if it's what you want. But I'll be sorry to see you go."

"I know, I'm going to miss you, too," Jessica said. "Why don't you come over for dinner this week?"

"That would be great. What night?" Emily sounded surprised but pleased by the invitation.

"You're busier than me. You pick."

Emily paused. "How about Thursday? Can I bring anything?"

Jessica thought a moment. "Maybe some dessert . . . but nothing with blueberries, please."

Emily laughed. "I hear you."

ACCEPTING THE JOB SUDDENLY MADE THE MOVE SEEM much more real to Jessica. Her new boss wanted her to start in two weeks, which meant she had to organize things quickly. She took herself out to lunch at the Beanery and found a quiet table in the corner where she started to make lists on a yellow legal pad.

She had nearly filled the page, and worked her way through half a roast vegetable and brie roll-up, when someone called her name. She looked up, not recognizing the voice. Then she saw Sam's niece Lauren coming toward her. Jessica's heart skipped a beat as she wondered if Lauren was with Sam. But she was with her mother, Molly, who was carrying in two trays of pastry.

With her dark eyes and thick lashes, Lauren resembled her uncle so strongly, it was almost hard to look at her. Jessica made herself smile anyway. "Hi, Lauren. What's up?"

Lauren shrugged. "School, shopping. We're going to the outlet stores at Southport."

"That sounds like fun," Jessica replied.

Lauren rolled her eyes. "Mom never gets me anything I really like. She always says, 'No way, that style looks too old for you,'" Lauren said, doing a perfect imitation of her mother.

"Well, maybe you'll be luckier this time," Jessica said.

Outlet stores or not, buying new school clothes for two kids had to really cost, Jessica thought, feeling an unexpected moment of sympathy for Molly.

"How is your cat? Are the kittens ready to leave her yet?" Lauren practically whispered.

Jessica didn't understand the sudden need for privacy, but found herself whispering back. "Yes, quite ready. They're eating me out of house and home. I'm moving in a couple of weeks, and I need to find homes for all of them."

"Sam asked Mom if we could have one," Lauren said. The sound of his name spoken out loud gave Jessica a secret pang. "But every time we ask her, she says we'll talk about it later."

"Oh . . . well, I don't think that's such a good sign," Jessica said sympathetically.

Just then Molly appeared beside her daughter. "Come on, Lauren. We have to go."

She looked at Jessica but seemed too uncomfortable to say hello.

Jessica felt her own resentment of Molly ebbing—why hold a grudge when she was moving? "Hi, Molly," she said. "How are you?"

"In a rush, as usual." Molly gave her daughter a parental glare, but Lauren ignored her as she tugged on Molly's arm.

"Jessica's moving, Mom, and she has to get rid of her kittens. Right away." Lauren had a flair for drama, Jessica noted, putting a critical spin on the situation.

"You're moving?" Jessica couldn't help enjoying Molly's unguarded look of surprise. "When?"

"In about two weeks." Jessica set her pen down on the pad. "I'm moving back to Boston."

"Oh . . . I hadn't heard that."

"I just found out for sure this morning." Jessica paused, wondering if she should say more. Why not? Her imminent departure made her bolder—bold enough to call Molly Willoughby's bluff. "I'm sure you're happy to hear the news."

Molly blinked hard, then had the grace to look embarrassed. "I guess I would be . . . if my brother didn't look so miserable."

Sam looked miserable? Over her? Is that what she was saying? The tidbit was definitely something to tuck away and take out later, for closer inspection, Jessica thought, feeling her spirits lift a notch.

"Mom . . . can't we please take a kitten?" Lauren hung on her mother's arm with a plaintive expression. "Jessica might have to give them away to a place where they destroy animals."

Molly shook her head, her expression half-annoyed, half-adoring. "This one is going to law school," she told Jessica. "Even I can't win an argument with her."

Lauren's eyes danced with excitement. "Then we can have a kitten?"

"All right, we'll take one," Molly relented. "But you guys have to take care of it. I mean it."

Lauren hopped up and down and clapped her hands. "Yes! Thanks, Mommy. Thank you, thank you . . ." Lauren's words were smothered as she hugged her mother.

Molly looked down at Jessica over Lauren's dark head. "Want to trade—two cats for one thirteen-year-old girl?"

"Take three cats and it's a deal," Jessica replied.

Molly's sense of humor seemed so familiar—undoubtedly a trait that ran in the family. To Jessica it was yet more proof that she was making the right decision. She had to leave Cape Light, where everything and everyone made her think of Sam.

THE DISH SEEMED EASY ENOUGH WHEN SAM MADE IT for her. He just chopped some onions and mushrooms and peppers and . . . stuff. She remembered him cutting the chicken in chunks and browning it. Then he added rice. But had he cooked the rice in the same pan or cooked it separately? Jessica now wondered. It wasn't at all the right color, she noticed. Did he add something when she wasn't looking?

She let the concoction cook awhile, then tasted it. It wasn't quite right. It wasn't terrible, either. Actually, it wasn't nearly as bad as some of her other culinary attempts. But it didn't taste like Sam's. And she couldn't call him to help her figure out the missing ingredients.

Jessica was dressing the salad when Emily arrived.

"Do you mind hanging out with me in the kitchen while I finish up?" she asked, pouring them each a glass of iced tea.

"Not at all," Emily assured her.

"Good," Jessica said. "Here, taste this." She offered her sister a spoonful of the entree. "I think it's missing something."

Emily took a taste. "Mmmm . . . this is good. What is it?"

"Ummm . . . it's called Chicken Warwick," she said quickly, "but that's sort of a joke."

"A private one?" Emily guessed. "That's all right, don't explain. It tastes delicious, whatever you want to call it."

"But doesn't it need something?" Jessica asked, tasting a little again. "Maybe some salt or pepper?"

Emily shrugged. "You're the expert."

"A little more of both, I think," Jessica replied, adding more spices. She stirred it around and tasted again.

Of course. That was it. It was just right now, but somehow getting the flavor right made her even lonelier for Sam.

When they sat down to eat a few minutes later, Emily asked Jessica all about her new job in Boston. Despite her sadness about moving, Jessica was determined to be positive. She hadn't asked Emily over to listen to a lot of whining. She wasn't going to mention Sam, either, she decided. What good would that do?

But Emily was the one who brought his name up once they had finished their dinner.

"Does Sam know you're moving?" she asked quietly as Jessica cleared away the dishes.

"He might by now. I ran into Molly a few days ago at the Beanery. So she knows. And Molly has always been very reliable at getting information back to him quickly," Jessica added with an edge to her voice.

Emily shrugged. "Well, Sam probably does know by now, if Molly knows."

"I'll tell you something funny. She told me she would have been happy to hear it, too, 'if her brother didn't look so miserable,' " Jessica said. She glanced at Emily. "Do you think that means Sam is sorry?"

Emily picked up the empty salad bowl and followed Jessica to the sink. "It sounds as if you're both sorry— and both too stubborn to admit it."

Jessica turned to her, about to reply, then felt her lip tremble and her eyes fill with tears. "I just . . . really love him" was the best she could manage. She pressed her hand to her forehead and sniffed hard.

Emily folded her into her arms. "I know you do. But you have to tell *him* that. Not me," she said gently.

"How? I saw him at the green on Sunday. He won't even look at me."

Emily stroked her sister's hair. "I think you just need to pick up the phone and call him. Let him know you're leaving and give him one more chance." Emily paused, her words sinking in. "Finding someone you really love is an astounding thing—such a precious blessing. You have to fight for it. Fight for him . . . and yourself," she urged in a low, determined tone. "Didn't you ever hear the expression 'Love has no pride'?"

Jessica shook her head and wiped her nose. "I guess so . . . but I never understood it until now."

She sighed and looked up at her sister. "It's not just my pride. I'm scared," she confessed. "He might say he doesn't have any feelings for me anymore. I'm scared of that, of course. And if we do get back together, I'm afraid I might not really make him happy. Or someday he won't be happy with me."

Jessica felt a fresh wave of tears overtake her, her face crumpling up despite her will not to give in. Emily rubbed her shoulder but didn't speak for a long time.

Finally she said, "I don't think Sam is waiting for a woman to come along and make him happy. I think he's content with himself and his life. He knows who he is and what he wants. I think he's just looking for someone to share all that with him, to be his true partner, come what may."

"I want to be that person . . . but I'm not sure that loving him makes me the one."

Emily watched her for a moment, then quietly asked, "Have you prayed about it?"

Jessica glanced at her, surprised that her sister had noticed her halting, fledgling faith.

"Yes, I have . . . a little," she admitted.

"Well, maybe you ought to stop worrying, then, and give this one over to God. Don't give Him too much advice about what should happen," she suggested with a smile. "Just pray and see if the answer comes to you."

Jessica took a deep breath. "All right. I'll try it. I'll try anything now, I guess." She smiled at Emily, feeling grateful for her company and advice. It was so wonderful to be closer to her sister, like a best friend but even better somehow because they shared the same history and family ties.

She regretted that she waited so long to let Emily get close to her. She knew in her heart that Emily had always wanted them to be there for each other. *Maybe there is some good to come out of this heartbreak over Sam*, Jessica thought. She may have lost Sam, but at least she had gained a sister.

Jessica made some coffee to serve with the lemon meringue pie that Emily had brought. They decided to have dessert outside on the porch.

"Your garden looks wonderful," Emily said as they stepped outside. "Still green and blooming despite the heat."

Jessica shrugged. "I probably wasted money, since I'm leaving so soon, but when certain flowers peaked in late July, I put in some late-blooming plants that will carry on until the first frost."

"You must get that from Mother," Emily said admiringly. "I only made a really good garden once, when I lived down in Maryland. I don't have a green thumb like you two. But I did have the time down there, and the warmer weather helped."

Jessica knew that her sister was referring to the year when she was married to Tim Sutton.

Jessica barely remembered Tim. The romance had been a secret from Emily's family, and Jessica only met Tim once or twice. She was probably about eight years old at the time.

It was interesting, Jessica thought, that Lillian disapproved of Tim as a match for Emily the same way she now shunned Sam. Of course, Emily had been so much younger and more under her parents' control.

Or so they thought, before she surprised them all by running away with her boyfriend and getting married.

Jessica didn't really know much of the story after that point. She had never really asked Emily about that brief time, she realized.

But she felt so much closer to Emily lately, especially tonight, and she wanted to know. Maybe hearing about it would help her understand her own confused feelings about Sam.

"What was it like, being married to Tim?" Jessica asked. "You never talk about it."

"It was wonderful. Truly," Emily said with unexpected emotion. "I loved Tim very much and he loved me. That time was probably the happiest in my life," she confessed.

She sighed and glanced at Jessica. "I missed him for a very long time. I still do, in a way. But it was so long ago now, sometimes it feels as if I'm trying to remember a very sweet, faded dream."

Emily's tone wasn't sad or self-pitying, but Jessica ached for her sister's loss.

"But we were very young," Emily went on. "Who knows what would have happened? Maybe our marriage wouldn't have made it over the long run."

"It sounds to me as if it would have," Jessica said.

A distant look came into Emily's eyes, and she smiled. "I think so, too."

They were both quiet for a long time, then Jessica said, "When I heard that Tim had died, I felt so sorry for you, being all alone down there. But I still didn't think you would ever come home."

"I had to at that point. Or thought I did. It felt as though I lost my spirit when Tim died. I didn't have anything more to rebel about, I guess." Emily glanced at her, then out at the garden again. ". . . And something else happened that . . . complicated things," she said slowly. "Something I don't think you know about."

"What was that?" Jessica asked curiously.

"I was pregnant when Tim died. I had a child about a week later while I was in the hospital, recovering from the accident."

Jessica felt a jolt. Had she really heard Emily correctly? She was so stunned she couldn't speak for a moment.

"No . . . I didn't know that. No one ever told me," she said, sitting up straight.

"She was a baby girl. I only saw her one time. Her eyes were very blue—they say most babies' are at that age. Then they change. I don't know what color they'd be by now," she said softly.

Jessica was quiet. Stunned, actually. Did she really have a niece somewhere—a grown woman by now—whom she had never even met, had never been aware of until this very moment?

"Wh-what happened? What happened to the baby?"

"I couldn't keep her. I had to give her up for adoption."

"That must have been so hard," Jessica said.

Emily's expression grew taut, and she pursed her mouth, as if the words spoken aloud were bitter tasting. Jessica moved closer to her on the step and put her arm around her shoulder. She didn't know what to say.

"I got to hold her once. I wasn't even supposed to see her, but a sympathetic nurse snuck the baby in and gave her to me for a few minutes."

Emily shut her eyes, remembering how she was so afraid to move, even to breathe, as she studied her daughter's tiny face, snub nose, and perfectly formed little fingers. Her daughter, the one link to the man she loved so dearly.

"Then she was taken away. That's all I ever saw of her," Emily explained in a thick voice.

It had only been a few minutes, a quarter hour at best. But it was long enough for Emily to have fallen totally and irrevocably in love—a love that had survived on nothing but bitter tears and regrets for all these years. It was Emily's deepest sorrow, her greatest mistake. An irreversible one.

"You must have felt so alone," Jessica said.

"Mother came down to help me. When she saw that I was pregnant, she . . . she really wanted me to give the baby up," Emily said. "You know how she can be."

"Yes, I know," Jessica said slowly, staring at her sister.

"Mother took charge," Emily went on. "She said I was only a teenager, uneducated, and widowed—that it wouldn't be fair to the baby to keep it. She said I would never be able to support it and give it a proper home. So she—arranged everything."

Jessica felt a chill go through her as she began to understand Lillian's role in all this.

Emily's hands were shaking so badly she put down her coffee cup, but she was determined to go on with her story. "I was so overwhelmed with grief over Tim, I probably wasn't thinking clearly. I wasn't old enough to make that kind of decision," she tried to explain. "To understand what I was giving up."

"Mother made you do it, you mean," Jessica summed it up for her. When Emily didn't reply, she added, "Why didn't you bring the baby back up here, so that Mom and Dad could help you take care of her?"

Emily remembered exactly what their mother had said when she asked that very question.

"Take you in with this child? Give me one good reason after the way you disobeyed us, Emily. The way you disdained our wishes, rejected everything we tried to teach you. You shamed our family and made a fool of your father and me. You thought you knew everything, didn't you? Well, here's your chance to prove it, then. Why should we help a foolish, insolent girl who knows everything?"

Emily took a deep breath, shaking off the memory. Finally, replying to Jessica, she said, "Mother didn't want that. She said it was fine for me to come back. She would help me go to college and get a degree. But not with the baby." Staring straight ahead, Emily squeezed her sister's hand. "You know how she felt about Tim. She considered anything connected to him a disgrace. I guess she saw her chance to erase the entire episode from the family history."

Emily could practically hear her mother's voice once more, sharp and clear and relentless. How many nights had she lain awake, going over the scene again and again in her mind? Trying to see how it could have come out differently, what she might have said or done.

"You can't keep the child, it's unthinkable," Lillian had insisted. "How will you feed it or even keep a roof over your head? What kind of job will you find—waiting tables or working as a checkout girl in a supermarket? Or maybe you'll marry another fisherman? Is that the kind of marginal, hand-to-mouth existence you want for your baby and yourself?"

"Mother told me I was being selfish," Emily recalled. "She said I always thought of myself first, and I had made a complete mess of my life the day I turned my back on my family and ran off with Tim. She said this was my one chance to do the right thing for myself and the child."

Emily felt her sister gently rubbing her shoulder, and she turned to face Jessica again, as if waking up from a nightmare.

"It was as if she just wanted me to pick up where I left off when I ran away with Tim. Getting back on track again, Mother called it." Emily wrapped her arms around herself, shivering despite the warmth of the August night. "Mother more or less talked me into pretending that Tim and my entire life with him—our love . . . our child— never existed."

"What about Dad? Did he know?" Jessica asked quietly. She didn't want to press her sister, but she needed to know the whole story, to try to make sense of what her sister had kept hidden for years.

"You know how Dad was," Emily said wearily. "He was up here, with you. I only spoke to him over the phone a few times. He was happy and relieved I survived the accident—and sincerely sorry about Tim. But he didn't have much to say about the baby. I think he felt bad for me, but he didn't have the courage or strength to go against Mother," Emily told her. "I tried. But I didn't win."

"I'm sure that Mother believed she was doing the right thing," Jessica said, "but the way she treated you—and your daughter—was completely unfair."

"Unfair?" Emily echoed in a bleak tone. "Well, maybe, but life isn't fair, is it? I was weak, Jessica, and Mother was the strong one. I should have fought for my baby."

Emily's head dropped, and Jessica could see she was crying. "Sometimes I still can't believe that I did it—let her persuade me. I'm so ashamed. Maybe that's why I never told you."

"It's okay, Emily. I understand, really," Jessica assured her. "I'm so sorry for what you've been through."

It was Jessica's turn now to comfort her sister. She patted her back as Emily wept. Poor Emily. And to think that all these years Jessica resented her, because Emily was away at college when their father's scandal broke— and Jessica always thought Emily had it easier. Meanwhile her older sister had been dealing with so much, a grief that would have broken a lesser person.

Finally Emily looked up. "Thanks for saying that. But I should have told you sooner. . . . Can you forgive me?"

"Of course I can. Of course." She leaned over and hugged her older sister. "Does anyone else know? Besides Mother, I mean?"

"Just Reverend Ben," Emily said. "I've gone to speak to him a few times about it. Especially when I first came back."

When Emily returned to Cape Light, she felt more dead than alive, going through the mere motions of life, whatever Lillian wanted of her. Reverend Ben was some help, and at his urging, Emily began to attend church and slowly grew in faith. As he had promised, she found great comfort in God's love and mercy.

"Have you ever tried to find her?" Jessica asked her quietly.

Emily nodded. "Yes, I did. I tried for a long time. Mother wouldn't tell me anything, of course. She claimed it was a closed adoption, and she didn't know herself where the baby had gone. She wouldn't even tell me the name of the lawyer she used. But I found out the name of the agency that had handled it. About ten years ago I went down to Maryland to see them. I couldn't get any information, though. The best I could do was leave some documents, saying they could give out my name and whereabouts if my daughter ever tried to find me."

"Do you know if she's tried?"

"They won't tell me that, either," Emily replied.

"Is that why you've stayed here all this time? So that she can find you?"

"Part of the reason," she admitted. "I think about her all the time—where she might be, what she's doing, how she turned out. . . ." She sighed. "I pray to God she's been raised by loving parents. That's the most important thing, don't you think?"

"Yes," Jessica agreed, "I do."

"Every night I pray that someday I'll find her," Emily admitted. "That's about all I can do now," she added sadly.

"I'll pray for you, too," Jessica promised. "I'll pray that you find her."

"Thank you," Emily said quietly. Squeezing Jessica's hand, she managed a small smile.

"Maybe now that she's older, she'll come and find you on her own," Jessica said. "You see these stories on TV all the time."

"Yes, you do. It doesn't always turn out happily,

though," Emily reminded her. "Still, I'd give anything to see my daughter again."

A short time later they went back inside. Jessica showed Emily some pieces of furniture that she acquired since coming to town that she couldn't take back to Boston. "My place is so small there. I love them," she said, running her hand over the satiny curve of her favorite antique chair, "but most of it just won't fit. It would make me happy if you'd take something."

As Emily looked at the pieces that Jessica was offering, two of Elsie's kittens popped out from under the couch and ran straight to Emily.

Emily bent down and picked one up, then continued to look at the furniture. The cat squirmed a bit in her grasp, but Emily quickly calmed it with some expert ear scratching. Jessica noticed that the small cat was soon purring ecstatically.

"Hey, you're really good at that," she noted. "You wouldn't want to take him home, would you? I have to find homes for all six, and I've only got one booked so far."

Emily looked doubtful, then looked down at the kitten, who had stuck himself to her chest, as if it had Velcro paws.

"I never approved of wearing fur," she said dryly. "But they are sort of cute," she admitted. "The thing is, I'm out so much. He may get lonely."

Jessica thought for only a beat. She bent down and scooped up another one, who let out a plaintive meow at the handling. "Then take two, by all means. A matched set," she said, holding the two spotted kittens side by side. "I've always heard that you should keep cats in pairs," she offered encouragingly.

"Oh, dear . . . this is some sales pitch," Emily said. She glanced from cat to cat, and a smile lit her face. "All right.

You'd better get a carton quickly, before I change my mind."

"No problem," Jessica promised, dashing to the broom closet where she had saved some boxes for just this purpose.

She also packed some food, litter, and cat toys in a shopping bag. "Here you go, the full starter kit." She handed her the carton and Emily put the cats inside, struggling to close the lid around contradictory little paws. Finally the cats were secure inside. For the moment, at least.

"I guess this makes it official," Emily said with a laugh. "I'm a classic spinster now. I think you need at least two cats to qualify."

"No, you're not," Jessica insisted. She so rarely heard Emily voice a discouraging word, that the admission caught her off guard. But tonight had been a night of surprises.

Jessica helped her sister carry the box and cat supplies to her car, then hugged Emily good night. "Thanks so much for coming," Jessica said sincerely. "I'm sorry I cried all over your beautiful silk blouse."

"I'm glad you did," Emily assured her with a warm smile. "I can always get another blouse. I'll never have another sister." With a brief wave, Emily and her new cats were gone.

CHAPTER FOURTEEN

～

$\mathcal{S}$ ARA WAS NOT AT WORK AGAIN. EMILY NOTICED right away as she took a seat at the counter in the Clam Box.

It was between shifts at the diner. Lunch was well over, and there was still an hour before people came in for supper. She had just stopped in for a quick bite to keep her stomach from growling later during the long, tedious planning meeting scheduled for that night.

Lucy greeted her and took her order.

"Sara's not here again today. Did she quit?" Emily asked abruptly.

Lucy's brows drew together in a frown. "Sara quit? Who told you that?"

"Well, she mentioned to me about a week or so ago that she might be leaving town soon. She wants to go back home, I think."

Lucy shook her head, looking baffled. "Well, if she does, it's news to me. As far as I know, she just has a bug or something." Lucy shrugged. She quickly wiped Emily's table with a damp rag and set down a paper place mat with a map of the local coastline and pictures of famous lighthouses.

"Oh . . . Sara's sick. Is it a cold?"

"The flu maybe. I don't know. She sounded terrible over the phone, so I just told her to stay in and take it easy. I'm going to bring her out some soup or something when I leave," Lucy added. "You know the way young women are—they don't take care of themselves at all," she said, shaking her head.

She turned on the heel of her soft-soled shoe. "Sara better not quit on me now. I need her too much. She's the best waitress we ever had around here. . . ."

Emily wanted to agree, but Lucy was by now too far away to hear her. She checked her watch, then called over the counter and asked Lucy to give her the sandwich to go. "And give me a container of chicken soup if you have any. I have time to go see Sara. I'll take her some dinner."

Lucy glanced at her. "Are you sure?" When Emily nodded, Lucy said, "I guess it's just as well. I won't be done here until late. She might be asleep by then. I'll give you a roll and some ginger ale, too."

"And some orange juice," Emily suggested. "Do you have any fresh squeezed?"

"Good idea. I'll check," Lucy said, disappearing into the kitchen.

It sounded as if Sara had a bad summer cold. Orange juice was good for that, Emily thought. Stuck out there in those cottages, she probably wasn't taking care of herself. It might seem intrusive, she knew, to drop in on Sara unannounced. But she would try anyway. She could just stand at the door and give Sara the food, see if she looked okay.

Lucy soon had the care package ready, and Emily left for the cottages. She wouldn't stay long, she promised herself as she headed for her car. She just wanted to check on her.

At first when she arrived at Cranberry Cottages, Emily wasn't sure which was Sara's. But then it was apparent that only three were occupied, and she could guess quite accurately who lived in each by simply checking out the clotheslines.

One line held a family of bathing suits, from Dad's billowing trunks down to a ruffled baby one-piece. The next held two pairs of men's jeans and a blue T-shirt that said Police Athletic League. Luke McAllister had moved in to number three.

Number five had to be Sara's, she surmised, walking toward it. She saw two Clam Box T-shirts on the clothes-line, which confirmed it.

A small light was on in the kitchen and living-room area, but Emily knocked twice and no one answered. *Sara must be asleep*, she thought. *I'll just leave this stuff here with a note and hope raccoons don't see it first.* She didn't want to wake Sara if she was sleeping.

An instant later the inner door opened, and Emily saw Sara's pale face behind the screen.

"I didn't mean to bother you," Emily began, "but Lucy told me you've been sick, and I just wanted to check on you." She held up the bag from the Clam Box. "I brought you some soup—chicken noodle. It's supposed to be good for a cold."

"I'm not sure if I have a cold exactly," Sara said slowly. "But soup sounds good. Thanks." She opened the door to her and took the bag. "Why don't you come in for a minute? I don't think I'm contagious or anything."

"I didn't even think of that," Emily said as she entered the cottage. "I really don't get sick much, no matter who coughs or sneezes in my direction."

"Well, thanks for coming and bringing this stuff anyway. That was nice of you." Sara smiled and tightened the sash on her bathrobe.

"It was no trouble. Lucy and I were worried about you." *And you don't seem the type who would ask for help, even if you needed it,* she nearly added.

"Sit down." Sara gestured to a chair at the cluttered kitchen table. "I'm just going to heat up the soup. Can I get you anything?"

Emily suddenly remembered her own dinner was wrapped up in the same bag. "I think I have a sandwich in there somewhere . . . and some coffee."

Sara peered inside the bag and found the food. She put the sandwich on a dish and gave it to Emily along with the container of coffee.

"Thanks . . . but you mustn't serve me. That's not the idea. Come, sit down. I'll reheat the soup for you," Emily said, getting out of her chair.

What had she been thinking? The girl was sick. She didn't want to impose on her.

"Oh . . . okay. If you insist," Sara said as Emily shooed her away from the stove. "I just need to get something in my bedroom. I'll be right back."

Emily nodded. She found a pot on the drain board, poured the soup into it, and set it on the stove over a low flame. Then she walked over to the small table, covered with books and papers, and tried to clear a spot. The table of a writer who lived alone, Emily thought with a secret smile.

She didn't want to disturb any of Sara's personal things, but she did need a clear space to set the bowl on, Emily reasoned.

She saw an open notebook with Sara's handwriting covering both pages, and quickly closed it and put it aside. It looked very private, and Emily was a stickler about respecting a person's privacy.

Sara came back into the room and stopped in her

tracks. Emily had just finished making a neat pile of the books and stacking up the papers. "I just wanted to clear a space for your soup bowl," she explained. "I hope you didn't have your books in any special order?"

"Ummm . . . no, not really," Sara replied, shaking her head. She looked even paler than before, Emily noticed. She wondered if Sara was running a fever.

"Have a seat. The soup should be ready," Emily said, walking back to the stove. She found a small dish and put out the roll and the two drinks. "You need lots of fluids when you're sick like this."

Thanks, Mom, Sara almost replied sarcastically but bit back the reply in time.

"Yes, you're right," she said blandly. She took the large cup of ginger ale and sipped on the straw.

"Maybe you've just been working too hard at the diner," Emily suggested. She paused to pour out the soup. "I'm sorry if I spoke out of turn when I asked after you tonight. I thought you had left town and mentioned to Lucy that you were planning on it. But she didn't seem to know anything about that."

"Oh, well, the thing is, they're so busy there right now. And on top of it, Lucy is trying to convince Charlie to let her go back to school. If I left her shorthanded, that would hurt her case, and I really hope she can persuade him."

Emily carefully lifted the bowl of hot soup and carried it to the table. "Lucy wants to go to college? Good for her," she said. "She's a very bright woman. I think it would be great for her."

"So do I." Sara leaned back as Emily set down the soup.

"Oh, the spoon. How dumb of me. I'd make a terrible waitress, I think," Emily said, returning to the kitchen.

"Top drawer to the right of the sink," Sara directed her. "Well, you seem to be doing okay as mayor."

Emily returned with the spoon and sat down to her

sandwich. "Thanks, I hope the voters think so in the fall."

"How is the campaign going?" Sara asked, taking a sip of soup.

Emily lifted one shoulder. "It always seems great at first. Like a romance—lots of high energy and fine promises. Later it's like a marathon. The going gets tougher and you really have to dig in to go the limit."

Sara smiled at the analogy. "Think you'll make it?"

"Me? I'm like the tortoise, slow and steady. I don't burn myself out on the first lap or two. Charlie looks like he's running rings around me now. But I can't see how he'll keep up this pace months from now."

"Let's hope he runs out of gas *real* soon," Sara said, making Emily laugh. She wondered if Sara would still be around at election time. But how could that be? The girl would surely be long gone by then. Back to Maryland or wherever.

"Do you miss your family, Sara?" she asked curiously. "They must miss you."

"I speak to my mom about once a week," Sara answered, tearing off a piece of the roll. "And sometimes I write a letter, or my parents write me."

"Any sisters or brothers?"

Sara shook her head. "An only child." *Lots of adopted children are*, she added silently.

"Have you ever been married?" she suddenly asked Emily.

Emily looked surprised by the question, but then her expression relaxed again. "Yes, a long time ago. I was just about your age—even younger, actually. That's when I lived down in Maryland," she added, taking a bite of her sandwich. "My husband's name was Tim. Tim Sutton. We met up here, in Cape Light, when I was a senior in high school. He was a few years older, a lobster fisherman," she added. "After I graduated we decided to elope and ran away to Maryland."

Sara's eyes widened. Tim Sutton. That was the name on her birth certificate. So he had been her father, after all. And it seemed he hadn't abandoned Emily when she was pregnant, as Sara often imagined.

Sara suddenly felt so disturbed, she couldn't swallow another mouthful. She pushed the bowl away.

Emily looked at her with concern. "Are you feeling all right?" she asked quietly.

"Uh . . . sure. I'm okay. Just not as hungry as I thought." She sat up and tried to assume a more relaxed expression. "What was he like—your husband, I mean."

"Oh . . . I don't know. How would I describe him?" Emily's expression softened, and Sara could almost see a love-struck teenager in her eyes. "He was just a wonderful person. Smart, kind, funny. Quiet sometimes. He loved music and working on the water. He loved me," she added wistfully.

Sara swallowed hard, but she forced herself to ask more questions, knowing she might never have this chance again.

"So what happened next? Running off to get married sounds very romantic."

"Yes, it was." Emily nodded. "We were together for less than two years. Then Tim was killed in a car accident. . . . I was in the accident, too, but I was lucky. Only a few injuries. Nothing serious. I decided not to stay alone down in Maryland and came back up here."

"Oh . . . how sad," Sara said, genuinely moved. Her father had died in a car accident. But was he her father? She judged Emily to be in her early forties, although she looked younger. The time frame seemed right. But Emily never mentioned having a baby.

"Well, that was long ago. I didn't mean to depress you," Emily added. "Honestly, I came to cheer you up, not tell you sad stories."

"I was the one who asked," Sara said carefully. "And

it was really interesting hearing about Tim and when you lived in Maryland. Thanks for telling me."

Emily nodded. "That's okay."

Emily suddenly found it curious that she hadn't told anyone this story in years and now was relating it twice in nearly as many days. Did that mean something? It almost felt as if there were something in her past that was trying to surface—only she had no idea what it could be.

"What about children?" Sara asked suddenly. "Did you ever have any?"

But Emily didn't know how to answer the question. Finally she said, "I never had the pleasure of raising a child—or the blessing of that experience."

No wonder Emily was so successful in politics, Sara thought. When backed against a wall, she could adeptly— and truthfully—sidestep the answer.

But Sara knew that Emily's reply told only half the story. She saw the sadness in Emily's eyes—a mirror image of her own blue eyes—and knew Emily hadn't purposely misled her. The truth was painful to her. Painful still, after all these years.

Sara felt the sudden impulse to reveal herself. *Why not?* she wondered. Would she ever find a better time? It suddenly seemed fated that Emily came here like this tonight, to see her, just so they could each tell each other the truth.

Sara's mind raced, trying to frame the right words— to start at least.

"Emily, there's something I need to tell you, something important," Sara began.

"What is it? Is something wrong?"

"No . . . not really." Sara shook her head, not knowing how to say it. Feeling restless, she got up from her chair. "Well, yes. There is something wrong, a problem I have. You can help me. In fact . . . you're the only one," she added, meeting Emily's blue gaze.

"I'd like to help, Sara, if I can." Emily stared up at her, looking genuinely puzzled.

Sara swallowed hard. Her throat suddenly felt tight. *I'm your daughter*, she wanted to say. *I'm the baby you gave up for adoption twenty years ago, back in Maryland.*

Still, she couldn't speak. The words just wouldn't come out. She felt her stomach twist into a knot, as if she were about to throw up.

"Are you all right?" Emily asked. "You're suddenly looking awfully pale. Maybe you should sit down again," she suggested, rising to her feet so that they stood face-to-face.

Sara glanced at Emily. Her expression was so open and caring. It was so hard to tell her the truth. But she had to do it.

This was it. Now or never.

"I need to tell you something. I hope you don't get upset . . . or angry," Sara said quietly.

"I'll try my best not to," Emily promised. "I'm pretty thick skinned," she added with a mild smile. "What is this about? Do you need me to help out with some problem in town . . . a parking ticket? A problem with Charlie Bates perhaps?"

Sara could tell that Emily was half-joking, trying to encourage her to speak. But the questions were only distracting. She shook her head impatiently.

"No, it's nothing like that," she said.

Emily waited, giving Sara a thoughtful look. When Sara remained quiet, she said, "Is this about your future— what we spoke about the other day? Is it something about your writing?" she probed.

Sara sat down heavily in the chair. She couldn't tell her. She just couldn't do it. Maybe because she didn't feel well tonight. She just couldn't handle this.

She felt Emily watching her, waiting. She needed to

say something, come up with some plausible explanation for her "problem." But what?

"Yes . . . it is about my writing," Sara said finally in a halting tone. "I've written this story, and you're a character in it. Well, not exactly, but someone very much like you," she added, unable to look at Emily.

"I think it's pretty good," she went on. "When it's finished, I'm going to submit it to some magazines, see if I can get it published. I just thought I ought to tell you. Just in case someone takes it."

It wasn't the truth, but it wasn't quite a lie, either, Sara reasoned. She had been working on a story about a young woman, like herself, trying to confront her birth mother. The story wasn't anywhere near finished, though, and Sara doubted she would send it out even when it was.

"Well . . . that's a first for me," Emily said, looking surprised. "I feel . . . complimented, I suppose. Thank you for putting me in a story."

"But you don't even know what it's about," Sara said.

"Will I be upset if I read it?" Emily asked, though she sounded more amused than upset by the prospect.

"You might be," Sara admitted. "I guess that's why I wanted to tell you." For goodness' sake, why had she ever come up with this excuse? It was getting more complicated by the minute.

"Don't worry about it," Emily advised. "As mayor, I'm used to having all sorts of things written about me. Besides, I believe in creative freedom. If I gave you an idea for a character, use it. Write whatever it is you need to write." Emily gazed at her and shrugged. "Maybe you can let me read it sometime when it's finished."

Sara glanced at her, then looked away. "Okay, that's a good idea," she said in a flat tone. Then, wondering if she had unintentionally hurt Emily's feelings, she added, "It's nothing insulting or anything that shows you—I mean, the character like you—in a bad light."

"Okay, don't worry about it. After all, we're friends, right?"

"Yes," Sara said, surprised to realize that it was true.

Emily smiled at her, then glanced down at her watch. "Oh, dear, I had no idea what time it was. I've really got to run. They must be wondering where I am."

Emily started for the door, then turned back for a moment. "If you're still feeling sick, don't rush back to work. Lucy and Charlie can survive without you for a few days. And if you need anything, call my office, okay?"

"Okay," Sara promised, though she doubted she'd ever take Emily up on that offer. But it made her feel warm inside to realize that Emily genuinely liked her and cared about her.

Once Emily had gone, Sara stretched out on her bed. Her head was pounding. *If only I could have told her,* Sara thought. *I'd be so relieved to be free of this secret. If only Emily glanced down and read just a few lines of my journal. . . .*

But Sara had been watching silently from the doorway, and she knew for a fact that Emily just shut the open journal and put it aside. Very honorable, she thought. Or just not terribly curious.

Either way, they still had the secret between them. And yet Sara's feeling about it had changed. After hearing the story of Emily's marriage, Sara was positive that her mother had not made the decision lightly to give her up. She no longer assumed the worst.

Instead, she now saw her mother as a very romantic and even tragic figure—at least, she was when she was young. Defying her parents—Lillian mostly, Sara suspected—to marry the man she loved. When and if she ever heard the real reason Emily had given her up for adoption, Sara was fairly certain now she could forgive her.

But would she ever summon the courage to tell her the

truth? Could she take it upon herself to mess up Emily's well-ordered life? She wasn't sure now if that was the responsible thing to do. Perhaps she ought to just go back to Maryland.

But having gotten so much closer to Emily tonight—so very close to telling her—made it even harder to leave. She would stay just a while longer. Lucy would appreciate it, too.

Sara crawled under the covers and turned off her light. It seemed she was making ties here, despite her plan not to. Emily, Lillian, Lucy—even customers who came into the diner regularly, like Tucker Tulley, who was always very nice to her.

Then there was Luke McAllister, her secret favorite and new neighbor, as well.

It was funny how that happens sometimes, no matter how hard you try to keep your distance. . . .

SAM SAT ATTENTIVELY IN BIBLE COMMUNITY Church's recreation hall, Molly and Jill on one side, Digger and Grace and Harry Reilly on the other. Lauren was up on stage, sitting gracefully at the black piano which sat in the middle of the stage—a large, shiny baby grand, donated to the church years ago by some wealthy widow, Sam recalled. Carolyn Lewis had since made very good use of it. Today it had been rolled out and polished to a mirror sheen for the recital of her summer piano students.

This was Lauren's first public performance. When she'd handed Sam the invitation, he'd known he wouldn't miss it for the world. They were all so proud of Lauren. Molly was positively beaming, and Grace was, too, pleased to see that Julie's old piano was being put to such good use. As Lauren played, Sam noticed Grace dab her eyes now and again. He even noticed Harry patting her hand at one point.

Molly was making them all a special dinner at her apartment afterward to celebrate. Everyone who helped moved the piano from Grace's barn was invited—except Jessica, he realized.

Molly thought that seeing Jessica would be too hard on him. But in a certain way, it made no difference at all, he reflected. Jessica might as well be sitting right beside him at that very moment. He was always that conscious of her. Her image was always in his mind—in his aching heart. He could almost smell her perfume. He couldn't help it though, God knew, he tried.

He thought about the night they moved the piano, when she went back with him to his apartment. They had been so close that night. He hadn't even seen it at the time, but looking back, he could see that they had just about turned a corner that night, gotten it all settled and right between them.

And then soon after that, somehow, they began to lose the thread. They lost it completely by her birthday, when she refused to take the sailboat. He had been very good about that, he reflected wryly, very understanding. He jumped in the boat and left her standing there on the dock, shouting after him. Then he didn't call her for almost two weeks.

I sure showed her, Sam silently lamented.

He almost couldn't blame her for going on a date with that guy from Boston. He had been so blown away, he couldn't see straight when Molly told him the news.

So now Jessica was moving back to the city. He had heard that tomorrow was the big day. He crossed his arms tightly over his chest and shifted in his chair. He missed her so much, he could hardly stand it sometimes. He could just manage to keep himself from jumping in his truck and driving to her house, standing at her door until she let him in.

But obviously, Jessica didn't feel the same way. He

would have heard from her by now if she cared at all—
at least a note telling him she was going. Good-bye and
good luck. Anything at all. She would have done . . .
something. Wouldn't she?

Suddenly everyone around him started clapping hard,
and Sam nearly jumped in his chair. He joined in the
applause, realizing that Lauren had finished her piece and
he had barely heard a note of it.

Later he walked with Digger out to the harbor, neither
of them saying much. Digger knew all about Sam's trouble with Jessica, but he was never one to offer unsolicited
advice. That was one of the reasons Sam valued the old
man's friendship so much.

"She's moving tomorrow," Sam said as they sat on the
edge of the dock, their legs dangling over the water.

"I heard that myself," Digger admitted, filling his pipe.

"I don't know what to do," Sam said honestly. "She's
never tried to call me or see me. She could have written
me a note or something, don't you think?"

"Well, you got until tomorrow to do something.
There's still time. You know what they say in the ball
game—it ain't over till it's over."

"If this is a ball game, Digger, it's the bottom of the
ninth, two outs, no men on base, and a blind man coming
up to bat."

Digger took a long thoughtful draw as he lit up.
"Sounds like the Red Sox are playing . . . but don't tell
Harry I said that."

Sam had to laugh, despite his aching heart. "I just can't
do anything about it," he admitted. "It's over. Jessica is
going back to Boston, just as she always said she would.
I don't know what else I can do."

Digger glanced at him, then stared out at the water and
sky. "If you've done all that you can, and you feel settled
in your heart, then that's it. You have to let it go. Maybe

her leaving tomorrow will be a help to you. Maybe then you'll be ready to give it up to God, son."

Sam didn't reply. Had he done all he could? His heart didn't feel anywhere close to settled. His faith had yielded some comfort, of course, and so had his talks with Reverend Ben.

But this was a bad one. Worse than anything he had ever gone through. His acute pain only seemed to be more evidence that Jessica was the one, after all.

If not, how could he love her so much—or feel this bad?

"Looks like some heavy weather moving in," Digger observed. "You ought to go out and check your house. You wouldn't want that new roof flying off or anything."

"I heard it will be light rain. Nobody's mentioned a storm or anything about high winds."

Digger shrugged and relit his pipe. "It's that radar tracking. It always confuses them. I'm looking straight out at the weather, and I'm telling you, a storm front is moving in," he insisted. "A big one. Should be raging out there by this time tomorrow. Harry believes me," he added. "We pulled a lot of boats out of the water today."

Sam looked out at the twilight sky. It was a balmy night, the air heavy and moist. A low bank of clouds clung to the horizon. It felt like it might rain later—but more like a shower to break the humidity than the kind of storm Digger was predicting. The air was so calm, there was hardly a sailboat to be found out on the water.

But if Digger said it was going to rain, he'd better take heed. He couldn't go out to the house tonight, but maybe very early tomorrow morning, before it got too heavy.

It would be better to get out of the village while Jessica was moving, anyway. Sam didn't want to do anything rash or foolish. Or totally humiliating.

*   *   *

JESSICA WAS PACKING UP THE LAST OF HER BELONG-
ings when she heard a sharp knock on the door. She was
expecting Emily, stopping over for a last-minute good-
bye.

She pulled open the door to find Molly with her two
daughters. The girls looked up at Jessica expectantly.

"We came to get the cat," Molly said, not sounding
totally pleased about the prospect. "Did you get our message?"

"Oh, yes . . . of course." They had left a message, a day
or so ago, but Jessica had been so busy, it totally slipped
her mind.

"Come on in. I have two left. Let me show them to
you and you can choose."

She shook the food box, and the two remaining kittens
scrambled into the kitchen. Lauren and Jill practically
melted at the sight of them. Each girl picked up one and
cradled it gently in her arms. Then they both turned to
look imploringly at their mother.

Molly rolled her eyes and shot Jessica a humorous
glance. "I knew I was going to get paid back for being
mean to you," she admitted. "Looks like I'll have to take
both of these cats, when I didn't even want one."

Jessica found it hard to resist laughing. She didn't feel
any rancor toward Molly anymore, she realized. In fact,
she had to admire her spunk and her spirit. Maybe given
some time, they would have gotten along.

"I'm sorry for yelling at your mother, too," Molly admitted in the same feisty tone. "I'm hardly ever that nasty
to defenseless old ladies."

"Don't worry, my mother is hardly defenseless," Jessica replied with a sly smile. "I'm sure she deserved it."

Jessica had a sudden impulse to ask Molly about Sam.
Maybe she could just ask her to tell Sam she said good-
bye. But as the girls hugged their cats and thanked her,
Jessica lost her nerve.

"Good-bye," Molly said curtly. "I wish you well."

They left and the apartment suddenly seemed very quiet and empty, with boxes piled everywhere and most of her furniture given away to either Emily or Suzanne. Jessica felt exhausted and was glad of it.

She fell asleep almost instantly, a blessed one-night reprieve from thinking about Sam.

Jessica woke to rain but was not surprised. The weather reports from Cape Light down to Boston had all predicted it. She had moved before in the rain. It made things messier and slower and even more frustrating, but movers kept moving. They didn't stop for a few raindrops.

But by mid-morning the winds picked up, and the skies grew darker. The movers were almost an hour late, and Jessica called the main office. The dispatcher assured her that the truck was on its way, just caught in slow traffic on the turnpike, due to the bad weather. "Sit tight. They'll be there soon," he promised.

But as the next hour passed, the winds became fierce. Jessica saw treetops bent backward and her garden flattened nearly to the ground. The rain fell steadily in wind-blown sheets, and distant rumbles of lightning and thunder broke the heavy silence all around her.

The phone rang. Predictably, it was the moving company, calling to say the move would be delayed indefinitely. No kidding, Jessica nearly replied, but the lights flashed, and she lost the connection.

Although the lights came back on a few minutes later, she didn't bother calling back. What was the sense? She'd check in with them after the storm and see how things stood.

Meanwhile, she had been thinking about Sam every minute since she opened her eyes. Why hadn't she forced herself to go to see him? She had asked herself that all morning, thinking that if she only had the chance, she would just do it.

Well, here was the chance, she realized. The unforeseen delay felt to her like a sign that she had to follow through and see him one last time. It wasn't going to be easy, she thought, glancing outside, but she would manage. She hoped she would find him in the village—at his shop or at his apartment.

But she would find him, no matter what. Totally determined now, she opened a box and dug through it until she found her high rubber boots. She pulled them on along with her yellow slicker.

Just as she was about to leave, the lights flashed again. This time they went dead with an ominous sound. Jessica waited a moment, but the power didn't return. It was out for a while, she surmised. She suddenly thought about her mother. She ought to call her and make sure she was all right, but her phone required electricity and so did her mother's. It would be best to just drive out there right away, she thought.

Okay, she had a plan. First she would check on her mother, then she would find Sam. No matter what, she would see him before she left, she promised herself.

It was much worse outside than Jessica had expected. Not only were the streets flooded, but fallen branches and downed power lines made the driving even slower. Carefully she steered through the narrow neighborhood lanes, which ran with water like miniature rivers.

It seemed like an hour later when she pulled into her mother's driveway. Through the rainswept windshield she recognized Emily's car and felt a sense of relief. It seemed they had both had the same idea.

Emily met her at the door, equally relieved to see her. "I tried calling your house, but I didn't get an answer. Then I realized without the power, your phone was off, too."

"I'm glad you've come. You're both good girls," their mother said, looking from one daughter to another. She looked shaken and unsettled by the storm, Jessica thought. Not her usual self at all.

"Let's go into town," Emily suggested. "I need to be near my office, and you shouldn't stay out here alone with Mother. Besides, my Jeep can handle the water on the roads, and I hate to think of you driving anywhere today in that little car of yours."

"Emily is right," Lillian agreed. "Let's go into town. Who knows when the power will come back on? I don't like being stuck out here like this."

"All right, Mother. I'll get your raincoat and hat," Jessica said, going off to the hall closet. She wanted to go to the village anyway, to look for Sam.

Emily and Jessica helped Lillian into Emily's Jeep Cherokee and then set off for the village.

"Maybe this wasn't such a sensible idea after all," their mother said from the backseat after they had driven only a block. "We should turn back."

"Don't worry. I have my cell phone with me. If we get stuck, someone will come get us," Emily promised

When they finally turned onto Main Street, the village looked like a windswept ghost town. The street was flooded with water on either side of the median, rushing downhill to the harbor like twin, wild rivers. Shops and restaurants were closed, torn awnings and broken signs flapping in the wind. A few storefront windows had already been boarded over, where a flying branch or other debris had crashed through.

"Heavens, I've never seen anything like this," Jessica said, gazing around.

"I have," Lillian told them. "But that was years ago. You were just a baby," she said to Emily. "And you weren't even born yet," she added to Jessica with uncharacteristic nostalgia. "*That* was a storm. It took the town a month to clean up."

"Looks to me like a month's worth of damage already," Emily observed grimly as she headed for the Village Hall. "And it isn't over yet."

"I can't believe it," Jessica said. "It looks like the Clam Box is open. Aren't those lights in the windows?"

"It's candlelight," Emily replied. She slowed down and tried to park as best as she could. "Let's go in. It looks like the only sign of life around."

Inside the Clam Box it appeared that a strange kind of party was going on. Everyone in town seemed to be there, even Felicity and Jonathan Bean. Lucy and Charlie had put small glass candleholders on each table and lined the counter with them as well.

Charlie had a few large battery-powered camping lanterns hanging over the grill and was cooking what he could. Lucy and Sara each walked around with a flashlight to help them serve.

As she and Emily carefully led their mother to a nearby table, Jessica glanced around for Sam. She didn't see him and felt a keen stab of disappointment. She hadn't seen his truck parked by Grace's shop, either, when she drove by earlier. Had he left town for some reason? She glanced around the diner again. Digger Hegman might know. While Emily settled Lillian and talked to Sara about what there was to eat, Jessica slipped away to talk to Digger about Sam.

Digger smiled, seeming happy to see her again.

"Do you know where Sam is?" she asked him.

"I think he went out to his house on the pond early this morning, before the rain got too heavy. But he must have come back to the village by now. Or else maybe he's stuck out there with the low roads washed out."

Jessica considered this. Yes, the low roads by the pond would be filled with water, unpassable by now in this storm. Without giving it a second thought, she sent up a silent prayer for Sam's safety, frightened to think he might be out driving in this weather.

Carefully watching her expression, Digger said, "Don't worry. Sam's okay. He's smart enough to stay off the road in a storm like this."

"Thanks, Digger," Jessica said, hoping that was true. She returned to her sister and mother, where the waitress asked her what she wanted. Jessica suddenly wasn't hungry at all; she ordered only a cup of hot tea. Her gaze remained on the door, hoping Sam's familiar face would be the next to enter.

Then Emily's cell phone sounded in her purse, and she took it out to answer it. Jessica saw her sister's face grow pale with worry, and she knew there was bad news. "When?" Emily asked, then, "Yes, I understand."

She shut off the phone and covered Jessica's hand with her own. "The police found Sam's truck crashed into a tree here in town. They've called an ambulance. Sam's been hurt, but they don't know how badly."

Jessica breathed in sharply and pressed her hand over her mouth to keep from screaming out loud. "No . . . it can't be. Maybe it was someone else," she said, wide-eyed with shock. "It could be a truck that looks just like Sam's."

"There was no mistake, dear," Emily said softly. She put her arm around Jessica's shoulder. "I'm so sorry." She met Jessica's gaze. "Let's pray for him, okay?"

Jessica nodded and squeezed her eyes shut, sending up a heartfelt prayer for Sam's survival. When she opened her eyes again, she stood up. "I have to go to him. Can I take your truck?" she asked Emily.

"Of course you can." She pulled out the keys and gave them to her sister. "Take this phone, too. But please be careful. Drive very slowly," she urged her in a worried tone.

"Jessica, you can't be serious!" Lillian said. "Emily, she can't go out driving around in this weather. That's just—insane. Do you want to have a car crash, too?" she asked Jessica.

Jessica glanced at her mother then back at Emily. "Where are they taking him?"

"Newburyport. That's the closest hospital with a head trauma unit."

Head trauma? Oh, dear God . . . Jessica felt the room spin for a moment and gripped the edge of the chair. Emily grabbed her hand.

"Mother's right, you can't go by yourself—and I can't leave town right now," she added, looking torn.

"I can take her there." The women turned to see Reverend Ben standing beside Jessica. He put his hand on her shoulder in a steadying, reassuring gesture.

Jessica didn't know what to say. She was so grateful she couldn't find the words.

"Thank you, Reverend. I can't thank you enough," Emily said.

"Don't mention it. I was just sitting over there at the counter, and I couldn't help but overhear. I do hope Sam will be all right," he said, looking at Jessica again.

She just nodded. With Reverend Ben stepping in, she noticed that her mother did not dare to object.

Jessica gave Emily a quick hug, then she and the Reverend left. It was slow going at first—it took a maddeningly long time just to get out of town—but finally they reached the higher road that led to Newburyport, and the reverend was able to drive at a reasonable but careful pace.

He didn't say much, concentrating on the road. Besides, they both knew there wasn't much to say.

Jessica prayed the entire drive. She knew you couldn't make a deal with God, but if you could, she would give up ever seeing Sam again, if only he would be okay.

Is this what it means to have faith? she wondered. She had been trying very earnestly these past weeks to pray and read the Bible. Maybe she did it all wrong. Maybe it just wasn't enough.

She squeezed her eyes shut and again tried to pray for Sam's safety. But she felt a sudden emptiness, as if she had just stepped off a cliff.

Are you there, God? I'm sorry . . . I'm not sure if I believe. I want to. I need to. Everything just seems so hopeless right now, she silently confessed. She felt tears slipping down her cheeks but didn't bother to push them away. *I love Sam. Please don't let him die,* she prayed. *Please help us. . . .*

Finally they pulled up to the hospital, and moments later they were in the emergency room. Jessica was so upset, she could barely see straight. She was so thankful for Reverend Ben, who quickly helped her locate Sam.

"He's in intensive care," the nurse at the desk told them. "Only family members are permitted to visit right now. Are you family?" she asked, looking first at the reverend and then at Jessica.

"Well, not exactly, no," the reverend admitted. "But I am the young man's minister and this," he said, gesturing toward Jessica, "is his . . . well, his girlfriend. More than that, actually. I'm sure it would do Sam a world of good if he were allowed to visit with her. Family or not," he added slowly.

Jessica looked at her hopefully and finally the nurse relented. "All right, you can see him. But only for five minutes," she warned. She got up from her station and led Jessica to Sam's bed in a small, curtained-off area. "Remember, five minutes," she said firmly.

Jessica just nodded. That would be more than enough time to tell him how much she loved him. She wouldn't waste another second, she vowed.

She walked up to the bed, telling herself it would be okay. But when she opened the curtain and caught sight of Sam's bandaged head, she felt herself go weak with shock.

Sam's eyes were closed. Dozens of tubes and wires were attached to his body and connected to an array of bedside machinery. Her gaze traced a row of dark stitches across one side of his head. His face was ashen, with dark circles under his eyes.

Was he conscious? What if he didn't hear her? she thought frantically. Or what if he did and still couldn't forgive her?

She knew in an instant what she would do. She would stay in Cape Light for as long as it might take for Sam to know how much she loved him.

At least God had spared his life. She sent up a swift prayer of thanks and felt tears fill her eyes again.

She reached out and softly touched his cheek with her hand.

As if sensing her presence, he slowly opened his eyes.

"Sam?" Her voice was shaking. "Can you hear me?"

"I have to be dreaming," he murmured. "Or it's the painkillers kicking in . . . or else I've passed on and am getting my heavenly reward."

"No, thank God," she whispered. "You are very much alive, Sam Morgan." She leaned over and kissed him softly on the mouth. "I love you so much. So very, very much."

The tears filled her eyes and her throat felt thick. She couldn't speak. She sat on the edge of the bed and took his hand.

"Do you believe me—and can you forgive me?" she asked him.

"Of course I do, Jessie," he whispered, staring into her eyes. "I love you with all my heart. . . . I'm sorry, too. I acted like a complete fool."

She shook her head, her vision suddenly blurred with

tears. "That doesn't matter now. You're going to be all right. And we're together."

With the arm that was free of IV lines, he reached up and buried his hand in her hair, pulling her face down to his. They kissed again, and she felt his strong heart beating under her hand.

At last she lifted her head. "Where were you going in the rain?" she asked curiously. "You could have killed yourself."

"I was trying to see you."

"But Digger said you went out to the house."

"I did, in the morning, before it got too bad out. But being out there only made me feel worse. Since the day you came out there with me, I kept picturing us living there together when it's finished. It was too painful being out there, thinking you would never share it with me. I turned around and headed back to town—to your place. I was hoping I could catch you before you left. But then a tree got in the way."

She put her hand on his cheek. "Don't think about that now," she soothed him. "I wasn't going to leave without seeing you. I was on my way to find you when the storm got really awful. Emily got the call about your accident, and I came right over."

"So you did." He managed a smile for a moment, but she could see he was in pain. He took her hand and pressed it to his lips. There was no need for more words now, she thought. They would have time to talk things through. A lifetime, she thought.

As if reading her mind, he said, "I don't want to be away from you ever again. Not even for a day, Jessica. I want you to be my wife, my partner. If you're still unsure, I can wait as long as necessary."

"You don't have to wait," she told him. Tears were streaming down her cheeks now, but this time they were tears of joy. "I know now for sure. I never really wanted to leave here—or leave you. Not for one minute. I just didn't think I had any choice." She gave him a tender smile. "It's almost funny how much that all changed. Now I want to live here—in Cape Light or wherever life leads us. As long as it's together."

Jessica didn't even notice that the nurse did not return to ask her to leave after five minutes, or even fifteen. Later, though, she wondered if maybe Reverend Ben had something to do with that.

When Sam's father and mother arrived a short time later and found Jessica and Sam holding each other, they didn't seem surprised. After making sure that their son was going to be fine, their attention turned to Jessica.

"Have you been here very long?" Joe asked her gently.

"Long enough to decide we're getting married," Sam cut in. His mother laughed, but Jessica saw tears in her eyes.

"I had a feeling about this," Joe said to his son. "You've been walking around like a loon for weeks now."

Marie just smiled and hugged Jessica. "Welcome to the family," she said sincerely.

"Thank you," Jessica said. She did feel welcomed.

She felt as if she were about to start a whole new life. A beautiful adventure with the man she truly loved, an endless sail on a bountiful sea.

Her mother would object of course. She might not even speak to her. But someday she would come around, Jessica was almost sure of it. Emily, of course, would be thrilled for her. She could hardly wait to share the news with her sister.

Jessica smiled down at Sam. His dark eyes were shining with love, warming her like the sun. She knew she had never been happier.

*   *   *

As LILLIAN PREDICTED, THE STORM LEFT THE TOWN in havoc. But the friendly spirit on Main Street was a heartening sight as shopkeepers helped each other, bailing out flooded basements and restoring damaged storefronts.

The workmen in town were overwhelmed with repair jobs and busy night and day. Harry Reilly had his hands full, dredging up boats that had sunk in the harbor. Digger was in his glory, feeling very much in demand as he helped out with many of the repairs.

Out of the storm-swept debris Charlie Bates had dredged up new campaign issues—repair of the outdated storm drains, which Emily had opposed when it was raised last year, and purchasing more emergency vehicles for the police and fire departments. There might be even more before he was through, he thought happily. He believed he might win on this. Then where would Lucy be with her going-back-to-college plans? Charlie had a feeling there were more negotiations in his future.

Right before the storm, Lucy presented him with a list of expenses and a plan for how she was going to manage her time. She had been accepted at the community college in Southport, so it was hard to hold the line. Seeing how much it meant to her—not that he really understood—he had to relent and agree that she could try it. One course, to start.

At that rate she would be ready to retire by the time she earned her nursing degree, she argued. Well then, she would have something to do in her old age, after they sold the diner, he countered. That was his final offer, take it or leave it. So she had taken it. At least life at home was more livable now. And though he would never admit it, he was actually getting a kick out of seeing Lucy look so happy.

Charlie knew that if he won the election, that would change everything. But they would cross that bridge when they came to it, he told himself.

The Bateses were both glad that Sara Franklin was staying awhile. Charlie didn't get it. A girl with her education waits tables for a living? He couldn't figure that one. She was an odd duck if you asked him, but a hard worker. They needed her now, so he tried to be nicer to her. At least nicer than he usually was to the waitresses.

He had done his best during the storm to help the town and more during the cleanup. People would remember that on election day, he was sure of it.

Emily, on the other hand, tried not to turn the storm into an issue. It had been, after all, an act of God. A freak occurrence for this time of year, which no one had been prepared for, and which no one—except Digger Hegman—had expected.

She was going to take this campaign one day a time, focusing on her present job as mayor, not on her future term. If she wasn't reelected, so be it. She had her health, her own home, and two cats who didn't have names yet. Her sister would be living here, marrying Sam, and soon giving her a niece or nephew, she had no doubt. Emily counted her blessings and knew she had many. The big storm seemed to clear the dank air in her mind and spirit, and she anticipated autumn with a fresh outlook.

There had not been much damage at all to Bible Community Church, despite its close location to the waterfront. Ben was watching a glazier replace a few broken sections of a stained-glass window when the mail carrier handed him a bundle of letters.

Ben leafed through them with only half his attention. Then a postcard caught his eye, a desert scene, eerily beautiful and as different from the coastal landscape of Cape Light as the surface of the moon.

He quickly turned over the card, stretching out his arm to read the close, clear script without the delay of finding his glasses. It was from Mark. He had a new address in Arizona, but no phone number. He said he was doing fine.

He said he would write a much longer letter or call soon.

Well, that was good news, Ben thought, looking up. *Thank you, Heavenly Father*, he silently prayed. Then he checked the address at the bottom of the card and finally patted his pockets for his glasses. He couldn't be reading this right, could he? With the glasses in place, Ben tried it again. He felt his heart skip a beat as he reread the return address on the card. Mark was now staying in a Buddhist ashram. What could this mean?

Several days later Ben had to admit he was still fairly stunned by the news. He hadn't even mentioned it to Carolyn. He was thinking about the problem as he sat on a bench in the green, an unread newspaper open on his lap.

Ben looked up to see Luke McAllister walking toward him. He raised his hand in greeting and smiled. He had not seen Luke since the storm and wondered how he was getting on.

"Hello, Luke. It's been a while," Ben greeted him. "I never did get to congratulate you on buying Dr. Elliot's land. I want to wish you the best of luck."

"Thanks." Luke nodded. "I think it was the right thing to do. I feel pretty good about it, though I still have no idea what I'm going to do there."

He sat on the end of the bench and leaned forward, resting his elbows on his knees. "I keep thinking about what you said to me that night on the beach, Reverend. How one thing leads to another?"

Ben nodded. "Yes, I remember."

"Well, it's true. Taking that first step was a good thing. And now I want to take the next step. I feel as if I want to do something good in the world . . . but I don't know what. Or even if I'll do it here in Cape Light." He met Ben's gaze. "Sounds pretty lame, right?"

"No, not at all. From small seeds mighty oaks grow."

Luke nodded. "That's what people say. I'm still at the seed stage, that's for sure."

Ben smiled and touched his beard. "Come by and talk to me sometime if you like. I'm always in my office, or not very far away."

"I will. Thanks." Luke nodded and rose to go.

"I'll pray for you, Luke. For the fruition of your good intentions."

"Thank you, Reverend. I'll pray for you," Luke replied. He looked perfectly serious, Ben thought, though a smile danced in his gray eyes.

Ben laughed. "Thanks. One always needs prayers. Even in my profession."

ON THE DAY THAT SAM WAS RELEASED FROM THE HOS-pital, Jessica drove them out to Sam's house in his truck. The narrow dirt road leading down to the house was still muddy and wet in patches.

Sam gave a low whistle. "Ten days later, and you can still see traces of the storm," he said.

Jessica knew he was worried about what kind of damage they would find at the house. They walked around the outside first, checking for loose shingles and broken windows. But they soon realized that Sam had managed to secure the house well before the heavy winds hit, and little had been disturbed.

It was a bright sunny day, and Jessica coaxed him to take a walk to the pond before they went in. She felt so content with his arm around her shoulder as they walked down the overgrown path, there was no need to speak.

When the path opened again, Jessica gazed out at the pond, remembering the time Sam had taken her here. That seemed so long ago now, though it wasn't really. She would be very happy living here with him, she thought. She could hardly wait.

He turned her face up to his and gave her a slow, sound kiss. "I love you," he said quietly. He had told her this about a million times since his accident, but she could never hear it enough.

"I love you, Sam," she answered. "We're so lucky. So blessed, it's hard to believe it."

"Yes, I know exactly what you mean. I can't wait until the wedding, though. Three months seems a long time. I wish it were sooner."

"Three months?" Jessica echoed. This was the first Sam had mentioned an actual date, and his time line was a bit of a shock. "Three months isn't very long to plan a wedding," she told him. "It's no time at all!"

He smiled at her indulgently. "Don't worry, it will all turn out fine. I can't see how it couldn't be the happiest day of my life if I'm marrying you. And don't worry about the house," he added, glancing back over his shoulder. "It will be done in time. At least enough to live in comfortably."

"I wasn't worried," she assured him.

"I realize it's not the house you may have wanted," he acknowledged. "Maybe someday we'll get another more to your liking."

She turned her head to one side, looking at him, then back at the house.

"You're right, it's not the house I imagined. And you're not the man I imagined," she added, looking back at him. "But both are much more wonderful than anything I ever wished for or could envision. I can see now that God had some very special plans in mind for me."

A slow warm smile spread across Sam's face, warming her heart. "So do I," he said, pulling her close again.

Jessica melted into his embrace, feeling his strength and love surround her. Sam was all she ever needed, all she ever wanted. No one else would ever replace him in her heart.

Jessica knew now she would always feel cherished and protected in his arms. And she would always be happy here, in this house and in Cape Light.